A CORPSE AT THE
OPERA HOUSE

ALLEN & UNWIN

FICTION

A Corpse At The Opera House

A Crimes For a Summer Christmas Anthology

Edited by Stephen Knight

ALLEN & UNWIN

First published in 1992
Allen & Unwin Pty Ltd
9 Atchison St, St Leonards, NSW 2065 Australia

National Library of Australia
Cataloguing-in-Publication entry:

A Corpse at the Opera House: a crimes for a summer Christmas anthology.

ISBN 1 86373 321 3.

1. Detective and mystery stories, Australian. I. Knight, Stephen, 1940– .

A823.08720803

Set in 10½/12pt Goudy Old Style by DOCUPRO
Printed by Australian Print Group, Maryborough, Victoria

1 3 5 7 9 10 8 6 4 2

CONTENTS

Having lectured and written about literature of many kinds from the medieval period to the present, Stephen Knight has a special interest in the relationship between narrative and its social context. That led to a book on the legend of King Arthur and another, in progress, on Robin Hood; his latest is *The Selling of the Australian Mind*, about our own context.

His interests also led to the study of crime fiction, on which he has written an academic book and, with fewer long words, he has reviewed thrillers for the *Sydney Morning Herald* for ten years.

Stephen Knight is now Professor of English at the University of Melbourne after teaching for a long term at Sydney University. He is father to Lizzie and David and both husband and estate labourer to well-known gardening writer, Maggie Knight.

Stephen Knight

INTRODUCTION

Everyone agrees there is a place in Australian culture for crime fiction. But is there a location as well?

Setting was either a puzzle or a problem in the mysteries and thrillers produced in the past almost secretly by Australian crime writers. The problem was over-assertion: fire, flood, snakes and wombats would swarm across otherwise lifeless pages. Even Arthur Upfield takes a tourist-eye-view, with highly coloured settings to match his whitewash of Aboriginal reality.

Other texts were puzzles because they bore no trace of place. Though published in Melbourne and imbued with its context of police corruption, Judah Waten's *Shares in Murder* has no actual localisation. Perhaps legal caution was the cause there, but a zero setting can have other origins: *Murder Pie*, the mystery by many hands (including Walter Murdoch and 'Marjorie Barnard Eldershaw') which appeared in 1936, curiously combined elements of Sydney and Melbourne, both unnamed, for a bland international appeal. A foreign setting could promise wider rewards: J.M. Walsh, whose first major novel *The Lost Valley* is a gripping Gippsland adventure, actually relocated his draft of *The White Mask* to Europe when he sailed off seeking his fortune in 1920s London. Into the 1940s the pattern of translocation persevered, and many a youth found from Carter Brown that manly excitement spoke with an American accent. There's a strangely neutral effect about such literally displaced work, as if these skilled and often quite insightful writers could speak of everything except their own country.

It was not always so. The earliest Australian thriller writers, like J.S. Borlase, Marcus Clarke (a student of the form), 'Rolf Boldrewood', and the prolific Mary Fortune—writing as W.W. and Waif Wander—all employed local settings as a matter of interest and focus of concern. From mine and bush camp to the roaring streets of Marvellous Melbourne and Spurious Sydney, there was a place for crime writing and a strongly developed criminography of place.

In recent years, partly through the recognition of those forerunners, local habitation has come to delimit Australian crime fiction, and anything set overseas was excluded from the post-colonial canon. Helen Simpson's London-based Sir John Saumarez stories are not included, but definitely embraced is Conan Doyle's gripping yarn of Western Districts gold, 'The Gully of Bluemansdyke', and so in part is E.W. Hornung, who lived briefly in the Riverina and originated Raffles in Victoria—not to mention Stingaree, the Gentleman Bush-ranger.

So if we define Australianness in crime writing through this sense of place, we should applaud recent writers who find in the cities and country towns of a recognisable Australia narratives that can be identified through their characters and their tensions as part of our world.

That achievement was clear in the two volumes of the *Crimes for a Summer Christmas* series. Authors were invited to produce something suitable under a title suggesting a southern festivity, and they wrote in many modes about an Australia here and now. The stress they laid on the *here* was central in realising a *now* that was vividly inhabited.

But in *A Corpse at the Opera House*, place is especially foregrounded. From the two previous *Crimes* anthologies there emerged something like an informal college of Australian crime writers, and the editorial brains trust at Allen & Unwin decided to adventure a collective stimulus. This was a little like the London Detection Club's 1930 book of stories with the same focus. In *Ask a Policeman* a number of major writers (including Dorothy Sayers and our own Helen Simpson) provided solutions to a barely told mystery plot, and the result was much more than mechanical: flair can flourish within firm guidelines.

A modern and Australian version of such a 'stimulus' was the challenge. We wrote to a set of selected authors, light hands at dark thoughts, and invited them to create a story which responded in some way to a particular paragraph:

A body lay on the steps. One hand rested just above the level of the water and a narrow watchband was visible above the cuff

of the light-coloured coat. Dark hair curled damply to the nape
of the neck. The legs were a little apart: the new sole of a
woven brown leather shoe faced upwards.

No marks could be seen on the head or hands, but beside the
face lay two items, a train ticket from Adelaide and a small
silver rose. A dawn walker had called the police from The
Rocks station; they arrived as the mist was lifting from the
Opera House.

Authors were told that the title of the anthology would be *A Corpse
at the Opera House*, but they did not need to use that title, and were
given all rights to ignore, change or rough-handle how they liked the
original stimulus.

So they did. Some from interstate, plotting with insouciant region-
alism, transplanted the whole location. Some used the setting as a
focal point of Sydney's self-consciousness, in its conflicted present or
troubled history. Others settled other scores, social, literary—possibly
even personal. The one feature on which all the authors agreed was
that their stories had nothing to do with opera or theatre. Literary
folk to the last, hungry for words and refreshment, their fictions tended
to describe an arc between restaurants and the deadly harbour.

Equally revealing differences formed around the corpse on the Opera
House steps (and there *are* some steps, over-hasty critics might note).
Particularly startling were the variations on the silver rose, and across
the range of stories the mystery was resolved by agents of remarkably
different kinds, each bearing some version of value to the writer and,
by persuasion, the reader.

Private eyes appear, smiling lone wolves of the criminal forests.
Peter Corris's Cliff Hardy is in ironical inquiring mode, making a
mediated past provide present clarification in a story of violence
contained. Jean Bedford's up-to-date woman consulting detective is,
unlike many of those modern challengers to a male domain, engaged
with criminal mysteries themselves conceivably caused by women.

Private detectives as a force have never in Australia achieved their
American dominance, and in this collection, too, detection mostly
remains amateur. In some cases the standard is professional as in Brian
Castro's elegant hall of literary mirrors focusing on a forensic scientist;
the inquirer in Kate Stephens's story is as effective with a different
wisdom, reading Aboriginal meanings with authentic feeling on the
fatal shore of Bennelong Point. Functional, too, is Mrs Mavis Levack,

cleaner to the Opera House and self-appointed remover of criminal stains: Marele Day's new invention stands about as far from cool, tall Claudia Valentine as you could imagine, but Mavis wouldn't care. A much less purposeful inquirer is the unfortunately credible academic who wavers through Janette Turner Hospital's epic of violence, passion and human humiliation, finding little to believe in beyond the Opera House bar. His mastery is so minuscule, he might better be seen as not an inquirer but merely a character in a different sub-genre, the multifarious mystery where events reveal their own meaning.

Several of these energetic enigmas were woven around the body in the harbour. As is his practice, Martin Long crosses history and distance, but this time without formal detection, in his clifftop encounter of deadly knowledge and brutal innocence. Marion Halligan's exotic escapade in literary death is literally focused on the Opera House steps, through a telescope; water, alcohol and critical bile flow freely, with malice aforethought on all sides.

One version of the detective-free mystery remains particularly popular in this country, the melodrama seen from the criminal's viewpoint. No doubt historical reasons explain why many Australians empathise with the anxieties of the extralegal classes. The tradition of Donohoe and Kelly thrives in Robert Hood's casually tough tale of a contract oddly fulfilled (set where the author won a holiday for a previous story—they never relax), while Steve Wright shows the humorous potential of these sinful sagas with more about his amiable villain Winston, embarrassed by his name but never by his behaviour.

Presenting contrasted glimpses of the Opera House as a site of crime, providing variant versions of what in our society might be held truly criminal and how it is best detected, all the stories mentioned so far share one remarkable feature: the police play no significant role.

But A Corpse at the Opera House does include police procedures. Few official detectives could be more persevering than Elizabeth Jolley's Chief Inspector Blunt, who here follows his earlier trials with Miss Porch (in Crimes for a Summer Christmas) with metaphysical, not to say postmodern, torture at the whimsical hands of Lady Meredith. An equally serious but less befuddled policeman appears in Robert Wallace's drama of constrained passion in a Victorian boarding school. Even less impressive figures are cut by the constabulary in two closely worked stories of crime with hidden depths: Archie Weller's unfolding of small-town malice in the West, and Garry Disher's layout of deep-laid corruption behind murder in leafy Melbourne. Striking indeed—even arresting—is the fact that the four stories featuring police detectives, of whatever dubious kinds, are all set outside New South Wales.

If a Sydney setting implies escaping from the police, that is itself a part of Australian self-consciousness. The beliefs of a region are realised in its myths of control, even if, perhaps especially if, the medium is partly playful. Writers have their own charges to face, and one of those is wayward independence, a freedom of spirit on which editors sometimes frown. But editing this volume has shown that independence in good crime writers is part of a professional skill which is never errant, though it may take complex paths.

In answer to our challenge of a 'stimulus' worded to suggest many possibilities, the authors have woven a mesh of interpretation and human veracity. Stimulus has returned as stimulation: the game of incitement becomes a play of imagination. Though they may have preferred the restaurants to the musical bars and only their plots are operatic, no aria was ever eerier and the result is a fully dramatic chorus. Thanks to their manifold talents, the *Corpse at the Opera House* is in vivid vital voice.

Stephen Knight
Melbourne 1992

Peter Corris was born in Stawell in the Wimmera, grew up in Melbourne and has lived in Sydney since 1976. He spent the 60s studying (BA, MA, PhD), and the first half of the 70s teaching history in tertiary institutions. From 1976 he worked as a journalist (literary editor of the *National Times* 1978–80) and writer. He has been a full-time professional writer since 1983 when *The Empty Beach*, the fourth of his Cliff Hardy private eye novels became a bestseller.

Peter Corris is married to the writer Jean Bedford. They have three daughters and divide their time between a Federation house in Marrickville in Sydney's inner-west and a log cabin at Coledale on the Illawarra coast. His interests are his family, reading and writing, films and sport, including learning to play golf. He has published more than 30 books of fiction and his plan is not to stop.

Peter Corris
GHOST WRITER

The magazine was old and faded, the paper yellowed and crisp. I treated it gently, opening it to the page which had been marked by a Post-it. The article was entitled 'Death Duo' and it went for atmosphere right from the jump. I read:

> A body lay on the steps. One hand rested just above the level of the water and a narrow watchband was visible above the cuff of a light-coloured coat. Dark hair curled damply to the nape of the neck. The legs were a little apart: the new sole of a woven brown leather shoe faced upwards.
>
> No marks could be seen on the head or hands, but beside the face lay two items, a train ticket from Adelaide and a small silver rose. A dawn walker had called the police from The Rocks station; they arrived as the mist was lifting from the Opera House . . .

I skimmed another few paragraphs and put the magazine down. 'I remember it,' I said. 'Vaguely—she really made a name for herself with that piece.'

The woman sitting in the client chair in my Darlinghurst office nodded. Dark red hair waltzed around a pale, perfect face—huge green eyes, sculpted nose, cheekbones, put-it-here lips. Physically, Madeline Ozal had everything women dream of having and men lust after. Furthermore, she had a quality that was probably worth around a million a year to her as an actress—she riveted your attention so that it didn't matter what she said or how she said it, you just wanted to hear more, and watch.

'Valerie Drew,' she said. 'God, what a bitch.'

I watched the way her lip curled. You read about it, lip-curling, actually seeing it was unnerving. 'She was a very successful writer,' I said. 'Went on from journalism into—'

Madeline Ozal's hand-waving dismissal was like a signal to take your own life without a moment's regret. 'I don't want to hear about it. I know all about her prizes and husbands and real estate holdings. She was a slut and the world's a better place without her.'

'I'm confused. I'm not used to dealing with celebrities, alive or dead. What—?'

She reached out and grabbed the twenty-year-old magazine. Its yellowed pages fluttered as she shook it. 'Valerie Drew implied that the woman they found in the water a few hours later had killed the man and then drowned herself. That's all bullshit. All that silver rose crap . . .'

Vague was the right word for my recollection of the case. It had happened before I got into the private inquiries business and I'd read about it in the tabloids and magazines like any other voyeur. 'Forgive me, Miss Ozal, but this is all old history. I'll be blunt—what's it to you?'

The big eyes filled with tears. 'Cliff, they were my Mummy and Daddy. She didn't kill him and she didn't kill herself. I was just a baby. They couldn't have.'

The whole story came out then over coffee and tissues. Madeline Ozal had been brought up by her mother's sister who was married to a Turk. Hence the name. The name on her birth certificate was Macquarie, daughter of Ernest, whose occupation was given as 'playwright' and Josephine, née Peters.

'Madeline Macquarie,' she said. 'Not as good, is it?'

I shrugged as I made notes. 'Is it important?'

'You bet. No-one would ever have heard of Norma Jean Baker.'

'What about Meryl Streep?'

She laughed. 'You've got a point. Kurt Butler told me you weren't dumb, not that Kurt's all that well-equipped to judge.'

Butler was an actor I'd bodyguarded some years ago. I hadn't seen his name in lights lately, but it's always nice to be well-thought of, even by a has-been. Madeline Ozal was no has-been—she was big and getting bigger. 'I had a bit part in one of his movies,' I said. 'I threw someone off a building or fell off myself. I can't remember which.'

She laughed again. 'In Kurt's movies it hardly matters. Look, the only people who know about my parents are my aunt and uncle and now you. But soon the whole world's going to know.'

This sounded like the nitty-gritty, worth getting a contract form out of the desk for. 'You're expecting to be blackmailed?'

'No. I'm writing my biography . . . well, I'm sort of writing it.'

Astonishment made me rude. 'You can't be a day over twenty-five. What's there to write about?'

She smiled, showing perfect white teeth, nicely spaced. 'I was brought up by an insane woman who ate twenty-four hours a day and was terrified of going to sleep on account of nightmares. Plus I've been in the movie business here and in the States for ten years. You'd be surprised. No, I'm going to reveal the truth about being an orphan in the book. It's a big selling point.'

I started to reassess her. So far, the only grounds she'd given for casting doubt on the standard account of the Macquaries' death was that they had had *her*. Now it was a selling point.

She leaned forward across the desk. She was wearing a white silk shirt buttoned to the neck. Nothing so crude as cleavage, but the way she moved made me want to close my eyes and count to ten. Her voice was soft and came from deep in her throat. 'It'd be a much bigger story,' she said, 'if I could prove who really killed them.'

I put my pen down and leaned back in my chair, stomach in, chin up. 'I suppose it would.'

'That's why I'm here. Peter says it'll make a great chapter. Oops . . . ' She dug into her leather shoulder bag and pulled out a notebook that had a gold pen clipped to it. 'I'm supposed to be taking notes. How tall are you?'

'Six foot and half an inch. Who's—?'

'What's that in centimetres?'

'I don't know. I was that tall before centimetres got here. Who's Peter?'

'Peter Drewe. He's helping me with the book. Are you married?'

'No.' I wrote the name on my pad and added 'ghost writer.' 'Any relation?'

'He's Valerie's son. We're lovers . . . sort of.'

'Uh huh.'

The green eyes were dry now and piercing. 'I can read upside down. Ghost writer is unkind. You don't like me.'

'I don't see how I can help you, Miss Ozal.'

She put her gold pen and suede-bound notebook away. 'Peter has some leads. We want you to check them out. We'll pay your standard fees.'

It all sounded odd, but I was intrigued by the cast of characters and the few routine jobs I had on hand would allow me to spend some time on it. I told her the damage, she signed the contract and I agreed to telephone Peter Drewe. She smiled and we shook hands. I tried not to watch the way she put on her coat, shouldered her bag, flicked back her hair. I tried.

Peter Drewe lived in a flat on the corner of Crown and Burton Streets, Darlinghurst. The building was called 'Royal Court', which was a bit too much monarchism in one address for my taste. Nice place though, good security door, wide staircase, vaguely art deco trappings. Drewe was a dark, thin, nervous type who licked his lips a lot. His one-bedroom flat was neat and admirably organised for writing and fucking. His word processor sat on a desk with fold-out attachments to carry books and papers. His writing chair was an engineering miracle. I caught a glimpse of the bedroom—mirrors, satin sheets, uh huh.

'Maddy's aunt won't talk to me,' Drewe said, after we'd kicked it around for a while. 'She doesn't approve of me. But I'm sure she knows a lot more than she's ever told Maddy.'

'Did she talk to your mother?'

'No. She wasn't in the picture then. Maddy was in hospital with some childhood illness when her parents died. The aunt claimed her about a week later. Valerie wrote her piece within forty-eight hours of the finding of the bodies. That was her way in those days, apparently. She called it "tasting the cum".'

'Miss Ozal said you had some leads. Is that it—talk to the aunt?'

'No. You could see the cop who worked on the case. One Ron Fisher. He got booted off the force later and won't talk to reporters.'

He gave me the names, addresses and numbers. 'Have you got a theory, Mr Drewe?'

He shook his head and licked his thin lips. 'Not really. Valerie said Ernest had a mistress in Adelaide and that Josephine killed him on that account. The silver rose was a gift for the mistress or from her,

I forget which. My only theory is that she was completely wrong about those things.'

'Why d'you say that?'

'Why not? She was wrong about everything else in her fucking life.'

I stood in the street outside my office building. Ron Fisher lived in Gymea. My car was parked close by, about the same distance away as the telephone. *You're not that keen*, I thought. I went upstairs, hauled out the cask of red, drew off a glass and let my fingers do the driving.

'Fisher.' A harsh Rothmans and Toohey's Old voice.

'My name's Hardy, Mr Fisher. I'm a PEA. Frank Parker'll give you the word on me if you want it.'

'I've heard of you. What is it?'

'I wanted to talk about a case of yours. Old one—the body on the Opera House steps and the floater.'

'Talk, then.'

'The inquests said heart failure and drowning.'

'That's right.'

'What do you say?'

'Mate, I had so many problems back then I was relieved when I came up with sweet fuck-all. They were both nuts—drunks and coke freaks. My guess is his ticker gave out on him when he was high and she thought she could walk on the water.'

'What happened to the train ticket and the rose?'

'The what? Oh, shit, who knows? They went to whoever got the effects. There'd be a record at the station, maybe. I was a Dee at the Rocks.'

I could hear the regret in his voice along with the bitterness. I thanked him and hung up. One thing leads to another—there's nothing wrong with visiting police stations, some of the best people do it. I drove to the station. The sergeant behind the desk looked old enough to have been in the force in Ron Fisher's time and I took the risk of mentioning his name. Coppers are clannish and whatever it was that had led to Fisher's expulsion hadn't tarnished his name among his fellows. The sergeant clicked his tongue, muttered 'Poor bugger' and obligingly sent a constable to fetch a record book dating back to the time in question.

When it arrived the book was both dusty and damp but it yielded the information: the personal effects of Ernest and Josephine Macquarie had eventually been handed over to the drowned woman's sister, Mrs Isabel Ozal. At that time her address had been in Kingsford, now it was in Dover Heights. I thanked the sergeant and handed the book back.

'How's old Ron?' he said.

'Sounds bitter.'

'Poor bugger.'

As an ex-surfer and still keen swimmer, I always see Dover Heights as a frustrating place for everyone except suicides and those maniacs who jump off cliffs with ropes tied to their feet. There's no other quick way to reach the water. I parked under some plane trees and gave the Ozal house the once-over. Nice place—end of the street, elevated double-fronted brick bungalow, 180-degree views to New Zealand and a piece of the cliff almost in the backyard.

I'd telephoned, intending to spin some yarn or other, but there had been no answer. The house looked occupied; there was a brown Celica in the driveway and the venetian blinds to the front rooms were open. Time again for Hardy to play it by ear, hoping not to get thrown out on it.

I stepped over the low gate and walked up a cement path to the front porch. The door was open and music was pouring out from the house. Italian opera, a warbling soprano and a fruity tenor. No point in knocking, nothing could be heard over the din. I walked down the wide passage past a polished table carrying a crystal vase full of dead flowers. The dry petals were scattered across the thick beige carpet. There were two sets of rooms off the passage which made a turn to the right into a big sitting room filled with late afternoon light. Its huge windows looked straight out to sea.

A trick of the light saved me. As I faced the window I caught a glimpse of a reflection, a blur of movement above the level of my head. I jumped sideways, spinning around as the axe blade whooshed down, missing me and hitting a low glass-topped coffee table. The glass shattered, shards flew and the axe skittered away to smash into a big earthenware pot. The pot disintegrated. I struggled to get my balance amid the flying glass and bits of pottery. The man rushed at me, his fists knotted and flailing. He was small but wiry and imbued with hysterical strength. He landed a wild swing to the ribs which hurt. I ducked away from the next swing and gave him a short right to the ear. He bellowed and came at me with his hands stretching for a strangler's grip. I grabbed his thumbs, exerted pressure and he was out of action. He sank to his knees. He was in his socks and his feet had been cut by the glass. Blood flowed across the dusty surface of the polished boards.

All the fight had left him. I eased him onto a couch. He sat there, staring at the darkening ocean view. I found the bathroom, wet a towel and came back to find he hadn't moved a muscle. I peeled off his socks and got to work on his feet. The cuts weren't deep but blood still seeped from them. I wrapped the towel around them and looked around for some anti-shock medication. There was a drinks tray in the corner of the room—I poured out two big brandies and put his in his hand. He drank it in a gulp and held out the glass for more. I obliged. The drink put some colour into his drained, haggard face. He was about sixty, olive-complexioned, with sparse iron grey hair. He wore a silk shirt that smelled of alcohol and sweat and vomit; his well-cut slacks were creased and stained. The socks hadn't been too clean, either.

'Are you Kemal Ozal?' I said.

He nodded and sipped his drink. 'Yes. She has left me. I was crazy. I thought you were the man. I am sorry.'

'Your wife has left you?'

'Yes.'

'When?'

He sat stiffly, not seeming to find it odd to be answering questions from a total stranger whom he'd tried to kill. 'They came, Madeline and the son of that terrible woman. They talked. After they went, Isabel told me that she was leaving me. She said she was in love with another man. I could say nothing, think nothing. I loved her. I did not care that she became so fat. I loved her fat. She left and I began to drink. I am a Muslim. I am not used to drinking. I was sick. I took many sleeping pills but they did not work. I thought you were the man. I am sorry.'

'Is there someone who can look after you, Mr Ozal?'

The tension and rigidity seemed to flow out of him. His eyes fluttered closed, opened and shut down again. 'I am all right,' he slurred. 'Just tired.' He knocked back the rest of his brandy without opening his eyes again and slipped sideways on the couch. He snored softly. I stuffed a cushion under his head and lifted his feet, still wrapped in the towel, up level with his head. The bleeding had stopped and his pulse was strong. There may be nothing in the law books to support it, but I reckoned I'd earned the right to search the house.

Houses can tell you a lot about the people who occupy them, but only when the people actually live there and do their own cleaning. The Ozal house was very little lived in and was evidently cleaned professionally. I found nothing of interest until I got to Mrs Ozal's bedroom. It looked as if it had been searched by a mad gorilla. Clothes and shoes and spare bed-linen were scattered everywhere; a few books lay open on the floor; the contents of a writing desk had been rifled and distributed across the bed which had been moved from its usual position. Conclusion: someone had been searching for something in great haste, not the best way to do it.

I took my time, examined the furniture and fittings carefully, and, down behind the dressing table, trapped just above the skirting board, I found a small, hinged case not much bigger than a powder compact. It was elaborately carved with gold inlay and possibly made of ivory. I snapped it open. It was lined with velvet and designed to hold a small object in the shape of a rose. I turned my attention to the debris on the bed and found four pieces of crisp, faded paper—a train ticket with booked sleeper, Adelaide to Sydney, torn savagely across twice. A collection of newspaper clippings of articles by Valerie Drewe had been ripped to shreds. Several other newspaper cuttings had been crumpled. I smoothed them and discovered that they recorded radio programs for Wednesdays, twenty years back. The 8pm 'Radio Theatre' timeslot was underlined. There were also some torn photographs—old ones showing a slim, pretty woman and later pictures of the same person twenty years older and fifty kilos heavier.

Kemal Ozal was sleeping peacefully when I left the house. I'd put a carafe of water with a glass and a strip of Panadol tablets on the floor beside the couch. Also a packet of Bandaids.

When I got home I made a toasted sandwich, poured a glass of cask white and sat down with a ballpoint and paper to try to figure out what I had. The one glass became two and then three and four before I reached any conclusions. Four-glass conclusions don't always mean very much, but I called a few people I knew in the journalism business and picked their brains about Peter Drewe. As a four-glass conclusion, this one was shaping up pretty well.

After making two phone calls, one to Madeline Ozal's agent and another to Peter Drewe, I spent the morning in the Mitchell Library and then walked to Darlinghurst. I buzzed Peter Drewe's flat and he answered immediately. He met me at his door and suggested that we go up on the roof. It was a mild day, two o'clock in the afternoon, and he had a six-pack of Cooper's in his hands. I agreed. We sat on upturned terracotta garden pots and looked out over the city skyline. Drewe ripped the tops off two bottles and handed one to me.

'Cheers.' He drank and wiped his mouth. I realised that it wasn't his first drink of the day by a long shot.

I sipped the beer. 'It was your idea, the biography of Maddy, wasn't it?'

'Who told you that?'

'Her agent. You made the approach. You've got a reputation as a political journalist. This is a bit out of your usual territory, wouldn't you say?'

He shrugged loosely. 'Saw the chance to make a buck.'

'I don't think so. Your mother died three months ago. A week later you made contact with Madeline Ozal. Your colleagues report on a personality change—from being a hot-shot political reporter, rooting everything in sight, you became detached, almost ascetic.'

'Bullshit.' He lifted his bottle. 'Is this being ascetic?'

'You're under pressure, son. Why don't you screw Maddy?'

'Who says I don't?'

'She implied it.'

'OK. So what?'

I produced the ivory case and opened it. 'I found it in Maddy's aunt's room. She's missing, but she tore the place apart looking for this.'

He drained his stubby and opened another. 'Go on.'

'You and Maddy went to see Isabel Ozal. Whatever you said to her caused her to leave her husband. She said she was in love with another man.'

He smiled. 'She must have weighed close to a hundred kilos.'

'Yes. I think she was lying. About now, not about then. I think she had an affair with Ernest Macquarie, her brother-in-law.'

'Proof?'

'I have some, of a kind.'

'Tell me. That's what you were hired for.'

I shook my head. 'First, you tell me what you found when your mother died.'

He was opening and closing the catch of the ivory case. The clicking seemed to have a mesmeric effect on him. 'One of these,' he said. 'Identical to this. Except that the rose was inside. That was typical of Valerie. Isabel might lose her rose, but not Val.'

'So, you discovered a connection between Macquarie and your mother. Who's your father, Peter?'

His smile was bleak. 'She told me she didn't know. She told me that when I was too young to understand. Later, when I was old enough to understand and saw the way she lived, I believed her.'

'Kemal Ozal knew your mother. He called her "that terrible woman". Isabel had made a collection of her articles which she destroyed when she left. What did you say to her?'

He drained his second stubbie and reached for a third. His hands were shaking and he had trouble pulling the tab. I took the bottle, opened it, and handed it to him. 'Nothing, really,' he said. 'When Maddy was out of the room I told her that I knew everything. I mentioned the silver rose. I was bluffing. She didn't react at all. That's when . . .'

'That's when you decided that you might need to apply a little extra pressure. Me.'

He nodded and took a long pull on the bottle.

'Let me get this straight,' I said. 'You've spent three months taping Maddy's reminiscences of the dopey films she's worked on and the idiot actors she's fucked because you wanted to find out—'

'Whether we had the same father and who killed him. Right.'

'But you didn't learn anything.'

'Not much. Her mother was a very good-looking woman, like Isabel must have been. That seems to have been their stock in trade. I've got a theory that they were both part-time whores, but no proof. Ernest Macquarie was a failure. He called himself a playwright but he never had a play produced. I checked with the Theatre Guild. He wrote advertising copy when he wasn't drinking, probably when he was, too.'

'You shouldn't be so hard on him,' I said. 'I think he was your dad.'

He glared at me drunkenly and pushed back the lank, dark hair that had fallen into his face. 'I was afraid of it,' he muttered.

'Because you're in love with Maddy?'

'Right. Fuck it. What's your evidence?'

'It's not evidence. You don't even have to listen.'

'I have to know.'

I told him then about the collection of radio play scripts I'd seen in the Mitchell Library. They'd been published by a small, now defunct press under the name 'E. Mack', but the library had identified Macquarie as the author. *The Silver Roses* was about a man who had a wife and two mistresses, one of them his wife's sister. The wife knew nothing. The mistresses knew about the wife but not about each other. Separately, each threatened to kill him if he slept with anyone other than her and his wife. The Lothario in the play liked games. He gave each of the women a silver rose and the play revolved around the danger to him when one of these roses got lost or found, I forget which, compromisingly for him.

Drewe listened in silence. When I finished he said, 'It sounds stupid.'

I stood up. 'I'm no critic, but I thought it was one of the dumbest things I've ever read.'

'You think Isabel found out about Valerie and killed him along with the wife?'

'Possibly. Or each one found out about the other and they did it together. Valerie's article could have been written to protect them by putting the blame on the wife. We'll never know.'

'What about the ticket from Adelaide? What's the significance of that?'

I shrugged. 'What does it matter?'

Two days later they fished Mrs Ozal out of the harbour. I used my contacts to get a look at the autopsy report. Her stomach was full of booze and pills and salt water. In the language of the report, they found a small silver rose in one of her 'body cavities'.

Brian Castro is the author of the novels *Birds Of Passage* (1983), *Pomeroy* (1990) and *Double-Wolf* (1991), all published by Allen & Unwin.

Born in Hong Kong in 1950, he came to Australia in 1961. He began publishing short stories in 1970 while at Sydney University, and has since worked in Australia and Europe as a teacher, journalist and lecturer. He was the recipient of a number of awards for his writing and was recently granted a Fellowship from the Literature Board of the Australia Council.

Though not specifically a crime writer, Brian Castro enjoys interrogating genres. Having once aspired to be a barrister, he is still very interested in court proceedings, from which, he says, one can learn a great deal about fiction.

He lives in the Blue Mountains outside Sydney.

Brian Castro

PORTFOLIO

I love harbours.

No body arrives through them anymore . . . except on funships which cruise the Pacific on ice and every now and then you see one come off when the partying's over. Out of the bottom deck in a steel container from the coolroom. Usually heart attacks. Usually *in flagrante*. I used to go up onto the farewell railings to watch them slip the hemp, pissed off at the mock sentimentality, the paper streamers, the screaming. Two weeks at sea and they'd be back. Most of them. I can pick the ones on their last voyage. You look for bellies. Baldness helps . . . they think they're virile. Then if there's a red face which goes with beef, I mean beef, not muscle, which they think they've got, then you've guessed right.

I love harbours.

Invitation au voyage. Interludes. Mahler's Fifth. It all swirls when I think of harbours. Nights when lights flare and smells come upwind out of the past you hear the creakings of yearning and regret. No longer mainstream, harbours are working ports or they're backwaters. Everything else comes in by air. I didn't want to do the airports. They were always too hot. So I covered the waterfront. Sometimes at night the moon slips over the water like a lemon in an oily pan. I can get lyrical. Maybe it's the salt in the air. My reports are a little flowery too: *The projectile skied down the carotid canal and debouched into the jugular foramen, dancing in the occipital before splaying the meningeal arteries.*

Not such a delicate matter when it came to Hemingway.

Yes, Hemingway. The last time I saw Nelson Algren we were talking about how Hemingway put the shotgun to his head. It must have been in the early sixties, and the steamer was standing off Kowloon and he was writing a story, so he told me, about a visit to a brothel, and he didn't know a damned thing about Hong Kong brothels and he tried to find out from me. He had a terrible frown. He frowned when he smiled. I was fresh out of Sydney University, still without a medical degree, and was visiting the folks back home. A son who didn't make good. The sea ran with slick and there was a chop. I fed him the lot. I said he'd end floating ass-up in the harbour if he tried the hypodermics.

'Brothels here ain't just sex,' I said.

His eyes opened a millimetre.

'You ever been to Chicago?'

It was bullshit time.

No, what makes me think of Algren standing against the rail on that greasy steamer was his obsession with Hemingway.

'It's easy,' he said in that blocked-sinus way of his, 'to replace art by profundity . . . Ernest took the risks of art.'

'Maybe it was more profound to put a gun to one's head,' I said.

I was young.

'You'll find that out in time,' Algren said, looking at me. 'Don't be a critic unless you can do an autopsy.'

The latter I could do. The launch came out then, and Algren said goodbye, flicking a cigarette into the water. I can still see him standing at the rail, the air-funnel behind him like a huge blunderbuss as I thumped homeward, already thinking of another place. For expatriate Australians in Hong Kong, the end of the fifties was the end of an era. My father, the great engineer, had succeeded in building an airport runway straight out into Kowloon Bay. But now that party was over.

I love harbours.

Thirty years after Hemingway's death, the sun still rises over Sydney Harbour. Sickly, sometimes in the mist, but it's there. The Opera House gapes like a shark-jaw trophy. I am still junior district coroner, balding, middle-aged, unmarried.

The nasal process shattered, vomer non-existent, particles of bone and cartilage spangled in the occipital . . . I had to use X-rays here. No metal fragments at all. He may have been kicked by a horse. That, at least would have been the pastoral explanation. But a harbour doesn't let up. Swallowing significance in making the most of an ordinary day, it allows things to surface at night. The body was floated towards me in the glare of lights . . . I can't swim. That's why water holds a fascination for me. Immerse dead flesh in water for some time and it fills out a bit. No obvious signs of violence.

I was going to run the saw for a transverse section when they told me she was waiting outside. You see, there's always a woman. Harbours disgorge bodies and there's always a gorgeous woman wearing diamonds on her throat in the wake of things. They say men like me can think only of flesh. Desire dissipates after a few post-mortems. It's the smell. But allow me this: Allow me words, and Lydia L'Emballeuse had the most seductive vocabulary a man like me could imagine.

Of course I knew he was her husband before they told me. There was no wallet, no plastic driver's licence; just a little silver rose. For me, not so boring. A murder, finally.

I was down in Adelaide a month before, for the Arts Festival. I frequented all these things, sucking all I could out of them, prising the metaphysical from the flesh. It's the job. Nothing is quite as . . . indifferent, as death, despite what the poets see in it. I rubbed shoulders with the literati, wanted to know what *they* thought. In Hindley Street, at the height of a superb lasagne, the police called me away, much to the delight of the writers. They who complained they never *knew* enough. 'Write only when there's something in the well,' Ernest once said.

Anyway, there were two bodies in the Torrens. All the local butchers on holidays and I always end up supplying the literati with their meat.

So, two nights later I was letting off a bit of steam in a jazz joint with a couple of playwrights when in came Lydia L'Emballeuse with her husband. Everyone knew them except me. I was lost for words and it was late, but a coroner always worked back. She was the daughter of a media mogul. Tall, horse-faced, I found her terribly seductive. He was a gigolo. He wore hand-made shoes. She sported a little silver rose on a platinum chain. I saw it glitter and swing in her cleavage when she leant forward. The name of that rose was Eros. She said nothing to me, just stared. I must have given off a whiff of chloroform. Presently she yawned. The party was dead.

Now she stood outside the lab in Sydney shaking in her thin silk dress. She obviously didn't want to recognise me. She put a hand on my arm and love rose, simple as that . . . like stepping into a warm bath on a cold day.

'Johnny was always drunk,' she wept, looking at me.

I knew from experience real weeping had no eye contact.

'He must have fallen into the water.'

She went into the most fearful howl then, and I knew that before things went further I had to shut her up.

'Your husband,' I said, 'I'm sorry to say, was murdered.'

She began shrieking, but it was muted.

'He was hit, once across the throat . . . probably with a steering lock, then a thin knife was thrust up his nostril,' I said, showing off. If she was grieving none of this would have made any sense, but people react in different ways.

'A steering lock?'

'Yeah, the hooked section gouged him behind the ear.'

Twenty-five years as a coroner melted to nothing before this woman. I found myself desperate to tell all. She sat down. Held her face in her hands. I tried to comfort her. When my hand touched her hair she said something rather strange. Try to imagine it: long dark hair which evinced a perfume overwhelming to a man who spent hours sniffing chloroform, embalming fluid, resinous blood, bowel products, toxins, malodorous secretions, cordite and explosives. She said . . . and it was in the form of a business deal, though tinged with the kind of drunken long-lunch generosity . . . that I could write it up as drunken happenstance, a funship mishap . . . to avoid scandal.

I could hardly do that, I said, the perfume on the edge of sweat, corrupted, magical.

'But you're bored,' she squeaked, 'you poor thing.' She sighed. '*I've* been bored for years. Are you moral? Do you read the Bible? Do you ever fall in love? God, he was a turd.'

'Who?'

'Johnny. A countersunk turd.'

I told you, she had great vocab. It had started to rain outside and the atmosphere in the office was oppressive.

'I'm not prejudiced,' I said. 'Neither homophobic nor misogynous.'

She took this to be compliance. We talked for two hours. I agreed to an interim statement. *Blood alcohol 0.5; traces of other substances; almost non-existent septum; an old scar on the abdomen; opened it up and divided the transversalis fascia; pushed up peritoneum and traced internal iliac. The man was haemorrhaging hours before he died.*

Open finding. It was the first time I had created a corpse.

'Are you good at your job?'

'I like to think so.'

'Then why aren't you Chief Coroner?'

I told her she had lived in the United States for too long. Here things still ground away a little fustily.

'I'm waiting for the C.C. to die.'

'You see?' she said. 'We're always waiting for somebody to die.' She bit at her nails.

'I'm happy where I am.'

'Oh yeah?'

She changed tack.

'I've seen you at literary venues.' She pronounced it *veenews*.

'Art,' I sighed, 'is unfortunately not as close to anatomy as it is to physics. None of those fractals and noodle maps. No chaos theory.'

'Maybe it cuts too close to the bone.'

We vibrated with understanding, conjoined by one evil amongst others. I put the silver rose into my pocket, and with that, pulled the shroud back over mystery. But life was too short to search out the seminal axis of our relationship . . . that universal human depth. Suffice to say, she taught me to swim.

I love harbours.

Lydia L'Emballeuse spent most of her time in gyms and I saw more sweaty lycra than midnight phosphorescence, but she had muscles in wonderful places, and she learned bad-mouthing in the gym and all this put together offered long aerobic desires to one whose crowning achievement was to make a sprint look like a marathon . . . but I was swimming, lie on me, lie to me, she moaned, lightly lightly, imagine you're a spermatozoon, gliding like a ray, butterfly strokes in a warm sea . . . and while she fishtailed over me and pushed me around I got fit, life was crusted with the hard edge of excitement and I became Chief Coroner and a respected reviewer on one of her father's papers. Status.

The scalpel became a bit blunt. When Lydia flew off to the States to sort out a few things . . . when she bought a newspaper or sacked a few hundred people . . . she left me a few toys. A sloop which I named the *Edmund Wilson*; a helicopter which I learned to fly from her Double Bay house, nonchalantly lighting my cigars over the drums of Avgas. She was generous with her girlfriends as well, though they were all unliterary, thinking Edmund was Woodrow's middle name, one even calling me 'Pudd'nhead', which was quite a compliment to her, believe me. I tacked out the Heads on sail and blade, iced champagne in hand to greet the jewelled mornings.

Sydney became one hell of a place. A couple of bodies surfaced and I shoved them back. Shark food. I was an environmentalist. I took on causes, became known as something of a critic, and was in the van of taste. I wasn't ungrateful. Every now and then I sailed to the international mooring beside the Opera House, the mooring reserved for round-the-world sailors, tied up and meditated on the origins of my luck. People came to gape. One grizzled old salt asked me if I'd ever crossed The Line.

'Yeah,' I said, 'between fiction and reality.'

Old fart.

In my pocket, a couple of dozen rejection slips I copied from a great critic:

The Chief Coroner regrets that it is impossible for him to:

- Read manuscripts
- Deliver lectures
- Autograph books
- Conduct post-mortems
- Answer questionnaires
- Write statements or reports to order
- Supply information
- Appear on 'panels'
- Allow his name to be used in fiction
- Supply photographs of himself

People were scared of me. Writers especially. Crime writers most of all. In my weekly column I exposed their fiction for what it was: fictional. 'No self-respecting sleuth would have made the mistake of confusing the *mastoid foramen* with the Sterno-mastoid' I wrote. 'A bullet through one is fatal, while a bullet passing through the other may simply be crippling.'

Mimesis was a deadly process if you didn't understand it. We all have a body, and we can all copy a crime, but not all of us can write.

Aye, there's the rub. I was never a benign critic because I was never a writer. The more I got into the literary game, the more curmudgeonly I became. A pariah of the first water. I made and destroyed reputations. I purported to have known Raymond Chandler. 'In '58, the year before he died,' I wrote, 'my family and I were holidaying in Southern California. It was damned hot.' And so a myth developed.

When Lydia L'Emballeuse came back from Copper Mountain, she

brought with her a book she had written. She flounced into the bedroom with an advance copy from Cape.

'They think it's one of the best novels ever written about marriage and violence . . . about the cusp of passion and hatred.'

The woman had no shame. Tanned and superfit, she jiggled, hands on hips as she said this, intersecting her intellect with curves. As if the publishers weren't aware she was the all-powerful Lydia L'Emballeuse. As if they would say anything else.

I thumbed through it. From the first sentence, interest flagged like a mid-life erection. Woman marries gigolo. Woman has a crisis. Gigolo is killed. Can't live with herself. Uses up men like Kleenex tissue. Discovers that her destiny, finally, is with other women. Becomes a famous crime writer.

For a woman with a great vocab, she had disintegrated into monosyllabic grunts. Minimalism passed for toughness. Dirty Realism for reflective depth, which she once seemed to possess. Maybe it was her wealth, her power, her words, of which she was totally unconscious. Now she flaunted them; made them obvious and was squeezing the life out of resonance. Gone the long afternoons and the tremors of the heart, the *mystery* that was missing from what was called 'mysteries.' It was crap and we were on the rocks.

I couldn't bring myself to endorse it. I kept silent for a while and then we drifted apart. After the din of sycophancy died, I began to write a scholarly piece on crime. I didn't refer to her novel, but that, too, became obvious. *I condemned by omission.* Now, if that was a sin, it was a venial one. I expected fireworks . . . her father ringing me, a political decision to have me stand down as Chief Coroner, social ostracism.

There was silence instead. So I vigorously made other reputations. A mere adjective like 'promising' rocketed sales. Then one winter afternoon, between writing articles and disembowelling a floater to keep my hand in, my car was stolen. My mood improved when Lydia L'Emballeuse rang and arranged to meet me for dinner in a restaurant, chosen, probably ironically, in The Rocks, and she was as nice as pie.

'I didn't expect you to like my novel,' she said, over coffee and cognac, the first time she brought up the subject. 'But I thought I'd given you enough time.'

'It's okay,' I said, suddenly feeling expansive. 'A critic must always get at the truth, whether a novelist does or not.'

Her eyes flickered. She was looking good.

'You mean, I didn't imagine it well enough?'

'Look, no offence, but women always think they have this detachment, but the secret is that they lack the practice. It's the practice that counts. Men have had ten thousand years of violence. What seems obvious is not so readily attainable. It's damned hard to realise how tough it is to kill. The body can't be disposed of in a sentence or two. I mean, cutting into dead flesh as I do once or twice a week is child's play compared to attacking live flesh. Life is more than energy, resistance . . . it's . . . it's *principle*, more than oneself. And that's what you have to realise in writing. It's a supernatural force.'

There was an icy smile on her face that would have snap-frozen tuna.

'Now don't get me wrong, Lydia, but I read somewhere the other day that eighty per cent of readers are women. That means you only need twenty per cent detachment, and that, Lydia, is not *practice*. That is what you haven't got. That's what's missing in your novel, in your life, in you. You're not filled out at all. No ambiguity. You're two-dimensional, flat . . . sorry, not physically . . . you haven't got the faintest whether your inferior cervical ganglion is at the back of your neck or in your crotch.'

I guess it was then that she hit me, to remind me of her presence; a right cross tuned by hours of pulleys and weights. Never mind particle physics. Old Newtonian principles still worked rather better than expected. The corner of my jaw transmitted the blow pretty well up the Fifth nerve. When I came to, she was gone.

That was the last time I saw Lydia. I balanced things up and concluded she'd probably thought she'd paid enough, but I knew she would probably go on paying for the rest of her life. Nobody can help you write, just as nobody can help you kill. Vicarious pleasure calls in its favours. I shuffled along the walkway towards the Opera House, looking back at the rooms in the Hyatt, trying to work out if the remote-controlled blinds in the end room which were closing and opening, closing and opening like a semaphore, were hers.

I guess that's when I began thinking of the time I met Nelson Algren. I met him once and only briefly on a steamer off Kowloon during a Number Seven typhoon warning to deliver a dinner invitation from my father. Algren never showed. He probably went to a brothel instead.

Sitting outside the Oyster Bar, nursing my jaw with a lump of ice, I thought about what he had said to me. Talking about the number

of times Hemingway might have pressured the trigger before writing
A *Farewell To Arms*, Algren frowned and turned to me and said:

'Anybody who can merge criticism with autopsy is the boy for me.'

A wave from a boat spewed over the rails and I felt myself powerfully
drawn to its reflux. Understanding, not mimesis; *that's* what artistry
is. An anatomy of criticism . . . *that* was the starting point. How to
place the knife; how to thrust it up the left nostril. *Then* write the
fiction.

After a couple of beers I took the scalpel out of my coat pocket.
Laid it next to the little silver rose. A study in graft. Then when a
ferry hooted and rumbled into the Quay, I flicked them into the
water. A wreath for Johnny and Lydia. From El Caballero de la Rosa.

I love harbours.

Now was that profundity, or was that art?

Elizabeth Jolley was born in England and educated there as well as in France and Germany. She served as a nurse during World War Two and migrated to Australia with her husband and children in 1959. She now lives in Western Australia. Elizabeth Jolley has published short fiction, novels and radio plays, and has won many awards including the Age Book of the Year (for *Mr Scobie's Riddle*), the New South Wales Premier's Award (for *Milk and Honey*), and the Miles Franklin Award (for *The Well*).

Elizabeth Jolley
LADY MEREDITH'S DAM

It is important for the patient to realise that if hypoglycaemia occurs it will probably happen about 3 or 4 hours after the injection of insulin.
(For symptoms see page 491)

(Evelyn Pearce
General Textbook of Nursing, 1942)

Sometimes a desperate heron stands at the edge of Lady Meredith's dam before flying off uttering harsh cries of disappointment.

This morning a body lies on the steps, one hand resting just above the level of the water. A narrow watchband is visible below the cuff of a light-coloured coat. Dark hair curls damply to the nape of the neck. The legs are a little apart; the new sole of a woven brown leather shoe faces upwards.

No marks can be seen on the head or hands; but beside the face are two items, a train ticket from Adelaide and a small silver rose.

'This one simply cannot have been murdered here,' Lady Meredith says to Chief Inspector Blunt. 'You see the train ticket in the mud there? He must have been murdered in Adelaide, otherwise why would he have the ticket? Everyone comes from somewhere. And it is clear that this person has come from Adelaide. And this small silver rose,' her ladyship bends down with a remarkable swiftness. 'This silver rose can't be his. I'll swear it just dropped from my Honitron and Mechlin mixture,' she says, quickly pinning the tarnished ornament to the lacey froth of her nightdress.

25

'As I was saying,' Lady Meredith continues, 'Adelaide's the place for action. Who does this corpse think he is anyway? He's got a nerve to lie where your father, Dorothea, and the subsequent Chirpies were found. Ah!' Lady Meredith adjusts her wiglet. 'You see, Dorothea, your father would not listen when I told him that the dam was not suitable for a yacht, and that no-one, simply no-one—who is anyone—has steps leading into a dam. Oh, by the way, Dorothea, I have not introduced you to Inspector Blunt,' Lady Meredith adds. 'Inspector Blunt has come to, er, help solve our mysteries. Um, the bodies we keep finding.'

The Honourable Dorothea squeezes the Inspector's hand in a bone crushing moment of welcome. 'You mustn't mind Mumsie,' she says in a low voice.

'Pleased to meet you, I'm sure.' Inspector Blunt does not know that Lady Meredith sums people up immediately on replies of this sort.

The Honourable Dorothea is tugging at her mother's arm with her incredibly strong fingers. (A family likeness considered to be an heirloom.)

'Yes, yes.' Lady Meredith is unconcerned. 'It's only a certain type,' she muses, 'who wears brown leather shoes. And d'you see, Dorothea, this man's not wearing any trousers and he's only got one foot, deah, and furthermore the sole is on the top of the foot. It *is* very important, you know, deah,' she turns to her daughter, 'to make on-the-spot observations.'

In the moment of silence which usually follows such wisdom the two women, as if from habit and the power of mutual decision, with a simultaneous movement, bend down and push the body, encouraging it to roll into the dam more completely. They then stand surveying their handiwork with the silent satisfaction of watching an unwanted corpse sink into the chill embrace of the salt laden waters of the old dam.

'Inspector,' Lady Meredith's rich voice rings out, 'could you please just give the corpse another push downwards? That's good! Thank you.' Lady Meredith then, arm in arm with the Hon Dorothea and Inspector Blunt, urges them forward across the tufts of grass and weeds.

'I think I see Nanny coming,' she says. 'She's got someone with her. It might be the new tutor. Come along, both of you, we must go and dress for breakfast.'

As they approach the house Lady Meredith stands still suddenly and strikes a dramatic pose, addressing her companions breathlessly.

'You know, it's absolutely clear from here that all the house needs is a moat, a drawbridge and a portcullis and we have a castle!' She sighs and walks on. Inspector Blunt tries, with his short legs, to keep up with his two companions.

On entering the house they are, all three, welcomed by several unintelligent but well-intentioned dogs.

'Failed Hounds,' the Honourable Dorothea says in a low voice to the Inspector. 'Mummy says all the brains were bred out of them years ago. You'll hear her explain this at dinner when she gets on to their unpleasant internal infections, a favourite topic for the meal table.'

Accompanied by the boisterous dogs they, all three, mount the stairs, leaving little pools of muddy water on the polished treads.

Part of a Personal Brief prepared in advance especially for Chief Inspector Blunt

. . . At Meredith Hall you will find a lifetime's supply of bathroom tissue stored in an enormous barn and watched over by two village simpletons (Lady Meredith prefers this title rather than that of idiots). These two valuable employees have the welfare of the bathroom tissue at heart. It is their duty to beat off with cudgels, especially made for the purpose, the rats who have discovered during discerning generations the suitability of the product for the ornamental shreddings in the linings of their numerous nests.

A word about Lady Meredith herself: Lady Meredith rose at an early age to the enviable state of being a millionairess because of her sweetly innocent yet apparently wise expression. She is not exactly beautiful or even pretty but she was born with a clinical look. An indefinable hygienic colouring and a smooth texture, in fact, a medicinal appearance which has caused people to want to photograph her, to paint her in oils and watercolours (gouache is being considered) and to make labels of her to put on natural products and on manufactured goods. It must be stated here that her blue eyes are blue with that vivid cornflower (the blue sort) intensity and, in spite of a naturally empty mind, the gaze from these eyes gives an impression that she is a deeply caring and understanding person, one who knows exactly what she is talking about. Furthermore she is capable of the right decision at the right moment, for example, which cereal to choose at breakfast and precisely when to rise from the dinner table. And, in between these, other decisions— what to have for lunch and whether to wear riding boots, Reeboks or her favourite carpet slippers. She dresses very simply in a plaid (of the ancient Meredith tartan) and her long hair is worn loose under a small matching hairpiece.

The enormous fortune has come about by an indiscretion early in her life when she allowed a Bathroom Adventurer to take advantage of her face. Literally, millions are stashed away in embarrassed banks and more conveniently, for immediate use, in the solid mahogany drawers where her underclothes and nighties are kept. Some of the money, as she is sometimes heard to say in a tired voice, is tied up in the land. And the rest, as has been mentioned, is in the form of a lifetime supply of a certain useful, but entirely lacking in glamour, commodity which is found in strategic places all over, or almost all over, the world. The enormous barn is within walking distance of the house. The two simpletons, in addition to their cudgel duties, are required to tear from the daily supply the wrappers which bear Lady Meredith's innocent yet wise face.

Inspector Blunt pauses in his reading of the Brief. He has never, in all his long experience, received a Brief like this one. He glances at the initials at the top of the page and sees it is written by a younger member of the force, an officer known to be a singer often accompanied by a lute. Inspector Blunt can remember all too well a tea-break which was taken up entirely by this enthusiastic young man explaining how well he understands the delicate quality and tone of the lute and how he has spent hours training for the necessary skill of controlling his naturally sexually ebullient voice to bring it in line with the sexually controlled lute.

Crushing the Brief into his hip pocket he goes in search of the Hon Dorothea and her new tutor, a visit to the stables having been promised.

'If you mention, just mention identikit to Mummy,' the Hon Dorothea tells Chief Inspector Blunt when she takes him to the stables with the new tutor, Herr Hood, in order to inspect their respective mounts. 'Just the word "identikit" sends her into a flat spin.' The Hon Dorothea's good-natured, large face is suddenly an uncomfortable red.

'Years ago,' she goes on, 'a small boy toddled up here as if from nowhere.' She indicates with a massive gesture the gravel sweep which disappears between the soft greens of an earlier judicious planting. 'Olives,' she explains as the two men look towards the trees. 'This child,' she continues, 'was crying bitterly. "He's lorst," Mummy said, and she told me to call off the dogs. "Call orf the dogs!" she said. Mummy's so tender-hearted. She tried to get the child to say where he had come from. "He's out of nappies," she said. She's always very observant. She noticed he had very expensive clothes. You know, a tiny Harris tweed and little Startrite shoes. To cut a long story short, Mummy thought he needed—that he might want to—you know, relieve himself, so she pulled down his little knitted undercarriage, only his jacket was Harris, you understand. He cried all the more, it was such a cold morning. As he didn't perform she pulled him up again, you know, put him all back together in his little knitteds.'

'Later she worried dreadfully. She was afraid that, by her action, she'd done him an unspeakable harm and he wouldn't remember and wouldn't know, in later years, why he had turned out the way he had. And she imagines him being psychoanalysed and being encouraged to draw a picture and, in that way, all these years later, she will be recognised from his drawing and perhaps have to appear in court on a charge . . . Identikit,' the Hon Dorothea draws breath. 'Mumsie can see it quite plainly. *Police want to question this woman 172 cm Blonde but could be grey or bald now.*'

They are in the stable in the presence of two of the most enormous horses, both at least seventeen hands, grey, raw-boned and both sharing the same off-white shade and unkempt style of mane and tail.

'This is Lucy,' the Hon Dorothea says proudly, 'and this is Charger.' She turns to the two men. 'Yours for the season. Their sex is indeterminate,' she adds. Both horses rear alarmingly and stamp. A sign of being well-bred, the Hon Dorothea offers in explanation, adding that it was, after all, rather a womanly way to carry on but then again it was behaviour associated with stallions also.

'About the murders,' the Hon Dorothea, opening the stable door, waits for her two companions to leave first. 'It all seems simple.' The Hon Dorothea bites an unwashed carrot. 'Almost as soon as Mummy remarries, something happens to her new husband. Poor Daddy was the first and then Bruno and then the Chirpies, the last being Chirpy the third. At present Mummy hasn't a husband, unless the corpse in the dam counts as one.' The Hon Dorothea is silent for a few minutes and then she tells the new tutor that she can't spell for toffee, that she can't even spell horse though she can sit one well enough. She adds that she hopes that the Inspector and Herr Hood will stay for a long time.

'And Inspector,' she turns to Inspector Blunt, 'do you think, as there are no murderable husbands at present, that Herr Hood should stay hidden? Might the murderer pick on him next?' She consults her watch, a very large one on a very narrow band which hardly reaches round her strong, competent wrist. 'We must hurry,' she says, 'we shall be late for afternoon tea. I know Nanny's dying to meet you both.'

Chief Inspector Blunt is mildly surprised when Herr Hood clicks his heels and asks the Hon Dorothea for an Ex.

'I should enjoy to borrow Ex.'

'Oh, Herr Hood. I've just told you, there aren't any. They've all gone. Kaput!' She flicks her large fingers. 'The husbands. They have all gone. Dead.'

'Exe,' the tutor makes chopping movements. The Hon Dorothea, quick on body language, laughs and tells him she will get Plant to send one up to his room. 'And now,' she goes on, 'I'll meet you both on the top landing, say, in a quarter of an hour. Nanny can't bear for us to be late.'

As the two men, at a respectful distance, follow the Hon Dorothea to the house, the tutor explains, with suitable hesitation, that there is a German word which means dung beetle. He asks the Inspector if he knows the word because he feels sure that this word, when translated back into the original German, could be an expression of extreme intimacy and affection . He explains that as he watches his new pupil leaping across the mud in the stable yard, he longs to rush after her calling out the appropriate word.

Chief Inspector Blunt, in return, admits his ignorance.

Visiting Nanny for afternoon tea is a custom kept alive at Meredith Manor. Chief Inspector Blunt has heard of such unusual customs and is interested to take part in the experience. Apparently the idea is to creep up the top staircase, avoiding the squeaky boards, and to peep coyly round the partly open door of the nursery where Nanny sits with her tea tray waiting, with a twinkle in her eye, for the family to bring their secrets.

The words to say with the coy peep are, 'It's only me, Nanny. May

I come in?' and Nanny replies in her comfortable way, 'Of course you may come in, darling.'

It amuses the Inspector to discover that it is quite in order on these occasions to play a prank. The more jovial climb the gable stairs armed with sofa cushions which can be thrown playfully at Nanny, knocking off her spectacles and sending the tea tray flying onto the faded roses of the nursery carpet.

Visitors to the Manor visit Nanny only in the presence of family. Nanny ignores the visitors while she regales the company with memories and anecdotes.

The Inspector understands almost at once that she makes it clear that if the visitor is not family then he or she does not count at all but may receive the tiniest sidelong glance when a murmuring of praise or amazement or gratitude is expected after the telling of an unusually long and boring family reminiscence. Unaccustomed as he is to making such murmurings, Chief Inspector Blunt tries a few tentative bleatings, realising that if a lamb was present in the room it would run at once to him for immediate refreshment and consolation.

While Nanny is relating that the Hon Dorothea at three months copied out recipes from the cornflakes packet in the best running writing you ever saw—'She was, dears, making a special little cookbook for her very own Nanny'—it is clear to the Inspector that Herr Hood is anticipating with hot fingertips, the cool, impersonal, sharp edge of the ordered and expected axe. The Inspector is sure that Herr Hood is, in his mind, testing the weight of the forthcoming axe so much so that it is possible to see, as if through his jacket (a good quality Austrian Loden cloth), that the muscles of his right arm have gone into a painful spasm. He can see Herr Hood's lips moving in secret; the young man is obviously trying out another German word which might translate into English as dung beetle. Herr Hood, catching sight of the Inspector's steadfast gaze, says with a little shrugged-off bow, 'Ziss word is not good, it does not produce the necessary hiss.'

Chief Inspector Blunt, Razor or Sharpie to his friends, sometimes wonders if his Creator has plagiarised him from somewhere. To the erroneous he is 'That Fat Faced Idiot', and to his wife and daughter he is Brian and Poppet respectively, though Mrs Blunt does sometimes refer to him as Mr Blunt or The Inspector.

Inspector Blunt is not accustomed to life at a lengthy house party. He reflects, while toying with a cutlet, that eleven months is a long time for a party. A glass of beer or a mug of Milo in an armchair in front of the TV with Mrs Blunt beside him in another armchair is party enough for him.

After talking to a few of the guests at intervals during the day he has not discovered as much as he had hoped to, but it does seem to him, when he thinks about it, that the guests are staying on not because they are particularly happy or comfortable but because there are marked physical difficulties connected with removing themselves and their luggage.

Meredith Manor, the Inspector muses over his cutlet, is the most isolated property he has ever visited. An uneasiness accompanies the problem about his own ability to, in plain words, get the hell out of the place. The last part of the journey, on the way to Meredith Manor, was prefaced by some weather-worn, scarcely readable warnings on a piece of wood nailed to a stump telling travellers to notify the Roads Board, the Custodians of the Environment Society, the Post Mistress and the District Nurse before travelling the road. That the gravel road was scarcely used was evident from the enormous ridges, the gullies and the potholes. Gaunt rusted farm machinery, abandoned along the way, did not suggest anything except that it was obsolete and possibly the cause of heartbreaking failure. The invasions of saltbush at ever closer intervals made it clear that penetration required the ultimate in determination inspired by a mounting panic.

Inspector Blunt, being a man of little or no imagination, does not know the meaning of fear but he has to admit to himself, as some little dishes of a soft junket are handed round, that when he finally emerged from the saltbush and found himself in an immense bald paddock with no sign of a continuing road or track it was all he could do not to burst into tears. Setting his direction by the fast-setting sun, he drove his exhausted car wildly across the bleached weeds and came upon the dam, ugly at dusk and sinister with the remains of a wrecked yacht, an unusual find in a dam, and what was without doubt a partly clothed body face-down in the water. The corpse, though wearing a light overcoat, seemed to lack trousers and a band of pale skin on one wrist told the Inspector that the victim must have been wearing a watch which had been removed.

Lady Meredith at the head of a long dining table is nearing the end of her third bottle of *Domaine de Plaisir*.

'Bring another bottle of this delicious port, Plant,' she says, 'and, Plant, bring another glass. I am sure the Inspector would like to look upon the grape.'

'Certainly, madam.' Plant is respectful and his hands encased in gloves are efficient. 'Madam will perhaps notice,' he says, 'the wine is Chardonnay with a remarkable crisp flintiness, a characteristic of the vintage.'

'Yairs,' Lady Meredith yawns into her stole. 'Flint is *the* word, isn't it, Inspector Flint?'

'Blunt,' the Inspector replies. 'I am a plain man, your ladyship.' He feels quite rightly that he has not made this long journey (his car is a complete write-off, as they say back in the Office, and the last part, from the dam onwards, had to be on foot, one uncomfortable foot after another, his boots pinching till he had a veritable embroidery of intricate little lines of pain all over his face) to sit over dinner and talk about wine. The name of the wine means nothing to him and as for 'crisp' and 'flint' the words would be better put to use to describe a lettuce and a good main road. Anything would be better than that desiccated gravel . . .

The guests are drooping on both sides of the long table. The candles too are melting and leaning over.

Inspector Blunt casts a knowledgeable eye over the company. One of them, or a member of the household, is a murderer. They are all, himself included, in danger. He feels tired.

It is disclosed during desultory conversation following the junkets that Lady Meredith has made a significant discovery earlier in the day. This discovery being some drag marks originating in the middle of the large and distant paddock affectionately known as 'the Home paddock.' After following the drag marks for some several kilometres Lady Meredith explains that she noticed the two drags became one.

'He must have lorst one of his legs,' Lady M says. 'The marks then stopped altogether about halfway to the dam. I can only say,' Lady M, with a quick upward movement of the chin (characteristic of those of noble birth), catches a stray morsel of junket and adds: 'he must have been carried lock, stock and barrel for the last part of the journey.'

'I wonder,' murmurs an unsuspecting guest, 'what was in the barrel and what has happened to it.'

Lady Meredith fixes the guests in turn with her well bred stare.

The new tutor, Herr Hood, the Inspector notices, is managing his maiden appearance at the dining table by talking to himself. He is, the Inspector hears him distinctly, trying to recapture the German for dung beetle. It is clearly something inherent to his upbringing, a useful insult, powerful in its original form.

Not knowing that white damask table napkins are left by the well bred in a crumpled heap on the white damask tablecloth, Chief Inspector Blunt tries to fold his serviette (not knowing that it should be called a napkin) while at the same time watching Herr Hood. Herr Hood, with narrowed eyes, is internalising over a comprehensive map which he made earlier, in his head, of Nanny's cosy sitting room.

Both men, taking a casual stroll before dinner, had paced together on the top terrace, during which time Herr Hood confided in the Inspector that he was extremely disturbed because of being offered, in a department store earlier, a colour rinse to put through his hair. Apparently such an experience had never happened to him before and he was wishing, he explained to Inspector Blunt, that he had come straight to the Manor instead of prowling through a preview of the mid-season sales. The unexpected proposition had come from a girl he presumed to be a hairdresser out on a lunch-break. She had a small paper bag in one hand. He was certain, he said, on thinking it over, that in the bag she was carrying a warm meat pie or a sausage roll.

The two men, still strolling, had agreed about the isolation of the Manor. They had paused to gaze together at the clock golf, played by remote control from the yellow plastic banana lounges on the lower rocky outcrop. They had walked together, with measured steps, the circumference of the tennis courts. They had admired the swimming pool and wildlife lake (the dam), the ornamental urns and pillars, placed at apparently random spots, and had marvelled together at Nanny's tales. Especially they agreed, Nanny had been in a sort of trance while she delivered a rerun of the Honourable Dorothea's birth. Herr Hood explained to the Inspector that he had been told, he had it on authority, that the Honourable Dorothea rode a Grey as if she had been born on it.

Finally, from the precipitous edge of the top terrace they had looked at the view of the surrounding paddocks. From the sun-rotted cane chairs to the faded bleached horizon, there seemed to be no life at all. They had pondered on the fate of lost sheep wandering, spreading fan-like beneath the dome of the relentless sky, showing signs, to those who understood, of the stress of starvation during the season of thin, poor quality stubble.

'Do you have an initial?' Inspector Blunt, taking advantage of the solitude, had surprised the tutor.

'Ach Ja!' Herr Hood, understanding suddenly, said. 'I have two,' unable to keep the pride out of his voice, 'two R's.' He gave a guttural laugh. 'Two R's.'

'Thank you.' Inspector Blunt entered the information in his notebook, some vague, slightly troublesome memory, persisting, caused him to add the words 'only has two of the three R's'.

Herr Hood had continued with his guttural laugh as they turned to go back to the Manor.

'Robin und Raskolnikov,' he managed at last alongside the laughter, enjoying his little joke which was naturally lost upon the Inspector.

Chief Inspector Blunt allows himself a little relaxation in the small hours. How much simpler the job would be, for example, if reduced in location to the carpark by the familiar Variety Store supermarket where two men in dirty, crumpled, cream-coloured safari suits, one afternoon, began to loiter. Inspector Blunt keeps a cassette in his Walkman. He listens frequently to the fragment of hoarse conversation in the hope of picking up an odd clue previously overlooked.

'What about that red Porsche? Yeah that, over there. I love red. Always wanted red—' the voice is interrupted.

'Naw! Don't be daft. Red and a Porsche! You must be off yer brain. Use yer loaf. It's white we want. Whites is everywhere. Red's conspicuous. Whites look alikes. That's what.'

The conversation, such as it is, is drowned then in the noise of a car engine, a baby crying and the aristocratic, indignant voices of two Siamese cats. It is forever to Inspector Blunt's chagrin that the car, the baby, the two Siamese cats and the safari suits were discovered almost at once, abandoned, in a nearby suburban street. 'It's like Christmas Day every day,' an elderly pensioner told reporters . . .

Why couldn't *this* case be cut and dried, Inspector Blunt strokes his chin, like the great Cat, Car and Baby Robbery. It would be easier, he reflects, if he could sit now and build houses with playing cards in the manner of a distinguished fellow in the field, but these days even playing cards are not what they used to be.

Baffled by isolation and the house party and his sudden loss of energy, the Inspector longs for a cup of tea. He is missing the welcome and regular visits of the Office Tea Lady and her pearls of wisdom. He can almost hear them:

'A fewell (fool) and her money is soon parted,' with special reference to the scattered ornamental pillars and. an extravagance of banana lounges.

And 'Where there's more money than sense!', a remark applicable to the brick paving squandered over large areas. His thoughts are restful even though he needs his tea badly. He tries to remember the Tea Lady's name and is disturbed in his pleasant reverie by a scream and a crash as of buckets falling from a great height.

'Drat!' Lady Meredith's voice is not hard to hear. 'Just when I was hoping to take Hunter out and do a bit of mustering. Why can't these kitchen gels learn to turn round and go down the back stairs without falling down them? If they must fall, why don't they fall in silence?'

'Mumsie,' the Honourable Dorothea can be heard replying in more subdued tones, 'it's because they're walking backwards bobbing curtsies and they go on bobbing right to the top of the stairs still *backwards*, Darling, do you see? It was your own idea.'

When all is quiet once more Inspector Blunt peers round his door and crosses the landing stealthily. He finds the Hon Dorothea sitting on the stairs with an enormous hamper.

'It's a midnight feast,' she says. 'Have some. There's salami and pickles and tinned peaches. I'm initiating Herr Hood. I sewed up his pyjama legs and made an apple pie bed earlier this evening. And, as an extra, there's Epsom Salts in the sugar basin. Also I have plans for a midnight bathe. A sort of unexpected little treat for our visitors. One of our little ways.'

The Inspector, with some heavy breathing, sits down on the top stair next to Herr Hood's devoted pupil

'Give me the lowdown, m'dear,' he tries the gruff avuncular whisper attached now, for many years, to his name.

'It's all very simple really,' the Hon Dorothea says before sinking her big white teeth into a buttered roll. 'Almost everyone who comes here gets murdered. Well some disappear, presumed murdered,' the Hon Dorothea yawns. 'Every few weeks I have a new tutor. My schoolwork naturally suffers.' She gives a sigh and demolishes the roll. The Inspector, his little finger delicately crooked, approaches an olive with caution. You never know with olives. (He has been known to hold forth on the subject.) One thoughtless bite on an olive stone can be the death of a tooth. Harm can come to the whole denture.

The Hon Dorothea deals with a tin of peaches savagely.

'Fortunately I am rather bright,' she says.

'Quite,' the Inspector agrees.

'I mean, people wouldn't murder merely for money, would they?' She smiles at the Inspector who feels he is in the presence of someone with an even greater wisdom than his own about the intentions of the human animal. It is impossible not to pay homage mentally to the strong masculine wrists and the sturdy collarbones of this Lorelei—this Rhine Maiden of the paddocks. He can see how the Tutor, the true Romantic for whom the power of reason no longer operates, would regard his new protégé.

'What we really need is an illegitimate descendant of Sherlock Holmes or Hercule Poirot or even that man, whatshisname, Superintendent Adam Dalgliesh of Black Tower and Steen Clinic fame. We need someone of their calibre, inherited calibre I should say. They would have to be illegitimate in the absence of wives. Mummy,' the Hon Dorothea draws breath, 'Mummy herself is awfully good at discovering and tracking drag marks. Girl Guides, you see, but her Tracker Badge didn't take her far enough. Though she has done well with clues. A pair of spectacles in a Bible and some white hairs on a velvet collar. Unfortunately both these turned out to be her own though she swears they belonged to one of the dogs.' The Hon Dorothea pauses for a competent picking of her teeth with a sharpened match. She looks at the Inspector closely saying:

'I don't suppose you shoot up with cocaine or play the violin or write poetry or memoirs. I mean you're not quite in the same class . . .'

Inspector Blunt, failing to see that with the Hon Dorothea's expression of the need for one or all of the mentioned great names he has been insulted, struggles to his feet telling the Hon Dorothea that she has been most helpful and that he will now amble along the various passages pausing now and then with an ear and an eye pressed to a keyhole.

Inspector Blunt after his private nocturnal stroll returns to his room to sum up his findings, recording them in his notebook in his own distinctive black hand. Another more susceptible man might easily have been overpowered, intimidated is perhaps a better word, by yards of menacing chintz and a hideous wallpaper known to have kept more than one person awake for nights on end. In addition the wallpaper is pasted, whether on purpose or by accident, over the door, making it very difficult, once inside the room, to find the way out.

He lists the suspects.

One. Lady Meredith who explains the one bedside ornament she allows herself is a bottle of whisky; 'Sometimes two, Inspector, as the level sinks in one.' On being asked where she had spent the previous night she had replied, 'Here in Meredith Manor,' opening her blue eyes wide. 'Where else is there?'

Inspector Blunt, recording the interview now, underlines the words, *Does not pretend to be anywhere other than here.* He has not searched her room for weapons feeling, at the time, that it would be indelicate during a tête à tête to ask if she had any hidden.

Two. The Nanny. He reflects on Nanny and the way in which her eyes slip sideways during her fits of rambling nostalgia. He realises it is almost impossible to persuade her to talk about anything except the Honourable Dorothea, how she, the H Dotty, would never eat honey unless it was called white jam, for example. And for an elderly respectable virgin (her title of Mrs being purely an honorary one) when prized from her shell of memories, she has an inordinate interest in sexual matters. An example being in her own words, 'Does that creature in the Yellow Daisy Room ever have the hots for anyone? Being on her own the way she is what the hell does she do for sex?' and about the couple in the Blue Room: 'Take a look at them, will you. How can they be right in bed? Get a butchers of the size, will you.'

Inspector Blunt privately has to agree that there is an irretrievable incompatibility in size. He hears Nanny's inexorable voice, 'Be like a Murray Grey serving a starved Jersey.' She was unable to hide the scorn in her voice. 'She'd never be able to get the calf—*imagine the size of it*—out. Have to be hacked out, it would, in pieces.'

However, Nanny has seemed happy to speak out on Lady Meredith's husbands. 'Alike as peas. Couldn't tell them apart—the living from the dead.' Inspector Blunt notes that, at the conclusion of his visit to Nanny, he asked her if she minded the pranks being played on her. Nanny gave a wicked little chuckle saying with a wry expression, 'Mind? Why should I mind? It's only cushions when all's said and done. I save them up, you see, I save them up. I do my own thing with cushions.'

The Inspector recalls Lady Meredith describing her husbands as 'darlings every one of them, a bit chubby but who's minding? And yes, they were all named Chirpy latterly. It was easier to remember that way. And yes, they all possessed similar qualities, like knowing what was essential at the crucial moment, whether it was a half bottle of champagne or a whole case, pearls or diamonds, breakfast in bed or lunch—hot lunch in bed—or simply a plate or two of oysters on the terrace—that sort of thing.'

Three. The Hon Dorothea. 'She seems a sensible sort of girl.' Inspector Blunt writes with care. 'And would hardly have disposed of her own father.' As a father himself he is unable to see his own daughter, in his own words, 'doing him in'. What does the Honourable Dorothea stand to gain by disposing of anyone? Inspector Blunt, in his notebook, dismisses her and the Tutor from his list of suspects. The Tutor will be, in the expected pattern of events, quite rightly a ready-made target as the next victim. 'He even looks like a rat.' The Inspector argues comfortably, without an opponent, inside his own head. He reads back in his notebook, going over the results of having his ear pressed from one door to the next.

From the Blue Room:

Lovely hot water.

Yes, the wise virgin certainly got there first.

I assure you I used hardly any, *practically none.*

Oh yes? I *saw* the steam under the door, filled the whole passage it did and it's still lying as a mist out there over the paddocks. I thought you said you were having cold baths. In the brochure it says cold baths. I mean, what else at a fat farm? You great gross hunk of . . . You . . .

No one said anything about a fat farm. What brochure?

From the Yellow Daisy Room (as opposed to Yellow Room (plain)):

I'm right here. Right over the bloody conservatory. Anyone looking up can see right up my skirt. Listen! If someone doesn't come by soon and let me out of here I'll smash everything, that glass table, the mirrors, the windows, the floor—yes that's glass too and that religious statue. I suppose it is religious. I'm not used to being alone like this. I thought when I answered the advertisement I was coming for the holiday of a lifetime. Horses unlimited, that sort of thing. And, on top of all this, I'm starving.

From the Yellow Room (plain):

I can't stand it here another minute. All that dead grass right out to the ends of the earth and, I ask you, who cares whether fox's droppings are pointed at both ends. I mean what a thing to talk about at dinner. And those dogs. Imbeciles.

Aw Honey, Sugar Baby . . .

Don't you Honey and Sugar me! I wish I'd never come. I wish I'd never met you. This place! I only came for a weekend and it's been months. What's the idea? I want to go home to mother. I'm hungry. I never want to see boiled mutton ever again. I could kill everyone here, you first . . .

Awright, awright, Honey Blossom. Come to think of it I don't seem to be losing weight, any. It was supposed to be *The Last Diet to end all Diets*. It's not what it's cracked up to be. I'll go along with you on that and tell the truth I wouldn't pass up a piece of your Mom's apple pie just now . . .

Moments later, continuing his monaural (peculiar to himself) keyhole investigations, the Inspector encounters, at the foot of the attic stairs, the tutor who confesses to having in his room a blood-stained axe and a brass bound box containing memorabilia. He tells the Inspector that he feels sure that he is to be the next victim. He is on his way, he adds, to a moonlight swim with his pupil.

Inspector Blunt scribbles a reminder to himself to look up, in the nearest dictionary, the word memorabilia. He advises Herr Hood to leave at once.

'Just as soon as you've had your dip.'

'Yes, but how?' Hood asks. Both men share briefly, the Inspector is sure, an internal and desolate vision of endless paddocks and vague unfinished tracks.

'That's your problem,' Inspector Blunt, to his surprise, finds himself adopting an idiom quite foreign to him. He thinks he hears a strangled sob escaping from the tutor and turns away at once to avoid embarrassment.

The next door which claims Inspector Blunt's attention is studded with jewels and has a striking door knob which gives the impression of being valuable since it is padlocked to the door. Peering at the knob the Inspector decides it is either made of hand-beaten gold or is an extremely good imitation. He is, he realises, at the keyhole of the sumptuous apartment belonging to Plant (the indoor man) and Mrs Plant, the housekeeper. From a somewhat limited view it is clear that the Plants are modelling themselves on the Barrymores of Baskerville but are falling short, as they themselves realise, on the sinister. He cannot help overhearing their conversation:

'Ida, you are not sinister enough.'

'I know, Ted. What d'you suggest I do about it? You're not all that sinister yourself. But changing the subject, Ted, I can't see us ever getting this place to ourselves. People keep on coming here and what's more they stay on. Talk about breakfast trays! And bed linen. Where's it going to end, I ask you!' Before Plant can reply, Mrs Plant changes her tone to one of excitement, an excitement, Inspector Blunt thinks, tinged with fear.

'Ted!' Mrs Plant exclaims, 'you know I told you about what I did in the supermarket that time . . . '

'What did you do, Ida?' Plant, in waistcoat and shirt sleeves, is putting on his jacket in order to answer a distant bell. He pauses. 'What did you do, Ida?' He waits patiently for Mrs Plant to speak.

'It's the Inspector, Ted. It *was him* that day in the supermarket. I'd know that face anywhere. Remember? I told you I'd picked up a Juicy Fruit before I got to go through the checkout. The girl there had got talking to the woman ahead of me, it was her mother, see, and they were taking ages—talking and talking so I unwrapped the Juicy Fruit and popped the whole lot in my mouth there and then. There was this man behind me watching my every move and I told him, "it keeps me off the grog and the smokes", I said, and he said, "not to worry", just like that, "not to worry", and I said, "no", and then I said, "no, I tell a lie, it's my blood sugar. I'm in a sugar crisis. You know, hypoglycaemia", I told him. He said he knew, he had one at home, he told me he understood. Such a perfect gentleman. They don't come like that these days. It's him. The Inspector. I'd know that face anywhere. Where can I hide, Ted?'

'Not to worry, Ida,' Plant says. 'Just as soon as I've done her Ladyship we'll dip them Hounds. Talk about scary. This new paint, it's the tops. They won't lick this lot off in a hurry. This'll scare the pants off that Inspector of yours. Flooressent. Ida. See?'

Stunned by what he has heard and seen (Plant putting on his jacket) at the jewelled keyhole, Inspector Blunt, weak, light-headed, sweating, trembling, cold and shaky and faint makes at once for the attic stairs. Trying to feel his own pulse he discovers it is weak and rapid.

The discovery at dawn or, as Inspector Blunt prefers to put it, the dawn discovery of an axe buried, as if with tremendous force, in a pile of sofa cushions on Nanny's rocking chair sends the Inspector hot-foot across the paddocks to the dam.

'So this was her "own thing with sofa cushions",' he mutters as he pants for breath. He remembers too late the hints he was given, the watch flaunted on the Honourable Dorothea's heavy wrist and the pale streak on the wrist of the unhappy corpse where a watch strap had once nestled. Then there was the tutor, he recalls, asking for an axe, and the tutor himself announcing he was going for a moonlight swim with the Honourable Dorothea. How could he, a Chief Inspector, have ignored these signs?

As he approaches the dam he sees through the early morning mist the shadowy figures of Lady Meredith and the Honourable Dorothea, dressed, it seems, in their night clothes. Both are bending over the water near, he imagines, those foolish steps. Is he too late? He is not able to run faster.

'They never will listen,' Nanny is overtaking him on her scooter, 'and into the water they go. No-one pushes them, they walk in, some dive, showing off.' She continues over her shoulder as she passes.

'It's no use warning them, they never listen, they see water and in they go. I could go on about it till I lorst all me breath. On the top the water's warm enough but just you go down a bit and it's goodbye with a cramp. Jack Knife! Fools!' With a high-pitched laugh and an extra roar she's gone, her little machine leaping over the uneven ground.

The Inspector tries to run but seems to make no progress. He runs and runs and does not get any nearer to the little group at the edge of the water. A heron rises from the far side of the dam and with a raucous melancholy cry flies off slowly, in search of food.

'You've missed the whole of Bugs Bunny, the News and Weather *and* Sale of the Century *and* your favourite Matlock and what's more you've not eaten your sandwiches and you know what that does to you, not eating I mean, and your tea's stone cold.'

Chief Inspector Blunt, deep in his TV chair, opens one eye to see Mrs Blunt already eased out of her own chair. Hands on hips she asks him if he would like more tea, 'but I'd say a Milo would be more suitable.'

All those people in the rooms at Meredith Manor, the Inspector is ticking them off in his mind: the Plants, the Hounds, the guests in the Blue Room and the two Yellow Rooms and, in the stables, those Greys, the biggest, most formidable horses he has ever seen. All of them were red herrings.

'Herrings,' he says aloud, almost as a question.

'We've had tea,' Mrs Blunt makes an announcement of the fact, 'but seeing as you dozed off without eating yours I'll fix you some nice bread and butter. Your blood sugar's dropped I'll be bound.'

'I must have dropped off, Brenda,' Inspector Blunt makes one of his penetrating observations.

'You can say that again.' Mrs Blunt always enjoys a little quick-witted repartée at bedtime.

So many clues, left to himself the Inspector goes over, in his mind, the little silver rose and the Hon Dorothea's large bones, Nanny's stories and the Tutor's axe, so many clues, he sighs. Once again he is faced with something bigger than both himself and the force of which he is the Chief. The wise virgin, the Chirpies, the one called Bruno. Then, he mutters in a low voice as if counting and making a list, Honey Sugar and Blossom, Robin and/or Raskolnikov, Nanny, Plant and Mrs Plant, the Honourable Dorothea and Lady Meredith. He is still compiling his list when Mrs Blunt returns with her little tray.

'Sounds as if you're planning a really high class party,' she says.

The Inspector, thinking now of the Murray Grey and the starved Jersey, tells Mrs Blunt to remind him to invite a vet.

Archie Weller spent his early years on an
isolated farm in the south-west of Western
Australia. His first novel, *The Day of the Dog*,
was written and submitted to the inaugural
Australian/Vogel award within a period of 6
weeks in a spirit of anger after his release from
Broome gaol for what he regarded as a wrong-
ful conviction. The book was highly com-
mended by the judges. His collection of stories
entitled *Going Home* was published soon
afterwards.

Archie Weller
DEAD ROSES

No marks could be seen on the head or hands, but beside the face lay two items, a train ticket from Adelaide and a small silver rose.

Senior Constable Newbry stared down at the body that lay across the sandy track. The cheerful, piping notes of small birds seemed incongruous near this scene of violent death. The man's face was twisted in a caricature of grotesque surprise—even more grotesque now a small band of busy black ants was trailing over his face and into his gaping mouth.

Probably attracted by the blood, Senior Constable Newbry thought. There was enough around. The body lay in a pool of thick congealing blood that not even the grey sand of the bush track had entirely soaked away. He had not died quickly, this man. There were wounds from some sharp instrument in his shoulder, thigh and chest. There were signs of a desperate struggle for survival but no-one except his killer would have heard a thing as he died a lonely and savage death. Finally, his throat had been cut.

This was the Senior Constable's first murder case. He had been transferred to the out-of-the-way township of The Rocks for the very fact that it was a quiet place and he was due to retire soon. He had hoped to leave the force with a clean record of everything tackled, everything done. This seemed to be in jeopardy now.

Constable Millson came back from being sick behind the old tingle-tingle tree, his thin face white. He wouldn't be much use, Senior Constable Newbry thought. He wished he had one of his old mates with him now because he sensed this would be a hard nut to crack. He remembered an old mate of his from Melbourne telling him about a similar case involving a Macedonian, known among the Melbourne Underworld as the Turk, that had never been solved. The reason he thought of this now was because the only clue then to that murder had been a small ornament of some kind—he couldn't remember what just now. But he had this dithering youth, fresh out of the Academy, who, so far, had appeared none too bright. He wouldn't be able to find a cow in a dairy, the older man thought. The Rocks—the place where all the no-hopers ended up.

The Rocks—a conglomerate of weatherboard houses, peopled mostly by spiders and rats as the population dwindled—moving family by family up to the city. A store, a hall, a police station, post office and small hospital also, all made of dark stained weatherboard and every building covered by a red tin roof. Only the pub (named by some wit as The Opera House) was different in that it was made of river-mud bricks and had a green tin roof. It was just as dilapidated as the rest of the town, though, and the only thing even resembling an opera held there would have been The Beggars' Opera.

'Christ, Don, what do you think would have caused *that!!*' Constable Millson croaked.

It was his first case of any sort, never mind murder. He had only arrived from the Academy six months ago. Young, full of ideas, very respectful. In a bit of a hurry to get up in the world, though. Senior Constable Newbry had told him to relax; not be so conscientious. At least he had succeeded in getting the youngster to stop calling him sir or, worse yet, Senior Constable. Protocol was quite uncalled for in a place like The Rocks, which most people had never heard of.

They would now.

No-one likes dead bodies lying around. There would be a team of CIB men over here now, this afternoon, buzzing around everywhere like flies; stepping on everyone's toes like elephants. Ordering everyone around.

'Right! Let's get this area sealed off. There's some cord and markers in the car. Then call through on your mobile to Kalveston Central. I want you to stay here and make sure nothing's touched while I go over and find old Benny Higgins. His eyes might see something we don't.'

'What!? Stay here with him?' the young policeman said, aghast.

'Don't worry. He won't annoy you, laddie,' the grey old man called back as he strode away.

The pale leaves of the beautiful red tingle-tingle tree cast soft shadows over the prostrate body and the sickened Constable. Its hollowed-out black interior seemed a cave of mysterious thoughts.

That is just what the Senior Constable's mind was as he drove the three or four miles up the lumpy grey track that meandered through the forest and somehow found its way to town. It was not the main road—that was a thin, potholed strip of bitumen that eventually led out to the South Coast Highway—but it was really the only other road in the district, even though it led nowhere. The population of The Rocks was not overly huge, perhaps three hundred with another hundred itinerants, come down to do fruit-picking or shearing or hay-carting or whatever. But most of them kept to a well run circle and had become familiar faces in their seasonal work. The thing that made old Don Newbry morose was that this man who had got himself murdered on his patch was a total stranger.

What was this stranger doing out there on this road to nowhere in the middle of the night (or sometime last night, anyway). A stranger, what is more, who had come all the way from Adelaide to this—The Rocks—where no-one ever came, not even from Kalveston, the nearest thing the district had to a big city, some seventy miles away on the coast.

He found old Benny sunning himself on the pub verandah along with Doctor Fairchild, so he invited them both along. He would have to put the body in the Doctor's morgue anyway. It had been built to accommodate any accidents at the mill.

Marrilyn Henry had also been sunning herself on the verandah and looking around with interest in her black eyes at the sprawling town and huge shell of the sawmill that had made this town exist. She had hardly left the city in all her twenty-three years and, besides, her country was the red, barren beauty of up North. Well, her mother's country really. She had been talking to old Benny Higgins, the last of the Nyoongahs from this area, about the significance of the rock formation the town was named after.

Old Benny was about sixty, with long white hair streaked with yellow and a craggy brown face. He was reluctant to talk to a stranger—and a woman—about things *his* father had said were special to his family and tribe, even if she was of the same race.

Marrilyn had been angry when called into the editor's office last week and told, in the editor's high-handed manner, that she must go down South.

Apparently there was a man down there called Micky Sierra, whose father had come out from Italy in the 1930s and started up a sawmill with some of his relations. But during the Second World War most of them had been interned and sent to camps over East. After the war he had come back and, even though he had owned the mill and some of the land round about, he had never made much money. One son and the two daughters had gone back over East to their uncles, aunts and cousins. Another son was a builder in Perth and only the middle son, Michelangelo, had stayed looking after his father's mill. It was one of the last independent mills left operating in the country.

It would make a great feature about a battling Aussie, fighting against prejudice and hard times and still being able to survive and now about to get his reward by selling out to a big company. The editor said he had some leaked information that the whole area was to be developed into a woodchip industry. (Surprise, surprise, guess who owned the greater part of the shares in the process terminal that turned wood into chips?? None other than the . . . but best to let that slide. No need to worry your pretty little head about politics . . . someone more competent could do a follow-up story on that aspect.)

But there was some possibility that a pile of old rocks down there might be of tribal significance (not that there *was* any tribe there now—they were all long dead!). So could she go down and check out the authenticity of this claim, as well as get a story on Micky Sierra?

He didn't exactly say it but the impression was 'because you're an Aborigine and understand about this *Spirits and the land business.*'

She had never been anywhere near the land in her life. She had been fostered out to a white family when young and gone to an exclusive girls' school, then straight to university and a career in journalism. She had no interest in Spirits whatsoever.

But the editor thought it was just the story for their Aboriginal cadet reporter to work on, so here she sat, half-asleep on the verandah, listening to an old man's mumbled half answers and irrelevancies.

Until the arrival of Senior Constable Newbry and his exciting news.

When she asked if she could come too, Don looked at her in some surprise. Nice neat clothes, new shoes, a city hairstyle. Was she some sort of relation to old Benny? He didn't know he had any. Don looked inquiringly at the old man.

'I'm a reporter from Perth. I was doing another story here, you see, and it would certainly do my career no harm to get a scoop like this.' She smiled.

'Well, plenty of room in the back, Miss. But it's not a real nice sight. My young Constable himself was sick when he saw the remains,' Don replied, his grey eyes studying her.

Her smile faded but she set her jaw resolutely and followed the three men to the van. There was only room for three in the front, so she had to ride in the back where the prisoners were put. The garrulous old Doctor, seeing her plight and embarrassment, sat in with her to keep her company.

She saw the amusing side to this, though, as she was tossed to and fro by the lurching van. Her first—and she knew without a doubt—her last ride in a vehicle which had incarcerated so many of her people. Going to see a dead white man who could make her famous for a while, and another Aborigine was needed to find this white man's killer—who more likely than not would turn out to be white also. There was irony in all that.

So that is how Marrilyn Henry came to The Rocks. The black oily houses stared back at her forebodingly, like black patches in the heavy pressing bush round about, full of their own secrets and unwilling to share them with strangers. The huge rambling old sawmill stood lopsided upon the hill just on the edge of town, empty now except for clattering bits of tin, chattering rats, swooping silent bats and cautious feral cats. The huge old pile of sawdust lay like a red festering sore and the wind howled dismally through the blackened rafters.

When she arrived at the murder site she got quite a shock. The murdered man she had seen alive only last night in the pub. Indeed, he had spoken to her briefly about a few shots she had made during a pool game. Even she, who didn't believe in Spirits, shivered slightly.

Don asked her who else had been there and she mentioned the shearers, especially one called Danny Lacy, and an Italian she thought was called Pedro and a woman who briefly came into the pub: blonde hair, blue eyes, about thirty-five. Very flashy.

'Aah, yes. That'd be Marjorie Perrit. She was a barmaid there once,' Don said.

The investigation into the murdered man began routinely and she was enough of a reporter to know to keep in the investigating officer's good books so she could glean any titbits. Although it didn't seem as big a scoop as she had hoped. No other reporters came down and the piece she sent to the papers was badly hacked around and stuck on page twenty-six, at the bottom. Then she got a midnight phone call from her boss:

'Forget this bloody ponyarse who got himself stiffed.' (He liked to talk like editors in second-rate American movies.) 'It's getting really hot on this woodchip business and I want to be the first to break it. Now pull out your finger and get some juicy bits about Sierra being overpaid to clear out, or the government's lack of concern over indigenous people's religious and cultural rights, or *anything!!*'

At the same time as the editor's gravelly voice was spiralling over the airwaves, punctuated by much crackling and hissing of the ancient line, Don was having a meeting with the three CIB officers from Kalveston.

Benny's sharp eyes had found a few clues, as Don had known they would. The old man was a quiet and somewhat shy (some would have said sullen) man but when it came to tracking he was one of the best and many a time old Benny had been called out to find some child or city picnicker lost in the huge surrounds of the jarrah and eucalypt forest, or the frightening eeriness of the karri forest with its huge white ghostly trunks and mass of wattle trees below. It could get very cold in this semi-rainforest environment, going down to minus two or three degrees sometimes, and many a child owed its life to this mumbling old brown man with the sharp black eyes.

He had found a much-used tube of vivid crimson lipstick (but what this had to do with the murdered man no-one knew). Still, it was carefully packed away and sent to the lab for further analysis. A path through the bush led from the dead body back to town, coming out just behind The Opera House, and Benny said the way some of the branches were bent showed the person had come and gone the same way. He had also found a set of footprints on the sheltered side of the track that indicated the dead stranger had come up the road. A piece of tweed coat caught on the scraggly hands of a prickle bush and the half obscured footprint of what appeared to be a heavy industrial boot gave some clue as to the attacker. Also, perhaps not really a clue but included because it was found alongside the tweed coat fragment, was a strand of greasy sheep's wool.

So, Don reasoned, the attacker and the attacked had presumably arranged a meeting at the old tingle-tingle tree. And why not? It was a landmark almost as well known as the rock formation. Once there had been many of these strange giants growing in the bush here, both red and yellow tingle-tingle. They were strange because once they reached a certain height and age the bottom part of them hollowed out, forming living caves. The biggest and most famous one you could drive a car through but, even so, every one of them had been awesome trees.

Senior Constable Newbry pondered over what they had discovered so far. The attacker wore heavy boots and a tweed coat so was probably a man. But that description of footwear applied to just about every man in the district. So a local man kills a total stranger. Why? He couldn't think where the strand of wool or the lipstick fitted in. The former was probably just some wandering sheep and the lipstick some girl's dropped belonging.

The dead man had quite possibly come from Adelaide and they were waiting for reports from the CIB there. He had a penchant for flashy jewellery, two expensive rings on his fingers and an eighteen carat gold necklace around his neck. In his pockets were found a wallet containing about five hundred dollars in big bills, a series of costly TAB tickets, each one running into units of hundreds, and a pocket box of matches with the logo of a well known Perth brothel. Also a packet of very expensive cigars, of which only one had been smoked.

Why would a person of obvious means come down here in the first place? A tourist, perhaps? The only people here were unemployed sawyers, out of work farmers and ne'er-do-well larrikins with no fruit-picking and very little shearing and plenty of time and trouble on their hands. Yet this was no simple attempted robbery gone wrong. He could sense it was something bigger.

Despite his well filled wallet, expensive tastes and, if *he* had brought the ticket, his willingness to outlay a large amount of money to come over here, the clothes he wore were seedy and crumpled as though he had lived in them for some time. A brown coat, thin brown trousers, a stained yellow shirt, threadbare yellow socks and well worn hushpuppies. Not the sort of attire to go traipsing about the bush in at two o'clock in the morning (the time the Doctor had determined death to be) when it had been about minus one degree. Very misty and cold. He would have known it would be cold when he saw the mist rising off the river as he came into town. He must have really desperately wanted to see this person whom he had met beside the tree.

Why? Old Don Newbry asked himself again.

Marrilyn Henry set out the next morning to go and do her master's bidding.

She found out from the publican, where Michelangelo Sierra lived, just out of town in the original old sawmill of his father's. There was only one phone in town now for public use and that was at The Opera House. The other phone was at the police station so she couldn't ring to organise a meeting. She just hoped she could surprise him and trick him into saying something of interest by pretending she knew more than she did. She doubted it though. There was nothing in this town of the slightest interest to the rest of Australia.

Various members of the Sierra clan had cannibalised parts of the old mill to make houses of their own, so the skeleton of a former empire lay haphazardly around the sucker-populated clearing. It appeared Mick's house was the back part of the old mill and where the sawdust heap had lain there now was a wonderful garden tended by the loving hands of Mick's tough little Northern Italian wife, Anna.

Mick himself was a large, easy-going Southern Italian, with a huge gap-toothed grin and work-roughened hands.

Marrilyn saw him and two younger men fussing about with an old car so she drove up to them and put on her best reporter's smile. A smile guaranteed to soften the heart of a rock; a smile that said 'I'm your friend and I sympathise with you. Tell me all your problems so I can alert the world and we will sort them out.'

The smile worked for Mick who gave a cheery wave and stood up, stretching his back. Probably he wasn't too interested in car engines anyway, she thought, noticing how abruptly he moved over towards her in his ambling lurch.

The other two scowled at her and she noticed with a slight shock that one was a man she had had a run-in with at the pub last night. And he certainly had been no Pavarotti, she thought wryly. She hoped there would be no more trouble. She noticed several youngsters peering around doors in suspicion or wonder. Apparently visitors were a novelty to the Sierra clan. But Mick himself was a shining ray of friendliness.

'Gudday. I 'eard youse was comin'. So . . . ya wanna do a story ona ole Mick, ay? No worries!'

He helped her out of the car, bowing slightly. The smile on his face was huge, yet his eyes were shrewd. He would be a hard fish to catch, she reasoned and looked forward to the battle. The Migrant and the Original Owner both sparring about land the white Australians had an interest in.

Mick spoke with his hands a fair bit.

'Me nephew Pedro and me baby son, Giovanni!' He waved a huge paw in their direction.

Just then three other youths came out of the trees, talking and laughing between themselves until they spotted Marrilyn, when they froze—just like a mob of kangaroos she had once observed at the zoo as a child. Bodies still and black eyes fastened on her as though they had never seen an Aboriginal before. She felt flustered under their gaze but a burst of Italian from the youths at the car caused them to carry on laughing towards the house. Although one faded away back into the bush with an idle wave to his companions. She wondered if they had been out planting trees, for one carried a shovel and another several green plastic bags.

'I've met Pedro, last night. I suppose you might say he was The Rocks' welcoming committee as you say he is your nephew and they say this is your town,' she said coolly.

'Aah, sure,' Mick laughed. 'He tell me about this abo girl. I 'ear ya give 'im one good talkin' to, better than his mama, my sister never give him. Good job! 'E's too cheeky for 'is own good.'

For a moment her eyes flashed then she let it rest. How was he to know that 'abo' was as hurtful to her as 'wog' or 'dago' or 'refo' might be to him? Besides, it was not as bad as the snide remarks Pedro had made to her last night, nearly driving her from the room.

'Aah, ya just a boong! Give youse fancy clothes, like, and powder yersel' up an' put on all youse 'igh-falutin' ways, youse still just a gin. Garn, I got no time for ya! Black greenie, white greenie, youse all the bloody same. Youse fuck up the work for us and then go back to youse 'omes, clappin' yersel' ona back and say what a good job ya done savin' the fuckin' trees!!'

Then Pedro had waved a grubby finger near her face, causing her to step backwards in a hurry, spilling her red wine all over her dress.

'Another thing too! Don't come at that 'rock bein' a sacred site' bullshit. My uncle was born 'ere and grew up with the abos. 'E's got a lot of time for them 'oo got some claim to the place, youse can ask ole Benny 'iggins. But don't youse come in 'ere and start takin' away every bit of the country just 'cos youse a boong. It don't work that way down 'ere!'

There had been a commotion at the door then and four or five heavy-shouldered shearers had clumped in, bringing the scent of rain and the smell of lanoline and sheep shit on their clothes. Their rowdy voices had cut into the Italian youth's tirade that had begun when she innocently inquired did he work at the mill and did he know why the town was named The Rocks? She had tried to be cunning and had ended up the focus of attention of the whole pub, humiliated because of the volatile Italian. She noticed the publican glance at her then look away and heard the suppressed laughter of the only other customer in the pub (a man half-hidden in the shadows) when she spilt her drink. She blushed in shame and embarrassment. The noisy shearers in their heavy boots and with their loud voices had come just in time to cause a diversion.

She noticed two of the shearers were Nyoongahs—one a big-gutted, heavy-set man in his early thirties and the other a slender youth of perhaps nineteen. It was this youth who sidled over to her. His eyes were black and piercing and proud—as black as hers. He flashed her a showy, snowy, grin and she smelt the wine on him so she was afraid again. Growing up as she had with white people, most of their prejudices had rubbed off on her, so whenever she came across a drunken member of her own race, she was as embarrassed and disgusted or patronisingly sorry as her white counterparts. She had had no taste of the very social life Aboriginal families lead and the humour which a close family life nurtures; the humour helped along by social drinking. All she ever felt when she saw a drunk Aboriginal was curiosity as to whether they might be a relative. This uncertainty and unwillingness to face up to her Aboriginality made her wary in Nyoongah company.

She flashed him a shy smile.

'What ya talkin' about, Pedro, ya stupid dago!? Ya can't even talk English proper, anyways! Don't ya know "boong" means bum in the Koori language? I read it in a book one time, and what ya see 'ere sure ain't no bum, coodah!' the youth called out then rubbed his wool-greasy hand on the back of his jeans and stuck it out to her. 'Danny Lacy, that's me, and this is me Uncle Fraser (he introduced the other Nyoongah who nodded slightly then looked away, shy of this flash city stranger). We call 'im Fraze the Daze cos 'e dazes ya with 'is shearin'. And me mates, 'Oward, 'Orace and Pete. We shearers!!!' he cried out proudly.

They had been lucky to get work. Most of the farmers were shearing their own sheep now, the ones they hadn't yet shot. It was almost a pointless exercise since the price of wool was at an all-time low and there were huge stockpiles in every capital city. This job was a solid one though and the pay cheque, lower than in past years, was still better than a dole cheque, so the five shearers were happy and ready to make a party of it.

The three white men among them looked her up and down and then at each other and nodded, winked and nudged amongst themselves like a flock of blue and white or red galahs. They grinned at her through broken yellow teeth.

'Lost, are ya, darlin'? Only people 'oo get lost wind up in this dump, ay Charlie?' one asked the publican. 'Come and 'ave a bit of a sing-song at the old Opera House.'

'Course, then ya never git found again, ay!' another cackled.

'Unless, like, ya know, we could always go out of our way to help ya find yaself,' the first one said.

'Coooorr!! Nice legs,' the third one added to the conversation and giggled to himself as he nearly fell over.

'Ah, come on. These three couldn't organise a game of two-up in the Perth Mint. What ya say to a game of pool? You look like ya hung around a few pubs in ya time,' Danny said, touching her on the arm.

He had such a friendly smile and warm eyes and she felt so cold in this place that she accepted his invitation. Besides, his easy-going banter engulfed her in a spirit of camaraderie she had not felt in a long time. He was not after her body in any form. Rather, he had a pocketful of pay and who better to share it with than a nice woman. If she had told him to leave her alone he would have cheerfully gone over to his uncle and mates and this was the sort of companionship she sought now.

He fancied himself as a hybrid between John Travolta, James Dean and Vince from 'The Colour of Money', a film he had seen three times when it made its long awaited debut at the Kalveston drive-in. However, the only coat he had to wear was not the leather of James Dean but threadbare cloth hunched around his slender body and the only music 'John Travolta' had to dance to was Slim Dusty, or the Everley Brothers or Gene Pitney:

> If I didn't have a dime
> and I didn't take the time
> to play the Juke Box
> OOOH! Saturday night
> would have been a lonely night
> for me!!

That was one of his favourites and he played it over again and again.

And he could certainly play pool! He beat her time and again, much to the amusement of the three shearers and the scorn of the Italian. Uncle Fraser had gone home long ago, for he wasn't much of a one for parties. The man in the corner came out of the shadows to give paternalistic advice to the poor female who couldn't play tiddlywinks. When she was just playing with Danny Lacy her mistakes had not mattered. It had been a fun way to spend an evening. Now the stranger's drawling commentary and the audience of the other shearers, chipping in with unwanted hints, spoiled it all for her and she began making more and worse mistakes.

Once, during the uneven contest, a woman had walked in the door and the stranger had flashed her the smile he saved for women, apparently. Obviously she didn't feel like staying in a room full of drunk males so she left pretty quickly afterwards.

As the night wore on Danny became more drunk and his smile slipped, while his bright black eyes, the best part about him, blurred. He looked a miserable sight with his Jackie Howe singlet hanging out. She decided to leave. He wasn't too happy about that. She knew he would have liked to have been her boyfriend for the night. She knew with a woman's intuition that he desired her. All his body language the whole night long had told her that. He certainly was handsome enough and he was not unintelligent either, having an appealing rough philosophy on life. And he had been over East, shearing, so had some interesting stories to tell. But she had two or three boyfriends in Perth with whom she travelled the nightclub circuit and she wasn't really interested in a one night stand with a young shearer.

'Hey, hey, listen,' he stumbled, 'd'ya wanna smoke a nyaandi?' He pulled a bag out of his pocket and waved it. Rather incongruously now that the whole pub, empty though it was, had seen what he had, he learned forward and whispered, 'I got some, ya know. It makes ya real 'appy.' He clung to the side of the pool table in despair.

'I know,' she smiled at him. 'But I think you're happy enough. You should go home now. It's getting near closing time.' She patted him maternally on the shoulder. 'Thanks for a great night. I had fun.'

'Home?' he mumbled and ran his fingers through his hair, held down by liberal doses of hair oil like all his heroes of fantasy. 'Yeah, thanks,' he murmured and staggered off over to his three mates, who grinned at each other and put arms around his shoulder to cheer him up. As she went to her room one was suggesting a flagon of red would warm him up.

So that had been her little adventure in this small town. Someone else had had an even greater adventure, though—the stranger who had leered at her last night and spoken to her in a drawling cynical voice. That was part of her adventure too, of course, but that was for the police to work out. She was in charge of getting a great story.

If there was anything Mick loved more than cutting down trees it was talking, especially about his beloved father and much loved family. So he filled her in on the story of how his father struggled and suffered and yet still survived, just as Mick and his sons were doing today. She was the professional, sniffing around for exciting bylines in half-said sentences and blurry word pictures. She would come down again with a photographer and take some photos of the Sierra clan, she said, and this prompted him to bring out the old photo albums. There they all were, his brothers, Guiseppe and Luigi, who had been in Perth but now lived at Kalveston with his building business; his nephew Pedro over from the Eastern states for a visit and his nieces Angeline, Juanita and Rosa. And all the other little Sierras.

'Buono. It is good.' Mick beamed.

He told of his own interests, his three racehorses and seven greyhounds. Then the proposed purchase of the sawmill by the woodchip enterprise came into conversation, gently coaxed on by Marrilyn's innocent questions.

'What do you think about the fact that this proposed woodchip industry is going to interfere with what many archaeologists consider to be one of the most important Aboriginal sites in the southwest?' she lied.

In truth no-one knew or cared at all, except the editor, who wanted only to stir up excitement and expose possible government corruption for a good story.

'Say, I tell youse what I think all right!' Mick waved his hands in the air. 'You an abo, and I'm a ding, all right? If youse come over and started diggin' up the Pope's house I sure be pretty damn mad. Hey,' he waved his hands even harder, 'I don't like this bloody woodchip all right!? What youse think? Money from that woodchip goin' a go to Japan straightaway! Youse seen the unemployment in this town?! They employ bloody Japan no worries. No boys 'ere get work! I don't want that woodchip business 'ere and I tell 'im too. Fuck off! 'E come back again and again, offer me much more and more money, I still tell 'im fuck off. In the end 'e say all right stick your mill, we go ahead without you, pretty soon you go bung anyhow, we cut down all the trees, no more left for you. If I got just my mill, cut down few trees 'ere, few trees there, enough for business but no bloody kill the whole forest. All right! OK! Ever'body 'appy. I give them boys job an' look after tree. No worries. That woodchip come along,' he threw out his hands expressively, 'pfffft! Nothin' left. All gone bloody Japan.'

She was surprised and secretly elated. Here was a much better story than the editor had supposed. His story was to have been about how the government was paying off a small sawmill, a home-grown business that had been earning the state money for thirty years or so, so that some people in high places could make a killing. That still applied of course, but *her* version would have a lot more guts to it. She was disappointed that the murdered man seemed to have nothing to do with the sawmill business. *That* would have been an interesting slant indeed.

Meanwhile, on the cold, grey and chilling day, Don and the young Constable Millson were going about their interviews. Heeding the words of Marrilyn Henry from yesterday and knowing that possibly the clue to all this lay in the confines of The Opera House, they proceeded there early in the morning.

The rain fell in slanting icy curtains across the wildly buffeting trees, almost as though it was trying to hide from the rest of the world the unpleasantness this town had experienced. A few brave birds tried to fly into the heaving winds and scurrying clouds but they were cartwheeled across the gloomy black sky like so many leaves. Most of the people of The Rocks were snuffling and shuffling about inside their damp dark houses, probably thinking of the time some five years ago when the river burst its banks. It looked as though it would do it again, but right now that was the least of Don's worries.

He saw Marjorie Perrit hurrying through the swirling squalls on her way back to her new husband. She was one of the success stories of this town and God knows there weren't many of them. But she had met her husband a year ago when he bought up the old Matthews place as a hobby farm. He was quite a well known film producer, looking for a rural retreat. She was working as a barmaid in The Opera House at the time. Suddenly Marjorie had found herself cata-pulted into the social pages of the Australian press. But she, like him, was a shy and introverted person and they kept very much to themselves. Well, it took all sorts to make a town, even one as small and dull as The Rocks.

Don glanced beside him at Constable Millson as they pulled up alongside the hotel. He still seemed a bit pale. Hadn't recovered from the shock of yesterday, it appeared. Really, he'd have to do better than this if he was to ever rise in the force.

The first person to be seen when they entered the gloomy interior was a very sick looking Danny, nursing a beer and a bruised cheek-bone. Don walked across to him.

'How are you, Danny, mate? Still skinning the sheep?'

He knew all the Lacy family well and had a high regard for them. If, sometimes, they were a little wild, they were never really bad, just impetuous.

'Tryin' to, boss. Not much shearin' round though this year. Not much sheep round neither,' he said gloomily, then gave a faint smile. 'Got a job, but. Out on Rabinovitz's place. Shearin' five thousand, Mr Newbry. That's better than a poke in the arse with a brandin' iron, ay. No rams this time either.'

'Was that a ram got you with his horns there, Danny? I'd of thought you'd be more careful.'

'Aah!' his usually sharp eyes looked shifty and he shuffled his big boots. 'Goes with the trade,' he muttered.

'Did you see any strangers here, last night? Brown coat, brown trousers, yellow shirt. Age about thirty-five, forty. Black hair, blue eyes. About one eighty centimetres?' Don pressed.

'Nuh. Rob the town bank, did 'e?' Danny murmured and gave a feeble laugh at his joke.

'You were here, weren't you? What time did you leave?'

Curiously the youth flicked a glance at Constable Millson before looking at Don then lowering his gaze to his beer.

'Oh, you know, boss. Closin' time, like always. Me and the boys got paid up, ya see, so we 'ad a bit of a party.'

Don gazed at the youth for a long moment until Danny became noticeably edgy, then the old policeman put aside his notebook and nodded imperceptibly. 'I see.'

They set off back to the police station to see if any information had come from the lab in Kalveston. It was still too early.

'What do you reckon about Danny Lacy, Don?' Constable Millson said timidly. 'A bit of a roughie, ay . . . but not too bad.'

'I reckon I want to know why Danny's lying.'

'The bloke could of snuck out. If he didn't want anyone . . . '

'No, no, no! There's only one door to that brothel of a place. Danny *had* to see him. As well . . . why is he lying about that bruise on his face? That was no bloody ram's hoof or horn did that. I'd say it was some sort of sharp instrument.'

Don shuffled through a mass of papers on his desk.

'What do we know about Danny Lacy?' Then he answered his own question. 'Well, he's pretty clean. Once, when he was younger, he was up for break and enter in the Perrits' house, I think. Then, last year he was caught with a gram or two of marijuana.'

He leant back in his chair and closed his eyes, thinking.

The news came through at midday. The victim's name was William Abraham Clarendon alias William Abrahams, Abraham Lowenstein and Bill Clare. He had done time in Adelaide, Sydney and Queensland for various petty crimes involving fraud, forgery and simple cons or shams. In fact he was wanted in Adelaide on a charge of forging and uttering right now. He was, after all was said and done, a small-time con merchant and sometime blackmailer. Better off dead, really, thought Don unkindly. He had no time for these spiders who hunched in their nests of deceit and poisoned any they came across. But why did he have to die in this part of Australia? Possibly because he was on the run from the South Australian law and here was as good a place as any to lie low. What else was here to interest a meagre crook like him?

There was some other information that Don had actually already known. The TAB tickets had all been winners. All in all William Abraham Clarendon—or whoever he last called himself—had been an extremely wealthy man for perhaps the first time in his miserable life. And finally the report mentioned that, caught in one of the expensive rings, were several hairs, black, belonging to a young male and anointed with some kind of hair oil.

Aaaah, Don sighed, the wonders of modern science.

When they got back to the pub they were told by Charlie that the shearers had gone back to Rabinovitz's farm. He also contributed the information that the stranger had not only talked to Danny but had finished the evening playing pool with him after Marrilyn's departure.

The shearers were having a break when the police car nosed up to the shed. The rain fell with a whispering roar on the tin roof and now the machines were off there could be heard the nervous clattering of sheep's hooves and throaty baas. The five men were gathered around on the greasy floor, holding big mugs of steaming tea in their sweaty hands.

Don smiled his fatherly smile at them then shouted through the noise of the rain.

'Listen, Danny, can I have a word with you about last night? Charlie reckons you *did* see that bloke and I just want to get everything sorted out.'

Body language is an important factor in Aboriginal affairs, Don knew. A whole conversation can be held without one word being spoken. Why, then, did Danny look first to his uncle and why did his uncle give the faintest, almost imperceptible nod.

Danny moved warily forward, away from his circle of mates, still clutching his cup of tea like a shield in front of him.

'Aren't you cold, mate?' Don asked amiably. 'Go and get your coat while we sit in the car and get warm.'

'Nah, Don. I'm all right!' Danny said.

'Go and get his coat, Simon. He's making me cold just looking at him.'

Before Danny could object the Constable walked over and took Danny's old green coat from where it hung beside his name and tally for the day. When he brought it back Don realised that it was in fact a tweed material. It was just so old and worn the pattern had all but faded away. It was so greasy with sweat and lanoline from the sheep that bits of wool were stuck all over it.

He searched the pockets while Danny looked on in sudden resignation. All life seemed to go from his sparkling black eyes. The Senior Constable brought out a large plastic bag full of green vegetation and sniffed it. He looked first at the other shearers, who all looked elsewhere, and then at Danny with a triumphant, yet sad smile. He had liked this bubbly, friendly youth. Now it seemed he was in real trouble.

'A bit of the old ha ha weed, ay, Danny? Did our mate William get a bit nasty last night and threaten to dob you in? Is that it? So you said you'd meet him up the track by the big tree and you'd pay him your shearer's cheque to keep quiet. Except he wanted more, so you hit him a bit too hard? Was that how it happened?'

'I dunno what ya on about! I never 'it no one!' cried a fearful Danny.

'Well, can *you* tell me why your hairs are found in a dead man's hand?' Don said calmly, his grey eyes watching every little sign on Danny's face.

'Look! Ya got me for the drugs, fair enough. But I never killed 'im.'

'It's open and shut, matey,' Don said sadly and put his hand upon the thin brown arm. 'Come on along with us.'

'Ya can't lock me up! I only 'ad a fight with 'im. I couldn't stand gettin' locked up,' the youth cried wildly and looked around for a mate.

But there were none in this shed. The three white men looked away, ignoring the problem and Uncle Fraser, seemingly about to say something, bit his lip and stared at his nephew with dark smouldering eyes. The sheep stood impassively.

Danny threw the cup of tea at Constable Millson and made to run out the door but he was caught in the grip of Senior Constable Newbry. The young Constable recovered and rushed forward to man-handle the struggling youth into the back of the van. Don turned to face the uncle who had now stood up.

'Yes, Fraser? Do you have something to contribute?' Don asked.

'He can't stand to get locked up.'

'Well, he shouldn't go around committing crimes.'

'He never killed no one.'

'Now, Frase, you want to be careful. I seem to remember you're not long out of jail yourself on a manslaughter charge. If you've been involved in this it'll go bad for your parole, don't you reckon?'

The man gazed at the policeman for a long instance. Then he tossed the dregs of his tea upon the floor and turned towards the stands. Tea-break was over and work must go on.

Back in her hotel room Marrilyn heard the latest news from Charlie. Constable Millson had come in and told him how the youth had reacted to getting locked up. He had had to be restrained somewhat, so upset had he become. But they can't handle closed spaces, these bush abos, the young Constable said (with half a year's experience in the bush). They were going to transfer him to Kalveston Central tomorrow to the main jail, there to await trial, Constable Millson said with some importance. Charlie was secretly pleased about the huge tea stain all over the youngster's shirt. That must have hurt, he thought. It might have woken the dozy bastard up at last, he chuckled.

Marrilyn was by now convinced that here was a story she could build her name on. The wicked government (or members of it) first trying to pay Mick off then threatening to close his business down was the background. Maybe, if there *was* corruption on a government level, she could draw a conclusion by emphasising what happened to one who corrupted at a local level. He had his throat cut by an irate Nyoongah youth whose money he had undoubtedly stolen and whose pride he had shattered. What would happen if a government stole and shattered an emblem like the sacred rock formation out of town? But she was too tired to work on it tonight. She would write it up tomorrow. For now, she wanted a long hot shower, a hot bowl of homemade soup and a cuddle-up with her dreams in her bed. Fuck the story . . . and fuck the editor too—sideways she thought with uncharacteristic vengeance as she let the steaming water wash all her worries away. To think she had played pool with a killer last night and spoken with a dead man. Even though the murder was, most probably, an accident, it made her shiver just to think of it.

Don sat in the office at the police station and listened to the soothing song of the rain. But his thoughts were turbulent. He had known the Lacys for years and, rough though they may be, he could not think of any of them as murderers. Still, there was a first time for everything. It made him sad though.

When the phone call came through about midnight he was dozing in his chair. The rain had become harder now and he wondered again if the river would rise and flood the town like it had a few years ago. Everyone had helped that night with sandbags and brackets and he could not forget Marjorie Perrit (who had just begun work in the pub) even in all that gloom and mud, with her nail polish, eye shadow and bright lipstick. She was never without them, and it was the source of many a good joke. That was the sort of woman she was, however. There was even speculation she put makeup on instead of taking it off before she went to bed.

'Gee, it's good to see some people are industrious, Don,' came the Senior CIB Detective's jovial tones. 'I'm only ringing up to say that there are further developments on the Clarendon case. In fact we have it all wrapped up this end.'

'Didn't Simon get in touch with you today?' Don queried.

'No! What? Well, never mind, we've come up with this: the silver rose found by Clarendon's body yesterday—or one similar to it—was not owned by him but by his wife, whose maiden name was Roberts. Marjorie Roberts.'

Roberts. *Marjorie* Roberts. Now Don remembered what had seemed so strange to him when he had seen her yesterday. She had been wearing her lurid blue eye shadow and her revolting pink nail polish but, for a woman so vain, her lips were dry and bare. Indeed, now he thought about it her whole face had seemed older and haggard. Had she been without lipstick because she had lost it at the scene of the murder?

'She calls herself Marjorie Perrit now, I understand,' the CIB man carried on. 'She had a colourful life of her own. She was a high class prostitute and he was her pimp before they married. She ran a call-girl service in Adelaide about five years before they caught up with her for tax evasion. Whereupon she disappeared into thin air. Well, it seems that Clarendon saw her in the Adelaide papers with her new "husband" and, even though she has cleverly disguised herself he knew who she was all right and decided to try a little blackmail—only it never worked. The irony is, of course, that he had just entered Gambler's heaven and had won about two hundred thousand dollars on the TAB! But, once a greedy thief always a greedy thief.'

'Can we prove this? That she was the killer?'

'The silver rose was never his. It was always hers. She must have dropped it in the fight. Ask her what happened to her rose and see if she can answer you that!' the CIB officer said. It was always good to wrap up a case quickly and this one had looked like being a humdinger of a dandy with mysterious strangers and few real clues. 'Remember that lipstick? I'll bet you'll find it's hers. In any case she's wanted for tax evasion back in Adelaide so I'd grab her first thing tomorrow. Now, what was Constable Millson supposed to tell me and didn't?'

The Senior Officer had little time for the young Constable, Don knew. He considered the lad too vague and with no stomach for police work and, quite frankly, too lazy and stupid to make a truly good lawman. He decided to take some pressure off the young policeman.

'Nothing. It's OK. I can handle this.'

'Good. Well, don't forget to pick her up tomorrow and hit her with the facts, then we can close this case. And good riddance to bad rubbish, I say!'

After he put the phone down Don decided to go and tell Danny the good news. Why, he thought, I might even let the poor bugger go. We're after bigger fish than him and what would a charge of possession of cannabis get him? Six months' jail? It wasn't worth it to ruin a basically decent youth's life. Why not let him go? He's had a good scare now.

The two lock-up cells were in a separate section of the yard to the office and he had to walk through a thundering passage, as rain hurled icy javelins at the structures of law and order in this small town.

He could hardly hear himself think as he made his way to the far cell. It was as though all the demons from the very pits of hell, and the watery bowels of all the rivers and oceans had gathered in the sky to shriek over the injustice of mankind. He flung open the door as he snapped the light on, smiling to himself at the surprise he would give Danny.

The youth swung slowly in the middle of the room, a torn grey blanket around his neck and through the bars of the cell window. His face was a ghastly yellow and his eyes and tongue protruded like some terrible clown.

Don was really in trouble now. He could see the impeccable record he had built up painstakingly over the years being torn asunder. Right when he was due to retire too. To make matters worse, when he went out to detain Marjorie Perrit he found she had gone, 'Disappeared into thin air' he said angrily to young Constable Millson. He still didn't look too good and Don felt it was time for a permanent rest for Simon Millson. He just wasn't cut out to be a cop, shaking and white-faced two days after a murder. It just wasn't good enough and he was in too much trouble himself now to worry about watching his partner's most unreliable back. He didn't have much time either to listen to the woes of Marjorie's 'husband' who bewailed the fact the shame and scandal would surely ruin him but could give him no idea as to where she may have fled.

When Marrilyn heard about the fate that had befallen poor young Danny Lacy she could not help but think about the night they had been together. If she had let him come upstairs with her as he wished, he would have spent the night in a warm and exuberant dream and would have had a tight alibi and never gone to jail and thus been so frightened . . . so scared . . . that he hung himself. It wasn't only that. She remembered what old Benny Higgins had said to her in his gloomy cracked voice. 'Why ya think there isn't any Nyoongahs live around 'ere? Only me, cos I don't care no more!'

For a while she lay on her bed and cried. After all, he was only a young boy, really, hardly out of his teens. Perhaps he had thought of himself as a tough rugged man about town. But when you got right down to it he was just a child.

Most of all, though, she felt, for the first time, that he was of her blood. She felt ashamed of the way she had led her life up to now. Living the European dream of power and prestige and riches gotten in any manner conceivable. Did anyone really appreciate the stories she wrote—or even read them? What of her friends in the discos around town? When it came down to the raw truth they only associated with her because of her colour, so they could say they were liberal minded. When she had been alone in a strange, cold, atmosphere it had been a total stranger who had come to her defence and offered her protection, simply because she was of the same race.

Charlie had told her that after she left that night Danny had murdered the black ball with a resounding crack of the white and a flourish of his cue cum guitar, then whirled around and challenged the stranger to a game.

Then it was on. Oh, the stranger drew Danny Lacy out like a spider does an iridescent beetle, with cunning and patience and infinite trickery. He lost a few games, then brought in the subject of money— an item Danny had little of. So they began playing for twenty dollars and the stranger lost forty and he won twenty, then a hundred, and he cleaned Danny Lacy out. It was pure magic to watch the ease with which this shark wiped out this tiny fish in a little pond.

She lay on her bed most of the afternoon and then her mind was made up. She would go back to the roots of her being. She would, tonight, visit the rock formation and try to find the mystic magic of this land. She would try to find some of the simple joy of the youth Danny Lacy, who was so proud of his little life—so full of life! For so short a time.

And the night came down, purple and black and grey, with drifting rain and swirling mists. Whispering trees shook softly in the gentle wind and a constant pattering deluge drenched the town. The river rose slowly and surely, a rumbling brown snake with whitish yellow foam in patches on its back like a snake's peeling skin.

She set off about eleven o'clock, wanting desperately to be alone, so waiting until the pub closed and the loud arrogant Pedro had been ushered down the stairs. Then she set off on her journey of atonement.

It was further than she thought to the rocks, perhaps a half-hour walk going by her watch. By the time she arrived she was wet through. Yet, it seemed to her, the rain was kind on her skin and the trees seemed to chant out a long forgotten chorus. A tune of welcome for the lost Spirit returning home.

The rock formation appeared at last through the haze of misty drizzle bathed in bright moonlight, and what a wonder it really was. Once, to her, it would have only been a clump of rather untidy boulders, grey and misshapen, splotched with pale green or yellow lichen and miniature forests of luxuriant green moss. But now it stood, solemn and majestic, a tower of some ancient civilisation. It stood strong and powerful—forever—and she knew that this was a part of her. A part no foreign race could truly comprehend.

She moved up to the rocks and touched them with her hand. Scaly cold surface or soft moss surface. Spirits abounded here by the plenty and she was surrounded by an aura of such an ancient past it was almost tangible. The very boulders seemed to move and take shape: here a brave warrior, there a crouching woman, there an old wise man. Voices seemed to drift out of the mist and encircle her, feeling her out with cold tendrils tainted with stories from ages gone. Then, as she moved further into the tumbled towers to be away from the rain and closer to her new Gods, she came across something of an entirely different age from the one she travelled in so esoterically at the present.

She was pulled back to reality at once.

For there, in the many caves in the centre of the formation, were bags and bags—all green plastic and all very bulky.

She opened one and needed to look no further. Here was perhaps three million dollars worth of cannabis, all ready processed and set to go.

She was possessed of a surge of elation and fierce ambition which totally dispelled her recent feelings of affinity, compassion and spirituality.

Here was her story, she thought. This would constitute one of the state's biggest drug busts. She would bring in the slant of how a Sacred Site was being abused for gain and greed and how a youth (who admitted to her, on his last night alive, to smoking this weed) had died because of the oppressive laws of another race whose very existence was based on greed. His death gave the whole story just the right dramatic touch to make it front page stuff, she thought.

She closed up the bag and hurried back to The Opera House. The river had reached the bottom steps now but it seemed the old building would last another day and many more, for the heavy rain had abated and there was just the merest of drizzle. But she did not care for the river or the rain. Even the beauty of the rocks had faded. She had a story to write.

'I am sorry you had to find out about that,' came the soft voice from the shadows. 'Clarendon found out about my operations because of his scummy mates in jail and a lack of security among my people. But he is no loss really. Just a fool who thought he could blackmail me. Me?! Didn't he realise how big my operations are over East? So I brushed him off like the fly he was. But you? I could have liked you, Marrilyn Henry. I am sorry for the boy too, but he had to die. He knew too much of my operations, he was one of my drivers, you see. Young Millson will have to have an accident too, only because his usefulness has been outlived and he is becoming a nuisance. Anyhow, he is too much of a threat, having executed Danny. A policeman's lot is not a happy one . . . if you get my drift. Greed is a terrible curse and it comes in many guises, does it not? If you had not wanted your story so badly you would be leaving this town but now . . . Don't be so surprised. You were seen leaving, you see, and home is where the heart is, isn't that what they say? And this old Opera House is the only home you had in this town.'

A small silver rose arched out of the shadows and landed near her drenched new shoes.

'Just so those greedy ones over East will know who I am and who killed you, even if no-one else does. It only remains now for me to say, Arrivederci, signorina.'

A body lay on the steps. One hand rested just above the water and a narrow watchband was visible below the cuff of a light coloured coat. Dark hair curled damply to the nape of the neck. The legs were a little apart; the new sole of a woven brown leather shoe faced upwards.

Marion Halligan has been a reader all her life
and in the latter part of it has taken up writing.
She has earned her living by writing about
reading, by trying to convince the young they
should read and showing them how, and by
writing fiction for others to read and sometimes write about—see *The Living Hothouse*,
The Hanged Man in the Garden and *Spider Cup*.
She likes to eat and write about that too; her
latest book is an invitation to Eat My Words
for people who like to read about food and the
diverse matters associated with it. For relaxation she reads.

Marion Halligan

CRITICAL DIFFERENCES

Billy Dodds was telephoning all her friends and a few enemies. Have you heard? About Cynthia? Of course, Cynthia Saussure. Pissed. Entirely pissed. Yes, I know, never touches a drop, that's what she said, and we all saw. Mineral water with a twist of lemon. Yes. But I tell you, half seas over wasn't in it. Full seas over more like. Yeah, and on the high seas, too. Well, the Manly ferry, but that gets pretty elemental. I know, it's incredible, but you should always believe three incredible things before breakfast, and it's already dinner time.

Marco saw her, along with Adrian of course, and wait, I haven't told you the half of it yet. She had her hat pulled down over one eye, and her coat collar up, looking, Marco reckoned, even more private eye than usual, AND . . . she was singing! No, well, none of us did. Not doing a bad job apparently, the woman has even more talents than we suspected. At the top of her voice, what's more, sort of deep and loud, Marco says. *Nessun dorma*, I believe. Plus bits of *Il mio tesoro* with lots of dum dum de dums and all pretty slurred. Twirling round those pillars you get at the end of the deck, hanging over the rail . . . Oh drunks are always safe, the god of drunkenness looks after them. Marco and Adrian? Nothing at all, of course, you know what terrible cowards they are, filter off at the first sniff of trouble. Well, they stayed around long enough to see, curiosity's their other thing, but apparently she moved round, a kind of ghastly song and dance act, the way they describe it, and they left her to it. Of course they're telling everybody, Cynthia'll never live it down. Reading *NARB* will never be the same again.

Hang on, there's more. Oh yes, I haven't told you all yet. She had her pockets full of bottles. Isn't it priceless?

This particular conversation Billy Dodds had with her client, Clinton O'Malley, one cold misty evening in early winter. He lived in an apartment on top of one of those tall buildings intended to allow the rich to dwell in European style lives.

One of the pleasures of the penthouse terrace was the telescope. For looking at the stars? People could think that if they wanted to. For looking at the world, was how Clinton O'Malley explained it to himself. A writer deserves his material. It nipped the sting from the word voyeur, a terrace with harbour views: there's the bridge, what are the painters having for lunch? the riggers wearing on their feet? Official mansions: is the prime minister at home? Drinking mineral water on his lawn. Opera House: observe the caresses of the promenading lovers to your heart's content. Stars are dull in comparison.

Of course, Clinton O'Malley himself was a star. Tall and slenderly made, with black hair and blue eyes, but that was just the gilding of his lily. As was the first career, though he had climbed to the top of its tree. Already, although Clint was still or at least had the air of a young man, it was the stuff of legend. You remember the Girasole ad. *Follow us to the sun*, the dancing skipping happy families, all with a chunk of bread and yellow in their hands, the slogan flashing and them singing, real South of Music stuff, and the sun when they get to it beaming rays saying *good health living well vitamins nutrition healthy old age bouncing babies flourishing kiddies* and such. Sublime. Subliminal. The slogans coming zapping out of this big benign sun and all the little margarine pots on springy stems dancing on the spot and beaming back from their yellow petalled faces. *Girasole* they sing, *Girasole, Follow us to the sun*. The genius of that was ad-making history. *Girasole* sang the babies in their prams, the old men, the checkout chicks, the young mothers, the executives in the secrecy of lifts. Girasole margarine was on everybody's lips.

There was the floor polish too. *Take a shine to . . .* and there is a gorgeous woman cuddling a spray can, a ring on her finger sparkling and winking enough to put the Koh-in-or in the shade, *Take a shine to Diamontine* they sing, the woman and the can, and together they waltz over floors as sparkling as the diamond in the ring. You see the form? Both of them using the brilliant mixture of animation and realism that became Clinton O'Malley's trademark.

But he no longer cared about that. Was proud, of course, liked the well-doneness of it, but the moving on was what counted. The real words on the actual page. 896 of them. (Pages not words.) His best-selling novel set in Ireland. The story's just about as famous as the Girasole adventure. The young hero, peasant poverty, shoeless hardship, cruel landlords, green potatoes if any at all, the rich young Protestant beauty, the doomed love, the mist and bogs and Guinness and moonshine and blarney and all the pity and terror of the auld country and religious feud and lost inheritance and descent from kings and tragedy and can the doom be undone—but mustn't reveal the end. This was called *Two is Too Many* and was a best-seller even before it was printed. It had to be, the publishers had paid so much money for it. Seven figures, people kept mentioning in connection with it, that was how much was paid before it was even printed. Seven figures, in hushed voices, though just what they were wasn't mentioned.

Seven figures, Cynthia Saussure would say. She'd pause, take a drag on her cigarette, blow out the smoke in a long ruminative stream. The rhythm of her conversation would have been entirely ruined by her not smoking. Seven figures, inhale, pause, blow. It makes me think of seven belly dancers waggling their navels with diamonds in them, and Clinton O'Malley succumbing to all seven at once. Throaty laugh. Inhale, pause, blow again, while everyone pictured it. Clinton O'Malley didn't know she'd said this, not for certain, or how often, but he did know she'd described *Two Is Too Many* as 'Best-Selling Irish Tome or is it Tomb' because that was the heading she put on the review Don Mercurio wrote for the *New Austral Review of Books*. The headings were always Cynthia's and so was the choice of reviewers. Clinton O'Malley knew that Don Mercurio would have been carefully chosen to hate it.

Clint trained the telescope on the Opera House. To one side were steps, going into the water, a kind of landing stage, so you could arrive at performances by boat, in a Venetian manner. Of course this wasn't a time for performances, being the dawn hour, the mist only just lifted. But there was plenty of activity: police cars, vans, fluorescent tape, spectators, the one or two offering assistance warned away. The focus, he could see from his rooftop terrace, was the line where the land met the sea, where the water climbed up the steps or dropped back, according to the tide. Treacherous those steps could be when the tide was low, moss-grown and slippery. Venetian aspirations would need sure-footedness. He made a note of a satin-shod foot precarious on the oozing voracious tufts, an oyster-iridescent Yves St Laurent or maybe Issy Miyake gown held bunched away from the mud-soil of the merciless sea. His current book was being set in Sydney.

Clint enjoyed his morning run, and was disappointed if he had to miss even one day. Tautness of mind and body depended on it, he thought. But in the last week or so he had been less regular; a little doubt about the Achilles tendon, he would say if asked. That's why he was doing it vicariously this morning, by telescope, not in the flesh. He liked his route to be regular too. The streets downhill, pity the gardens were shut at this hour, across the Quay, on to the Opera House. Jogging round the Opera House was like being on a ship: so many times round the deck equals so many miles. Miles it was when there were ships like that. Back in a more certain and elegant world. Even a person as rich as Clint couldn't easily these days find a ship to travel on at leisure and run so many times so many miles round the deck every morning before breakfast. Keeping fit for the lazy shipboard life of meals and drinks and liaisons in bars. The number of times round the deck of that stationary great boat the Opera House was the only variation he allowed himself; always the route was fixed but this way the time could expand. If he was thinking well he'd often take a couple of extra turns.

Now on this vicarious morning's run he watched the turmoil round the Opera House. The silence of it, at this distance; the vision through the telescope so exact but no sound at all. Perhaps the afternoon papers would write it up. Tomorrow he'd be there in person, not just watching from afar. He was sure his foot would be up to a good jog tomorrow. Running round the deck, past the steps by that time empty of incident, whatever was happening now quite cleared away.

In the meantime there were the morning papers, Saturday and the book pages. There was still the *Times* review to come, it was late but surely they wouldn't not do it? And Newsfair. Maybe they'd manage to get beyond sour grapes at best-sellers and recognise literary merit when they saw it. Or maybe, and this was the real fear, the powerful poison of *NARB* would have tainted even them.

Clinton O'Malley shuddered when he thought of Cynthia Saussure. She looked like a powerful woman, tall, lean, of little flesh. Yellow as a haddock, said Billy Dodds his agent. She'd spent so many miserable years giving up smoking that she enjoyed malice against those who hadn't. Billy and Cynthia were ancient armed but affectionate enemies. Cynthia as editor of NARB often printed demolitions of Billy's clients' books, but also sometimes praise. I have to believe she's honest about it, said Billy, and so she is, often, probably, if wall-eyed and on occasions blind as a mole. But vengeful; I think not. Cynthia for her part regarded Billy as a bit of a tart, really just a whore, petal, selling her clients where the price is highest. Soliciting is soliciting is soliciting, however literary it pretends to be. But they were addicted to one another's cutting conversations, moved across crowded rooms towards one another with genuine anticipation.

Billy hadn't been much comfort over the NARB review. Just the usual narbed comment, she shrugged. Don't take it to heart, my love.

But why is she so negative, Clint asked. She doesn't seem to have made the slightest attempt to read what I wrote.

Not she, he. It's Don Mercurio, remember, who wrote the stuff.

Who's he? Some tinpot academic hack, sneered Clint.

Shh, said Billy. Not profitable my love to talk like that. One of our more literary critics. He's into deconstruction in a big way.

What's that?

Oh, she said, reflecting. It's a trendy way of taking authors apart.

Deconstruction, eh. Take out the con and you've got destruction, muttered Clint.

Marvellous, darling. Billy laughed. But suddenly seeing how forlorn he really was said, Hey, don't worry. What do you care? Ever heard of laughing all the way to the bank?

Don't say that. Don't ever say that.

Okay. Sorry. But there it is. Look, she said firmly. You can be literature, or you can sell. Be read by millions, doted on, adored, cried over. Who cares about that poxy arty stuff? Who's it *talking* to? You've got readers where it counts: among the people.

And it was true that the women's magazines ran glamorous photographs (especially the one graceful on a motorbike which you couldn't tell was a studio prop) with captions saying things like *Clint says it all* (that was with one elbow leaning on a stack of *Two is Too Many*) and *Clint's got it all*—that was the penthouse, the view, the telescope. I like to look at the stars, it quoted him as saying. The context of eternity, you know. His black hair curled over his forehead, his blue eyes gleamed. They did a good job, the women's magazines. A very neat package. No problems. The problems were with the literary journals. And *NARB* was the sharp end.

He'd met Cynthia Saussure at the launch of his book. Had gone out of his way to be charming to her. Had invited her to the dinner afterwards at the Thai Me Up Thai Me Down, which was very fashionable at the time and not so expensive that it made people nervous. I'll pay, he said to Billy and she said okay but make it modest. You don't want to give these people any hooks. And he hadn't, he was sure.

Cynthia was dressed in the clothes he was to recognise were her trademark. Pale trench coat, Burberry's, of course, black velvety fedora, tailored trousers, silk shirt. She looked like Lauren Bacall playing Humphrey Bogart. Well, she had brown hair, but it waved round her ears like Bacall's, and there was something in the wide-apart glint of her light-coloured eyes. And the hands in the pockets.

Do you carry a gun in there, he said to her, and she laughed. It was one of those exchanges that you mull over in the night afterwards looking for meanings, wondering if there are any, or is it just that the rest of the world is as inept at conversation as you.

But it had been a good evening. The steamed fish in banana leaves was particularly good, she said, though she hadn't drunk any of the Laurent Perrier champagne which he'd chosen as not too *trop*. But she explained that it was nothing personal.

This is my vice, petal, she said, waving a cigarette in his face so that he had to hold his breath to avoid the smoke. Imagine if I drank as well. Oh horrors. She shuddered her thin bones under the cream silk shirt while she took a sip of her mineral water. With a twist of lime, petal.

The smoking provided another of her trademarks: the cigarette holder. It was ivory (an antique, petal, the elephant would be dead by now anyway), the slender cylinder that held the cigarette being held in its turn in a kind of silver bud on the end of an even more slender stem that curved around in a loop like half the handle of a pair of scissors, so that smoking for her meant holding her hand in a fist with her forefinger curled through the loop. It was elegant and odd, it recalled Paris in the thirties, which was where it had come from. Was Cynthia herself French? Way back. Her ancestor had been chef in the French restaurant that flourished in Parramatta in the 1790s. An aristocrat who was a hobby cook in the manner of Marie Antoinette, he'd fled to England after the Revolution and then been deported for selling rabbit as partridge; he was lucky to escape hanging. Instead he gave his descendants the kudos of being practically first fleeters. Cynthia claimed to have got her thin arms from this ancestry, and if the sturdy legs came from there too, nobody noticed under the knife-edged crease of her trousers.

Clinton O'Malley had been prepared to find her immensely charming. He liked the admiration of women, enjoyed their affection, even if it was men that interested him. And then had come the review. Don Mercurio's sneering demolition in the *New Austral Review of Books*. It had seemed like a betrayal. And every other review had taken its tone from that. Gibing. Joking. 'Mr Girasole descends to fiction.' 'A new diamond mine for Señor Diamantine.' 'The novel as product and package.'

It doesn't matter, said Billy. Why should it worry you? And she pointed to where, on the same page as a review mentioning bankrupt imaginations and one syllable words (not true, open the book anywhere and check, not true) was a list of best-sellers with *Two is Too Many* in number one place. How many weeks has it been there? she demanded. How many will it stay there! She jabbed her finger at the page. That's what counts, my love.

You can say that, Billy, but what if *NARB* had said it was good, at the beginning, what might have followed?

I'm telling you, you're not to worry . . .

And what about this next book? (For the sequel to *Two is Too Many* where Colum and Maud migrate to Australia and start a pastoral dynasty was already in page proofs.) What if *NARB* pans this too and the rest follow like a mob of fucking sheep?

It's the people who count, still. Your fans, who buy you. Voting with their pockets, my love; that's the ticket.

What's wrong with wanting to be counted as literature, as well as popular? Clinton couldn't let it go. Peter Carey was in advertising, nobody holds that against him. He writes big books, like me, lots of adventures.

He started off in little magazines, said Billy. Never sold like you, even when he won the Booker.

Maybe if I won the Booker, said Clint.

Why not, said Billy.

Clint always had bottles of champagne in his fridge. Are you thirsty, he'd ask Billy, who liked to come to his place to talk business. So much more pleasant than the office. Rather, Billy would answer, I'm as dry as a wowsers' convention. Then he would open a bottle of champagne. He was making comparisons. They'd been through Krug and Bollinger and Tattinger and were up to Dom Perignon. Billy often had little matters to discuss with Clint that involved calling by his place.

I think you're being a bit neurotic, she said fondly, when Clint began to worry yet again about not being seen as literature. *NARB* doesn't have that much power. Cynthia likes you.

I don't think so, said Clint. Every time I think about that woman I feel sick. The sheer power . . .

This was a conversation he had tried to have with Cynthia herself, with surprisingly little success. It had been at one of the publishers' Christmas parties, Cynthia minus the trench coat, in a linen blazer instead but the fedora still in place, the finger of her elegant fist permanently curled through the silver loop of the ivory cigarette holder. He'd been chatting her up, playing his most charming self, a chase with a beast in view. He began by praising the seminal role played by *NARB* in Oz lit. Well, I prefer ovular, said Cynthia, but only in passing, she accepted the praise, even joined in, from her own angle. After a bit Clinton said, Tell me, how does it feel to be a person of such power?

Power? Petal, what do you mean, *power*?

Well, choosing which books get reviewed, and who reviews them. That can make or break reputations. Isn't that power?

But she appeared to be puzzled by this. Not to accept it at all. She did the best she could, to match up books and reviewers as honestly and yes as interestingly as she could. After all, that was important, if *NARB* didn't interest people then it was an entire failure. A reviewer like Don Mercurio was always good value, so witty and sharp, as well as perceptive.

But what if you knew he'd hate the book?

Petal, how could I know that? My reviewers are entirely free spirits. Imagine if I tried to influence them! She slid a hand like a knife across her throat. No, no. Their own mistresses entirely.

She patted his arm with the cigarette fist and moved on to where Billy and Don Mercurio had their heads together, giggling. Clinton was baffled, and hurt, then angry. Why should Cynthia lie like that? And why bring up Mercurio, why taunt him with Mercurio? It did not occur to him that Cynthia might not be thinking of him at all, that she might be speaking out of her own concerns and with no reference to a piece of writing she wasn't bothering to remember concerned him. He did not pause to think how many reviews passed through her hands every week. She is lying, he thought, and saw this as evidence of malice. More than malice, a careful and long-term plot.

It was a Friday night in early winter that Billy rang to tell Clint about Cynthia being drunk on the Manly ferry. This'll cheer you up, she said, and he thought it was a funny thing to say because how was her disgraceful behaviour going to help him any? On Sunday he rang Billy because yet again Newsfair was failing to do a review. She said, Listen, shall I pop round for a moment? in a rather small voice, and he replied Why not. He hadn't even time to open the Dom Perignon before she was spilling out her news, in an eager appalled way. She babbled and burbled, and the upshot was, Cynthia Saussure being dead. She must've fallen off that ferry, Billy said. Oh Clint, how terrible, we laughed and all the time she'd drowned. Was dead already.

I don't understand, said Clinton. Characters in his books often said this. You mean, that night when she was singing, she fell in the water and drowned?

Well, I suppose. Marco told me, he got it from Sam, Annette told him, she's Cynthia's cousin you know. They found her yesterday morning, the police did, washed up, Billy gulped, on those steps beside the Opera House.

And she was definitely drowned?

Well, washed up sounds like drowned, doesn't it?

How long had she been in the water?

I didn't ask. I presumed Thursday night till Saturday morning. That seems to be the sequence of events.

So the police think she fell off the ferry? Clinton filled Billy's glass for the third time.

That's what Marco was saying. Apparently quite a lot of people saw her, several people she knew were on the ferry, going to a party at Balmoral. The police have well and truly got that story. There's even talk of it being suicide, maybe getting drunk to be able to do it.

That doesn't sound like Cynthia somehow. Though of course you can't generalise. He frowned. Poor Cynthia.

In the water for all that time, and then washed up, Billy gulped again, on the steps beside the Opera House. That'd be the tides, wouldn't it? I expect the police understand that sort of thing. Bodies lost then washing up. Days later. I expect there's an established pattern. Though maybe the bottles, maybe they weighed her down. Oh, it's too awful.

It's terrible, said Clinton. What a terrible thing to happen. To such a wonderful lady. She'll be sorely missed.

He got another bottle of champagne, and they sat together on one of the white leather sofas and talked sadly about life and death and how close one was to the other. Outside a grey evening closed in, mist dripped into rain, the whole penthouse seemed to be in a cloud.

On Monday morning Clinton was back to jogging again, and for the rest of the week. No foot problems. His tread was light and his head clear. Sometimes he noticed his surroundings, a ferry sliding stately across the harbour, a water taxi slapping through the waves. No small craft sliding silently into the steps where the land meets the sea, where the body of the unfortunate Cynthia had been washed up. Where his lady in oyster satin held her skirts away from the treacherous moss. Perhaps he should name her Cynthia. In memoriam. Throw a wreath in the water.

During the week more details emerged about the death. That she'd been wearing her trench coat, and yes there were bottles in the pockets. That the fedora was there, bobbing on the water a few yards out. The cigarette holder too, the little silver rose still looped around her finger, her fingers still closed in that characteristic fist, but the ivory part snapped off. The jogger who'd found her told the papers about seeing the pale shape lying on the stairs, the tide already retreating so that it was partly out of the water, the moment of horror, then hope, because the head was out of the water, maybe it was somebody who had just stumbled, and then seeing the wetness of the hair, the skin of the hand white and puckered, suggesting a lengthy immersion, the legs slightly apart, the feet in their sodden brown leather shoes (the elegant expensive Beltrami lace-ups that were another feature of Cynthia's dress) drifting at the volition of the water, not their own.

But what actually killed her, Clinton asked, and Billy said, Well wasn't it the drowning, but nobody seemed to know for certain. Do the police suspect foul play, he wondered, but if they did they weren't saying. There was to be an inquest, but then that's standard with any unnatural death, isn't it? There was a wake, and everybody wept, and then they went to her favourite bar because of course she needed a good bar even though she didn't drink, and with good reason you'd have to say wouldn't you, pointed out somebody, look what happened when she did, and people got drunk and celebrated her life and the marvellous manner of her leaving it. So very Sydney. Death by drowning in the harbour she adored, said Marco, maudlin enough to proclaim Cynthia's entirely loving the idea. The poetry of it, it fills you with a kind of fearful joy, said someone. Clint started buying champagne. It was the best wake anyone could remember. And Cynthia's death the finest of any story she'd ever told.

Clinton O'Malley continues to jog around the Opera House every morning. X times around the deck equals so many miles. Kilometres. One day he'll work out the exact figures. Sometimes when he passes the moss-treacherous steps a laugh escapes him, which wrecks his breathing but he can cope with that. Cynthia's not Saussure now, he tells himself, and chuckles again. He thinks he's the first person to make this joke.

He says to himself, deconstruction is a game that others can learn; he reckons he's a pretty smart pupil. And improve on the instruction: what about decomposition, for instance. I compose, she decomposes. Round the Opera House again, past the steps, pity he couldn't have been the one to find the body given his habits not to mention his authorship of the whole thing but that was a luxury he had more sense than to allow himself. Far too dangerous. And at least he was able to watch it through his powerful telescope.

More word games: he plays about with the idea of contracts, it's very witty. There's other contracts than book contracts. One contract isn't the same as another, not at all. And sometimes it's good to be on the giving as well as the receiving end, of course it's more expensive but worth it, oh yes, worth it. Clever old Billy gave him the idea, the idle remark: Plenty of writers would like to put out a contract on her she said, but of course they never do, being writers they don't do it, they just put it into words, and that's where he's different, he's a writer but he's a doer too, and that's what gives his stuff its character and now one day somebody may see just what that's worth. A bit sad, of course, it could be one of the best plots he ever thinks up, not to mention takes part in, the drunken act on the ferry was absolute genius, he sings again in his head the slurred dum dum de dums of

Il mio tesoro, not aloud of course, that would really muck up his breathing. Great gear too, pity he couldn't keep the clothes, quite fancied himself in a trench and fedora, Saussure reincarnated as well as rubbed out, very rich. As well as the sadness, this marvellous plot and he's got to keep it a secret, but then of course the very finest artists work for their own satisfaction. That's what really counts, your own satisfaction.

Steve Wright was born in London and spent
the late sixties and early seventies travelling
the world before arriving in Australia. He's
been here ever since. He has a BA from the
Canberra College of Advanced Education and
spent a year at the Australian Film, Television
and Radio School studying screenwriting. He
has sold ice-creams in Regents Park and
planted trees in Canada but these days he
writes full time.

He has written various scripts for television
including the series 'Stringer' for the ABC. He
has been a journalist, written plays, films and
three novels featuring his emigre English
detective Barry Donovan who once described
himself as 'the Keith Richard of private eyes'.
Steve is happily married with one child and
lives on the coast south of Sydney.

Steve Wright
THE THREE OF SPADES

Sitting there on the bench, watching the dawn break over the misty harbour, Winston kept thinking about the three of spades. Such a nondescript card the three of spades. An ace or a picture had clout, meant something, but the three of spades? The three of spades was nowhere, especially when it joined the eight of diamonds and the ten of diamonds and the nine of diamonds. A little black card joining all those red ones, buggering up Jacko's chances of a running flush and making Winston's three kings, two up, one down, look better and better. That's what Winston thought anyway, face cool, butterflies hammering away inside his stomach, as he raised the bid to fifty with two kings showing. Everyone else had folded, only Jacko left, and Jacko hesitating as he contemplated the stake. Of course with three diamonds showing Jacko could have had two more face down but Winston had three in his hand and the chances of eight diamonds between them were slim. Sure, Jacko could have a possible run, runs were always possible, but Winston didn't think so. After so much bad luck, all night, Winston could feel a big win coming and even when Jacko slid two twenties and a ten into the pile Winston still felt confident that Jacko didn't have a run.

Next card, face down, one each. Winston picked up the four of hearts wishing all the time for another king or even an ace to match those already in place, up and down. Jacko folded back one corner of his card, looked at it and then leant back in his chair, at ease, comfortable. Believing this to be bluff Winston looked at the sixty bucks in an untidy pile beside his cards and threw fifty into the kitty. Then, leaning back, at ease, comfortable, Winston waited for Jacko to make his move. Jacko seemed to take a long while studying the remaining pile of coins that were Winston's before placing sixty bucks in the kitty and saying, 'Seeing as how that's all you've got left, Winston old mate, we'd better make it sixty.' Looking cool but feeling those butterflies start to collide, Winston wondered whether to go the ten, see Jacko, or up him and borrow ten from Carlo who was always good for a stake.

Winston went the ten. One by one Jacko turned over his cards to reveal a full house, threes and eights, beating Winston's three kings and leaving him broke, full of dead butterflies.

Winston took out his last cigarette and stopped thinking about the three of spades. As he flicked the empty packet into the oily water he started thinking instead about where he was going to find the fifteen hundred bucks he owed Seamless, which was the reason he'd been playing seven card stud all night in the first place. Seamless had said he wanted the money by midday and Winston shivered as he lit the cigarette with a book match from one of Seamless's clubs, The Blue Cockatoo, because Seamless had also said that he would break Winston's legs if he didn't get it. And Seamless was a man of his word. Everyone knew this and Wally Bremner knew this better than most because Wally wasn't walking so well these days. Winston shivered again. Wally had owed less than Winston.

Sucking on his last cigarette Winston stared blankly at the misty water turning steely blue and actually wondered if praying might be the answer. He remembered vaguely from his youth that this was something you did on your knees with thoughts of The Almighty in your head. Over the last twenty years Winston had probably only thought of The Almighty twice. The first time was when the Maori threatened to stick him with a filed down prison fork and the second was wondering whether Mardi Dennehy would remember him after he'd been away so long. On both occasions he'd had trouble conjuring up any image of his benefactor and, anyway, the Maori had decided to stick someone else and Mardi had remembered after a minute or two, so what was the point. Still, all the same, he liked his legs the way they were.

As Winston flicked the cigarette butt in the same direction as the packet he desperately wanted another but the cold was getting to him and he decided to walk instead. Better to go round by the Opera House, he thought, no sense retracing his steps. Maybe he'd find someone down on the Quay, a commuter or cabbie, to bludge a smoke from. It was still early for commuters but all this bad luck, all night and more, couldn't last could it? Luck, like everything else, had to change. Yeah. Had to.

In the distance, somewhere out to sea, a cloud's tip was turning white. The harbour lapped gently on the sandstone wall and seagulls strutted in search of food. But Winston saw and heard none of these things. Winston didn't even notice the Opera House as he approached, its fins sticking out of the mist like nuns in conference. Winston walked head down, hands in pockets, wondering what business The Almighty had with him and, if the answer was none, what he might do to reawaken his interest. So engrossed was Winston in this that he almost missed the dead body lying on the Opera House steps where it had been dumped as the tide receded.

When Winston did notice he continued walking a few steps thinking oh, there's a dead body on the Opera House steps, before suddenly coming to a halt. Winston's first reaction was to look around, see if anyone else was there, and, finding the place deserted still, Winston approached the dead body. Even from this far away Winston could tell the body was dead. Without life bodies like this looked incredibly still and with each step closer Winston could see no twitch or movement.

From the top of the steps Winston looked down. The body was male, face down, the water lapping around its legs. He was dressed in a light jacket, brown leather shoes, dark green trousers and Winston thought the clothes looked new, expensive. Winston looked around again and felt his heart quicken, the man was wearing *expensive* clothes. Still seeing no-one, not even a jogger, Winston went down the steps, get a closer look, check this out. Winston took a deep breath and crouched. The man had curly black hair, dark skin, Italian maybe—like his clothes. No marks, no bloating, no pale puffy skin bodies get after being in the water a long time, no shark bites, nothing. Winston wondered if he should roll him over, look at the face, but decided no, better not move him, he could get to the man's pockets without moving him. Feeling the butterflies start again Winston reached down, noticing for the first time the train ticket and the silver charm. These lay by the face and the right hand as if he'd been clutching them, trying to protect them from the water. Winston picked up the train ticket. It was one-way, Adelaide to Sydney, which made sense to Winston who had never liked Adelaide much and could understand anyone not wishing to return there. Why keep it though, thought Winston, as he replaced it on the step. The charm was a silver rose, the sort you might put on a bracelet or wear round your neck, for luck. Winston didn't pick it up. If this was the sort of luck the silver rose charm had brought the dead man then Winston wanted none of it and proceeded instead to search the dead man's pockets.

In the left-hand jacket pocket Winston found a packet of Marlboro, sodden but still intact, capable of salvation. Winston smiled thinking maybe his luck had changed after all. However what Winston found in the right-hand jacket pocket made him forget all about cigarettes, changing fortunes and even The Almighty. What Winston found in the right-hand jacket pocket took his breath away. Inside a plain manilla envelope, torn open at one end, was a wad of hundred dollar and fifty dollar bills as thick as your little finger.

For at least five seconds he just stared at it. Then he got jumpy and looked around him again, head swivelling on a neck of rubber. Winston stuffed the envelope in his own pocket, replaced the cigarettes and whispering thanks mate to the body went back up the steps, almost tripping on the top one. Bursting, Winston stuck his hands in his trouser pockets, tucked his chin down into his chest and began walking around the Opera House to the Quay, trying hard not to dance like Gene Kelly in that picture with all the rain in it.

On the way he passed a man walking his dogs, going in the opposite direction. Winston shuffled past in the lifting mist without eye contact, and the man walking his dogs did the same, hardly noticing Winston at all, thinking that Winston looked like just another loser.

'Good on you, Winston,' Seamless said without taking his eyes from the fifteen hundred dollars wrapped tightly in an elastic band in front of him on the desk. 'Frankly I wasn't sure if you'd get it but I'm glad you did. I'm glad that I don't have to extract any penalty.'

Not half as glad as Winston was, his legs growing more confident by the minute.

'It's always better to conduct business without penalties, don't you think?'

Winston nodded, trying hard not to appear the way he felt which was as close to ecstasy as a man of Winston's disposition could get, what with a debt cleared and still ahead by two thousand, seven hundred and fifty dollars.

'That's right,' Winston said, wanting to nail his feet to the floor, stop them tapping with excitement. 'Definitely.'

'Because business can be difficult enough without penalties, can't it?'

Winston nodded again, watching Seamless drag his eyes from the roll of money and get up from the desk, moving over to the window and staring out at the street below. Framed by the light like this Winston found it difficult not to stare at the way Seamless's hair so obviously changed from sandy to brown where the wig perched on top of his head like vanity itself, giving rise to the nickname by which Roger Davis was known on the street, but never, ever, to his face.

'Quite difficult enough,' Seamless continued like someone bearing the burden of power heavily on his shoulders before turning to Winston, causing him to flush slightly and lower his eyes.

'You know something, Winston?'

Winston, at a loss, said no.

'Business can be very hard when people don't do what you tell them.'

Winston agreed, all smiles, eyes down, thinking conversations with Seamless could be hard too when all you wanted to do was hand over the money, get to the pub and let the beer flow.

'Take today for example. I get bad news, upsetting news, and all because people don't do what I tell them.'

Winston knew the feeling but without Seamless's clout he seldom got to tell people what to do, let alone have them do it, feeling more like the three of spades to Seamless's ace or picture.

Seamless was staring out the window again, shaking his head, saying 'Bad for business is what it is, Winston, bad for business. And you know where the buck stops when business gets bad?'

Winston pausing, searching for the right answer, cleared his throat and offered, 'With you, Roger?'

'That's right, Winston. With me.' smoothing the brown part of his hair now. 'But, you see, someone like you understands that, don't you, Winston?'

Winston said he did.

'That's why doing business with you is . . .'

Seamless searching for the right word and Winston, so used to this question-answer routine, getting just a little cocky, said, 'A pleasure?'

This time it was Seamless who paused and Winston wished he hadn't been so quick to reply, not knowing how Seamless would take it. A few moments passed, Winston putting one foot on the other, to stop it from tapping, before Seamless said, 'A good choice of word, Winston. Yes, a pleasure is what it is doing business with someone like yourself who understands what it is to do what he's told.'

Winston felt relief rise and mix with the excitement he held in place like hot lava and thought that the greatest pleasure he could foresee was having Seamless say you may go now, Winston, and getting stuck into all that money. To hasten this along Winston said, 'It's a pleasure doing business with you too, Roger.'

'Thank you, Winston.'

'So, if that's all, I might, you know, get going . . . '

Still staring out the window Seamless said, 'One last thing, Winston . . . '

'Yes, Roger?'

'Feel free to tell me to mind my own business, but was it hard getting the money?'

At the end of the sentence Seamless turned and looked directly at Winston but to his surprise Winston just shrugged, replying 'I got lucky, Roger,' thinking go to hell you nosey bastard.

Seamless smiled and stroked the brown part of his head. 'That's good, Winston. I always like to hear of a man getting lucky.'

Winston made to get up but, feeling really cocky now, decided to play an ace or a picture, not the three anymore. He nodded toward the bundle of money on the desk and said, 'Aren't you going to count it?'

'Winston,' Seamless said, looking as hurt as someone like Seamless could in the course of business, 'haven't you understood anything I've said?'

Winston hesitating, wondering had he?

'Don't you realise that I trust you?'

Ah yes, of course, trust.

'And besides,' Seamless continued, 'if that money is not all there, I'll come looking for you and break both your legs.'

And the penalty, thought Winston. Don't forget the penalty.

When Winston walked into the pub he felt like a king amongst paupers. Wings on his feet, step light, nodding at a few locals hunched over their glasses, he walked up to the bar and waited to be served. Contemplating all sorts of drinks but settling for a beer, Winston remained at the bar wanting to shout drinks all round, but seeing no-one worthy of his generosity, he refrained. Others would show, he thought, blokes worth impressing. Till then he'd wait, contemplate what he'd do with the two thousand plus, besides pass a little across the bar right here and now. No hurry, plenty to contemplate.

Firstly, Winston thought about buying Mardi Dennehy something, like a ring or earrings. Women liked that sort of thing, didn't they? Then Winston wondered about buying her a ring, thinking about the connotations a ring had. Maybe earrings would be better. He thought about giving them to her in one of those little velvet boxes all wrapped up and how she'd say something like, oh Winston, for me, you shouldn't have. And he'd say, it's nothing, Mardi, just a little gift, get her to make him dinner and the rest. Thinking along these lines, Winston suddenly remembered the last time he'd seen Mardi and how cold she'd been, not going to any trouble with the dinner, frozen pie and peas and lumpy mashed potatoes, and how she'd made him leave before ten because she was feeling tired, worn out from too much work. Winston sipped his beer and wondered. Maybe he'd get her a bunch of flowers instead.

There was his brother too. His brother deserved something for all the help he'd given Winston when Winston got out, setting him up with a place to stay, a little cash. Maybe he'd get the kids some toys, pay his brother back that way, do it so that awful bitch of a wife of his got nothing and watch her quietly seethe as she thanked Winston on behalf of the kids for the nice toys.

Or maybe take his brother to the track, a day out. His brother wouldn't go near a TAB but didn't mind the track, especially Randwick. Winston liked going to the track too and with his luck transformed this idea grew on Winston until he realised the explaining he'd have to do to his brother about where the money Winston was staking him came from. Winston's brother wanted him to go straight, so saying he'd found it on a corpse would not do at all. Sure Winston could come up with other reasons for his new-found wealth but he knew his brother would get suspicious and all the explaining he'd have to do didn't appeal. Maybe he should forget about taking his brother to the track, just go himself. Or even ring Jacko, forget all about the three of spades, and see when the next card school was happening.

Winston, on his second beer, tried to think of other debts but apart from twenty bucks, here and there, could recall none. Seamless's fifteen hundred was the one that mattered and with this out of the way Winston could relax. He felt pleased the way he'd handled it with Seamless, not letting the man get on top of him too much. Sure he'd been nervous, everyone was around Seamless, but he'd held his own and even come back enough at the end to show Seamless that he was someone to reckon with, not some mug to be pushed around.

Smiling to himself, Winston sipped his beer when he heard a voice behind him saying, 'Hey, Winnie, how they hangin'?' Winston turned to see Vincent with his lopsided grin and cheap pimp clothes heading toward him. Vincent the motormouth, only halfways important but with no-one else around Winston dug into his pocket and with an expansive gesture at the barmaid insisted on shouting, saying have whatever you like. Vincent said he'd have a double Bundy and Coke and they fell to talking about this and that. Vincent didn't take long to finish his, starting to fish in his pocket for change but Winston, not far behind with his beer, insisted on going again. Pleased, Vincent had another double b and c, keeping his mouth shut and listening politely to whatever Winston had to say, figuring if the man wanted to shout him drinks it was the least he could do.

Winston wasn't bothered by Vincent's gall, ordering expensive drinks like that. Winston was pleased enough to buy someone a drink and get this session happening, hold court and let the good times roll. Buying drinks helped make you feel important and that's the way Winston wanted to feel. Truth was, Winston couldn't feel any other way with his luck the way it was. And Vincent wasn't so bad, for a bludging lowlife, quiet too for once. Only thing that really bothered Winston about Vincent was the way he insisted on calling him Winnie. Winston had enough trouble being called after the cigar smoking fat man without Vincent abbreviating it. If Winston did the same to his name then they'd be Winnie and Vinnie and how would that sound, for christsake? Like a couple of budgerigars or something.

Vincent went off to the Gents and with no-one to talk to, Winston started thinking about his name some more. He remembered the way his old man used to brag about his being conceived on V.E. Day whilst they were listening to Churchill's speech on the radio, providing the inspiration for naming their first-born. Winston's brother came along a few years later and, in keeping with this new family tradition, they called him Robert after that prick Menzies. Winston remembered how this story always earnt his father a few laughs at the club, in male company, no matter how often he told it. Winston thought that rather than being funny it displayed a distinct lack of imagination on the part of his mother and father but then he'd never thought either of them real smart. Devout Royalists too.

Winston got another round in when Vincent came back from the Gents but thinking about his name had taken the wind from his sails and a lull in conversation developed which Vincent took no time in filling. Sipping his double b and c rather than gulping it like there was no tomorrow, Vincent said, 'You heard the word on the street?'

Winston said he hadn't

'So you didn't hear about Seamless's money?'

Again Winston said he hadn't, all the while thinking, which money? Surely the sum of fifteen hundred that Winston had repaid him wasn't sufficient to start rumours on the street. Surely money like that was nothing to Seamless. Or almost nothing.

'You know there's been some bad blood between Seamless and Ronnie H? Well word is that Seamless decides to cancel his ticket, figures it's gonna be easier and cheaper in the long run, so he hires this Eyetalian bloke from Adelaide who dresses like Mr Cool . . . ' Vincent paused, taking a sip, gearing up for the story. 'Shit, Winnie, you're gonna love this . . . '

Winston wasn't so sure.

' . . . Anyway the Eyetalian comes over from Adelaide by train, he's got this thing about cars or something, and meets with Seamless at one of the clubs. Deal is he does the hit for ten grand, five up front and the rest after the job's finished. So they have a nice lunch, drink a little, talk about business and Seamless parts with five. Only stipulation Seamless has is the Eyetalian should keep a low profile and get the job done soon as possible. Anyway, what Seamless doesn't know is the bloke's a bit of a dipso and as soon's he's got a taste for the stuff he's away. He's spotted drinking around town at various establishments, whiling away the afternoon, waiting for some sheila he's got tucked away on the North side to finish work, go see her. In between drinks he does a bit of shopping, spends a bit of Seamless's dough, smartens himself up for the woman. Even buys her something, some charm or other, which he shows off in the pub, talking about *amore* and all that shit. Come evening he's three sheets to the wind but he's gotta go and see *amore* so he staggers down to the quay, catch a ferry 'cos he's got this thing about cars, you know. And you know what, Winnie?'

Unable to speak, Winston just nonchalantly shook his head.

'That's the last anyone sees of him until this morning when they fish him out of the harbour.'

Exercising his will Winston cleared his throat and said, 'No kidding?'

'Dead set. And whaddya reckon's happened when they fish him out?'

His legs cold like stone, Winston shrugged.

Vincent smiled his lopsided smile. 'The money's gone.' This struck Vincent as being the funniest thing since sliced bread and he chuckled away to himself. 'Yeah. All gone. Can you believe it? 'Course what no-one knows is what happened. Did the Eyetalian just take a spill, you know, drop the money and go overboard? Or did Ronnie H get wind of it somehow and get to him first, give him a little shove? Either way Seamless is not a happy man. Not only is he out of pocket by five grand but Ronnie H is still walking the streets, and there's every likelihood that Ronnie'll cop a whisper and bad blood'll get worse.' Vincent shook his head a little too happily. 'Can you believe that luck?'

Winston couldn't. More importantly, Winston couldn't believe *his* luck. He'd hardly touched his beer as Vincent told his story and now, mouth dry, he drained it. Vincent did the same and placed his empty glass on the bar, looking at Winston, waiting.

Winston felt giddy, mind whirling, no longer feeling like a king but back to a little card, thinking no presents, no more rounds, time to be poor again.

Prompted by Winston's silence and his empty glass, Vincent said, 'We going again, Winnie?'

'Why not, Vincent,' Winston said, the blood slowly returning to his legs. 'Must be your shout?'

Jean Bedford was born in England in 1946 and came to Australia in 1947. She graduated in Arts at Monash University and in TESL at the University of Papua New Guinea, has taught English as a second language, worked as a journalist and a publisher's editor, and taught creative writing classes. Her short stories have appeared in *Nation Review*, the *National Times*, the *Sydney Morning Herald* and *Meanjin* and have been widely anthologised. She is the author of *Country Girl Again* (1979), *Sister Kate* (1982), *Colouring In*, with Rosemary Creswell, (1986), *Love Child* (1986) and *A Lease Of Summer* (1990). She has also written two detective novels featuring private eye Anna Southwood—*Worse Than Death* (1991) and *To Make A Killing* (1992).

Jean Bedford is married to Peter Corris and divides her life between Sydney and the Illawarra coast. She has three daughters.

Jean Bedford
COUSIN TO DEATH

The young woman who stood on my doorstep when I answered her ring was barely out of her teens. She twisted a strand of bright chrysanthemum-orange hair in her fingers and gave me a wide nervous smile.

'Anna Southwood?' she said in a voice that made everything a tentative question.

'Yes,' I said. 'You must be Susie Miller. Come in.'

I made coffee and sat her down on the comfortable couch in my downstairs office. Toby, my cat, stretched and gave her a sniff and a glancing touch of pink nose, then settled again in his patch of sunlight on the floor.

'What a beautiful cat,' she said, fingering her earring now, a silver pendant rose, and confirming my theory about her intonation.

We talked desultorily for a few minutes about cat people and dog people, agreeing that we both fell into the former category. When I thought she had relaxed somewhat I got down to business.

'You said on the phone that you think your life is in danger,' I began. 'Do you want to tell me about it?'

She fidgeted with her hair, her jacket, her earring again. She took a sip of coffee and looked at me over the cup. She was startlingly pretty, with classic Edwardian features and that mop of outrageously coloured hair. Like a flower at its absolute peak of perfect blooming, the way some young women are for a brief while.

'Well?' I asked patiently.

'Someone's following me,' she blurted. 'I'm sure of it. They've found me.'

'Who? Who's found you, Susie? Don't you think you'd better start at the beginning?'

'That's the trouble,' she said. 'I don't know what the beginning is.' She thought for a moment, straightening the hem of her short green skirt. 'No, I suppose it started with the money . . . '

'It often does,' I said, opening my notepad and taking the top off my fine-point pen. 'What money?'

'My grandfather's money. He left it all to me. I was going to share it with my cousin, Emily, but she . . . she died.' Her voice broke before it could rise.

'When? And how did she die?'

'Oh, a couple of months ago. She fell out of a window.' Suddenly she was talking fast, as if she'd had it all bottled up and now she'd started she couldn't stop.

'We were on a holiday, at Coffs Harbour. I'd just got Grandad's money, and neither of us had ever been anywhere before. We lived in the country, right out past Armidale, with the old man. Our parents were all killed in the same car accident when we were little and he and Gran brought us up. She died years ago, so there was just us and him. He really made us work hard on the farm, and after we left school we hardly ever saw anybody. We didn't know till he died that he was rich.' Her face flushed with resentment and I guessed at the life of skimping and making-do the girls had grown up with. It went some way towards explaining the slight incongruity of her smart clothes—new and expensive—and her constant fussing with her accessories, as if she had to keep reassuring herself that all these nice things were really there and really hers.

'Why didn't he leave the money to both of you?' I said. 'It seems a bit unfair.'

'It was *incredibly* unfair,' she said vehemently. 'That's why I was going to share it. He didn't like Emily—he was always picking on her, about her clothes and her make-up and the way she used the farm peroxide to blonde her hair . . . ' She touched her own hair self-consciously. 'When he died we *both* went into town and had our hair dyed as bright as we could. I'd never dared to do anything like that while he was alive, but Emily persuaded me, and I'm *glad*. I hope he's spinning in his grave.'

She seemed to have run out of steam, so I prompted her again.

'So? You got the money, and then whatever's going on now started. Is that right?'

'Yes,' she said uncertainly. 'At least I suppose it must have started before that, really, with Emily and Wayne . . . '

'Wayne?'

She looked evasive, then took the plunge. 'Wayne was a bloke that Emily saw sometimes. She sneaked out to meet him at night and I covered up for her. He came to the farm once to try and talk to Grandad about asking her out properly, but he ran him off with the shotgun. He said he was white trash.' She laughed.

'If he'd known Wayne was part-Maori he would have had a heart attack.' she said. 'Anyway, she used to go off with Wayne, and . . . and I think they used to do drugs or something. Sometimes she was really strange when she got home.'

'Strange? In what way?'

'Oh, talking a lot, giggling, really high. Once she didn't sleep for three days.'

'Sounds like coke,' I said. 'Was Wayne a dealer?' It would make sense, I thought. If there was drug-dealing involved then threats to someone's life weren't all that bizarre. Perhaps Emily's death hadn't been an accident either.

'I don't know, but I thought he might be . . . sort of bent. You know? He didn't seem to have a job and he always had plenty of money from what Emily told me. They used to go to a pub in Armidale and he'd play cards. Once she told me he'd lost $3000 in one night.' Her expressive thick eyebrows rose in wonderment.

'He bought her presents, too—really expensive gold chains, perfume. She had to hide them in the old tankstand under our bedroom window. That's where we always used to hide our things from the old man when we were kids . . . I suppose some of them're still there.' A tear ran down her pale cheek. 'We just packed up and left when he died—couldn't wait to get out of there. Though I made Emily stay till I got someone in to feed the animals.'

'So . . . go on,' I said. 'You went to Coffs Harbour for a holiday. Did Wayne turn up there?'

'Yes. He was always hanging about. He and Emily went out just about every night, sometimes I went with them. He's all right,' she said. 'I mean, he was always friendly to me, didn't mind me tagging along.'

Especially if you had money, I thought, then told myself not to be so cynical. Perhaps Wayne *was* a nice bloke. Like cops, some dealers must be.

'Did you try any drugs yourself?' I asked, trying to work out how much might have been around.

'Oh, not really. I had a joint one night, but it made me sick. I was going to try coke, but I was sort of building up my courage, you know? Then Emily died and I didn't have the chance.'

'Okay, so tell me about how she died.'

'Well, I don't really know. She'd been out with Wayne and she didn't come back till really late. I heard her come in and then I went back to sleep. I didn't hear anything else, and in the morning she wasn't in bed and I thought she'd gone out again, or that she'd just come back to get something and then gone to Wayne's room.' She paused and thought for a bit, as if she was trying to get the sequence of events straight in her mind.

'The doors to the balcony were open, but I didn't go out there. We often left them open to get the breeze—our room was twelve storeys up. I was downstairs in the dining room having breakfast when the cops . . . the police . . . came in and started asking questions about a young woman staying at the hotel. Some derro had found the body—she was stuck on the iron railings round the basement.'

Her voice faltered, then she steadied herself with a determined lift of her chin. 'I had to go and identify her.' She fumbled in her bag and came up with a cigarette. 'Okay if I smoke?'

I fetched an ashtray and sat down again, with only the slightest twinge of desire when she lit up. I'd been off them again for nearly six months and it was just starting to be bearable.

'So what was the verdict?' I asked. 'There must have been an inquest?'

'Accidental death.' She looked startled. 'It was. I mean, Wayne said she'd been really drunk when he dropped her off at our room, and they found alcohol and traces of cocaine in her bloodstream. They figured she'd gone out to the balcony for some fresh air and just . . . overbalanced.' She stared at me. 'It was an accident,' she insisted. 'I'm sure I would have heard if Wayne had come in with her. I said that at the inquest.'

'Okay,' I said. 'Well that more or less brings us up to when you came to Sydney, does it? Now you'd better tell me why you're here and what you're afraid of.'

She started fiddling with her earring again, then saw me looking and took it out. 'It was my grandmother's,' she said. 'It's part of a set—earrings, brooch and necklace. Emily and I shared them after she died, we hid them from Grandad. He thought they'd been lost. He put the rest of her jewellery in a deposit box at the bank. But I've got it all, now.'

I looked at the little antique silver rose in perfect bud hanging between two tiny serrated leaves, its delicate stem ending in a lover's knot where it entered the ear. 'It's beautiful,' I said, and she gave me an uncertain glance and put it back in her ear.

I waited, and she finally stopped fidgeting and went on with her story. 'Well . . . things started happening while I was still at the hotel. Phone calls late at night, a man with a really strange voice asking for Emily, then sort of snorting when I said she'd died. That happened a few times, and then the last time he said he'd check it out and if she wasn't really dead she soon would be. I got frightened. Wayne had gone back to the bush and I didn't know who else they knew in Coffs. I thought . . . '

'Yes?'

'I thought perhaps it was some drug deal. Perhaps Emily was supposed to do something and she hadn't and they thought she was hiding from them. She'd seemed a bit . . . worried, or something, for a few days before she died. Perhaps she was in some sort of big trouble. I thought they might come after me. So I left and came to Sydney. I've always wanted to see Sydney.'

'And now?'

'I'm sure I'm being followed. It's just a feeling, but you know how you can tell if someone's staring at you?' I nodded and she went on more confidently. 'But when I turn around there's no-one there. And there are phone calls again. Asking for Emily . . . ' Her voice strangled on the last word and she put her head in her hands.

'It's spooky,' she said, and I had to crane forward to catch her muffled speech. 'You know, like one of those horror movies where the dead come back to life. It's frightening me. I don't know what to do.' She sniffed and scrabbled in her bag for a tissue, burying her face in it.

'Where are you staying?' I asked.

'At the Kings Cross Hyatt. I suppose I was stupid to register in my own name, wasn't I? But I thought it was just something to do with the scene at Coffs Harbour. I didn't think it'd follow me here. I've checked out now, but I don't know where to go. My luggage is all in the car.' She raised a tear-stained face and I fell.

'Well, I suppose you could stay here for a while, till we find out what's going on.' Her look of gratitude nearly made me regret the immediate wish to eat my words. I explained my terms to her and said I'd give it a couple of days and see what I could find out. The Sydney end could wait, I thought. She was safe enough at my place, and clearly whatever was going on had its origins in the girls' former lives. Anyway, there was nothing to show that the latest phone calls had been made in Sydney—or that the first ones had been made from Coffs. Susie didn't know whether they were STD or not, as they'd come through the hotel switchboards. Given that the caller hadn't known that Emily was dead, I thought it more likely that those calls came from somewhere else, perhaps Armidale, and there was only her vague impression of being followed to go on here. I sighed. It looked as if I'd have to go to Coffs Harbour, Armidale and points northwest. I got the address of the farm and the hotel where Emily had died, then booked myself a late-afternoon flight.

Susie wrote me a cheque from a hardly touched book, with the proud flourish of one unused to having her own account, and went out to get her bags. I took her upstairs and showed her the spare room and where everything was and did my packing. By the time I left she was happily curled up with Toby on the couch watching a video of *Gone With The Wind* and munching on potato crisps. She seemed to have an absolute faith in my ability to put things right, like a child who has finally told the adults about the nightmare and had it soothed away. I hoped I could deliver.

I've been to Coffs Harbour several times and never liked it. It seems to me to be the acme of tackiness, worse even than Surfers', and the Big Banana feels like exactly the right wry symbol for the place. I booked into the same hotel that Susie and Emily had stayed in and started on the staff. After the expected runaround I got onto the maid who had serviced their floor, a thin, drab-looking woman, and persuaded her to have a drink with me when she went off duty.

We sat in the hotel's 'Palm Court' room, surrounded by desert-island paraphernalia, and she astonished me by ordering a rum and tequila. 'I'm a part-time drunk,' she said, chuckling wickedly. 'But dedicated. I like experimenting with alcoholic combinations.' Her voice was educated and I was certain there was a story there, but there wasn't time for it.

I asked her if she remembered the cousins, and whether they'd had many visitors.

'Yes, I certainly do remember them,' she said. 'That one who died, she was an absolute tearaway. Parties most nights in the room, keeping her little cousin awake. Young Susan'd talk to me in the mornings when I was cleaning, and she'd always give me a large tip because of the extra mess. I felt she was completely out of her depth, but she adored her cousin, did everything she told her to do and always made excuses for her. A bit simple, if you ask me.' She was managing to talk fast through great mouthfuls of her drink.

'She had the money, I think, and she used to go out shopping every day, mostly bringing back presents for the other one. She left me a thank-you note and fifty dollars when she checked out. A nice kid, she was. I tried to see her after her cousin died, but she was too miserable to see anyone, just stayed in the room with the "do-not-disturb" sign up all the time.' She looked pointedly at her empty glass and I gestured at the waiter for another. He delivered it so quickly that I guessed they had them lined up under the bar for her.

'Were there regular visitors?' I asked. 'Anyone you saw there a lot?'

'Well, I go off duty at eight,' she said, taking a big swallow. 'Like tonight. Then I start drinking. Get three hours sleep and back on the job by nine am. So I don't know what happens inbetween—but there was one young man who had a room here, too. Wayne, his name was. He was that Emily's boyfriend and she spent half her nights in his room. I had to collect up her underwear, so I know. I used to feel sorry for the other one. She'd sit in her room watching telly, I think, too shy to go out and get a chap of her own, though she was just as pretty. More like sisters they were, to look at. Except Emily had . . . oomph. You know what I mean?'

I nodded, disappointed, though I hadn't really expected that she'd be able to tell me much. *A bit of background colour*, I told myself. *That's worth having anyway*. I finished my gin and tonic and left twenty dollars on the table for the rest of the night's drinks. No-one else on the staff had been able to tell me anything and I thought it was a waste of time staying there for long. I went to bed, planning to go out to the farm the next day and see if I could get any word on where Wayne was hanging out.

I had hired a zippy little Honda Accord and in the late morning, after doing the cryptic crossword, I set off up the mountains for a few hours' drive. I'd had a look at the map and realised I'd have to stay in Armidale overnight if I didn't want to arrive at the farm in the small hours, but that was good for tracing Wayne's connections.

I'd never been to Armidale before and I was surprised at how small and provincial the city was. No movie theatre, but pubs on practically every corner. Two Chinese restaurants, an Indian, a McDonalds, a Woolies and a row of banks. A few boutiques in between that were tax dodges if ever I saw them. Video shops. That was about it. I wondered what the students at the university did for kicks. Drinking seemed to be the only leisure activity offering. And drugs, of course. I had a late lunch at the surprisingly good Indian restaurant and then booked into the nearest pub for the night.

After I'd settled into my room, looking longingly at the old-fashioned deep bath, I went down to the bar. There were a few drinkers scattered about and a big blackboard announcing a Country & Western band for that night. I ordered a light beer and asked the barman if he knew Wayne Bradley. He didn't. Then I asked him if he knew which pubs had late-night poker games and he gave me an incredulous look and moved off into his storeroom.

I shrugged and turned around on my stool to examine the clientele: two old men nattering over their beer and racing forms; a middle-aged couple niggling at each other, the remains of their steak-and-chips counter-lunch still piled at one end of their table: a couple of blokes who looked like out-of-work cowboys staring morosely at the huge colour TV blaring out an American game show; a group of younger people around the pool table. They seemed the best bet. I watched them while I finished my beer, trying to work out if they were students ducking lectures or unemployed youth. It was impossible to tell. I put my glass down and went over to them.

'Anyone here know Wayne Bradley?' I asked in a friendly voice, taking care to wait until no-one was sighting down a cue. Four blank faces turned to me and then to each other. They all shook their heads, and a thin young man began crumbling chalk into his palm.

'Hang on,' one of the girls said. 'There's a Wayne who comes in here sometimes to listen to the band, but I don't know his other name.' There was no answering agreement from the others, so I gave her my room number and asked if she'd tell him I was looking for him if he came in later. She repeated the message dutifully but not with much conviction and I thanked her. I went out to the street wondering whether it was worth going into every pub—there seemed to be dozens of them—and how many light beers I could stand. Five, it turned out, before I got thoroughly sick of it. No-one had admitted to knowing Wayne, or which pubs had poker games, and I'd been propositioned three times by drunks.

It was dark by the time I got back to the Royal and there was the smell of frying. I made myself several black coffees in my room, had a long hot bath, put on jeans and a jumper and prepared to brave the bar again. I was picking up my bag and keys when there was a knock at the door. The young man standing there was tall and dark, with long wavy hair, a hoop earring, and dressed incongruously in a conservative pinstripe suit.

'Hear you're lookin' for me?' he said in a pleasant, New Zealand accented voice.

'If you're Wayne Bradley I am,' I said. 'Come in.' I mentally apologised to the girl in the bar. She'd given me a break.

I poured us both wine from the bottle I'd bought on the way in and sat on the bed. He sat in the one vinyl armchair, swivelling it around so that he could put his feet up on the oak-veneered dressing table. Apart from saying he'd like a drink he hadn't uttered a word, just sat there watching me and waiting to hear what I wanted.

'Are you making threatening phone calls to Susie Miller?' I asked him abruptly, seeing if it would shake his composure.

It did. 'Susie? Have you seen her? Where is she?' He swung his feet back onto the floor and leaned forward eagerly. 'I've been trying to track her down—she's bloody fallen off the edge of the world, I thought.'

'She's in Sydney,' I said. 'And someone's been ringing her, asking for Emily. Would you have any idea what that's about?'

The mention of Emily made his face contract painfully. *He really loved her*, I thought, and wondered why it surprised me so much.

'Emily's dead,' he said dully and took a swig of the wine.

'I know,' I said. 'Susie was getting the same sort of phone calls in Coffs Harbour, that's why she went to Sydney. Did she tell you about them?'

'No. I never saw her after Emily died. I didn't even find out till the next day. I had to go out of town early in the morning. Susie wouldn't come out or talk to me on the phone or anything. I tried to wait for her after the inquest but she had a cab waiting and just ran off. I left a couple of notes at the hotel for her, thanking her, you know, for clearing me at the inquest, and asking if I could do anything to help, but she never answered.' He shook his head and I filled his glass for him again. 'She never even told me when the funeral was. And then I had to go right out bush on a job, into Queensland, and when I got back I went to Coffs but they said she'd left the hotel. I don't know anything about any phone calls, but.'

'What sort of job?' I said and he looked puzzled. 'What sort of job in the bush?'

'Oh. I'm a sort of travelling salesman,' he said, grinning.

'What sort of things do you sell?'

'This and that. This and that,' he said vaguely, but in a mind-your-own-business tone. 'Anyway, how's Susie coping on her own? Fancy her going to Sydney by herself. I wouldn't have thought she had it in her.'

I thought Susie must have done some painful growing up when her cousin died. He'd be surprised if he saw her now, if what the maid had said was accurate. I said so, and he shook his head, disbelieving. He finished his drink and got up to go.

'Listen, tell Susie where I am, will you?' He handed me a card with an Armidale address and phone number on it. 'I didn't know where I was going to be after that last job—thought I might even stay in Queensland—so if she did want to contact me she couldn't. Anyway, tell her if I can do anything . . . ' He trailed off. 'I guess she doesn't want to see me though. I think she blames me for Emily being so out of it that she fell off the balcony. I wish I could talk to her, but.'

I thought he meant it. I'd decided I liked Wayne Bradley. He might be a dealer, but he had a straight sort of charm and friendliness about him too. I let him out, thinking that perhaps he was just a middle man, going between the big suppliers and buyers, not actually doling it out to the addicts on the streets. I don't know why that made it feel better, but it did.

I gave up on the idea of anything to eat and went to sleep to the rather comforting raucous rendering of 'Stand by Your Man' drifting up from the bar.

It was a long drive to the farm, nearly up to the Queensland border. I set off very early, just after daybreak, but it was well into the afternoon when I got there, having got lost several times and also having fallen asleep for an hour or so by the creek where I stopped for a break. It was beautiful country to drive through—rich red soil and forests of tall gums, and hardly any other traffic for miles on end, but I was relieved when I finally saw the tin letterbox with 'Miller' painted on it.

The rutted track led to a picture-book farmhouse—white painted weatherboard with deep verandahs, set back against small hills and looking out over pasture and large stands of timber to a wide river. There was an old ute parked by the shed and, as I pulled up, a round rosy smiling woman came out onto the verandah, adding to the picture-book feel of the place.

'Are you Mrs Rattray?' I asked. 'Susie Miller said I could come and have a look around.'

Her dumpling face creased into lines of concern. 'Susie? How is the poor girl? I thought she might come back here when Emily died, but she sent a note with the last cheque saying she was going to sell up.'

I followed her into the house, telling her that I thought Susie was fine, but she seemed determined to make a new life for herself. Mrs Rattray shook her head doubtfully while she pressed me into a kitchen chair and began to make tea. 'I don't know,' she said. 'She's not used to looking after herself, you know. What with the old man bullying her all her life, and that Emily bossing her about, she didn't have a mind of her own at all.'

I muttered something about the quiet ones surprising you when they get out from under, but she didn't looked convinced. I asked her about the girls, and about Wayne, but she didn't have much to add to what I'd already found out. She'd never met Wayne, but she'd heard about the old man running him off.

'Cursing and swearing, she was, the next day. That Emily. Good job old Jeb didn't hear her.'

I was surprised. 'Did you work here when their grandfather was alive?'

'Oh, just a day or so a week. I was here a lot of the time when the girls were little, when Elsie was sick. Afterwards he made the kids do most of the work, but I used to come up for the chooks and do a bit of baking. Now I come up most days again and tend to the animals. Susie sends me a cheque every month.'

She nattered on comfortably over the tea and fresh scones, mostly about what a tyrant the old man had been and what a sweet girl Susie was. She had no time at all for Emily: 'She was just plain wicked,' she said. 'Right from a baby. As soon as she could talk she was telling lies, blaming everything on Susie, getting her whipped for things *she'd* done. She was a thief, too. Always taking little trinkets out of her grandmother's jewel-box and then trying to make out I must have lost them, or worse. I caught her at it once, and she never forgot it. Oh, she led me a dance, played cruel tricks on me for years.' She sighed, and looked as sour as her jolly face would allow.

I finished the tea and said I'd like to have a look around. She bustled off happily into the yard and I explored the house. The downstairs parlour looked as if it had been kept for best, with stiff formal furniture, a large family Bible on the piano, and photographs on every surface. Quite a few were of the two girls, from about three onwards, which would have been when their parents died. They were very alike, two serious little faces staring from under thick elegant eyebrows and tightly drawn back dark hair. As they got older the differences began to emerge and it was clear which one was Emily. Susie never lost her bewildered sweet frown, but Emily began to look distinctly impish, even poking her tongue out in one picture. The most recent ones showed Emily with patchily bleached hair looking sulky while Susie still wore her dark curls in an old-fashioned page-boy, drawn back over her ears by tortoiseshell clips. No wonder she'd been so eager to be persuaded to her spectacular dye-job.

I went up to the bedrooms. They were bare and clean, the huge old double bed standing in the largest room with looming mahogany dressers grouped around it like an attendant chorus. Although there were several rooms upstairs, the girls had clearly always shared the small one at the back corner of the house, with its two narrow, neatly counterpaned beds. I looked out the window and saw the tankstand Susie had told me about. The room was minimally furnished, with a plain chest of drawers, a small upright wardrobe and two high-backed wooden chairs. There was a Bible on the table between the beds. I picked it up and saw Susie's large childish signature on the fly-leaf. I shivered slightly, as if the ghosts of those unhappy little girls still lingered.

I went back downstairs and wandered out onto the verandah. I couldn't remember why it had seemed so important to come all this way to see where the girls had lived. Obviously there was nothing more to be learned here about Wayne, or whatever shady deals Emily might have been involved in. But I had been convinced that the threats to Susie must have their roots somewhere in the past, and their past was here. Coffs Harbour had been their first move towards a future.

Mrs Rattray emerged from behind the shed, a basket full of brown speckled eggs in her hands. 'I'm off now,' she said cheerfully. 'There's plenty of snack food in the kitchen if you want to stay. The beds are all made up.' She waved and got into the ute, starting it with a great roar of exhaust fumes. I watched her bumping up the track and decided I might as well stay the night. I wouldn't get back to Armidale at any decent hour, anyway.

In the morning, after sleeping in one of the spare rooms, I had a cold buttered scone and cup of tea and got ready to go. I left a note thanking Mrs Rattray and went out to the car, then changed my mind and walked round to the old tankstand. I crawled underneath, through tendrils of honeysuckle and spider webs and over rotting pieces of lumber, to a dry little space beside the wall of the house, littered with cardboard boxes and paper packets. I opened some of them, squinting in the dim filtered light, and found plastic beads, a tattered and chewed kewpie doll, a couple of little tin brooches, faded ribbons—all the tat that the old man would have disapproved of as frivolous, I supposed. The last box I picked up seemed newer and more solid. I prised open the stapled top and saw the neat rows of plastic packets all full of white powder. 'Shit,' I said. Then, 'Shit, indeed.' I put the top back carefully and replaced the box. I crawled out backwards and brushed myself down, then went and sat in the car, trying to work it out.

I was still puzzling about it when I drove into Armidale's main street in the afternoon, and later while I had a bath in the hotel. I got dressed and then rang home. Susie answered on the second ring. I filled her in on what I'd been doing, except for finding the stash, and made sure she'd been all right. She seemed touched at my report of the meeting with Wayne and asked me for his address. 'I'll write to him,' she said. 'I know it wasn't really his fault.'

I told her I'd be coming home the next day and she put Toby near the phone to say hello. There was an outraged squeal and an exclamation from Susie, then a laugh. I should have told her Toby doesn't think he's a toy—or even a pet. I put the phone down thoughtfully then realised I was starving. I'd driven right through the day, stopping only once for petrol, too preoccupied to do anything about lunch or to even notice the spectacular scenery.

Over a pub mixed grill and a beer I went through it all again in my mind. It was taking a sort of shape, I thought, with a lot of what-ifs. Like, what if Emily had somehow hidden the stash, holding out, and the threatening phone calls were from its rightful (if that was the word) owners? Or what if the tankstand was just where Wayne usually put his wares between both ends of the negotiation? In that case, where did the phone calls fit in? Perhaps it was someone trying to cut Wayne out, who thought Emily might know where he hid it, and didn't believe she was dead. Or they knew she was dead but they thought Susie might know, and they were trying to frighten her before putting the word on her? Or what if Emily had been working with someone else to cut Wayne out, but she hadn't told them the hiding place yet? In which case, some of the above might still apply. I was going round in circles and nearly falling asleep in my dirty plate, so I went up to bed. I'd have to ask Susie about the coke tomorrow. *She might know something she doesn't know she knows*, I thought incoherently as I drifted off to sleep.

But when I got home she wasn't there. The spare key was on the table, everything was washed and put away, Toby had been fed and there was a note under the key in her characterless round script:

Anna,

Thanks for everything. I've decided to drop it and just move somewhere else for a while. I think I was silly to be frightened —it's nothing to do with me.
Yours sincerely,

Susie Miller.

There was another cheque, too, for five hundred dollars. I tore it up in my fury at the wasted time and energy, but I had to admit I was really angry because now I wouldn't get to the bottom of it. I toyed with the idea of ringing Wayne, perhaps just following it up a little bit more for my own satisfaction, but then realised that was futile. If I didn't know where Susie was, I couldn't do anything about the phone calls. I paced around the house for a while till I was reasonably calm and then went down to the office and checked the answer machine. There were a few interesting messages, so I put the violet folder marked 'Miller' away and tried to put it out of my mind.

A week later, after I'd dealt with some other fairly simple business, I realised the Miller case was still bothering me. I got out Wayne's card and dialled the Armidale number. A weary woman's voice answered. 'No,' she said. 'You can't talk to my brother. He's dead. I'm just here packing up his things.'

'What? What do you mean, dead? How?'

'Murdered,' she said. 'Stabbed. I don't know . . . some dirty drug business, I suppose. Or at least that's what the cops think.' Her voice became suspicious through its tired grief. 'Who are you?'

'Just a friend,' I said. 'I'm sorry.' I put the phone down to the sound of her sudden sob.

It looked as if the cutting out scenario was correct. If Emily had moved the stash without telling him and was working with someone else, his suppliers would have been getting very angry when he couldn't produce the profits. They wouldn't muck about when he couldn't come up with the stuff itself, too.

I was in the garden later that afternoon when the phone rang. I ran in and answered it with dirty hands. It was Susie.

'Anna,' she said breathlessly. 'Wayne's dead. And now I'm really in trouble. I told him where I was living in Sydney—and I think he told someone else. The phone calls have started again, but now they're asking for me, and threatening to kill me too, if I don't tell them where something is. I don't even know what it is they want.' She sounded strung out, hysterical. 'Anna, could I come and stay with you for a few days? I felt . . . safe . . . there. And will you try to find out who they are?'

I waited for a few moments. I was pissed off at her, but I did want to solve the case. 'Sure,' I said, 'but this time no sudden flits.'

'No,' she said, relief in her voice. 'I promise. I'll come round tonight, okay? I've got some things to do first.'

But she didn't arrive that night, nor the next day, and she didn't phone. It was the next weekend when I saw the item in the *Herald* about the young woman washed up on the Opera House steps. An early jogger had found her and there was a description of her clothes— new shoes were specified—but what made me rigid with shock was the mention of the small silver rose brooch and matching earrings. The police were treating it as a case of murder.

I put through a call to Glenn Sheedy, my friend the cop, and noticed my hands were shaking. 'Glenn,' I said, when he came on the line. 'Do you know anything about this Opera House corpse?'

'Not my bailiwick,' he said in his nicotine-ruined voice, 'but I can find out.'

He hung up before I could thank him and rang back about half an hour later.

'Black hair,' he said, by way of greeting. 'Recently dyed over blonde over black. Five feet tall; around fifty kilos. Blue eyes. Female cauca-sian aged approximately twenty-one years. Bashed on the head then shoved in the harbour. Slight scratch, possibly cat, on right arm. No leads. Okay? That help?'

'I think I know who she is,' I said. I gave him Susie's name and told him everything I knew about it. He said he'd pass it on and get back to me when there was any news.

I spent the rest of the weekend in suspense, waiting for the phone to ring, but it was Monday afternoon before Glenn got back to me. His voice was puzzled.

'Anna, you were in the right paddock, but you had the wrong cow.'

'What?'

'She's been positively identified—dental charts and that, plus a distinguishing mark, a star-shaped mole on her thigh. Some old duck who used to mind her up the bush pointed it out. They got her to come down to the city to make the ID. It wasn't Susan Miller at all, it was her cousin, Emily. Make any sense?'

'I think so,' I faltered after a while. 'Thanks Glenn. I'll ring you.'

I sat on the couch feeling stunned as it all reformed and raced around my head, finally falling into place. The way the hotel maid's and Mrs Rattray's descriptions of Susan had seemed a bit off-centre—the Susan I had met didn't seem simple, unable to look after herself, just a bit childish. But of course it was Emily. Emily the liar and the thief. The leader. The naughty girl who didn't inherit anything. The jealous spiteful girl who never forgot a grudge. Why should Susan have all the money? Or even any of it if she was going to share, as she probably was? Get her drunk, give her some coke, and while she's reeling from unaccustomed sensations, push her off the balcony. Then take all the money without waiting to inherit—easy enough to imitate that round schoolgirl signature—and get out of the drug trouble at the same time. Become Susan, go incommunicado. Don't see anyone who knew Susan at all well and get right away as soon as possible. It made sense.

And then what? Why did she come to me? Perhaps she'd worked out that Wayne would always be a threat—he wouldn't stay fooled that she was Susan, he was in love with wicked Emily. 'Oh shit,' I said out loud as I realised how thoroughly she'd played me for a sucker. She'd needed to find out where Wayne was, so she could put him out of the way. Especially if she'd hidden the coke consignment and was intending to deal on her own behalf. She had money of her own, though, by then. Still, I supposed that when you've always had nothing, no amount will ever be enough, and there had to have been a quarter of a million's worth of coke in that box. She'd made up the threatening phone calls to put me on his track, and as soon as she had his whereabouts she'd gone. Though perhaps she hadn't made them up—if I could believe anything, it was the story about the so-called Emily's situation.

I wondered about her last phone call, whether the heavies had really got to her finally, or whether she'd suddenly realised that I might have snooped around the tankstand and so I was a danger to her, too. Had she wanted my help? Or had she intended to kill me? I'd never know for sure; perhaps it was both—after all, she'd dyed her beautiful hair again, as if she was on the run, and *someone* had murdered her. The only thing that comforted me somewhat was the thought of all that coke rusting away under the old tankstand—that was one deal that had got away.

Robert Hood is the author of some twenty-five
published (and lots of unpublished) stories as
well as several plays and textbooks, an opera
libretto, two-and-a-half novels and a song
about lost love and Godzilla. His collection of
stories, *Day-Dreaming on Company Time*, was
a finalist in the Best Collection by a Single
Author category of the 1990 Readercon Small
Press Awards (held in Massachusetts, USA).
He won the *Canberra Times* National Short
Story Competition in 1975 and the Australian
Golden Dagger Award for mystery stories in
1988. Robert Hood works as a research assis-
tant and is described by his wife, sculptor and
poet Debbie Westbury, as a 'very sick man'.

Robert Hood lives in Coledale, NSW, with
Debbie and son Luke, and has committed no
major crimes.

Robert Hood
BLOODY HIDE

'That's her,' whispered 'Piss' Barall, pointing ostentatiously. The woman's hair was dark, cut neat at the back and wild on top, as though her hairdresser had run out of steam halfway up. She was carrying a leather bag and a scowl of intense concentration. 'Gail Veitch,' Piss added, in case I'd forgotten her name. 'She lives there.'

'Which floor?'

'Thirteenth.'

'Unlucky. What number?'

'135.'

I yanked him back from the window and shoved him into a chair. He shot me an indignant frown. Veitch ran an ID through a black scanner on one side of the doors. They opened and she strode in.

'What the hell you doin,' Crowe?' barked Piss.

'You were standing in my light,' I said.

Gail Veitch was a muck-journo for *Manhunter* magazine—nothing important, just low-level gossip and a bit of criminal innuendo. From a distance she'd looked stern, like she took herself too seriously. The curves were all there though, and in the right places, and her legs were long and suggestive. Even with that scowl, she had the sort of face some blokes would kill for.

My client wanted her dead.

'I ain't your bloody scratch board, Crowe,' Piss whined, 'Show me a bit of respect.'

I sat back, staring at him, and sucked at my half-empty coffee mug. Its contents had gone cold ages ago. Hot shit was just bearable, but cold? 'Get me another coffee,' I said.

Piss wobbled towards the café's counter and spoke to a harassed-looking woman behind the cappuccino machine. I might have asked McKimm for more money if I'd known he intended to inflict me with Piss. Bloody nuisance. He staggered back. Grinning.

'How do we do it?' he said, dumping coffee in front of me. 'You gonna hit her at home?'

'*We* don't do it at all, Piss.' I poked at his chest; it looked like people poked it all the time. 'Now you've pointed her out to me, you get lost. Right?'

'McKimm said—'

'McKimm's not here, mate. I can easily make this a double header if you keep annoying me.'

'I'd like to watch, Crowe. I'm looking out for a new career.' Piss was a runner and a junkie, as far as I knew. As an assassin, he'd make a great target.

'I work alone,' I said.

Fact is, I usually didn't do this sort of job at all. But McKimm had caught me on the hop. Been skint for weeks, thanks to a couple of mafioso bookies I'd fallen foul of. Rent overdue. Eating from cheap takeaways. That sort of thing.

'It's an easy hit,' McKimm said.

'Not my line, McKimm,' I told him. 'Get a professional from the Pink Pages.'

'Don't sell yourself short, Mike. You're a good man. I don't trust pros. They're all sociopaths.'

'And you prefer psychopaths, eh?'

McKimm scowled, as though he wasn't sure I was joking.

Veitch was a real bitch, he went on, not so much a woman as a leech. Surely I didn't have scruples. I told him amateur hitmen annoy everyone, pros and cops alike. He reckoned no one'd care.

'What've you got against her?'

'She's trying to blackmail me.' He scratched at his moustache as he talked. A lousy liar.

'What with? Pictures? Documents?'

'Sure.'

'So I'll beat her up a bit and get 'em back.'

'She won't give up,' he said. Maybe he was right, but I smelt a rat—a big, dirty one with shit all over its claws. As I saw it, Veitch was no threat at all. *Manhunter* was one of the country's least prestigious journals. Its 'exposés' amused rather than exposed. So why was McKimm so paranoid? And why me?

'Okay,' he said, his squinty eyes squeezing down even tighter. 'I'm not gonna argue. I'll be in Adelaide for the next week. While I'm out of town, I want her dead, Crowe . . . and you'll bloody do it, 'cause if you don't, I'm gonna tell Pukalski about the Kembla job. Capice?'

He was talking about a scam I'd pulled last winter, one that involved about a hundred thousand bucks, a crate-load of crack on a boat off Port Kembla and the South Coast's most successful crim. It'd come about almost by accident, unplanned—one of those little gifts the devil drops in your lap sometimes. Too bloody hard to resist, despite the risks. It made me a bit richer and Charlie Pukalski a bit poorer. Not enough to bankrupt him—just pocket money. But Pukalski follows a strict code of behaviour: he can shaft whoever he likes . . . nobody shafts him.

The money didn't last long. Payback on a few debts, a new BMW and a suit to go with it, then a couple of weeks on the Gold Coast. That lot saw my score out in a matter of months. Unfortunately, the crack disappeared too, along with the courier's corpse. The latter ended up feeding the sharks, but I'd hidden the junk; when I went back for it a day or two later, it was gone. Nice present for someone. Wish I knew who.

The courier was a bloke named Sorensen. One of Pukalski's most trusted. Bad-tempered prick with a face that made a pig-dog look like Sam Neill. When you shook his hand he gave off a stink of cheap cologne and sweat. Used to wear trendy clothes too big for him, really coarse cravats and a tie-clip with a silver rose on it. Puzzled me not only why Pukalski put up with him, but how he managed to pull the birds. I remember he'd been hanging around with this real looker at the time. I'd considered making a move on her myself, once I'd got rid of him. Frizzed-out hair. Blonde. Great legs. 'I'm on the wagon, Crowe,' Sorensen had said the day before the Kembla deal was due to go down. I'd asked him to come to the pub, so I could squeeze information from him. No go. 'Promised me girlfriend. She'd kill me if I got pissed, first opportunity.' Hardly a consideration he needed to worry about; I shot him in the gut the next night and pushed his weighted corpse into the sea.

By the time I got back from up north, his girlfriend wasn't around any more, though I didn't like to inquire too closely. I wasn't part of

Pukalski's organisation after all and hadn't even got near enough to the woman to tell if the padding was real.

'You're a dead man if Pukalski finds out what you did,' McKimm said. 'Sorensen was like a son.'

I studied his slick black hair, receding at the top and long at the back, and the folds of blubber wobbling about under his jawline. He licked his lips nervously. 'Don't know what you're talking about, McKimm,' I said.

'Sure,' he smirked, 'Sure you don't. So you'll do the job for money, eh?'

Getting into the building wasn't hard. It's in the middle of Sydney, with pedestrian traffic milling around it all day. Another body, even one as Neanderthal as mine, wasn't going to be noticed. I waited out of sight until I saw someone exit from the internal elevator and head for the front doors, then I walked toward them myself. They opened for the bloke coming out and I walked in. There was a doorman sitting behind a counter to the left. Apparently I didn't arouse his curiosity, even though he couldn't recognise me; he gave me a side-glance, then kept reading his newspaper. I strode across the foyer to the elevators.

The room I was after was at the end of an over-dressed corridor. Front door had a peep-hole, just under a big brass '135'. I stood slightly to one side so my worst feature, my face, was obscured, and knocked. It took Veitch a while to answer; she must have assumed I was another tenant, because she didn't worry about security. She opened the door without attaching a chain. 'Yes?' she said.

She was wearing a bathrobe and her hair was wet.

'Can I borrow a cup of sugar?' I said.

She frowned and I pushed hard on the door so she was forced to stagger backwards; I was slamming it shut behind me before she got her balance enough to start complaining. By then, there was fear swelling in her eyes. 'Crowe?' she growled, backing away, 'What do you want?'

She knew me. Odd. I grabbed her wrist as her hand reached towards the communicator on the wall. 'We'll keep this little visit to ourselves, eh?' I said, twisting hard. She squealed, then cursed as I let her go.

There was a small kitchen to the right, with a large space beyond it filled with bookshelves, grey leather divans and potted palms. Glass sliders led to a balcony. There were two doors on the wall at my left. Bedroom and bathroom, no doubt.

'We acquainted?' I asked.

'I hope not,' she said.

'Well, you shouldn't open your door to strangers. Didn't your mother teach you anything?'

'My mother got pregnant to a door-to-door salesman. What would she know?' She looked directly into my eyes, letting me feel their ice.

'I've been hired to kill you,' I said. For a moment her coolness broke. She looked at me aghast, but her mood shifted quickly. She hoped I was joking. 'I'm not joking,' I added, producing a 9 mm Glock handgun. Accurate little bugger. Polymer technology, they reckon. Ceramic. 'Make us a cup of coffee, eh?'

Her face was bloodless, though she didn't move. 'I need the caffeine,' I said.

She wet her lips, unsure of herself, and went into the kitchen. She filled the kettle, plugged its cord into a socket and pressed the switch. She glanced at me, then reached for some mugs. Her hand went to the cutlery drawer for a spoon. 'No knives,' I said. 'You wouldn't be able to take me anyway.'

'Sure of yourself, aren't you?' Her green eyes blazing.

'Practice,' I commented.

When we had our coffee, I gestured her through to the loungeroom. She glared at me, but went without trying anything. As she sat on the divan, her robe fell open above and below the tie around her waist, exposing the curve of one breast and a length of thigh. Deliberate? Perhaps. 'Well?' she said. 'When are you going to do it? Before or after you rape me?'

'Maybe I'm not going to do it at all.' I sipped at the coffee. It was hot and bitter.

'Oh?'

'You know Leon McKimm?' I watched her eyes, but the name provoked contempt rather than fear.

'Sure. He's a scumbag—and a resentful shit.'

'He wants you dead, so I guess the feeling's mutual. What's he resent?'

'Why don't you ask him . . . ?' I heard a sound and held up my hand to stop her. She frowned. The sound came again, a scraping on the far side of the front door. 'The balcony!' I said to Veitch. She protested, but I grabbed her and shoved her out. I locked the sliding glass and pulled a curtain across. The only way off the balcony was straight down thirteen floors to the street.

Piss was crouched on the other side of the peep-hole, made rounder and more grotesque by its fish-eye lens. He was fiddling with the lock. I growled, yanked open the door, grabbed him and pulled him into the room. He flew across the kitchen, hit the bench and crashed down on the vinyl tiles.

'I told you to get lost,' I said and kicked him in the gut for good measure. He wheezed.

'Shit, Crowe . . . '

'No one hassles me, Piss,' I said, giving him another to be going on with.

'Thought ya might need help.'

I pulled him to his feet. 'You're a fool.'

'Where's the bird?' he asked, with a sneer so smug it forced me to pound it hard. Several times. He tumbled into a corner and curled up, groaning.

When I let Veitch in, she looked at Piss as though he was something small and obscene that had squeezed under her door. 'Who's he?' she said.

'He's leaving.' I gestured at Piss to go. He crawled maybe a metre, then made it onto his feet. He walked even more drunkenly now, but he was heading out. Good enough. Veitch began to say something and I turned toward her, but saw from the corner of my eye that Piss had changed course. He was pulling a gun. 'Bastard!' I yelled, pushing myself back. My own gun came around. We must have both fired at the same time, because I only heard one shot. Piss shrieked and so did Veitch behind me. I staggered to get my balance as I watched a bloody hole appear in Piss's chest; the impact propelled him against the wall. He crashed, blood splashing across the pastel-toned wall-paper. I went over to him as he clawed at the floor, trying to reach his gun. Cordite smelt sharp in the air.

'What's the idea, Barall?' I said.

He looked up at me, his eyes going filmy. Muscles twitched on the side of his face. He wanted to say something, but the loose blood in him swelled up suddenly. He gasped, heaved scarlet bile and fell face-down. I prodded at him, but he didn't move.

'Is he dead?' Veitch said.

'I guess so.' I glanced around, noting a hole in the sliding glass door where Piss's bullet had escaped the room. 'You think we might have disturbed the neighbours?'

'The nearby apartments are all empty,' she said, 'till they get home at about six.'

I nodded. My coffee was sitting on one of her bookshelves where I'd left it. I went to it and took a sip. Still warm. Only instant, but I needed something.

'What was all that about?' Veitch said, not coming any closer, but not making any threatening moves either. 'Was he one of yours?'

'McKimm's.'

'Looked to me like he was trying to do you out of a job.'

'Yeah.' I studied her carefully. Not too many yuppies could go through what she'd gone through in the last fifteen minutes and still be coherent, let alone cunning.

'What do you plan to do with the body?' she said. I shrugged. She came closer, her fingers untying the knot at her waist. 'How about dealing with this body instead then?' As she spoke she shrugged off the bathrobe. 'After that, we should talk.'

When we got around to talking, she did most of it. While she babbled on about petty scandals among the rich and famous, the politics of the *Manhunter* office and the effect of recession on the cost of her make-up, she wandered around the unit like a junkie heading for a major withdrawal, smoking a particularly nasty-smelling brand of cigarette and making cups of coffee.

'Have you decided if you're going to kill me?' she asked.

I shrugged. She offered me something stronger than coffee; when I told her I never touched the stuff, she poured herself a triple Scotch. She delicately stepped over Piss's corpse whenever her energies took her in that direction.

'For god's sake, say something useful,' I said at last. She was drunk and I didn't think she'd make sense much longer. 'I can't stand any more of this shit.'

'Shit?' Her eyes narrowed at me. 'You've never heard of post-coital intimacy?'

It turned out she'd been McKimm's lover; she informed me of this with a sort of cool satisfaction. Of course, I was glad she hadn't told me before we went to bed, because it would've put me off, but it gave McKimm a motive. She'd thrown him over and taken most of the contents of his safe with her. He hadn't liked that.

'Why didn't he just say so?' I growled.

'Pride?' she suggested. If there was more to it than that, Veitch wasn't letting on.

She fell asleep about six-thirty. The sun had descended gurgling into smog haze and gathering cloud. I was feeling sore and bad tempered—the soreness from Veitch's aerobic style of fucking, the bad temper from frustration. I now knew a bit more about what McKimm was up to, but couldn't see how it helped me. I had an advance on the job and had screwed his woman, but he could still threaten me over that business with Pukalski—and he wanted Veitch dead. I didn't feel particularly happy about that; I would if I had to, but what guarantees did it give me? Anytime he liked, he could make me very unpopular with Pukalski. I didn't fancy having that particular sword hanging over my head. A fight with Pukalski wasn't on my agenda.

I got up and wandered out of the bedroom. On the balcony, evening air was cool and the cloud cover was thickening and starting to look damp. The pollution smelt like stale sweat. Sooner or later I might have to do it, I thought, feeling the weight of the gun in my hands. At least killing Veitch would buy me some time to deal with McKimm. Maybe I could set it up to look like she and Piss killed each other. An autopsy would tell the cops she died later than him, but what the hell? Maybe he only wounded her and she'd bled to death.

I stood watching the car lights on the street and the ant-like movement of nightlife below.

When I went back inside about a half hour later, the unit was empty except for Piss. I considered going after Veitch, but she was probably long gone. She would've had a car in the basement carpark and could be anywhere by now. I'd been careless.

She hadn't touched Piss's gun, which was lying in a pool of his blood. I doubted she'd phone the cops. Probably had secrets she'd rather not expose to too much legal scrutiny. But anything was possible. Time to clear out.

I got dressed, stripped the bed and remade it with clean sheets I found in a cupboard. Rubbed down parts of the furniture I thought I might have touched, as well as cups, teaspoons and the taps in the bathroom. I never use guns registered to me—the Glock had once belonged to a careless competition shooter. I got my prints off it, wondering if that particular shooter had had time to get another, and tossed it across the room as Veitch might have, after she'd killed Piss and panicked. Then I found a pair of Veitch's gloves and gave myself some time to search the place. Ten minutes, I said. The first surprise came from Veitch's jewellery box: a silver-rose tie-pin. It looked like the one Sorensen used to wear. A coincidence? I pocketed it and began rooting through correspondence piled on the coffee table—a sort of in-tray full of opened mail. It was hard handling the stuff because Veitch's gloves didn't fit me properly. Fingers too big to go right into the holes, and the tips flapped around. Must have looked comical. It pissed me off.

But it was worth it. A lurid card was scrawled with the message: CAN'T WAIT TO PLOUGH THE FOURTH ESTATE, HONEY. FRIDAY AFTER THE SHOW. I'LL MEET YOU IN THE BENNE-LONG AT EIGHT. I'M INCOMMUNICADO TILL THEN. DON'T CALL. Today was Friday. 'The fourth estate'? Journalism, of course. Veitch was a journalist. 'Bennelong'? That'd be the restaurant at the Opera House. And it was signed 'Charlie P.'. Were Pukalski and Veitch having an affair?

Why not? It made sense of McKimm's actions. He was jealous and wanted revenge. The oldest motive. But if Veitch was screwing Pukalski, McKimm wasn't about to take official responsibility for having her killed. Pukalski knew all the professionals. It'd get back to him.

I could see it clearly. McKimm would get me to do it, then set me up, through Piss. Maybe he'd told Piss to shoot me, so he could say to Pukalski: 'He stole your money and he humped your woman, then he murdered her. My man was following him, saw him do it and got him for you. Aren't I a great friend?' And why was Piss following me? McKimm had heard a rumour I'd conned Pukalski and wanted proof.

A dodgy story, but Pukalski probably would have bought it. After all, Veitch would've been dead and me too, and once Pukalski started poking around, he'd put together the Kembla affair easily enough. Someone would have seen me in the wrong place at the wrong time. Perhaps whoever took the crack. Easy.

And McKimm was in Adelaide.

I piled up the mail, took off Veitch's gloves and shoved them in my pocket. Then I used my handkerchief to open the door and a few minutes later was walking out of the place like I owned it, carrying a plastic shopping bag full of soiled sheets. The doorman didn't even look up. It was twenty to eight.

I hot-wired a car parked in the next block.

Rain like a fine mist was settling over the sails of the Opera House. I parked the car behind a bus along Circular Quay East; its owner could handle the fine.

Twelve minutes to eight. I dumped the bag of dirty sheets in a rubbish bin under the walkway and ran towards the Bennelong restaurant, which was sitting like a baby UFO on the stairs next to its mum. There were plenty of people about, coming from or going to shows, all done out in their finest togs and thinking the world was okay. I knew better. They'd just paid thirty bucks a ticket, were probably stuffed to the gills with rump steak, lobsters and designer hamburgers, awash with champagne and Tooheys Red. But what did they know? They lived in their nice houses with their bit of garden and their family and dog and they thought life was sweet. But people are dying all the time. Just over the hill in their favourite suburb some car's waiting to splatter their dog across the bitumen. Or a fruitcake's going to rape their wife. Murder their husband. Slit young Johnny up for kicks. You've got to think like a terrorist. Life wasn't meant to be easy.

'You're a cold bastard, Crowe,' my last woman had commented.

A man of the times.

Veitch was already in the restaurant. She was sitting at a table, anxiously sipping at a glass of wine. I watched her through the tinted windows, keeping myself hidden behind the crowds, trying to see if Pukalski had turned up. Veitch looked okay, considering how quickly she'd cleared out. Hair tidied. Bit of make-up. Red dress. No ornaments. Only what she could grab.

I entered the Opera House through the doors near the bus ranks, went up the stairs and through the Café Mozart to the restaurant's entrance. Staying out of Veitch's line of sight, I caught the eye of a waiter and gave him five bucks to take a message to the woman in the red dress, telling her Pukalski was waiting for her near the ticket office. Then I got out of the way. When she came out, I approached her from behind and grabbed her arm. 'Don't make a fuss,' I whispered.

Her eyes widened, but she controlled her instinctive panic. Her breathing was tight. 'Shit, Mike, I'm sorry I ran out on you,' she managed. 'I had a date.'

'Yeah,' I said, pushing her through the crowd. 'Pukalski. But we haven't finished our own business yet.'

I led her down the far side of the stairs and along the narrow path around the eastern side of the building. Couldn't risk leaving. Not bang on eight. I didn't want to take the chance Pukalski would spot us. Veitch was pretty docile, even dispirited.

I was beginning to form a bit of a plan, but it hadn't come together yet. How was it going to work? McKimm was in Adelaide. If I wanted to put Veitch's murder onto him, I was going to have to make some adjustments. Maybe once the shows had started I could spirit Veitch away, to somewhere quiet. Then wait for McKimm to get back the day after tomorrow and set him up. Or maybe I'd just kill them both straight out.

I couldn't see a solution so I just did what I always do. Pushed ahead, with an eye on the main chance. Something always turns up.

Halfway around the building, stairs rose from the walkway and ended high above against the sail, uselessly, to all intents. It was cold now, and a chill breeze turned the night air unfriendly. No-one was walking around this side. They were in the various auditoriums waiting for the curtains to rise, or still noshing on. Hopefully Pukalski was among them. Mist was thickening into a heavy pall. I pushed Veitch toward the base of the stairs. 'We'll wait here for a while,' I said.

'I'm freezing to death,' she whined.

'It'll save me trouble then.'

The sound of the harbour against nearby pylons was a low mumble. I listened to it and kept an eye out for Pukalski. 'What happens now?' Veitch said.

'We wait.'

'What are you doing this for, Crowe? It's stupid and you don't seem like a stupid man. You know I'm Pukalski's. You don't want to kill me.'

'Maybe.'

'You saved me from that other bloke. I like you.'

I looked at her and for a moment imagined she meant it. But her face was in shadow. 'You in love with Pukalski?' I asked.

'He's very rich, and he likes my tits.'

'They're good ones,' I said, looking at them. She breathed in to make them swell and I grinned, then looked away. Before I could say what was on my mind, someone appeared down the other end of the walkway, silhouetted against the fogged light. It was a man. A big man. Bigger than Pukalski.

'Look, Crowe,' Veitch said, touching my arm. 'You could join up with Pukalski. I mean on a permanent basis. He'd pay you well. It'd be regular work.'

The man was walking toward us. I couldn't tell if he was looking at us or past us to the light of the Harbour Restaurant spilling around the corner of the building.

'What do you say, Crowe?'

'Pukalski's a loser, even if he's got muscle. I'm better on my own.' I was watching the man, putting the pieces together. How had McKimm known about my part in the Kembla business? Suddenly it was obvious.

'You can't take him on, Crowe. Even you wouldn't have the hide.'

'I've got more bloody hide than a rhinoceros,' I said.

Veitch glanced toward the man now.

He was close. I recognised the weight of him, could see the texture of the light-coloured coat he was wearing. He'd been wearing it last time I saw him. Dark hair clung wetly to his scalp and neck. But, not as astute, Veitch only saw him as a stranger. She suddenly leapt up and flung herself in his path. 'Help me!' she yelled. The man grabbed her arm with one hand. The other was holding a silenced gun.

'I thought you were in Adelaide,' I said.

'I am. A dozen citizens'll swear it.'

'Leon?' Veitch cried, pulling away.

'Sit back down, Gail,' McKimm growled. I hadn't moved. Veitch flopped back onto the stone step. Her dress rode up her thighs and the light was good enough to let me see McKimm's eyes following the action.

'Piss's dead,' he growled.

'Sure. He got in the way.'

'You killed him?'

'No one hassles me, McKimm.'

He thought about that a moment. 'I followed you from her apartment building,' he said at last.

'Yeah,' I said, 'Planning a double-cross?'

'I wanted to make sure you killed her.'

'You could've done it yourself in the first place, McKimm. Tidier that way. More personal. Why didn't you?'

'I don't know what you're sayin', Crowe.'

'Why the bullshit about blackmail? Why didn't you just tell me she'd dumped on you?' He didn't answer. Pride stiffened his muscles and transformed his obsession into fury.

'Why haven't you killed her?' he growled.

'I screwed her instead,' I whispered savagely. 'Like you've been screwing me.'

I figured he'd react to my statement just the way he did. Anger and surprise. Both. His self-control wavered. He stepped toward me—but pulled back, remembering he had the gun. At that moment his mind was elsewhere, turning his reflexes against themselves. I kicked out, ramming my foot into his crotch. He screamed and buckled up; I was on my feet at once, but he had the presence of mind to move his gun to cover me. His finger tightened too soon. A bullet buzzed past me and ricocheted off the paving some metres behind, detonating like a cracker. I lashed out. He grunted back against the wall of the building, firing again and missing. I leapt at him. Grabbed the gun. Smashed his wrist between my hand and the stonework. He screeched and let his fingers loosen. As the gun skidded off, I pushed away and got it. 'Crowe . . . ' he said. I twisted, aimed towards his head, pulled the trigger. A liquid explosion of light and blood. His body jerked away from me, falling back onto the stairs.

Veitch staggered to the railing and threw up into the Harbour's already polluted water.

The wound wasn't that big, though a lot of what was in McKimm's head had leapt out through the hole and lumpy blood was still dripping down the stairs. He lay with one arm twisted under him, his watch-band visible below the cuff of his coat. One of his shoes had come off and was lying sole upward about a metre away.

Nothing like a bit of action to clear the head.

I felt in his coat pocket and found his wallet and two tickets. One was for a train ride from Adelaide to Sydney, dated the day after tomorrow and already cancelled. His proof that he hadn't been here. The other was a used plane ticket, dated yesterday. Same point of departure. Same destination. I screwed the first up and tossed it over the railing. I figured McKimm owed me, so I took his money. It'd look like robbery, if they wanted it that way.

'What do we do now, Crowe?' Veitch's voice sounded frail and distant.

I came up close to her and stared into her eyes. 'Does Pukalski know you've been playing around with McKimm?'

'No. He wouldn't like it.'

'Don't suppose you'd want him to know about you and McKimm flogging off his crack either.'

She blanched. 'What are you talking about?'

'This,' I said, showing her the tie-pin I'd found in her unit. 'You the one gave it to Sorensen in the first place?'

She licked her lips nervously.

'I was wondering how McKimm found out about me and the Port Kembla scam. It occurred to me the most likely candidate would be the one who stole the crack. McKimm himself? Maybe. I didn't remember him being around, but you never know. Then I found this pin.'

'Oh?' Her innocence was becoming token.

'That bird hanging around with Erl Sorensen was you.' I tossed the pin at McKimm's corpse. The shiny metal struck his chest, bounced and lay on the step, resting against the tip of his nose.

Veitch shrugged. 'I was young. He was a way in.'

'You had a mass of blonde hair then. I didn't recognise you, 'til I saw the rose. Then it made sense. My guess is you were there, in the background somewhere. You noticed I was up to something. Watched me closer than I watched you.' She was afraid, but holding it back. 'Pukalski know you were Sorensen's?' I asked suddenly.

'Sure. I said I was using Erl to get closer to Charlie.'

Pukalski'd like that. 'When you realised what I was up to you might have dobbed me in to Pukalski, but instead you thought you'd rather make some quick cash. Why McKimm?'

'I didn't know how to sell the stuff. It would've been too obvious.'

'And the two of you finished up fighting over the proceeds, eh?'

She nodded again, looking ill. I said nothing. 'What do you want?' she whispered.

'Go find Pukalski. Tell him what happened.'

'What did happen?'

'McKimm followed you. He tried to kill you. You wrestled with him and then shot him. I wasn't here. Use your imagination.'

'Why would McKimm try to kill me?'

''Cause Piss Barall told you McKimm pulled the Kembla job. You left Piss at your unit. Alive. You can find him there later. Pukalski'll think McKimm did it.'

She nodded. The fog was lower now, thick, almost blotting out the lights along the foreshores. 'Will this work, Crowe?' she said. 'It's crazy.'

'Sure,' I said, 'that's why it'll work.'

A dawn jogger found McKimm next morning, lying on the stairs with his punctured head resting against the stonework. She called the police from the Quay. They arrived as mist was lifting over the Opera House.

During the following week, Pukalski had several of McKimm's associates murdered. I guess it made him feel better. Piss Barall was never found at all—not that anyone was looking for him.

By Sunday I was in Melbourne.

I hadn't been to Bennelong Point on Friday night, of course. Everyone knows I hate opera.

Kate Stephens was born in Sydney in 1960 and apparently showed a keen interest in fabrication from an early age. She read prolifically as soon as she was able, started writing short stories at about the same time and has never really stopped. She moved to the South Coast in 1970 and left school five years later. English was about the only non-failure on her School Certificate. Kate Stephens attended tech for a year before embarking on a spotty career of unskilled labour.

Kate Stephens is still living on the South Coast, near a mangrove swamp. She won the Golden Dagger Award in 1989 and has had two other stories published. At present she is working on various short stories as well as an Australian novel of the futuristic kind.

Kate Stephens
FIRST VICTIM

There's nothing unusual about people dying in the middle of Sydney. It's just that you never expect to be the one who finds them.

It was close to dawn, and I was still walking. One of those mornings; throat hoarse from the piano bar of some grubby little subterranean pit off Macleay Street, sobriety approaching at a slow shamble. The grey steel acres of Garden Island far behind me, a rainbow-sized festoon of lights in the misty fug somewhere ahead that had to be the Bridge. The first Sunday of my holidays about to break and not a taxi to be had for love or money; but I was still drunk enough to be enjoying the walk in a maudlin sort of way, and if there's one eternal and nostalgia-producing thing about Sydney, it's got to be the Bridge.

And the Opera House, if you happen to be born into the right generation. I can remember watching it grow stage by stage on each exciting trip into the city; peering through the train's grimy windows, grabbing Mum's sleeve—look, it's got another sail now . . .

And here it was in front of me, twenty-five years down the track, and a ghost of the old fascination stirred. I'd go down to those wide sweeping steps and look at the Bridge as the sun came up. Bennelong Point, I thought fuzzily. Bennelong . . . a name from the dry bones of primary school history, when I'd woven a vague fantasy which starred him as my distant ancestor. On my natural mother's side, of course—it was to be years before I learned that she came from the Territory. But who knew about my father's side? Maybe, I thought, I could claim descent from the man who gave Bennelong his first taste of rum . . .

I sat on one of those wide steps and looked out over the harbour.

Boats and ferries all asleep, and only a broken string of cars on the Bridge. The sky was lightening, dimming the kaleidoscope of reflections on the water's slick black surface. I must have sat there for five minutes or more before I noticed the sprawled dark shape no more than thirty metres to my right, just above the tideline.

He was lying on his stomach, his head turned towards the gigantic sails of the building above. I knelt beside him, suddenly sober. The eyes were open and staring, but there was nothing alive in that face under its tangle of hair. Wide thick mouth, broad flat nose, skin much darker than my own. Pupils utterly black, just beginning to glaze over.

I drew back a little, my gaze taking in the rest of him. He wore a buff-coloured gaberdine coat and trousers to match, brand new from the look of them; so were his shoes, leather soles hardly scuffed at all. I followed the line of his stare to a small silver object a few inches away. A tie-pin, intricately wrought in the shape of a rose. Beside it was what I took at first for a scrap of rubbish, then I saw the words 'Adelaide–Sydney', and realised it was a train ticket. A glitter at his wrist caught my eye. A watch, its diamond-studded face not much wider than the narrow leather band, the kind of watch a man only wears when he's rich enough not to worry about how feminine it looks. Impossibly out of place on that calloused, capable-looking hand.

I could see no evidence of what had killed him. Nothing wrong with him, I thought stupidly, except that he's dead. Taking hold of his shoulder, I eased him half on his side. His shirt—light mauve, as expensive and unworn as the rest of his clothes—was open half to the waist. No wounds, only a number of old scars. I lowered him back down gently.

Fifteen minutes later I found a phone that worked, and called the police. Anonymously. I couldn't tell them anything they wouldn't find out for themselves. Then I caught the first of the early morning trains and sat staring blankly at the mist rising over the city, and as the last of the shock wore off the questions started to take shape.

It made the midday news. The body of a man was found on the Opera House steps early this morning. It is assumed he died of a drug overdose. Police say there are no suspicious circumstances. It is believed the man was in his mid-twenties, but his name is being withheld until relatives can be contacted. And now the weather.

I turned the radio off. Only an idiot expects to learn even half the story from the news, but I'd hoped for more than that. No mention of the fact that he was a full-blood Aborigine. No mention of the costly, brand-new clothes. The train ticket. The silver rose. Well, maybe none of these things were important, maybe it was all explained. Maybe—

Maybe it was time I went to see Uncle Mooroo. If anyone would know, it'd be him.

There's been a lot written about the problems of growing up with black skin in a white community. Caught between one culture and another; prejudice, poverty, what they like to call 'reduced living standards'; not to mention the insidious despair of being a member of a dispossessed race in a society that has no use for you. It's all been said, and I can't add to it. In fact, for the first half of my life, it hardly applied to me at all.

Sure, my skin was dark brown. But being the adopted son of Dr and Mrs Billingsley, living in one of Sydney's respectable northern suburbs, made a fair bit of difference. Popular psychology stated that heredity counts for virtually nothing against environment, and my parents believed this implicitly. So what if I was the only black kid at school? I was brought up white. The colour of my skin was no more significant, my father told me, than Johnny Gilbert's flaming red hair and freckles. None of the other kids seemed to put much importance on it either. Why should they? I'd grown up with them. I spoke like them, acted like them, went home every afternoon to a place just like theirs.

It wasn't until I was well into my teens that I started to wonder. Books and TV showed me scarred, naked, grizzle-bearded men and their families living in dusty, fly-ridden desert camps a world away from my safe solid house in its tree-lined street. There were scenes even more disturbing, too—corrugated iron shacks on the fringes, broken-down drunks and diseased, pot-bellied kids. Scaled-down city ghettoes, the increasingly ugly groundswell of hatred and violence. Faces in which I saw my own face, my hair, my skin, my features. My blood.

Then came the questions every adoptive parent dreads. My *real* mother? My *real* father? Who? Where? How had it come about that I was living in Waitara and calling myself Leonard Billingsley?

To cut it short, after a few years of inquiries—and some rigid opposition from Dr and Mrs Billingsley—I found out that Mary

Williams (no fixed address) had given birth to a male child (father white) in the shearing shed of a property near Yass.

'Is that what you wanted to find out?' said Mrs Billingsley. 'That your *real* mother didn't even know your father's name? Are you satisfied?'

No, I told her, I wasn't, and went on to discover that Mary Williams' family could be traced in two directions—to a mission in the Northern Territory, where she'd been born, and to Sydney's inner suburbs, where some of her relatives had ended up over the years. Redfern was closest. Enter Uncle Mooroo.

I never did find out exactly what relation he was to me. Uncle was the simplest thing to call him. Tall, spare, grizzle-bearded as the best of them, he spoke in accents as liquidly rich as melted chocolate and accepted our kinship without question. The deep lattice of lines on his face looked like it'd been put there by more than one lifetime's worth of experience, and the eyes under their grey bushy overhang had seen more than I'll ever know about.

From him I learned that Mary Williams had died of childbirth complications a few years after I'd been taken from her. Taken from her, those were his words; he didn't say she'd put me up for adoption, and I realised I didn't want to know the details. When a thing's done and nothing can change it, it's always easiest to believe it's for the best.

I settled down after that, passed my exams and took the engineering course that Dr and Mrs Billingsley had mapped out for me, and I even started feeling comfortable about calling them Mum and Dad again. But I still kept in contact with Uncle Mooroo. In him I discovered a wealth of information about my ancestors and their way of life. I never knew exactly where I'd find him; he might be at any one of a dozen addresses, depending on which nephew or great-niece or fifth cousin he happened to be living with. On the surface, I suppose it looked like he was shunted from place to place, but it wasn't like that at all. Uncle Mooroo shifted camp as it pleased him, and he knew everything that went on in that close-knit community to which I was only an occasional and uneasy visitor. If the nameless man on the Opera House steps had passed through even briefly, Uncle Mooroo would know who he was and where he came from. He might even know how and why the man had died. Whether he'd tell me was another matter, of course. Uncle Mooroo could describe in minute detail a kangaroo hunt, a family tree or a car chase through the back streets, but if he didn't want to talk about something it was a waste of breath to ask him.

I was halfway through telling him about my discovery when I realised that this was going to be one of those things. I kept talking anyway. I told him about the dead eyes gazing at the silver rose, the scarred, weatherbeaten skin, the grotesquely improbable clothes. He heard me out in silence, eyes fixed on something beyond the dirty window-glass, and for all I knew he might have been listening instead to the piercing and energetic squabbling of some children in the street below. When I'd finished, he nodded absently.

'Did he have any money on him?' he said, when I'd just about given up hope of him speaking.

'I don't know,' I replied. 'I didn't look.'

'You should've. If he did, y'coulda taken it.'

'What?' I wasn't even sure I'd heard him right. His stare shifted at last, and he stretched and sighed.

'Then him dyin' woulda been some use t' some bastard.'

I shook my head. The argument down in the street had gained volume, and at least one adult's voice. 'Did you know him, Uncle Mooroo?'

'Yeah.' Matter-of-fact. 'He was here a while back.'

'Who was he? Where'd he come from?'

'Up north.'

I considered giving up; I would have done, if I thought that was all he knew. Of if I thought his indifference was real. But two things were plain enough—that he had known about the man's death before I got there, and that something about it bothered him deeply.

'What was his name?'

'Names don't matter. He ain't got a name now.'

'Uncle Mooroo . . . ' I stopped, wondering what did matter. Then I went on, 'They reckoned on the news it was an overdose. But—what was he doing here? What was he doing in those clothes, for Christ's sake, when they hadn't even been worn, didn't look like they even *belonged* to him? I just don't understand. The whole thing stinks.'

Unexpectedly, he looked at me and smiled faintly. 'First time you seen a dead body, eh?'

I nodded, uncomfortably aware that I was sweating.

'Thought so.' He looked out the window again. A siren wailed to a halt a few streets away, and in the next room a baby started squalling. 'Seen yerself lyin' there, eh?'

I nodded slowly, though I hadn't realised it until then. 'I just want to know why he died,' I said.

'You found yerself a mystery,' he said after a moment. 'All these things that don't add up. Just like them shows on TV. Ferget it, Lenny. No mystery about why Bill Burragai died. He died cause he knew too much, simple as that.'

'What d'you mean? What did he know?'

Uncle Mooroo was silent for a long time. Then he drew a deep breath and scratched ponderously at his beard.

'I tell you some things,' he said, 'then you find out why he died. I tell you why he come here. He did paintings, up where he come from. Proper paintings, not . . . ' He gestured to the world outside the dirty windows, ' . . . ones like they hang on the wall. Then a while back, this feller heard. Rich feller, shits fifty-buck notes. He went to see Bill, brung him back here. Art galleries. Lectures. Big business. Bill found out too much. Bill died.'

Something small and cold walked up my spine. 'But what did he find out?'

A distant expression in those black eyes under their grey tangle. 'You go away,' he said. 'You come back in a few days, a week, then you tell me.'

And he gave me two names.

'Amanda Thomas? I'm Leonard Billingsley, I rang you this morning.'

'Oh, right. I'll buzz the door open.'

Two more doors and a safety chain later, I was in the kind of apartment that hovers on the edge of vogue but never quite gets there. The same could have been said of Amanda Thomas as she smiled at me from a face subtly made-up to seem even thinner than it was.

'I can give you half an hour, then I'm off to the gym. What did you want to ask me? You said it was about Bill.' She sat on a pallid corner-lounge, and waved a mauve-tipped hand towards an armchair of the same breed.

'Did you know him well?' I said as I sat down.

'Oh yes. I was one of the first people he met when Alex brought him down. I couldn't *believe* his paintings. I only heard about him last night. It was horrible. Do they know what he died from?'

Little to be heard in her voice but curiosity. Her eyes darted around the room as she spoke—not from nervousness, I realised, but habit.

'They're saying "accidental overdose",' I said, and saw that the approach was the right one; her eyes flicked back to me and settled.

'Is there something suspicious about this? Is that why you wanted to talk to me?'

I hesitated long enough to let her draw the conclusion that suited her. 'As I told you, Bill was a cousin of mine. I didn't know him, but my uncle . . . well, he wanted me to speak to someone who knew Bill over the last few years.' I'm not an inventive liar, but it didn't really matter at this stage. She'd scented trouble for someone else and her nose was twitching almost visibly.

'You're nothing to do with the police, are you? Or the press?'

'No.'

She looked almost disappointed. 'Have you talked to Alex?'

'Not yet.'

'He had more to do with Bill than I did. He was the one who discovered him, arranged the exhibitions. He would have *made* Bill. Ask him, he'll tell you.'

The note of scorn wasn't intended to be missed. 'I never saw Bill's paintings. Were they that good?'

'Of *course*. Brilliant. So vivid. Alex couldn't bear to let poor Bill out of his sight, in case some other vampire snapped him up.'

'Vampire?'

'Alex is a vampire. I should know, I worked with him for eight years. He's got an eye for what sells and a mind like a cash register, and *that's* as much as he knows or cares about art. But he stuffed himself up this time, didn't he?'

'Did he?' I wondered what the argument between her and Alex had been about.

'He had it all arranged,' she said, her eyes on the move again. 'All those overseas engagements. Only trouble was, no product. Bill stopped delivering the goods.'

'He stopped painting, you mean?'

'He turned out two or three over the last year. But the quality wasn't the same. Why do you want to know all this?'

I shrugged. 'My uncle wants to know.'

Surprisingly, this seemed to satisfy her, and she fastened her teeth back into Alex. 'Even Alex could see they weren't anywhere near as good. After all the hype he'd put into it—and hype costs money—it looked like he wasn't going to pull in any dividends. Nothing worth exhibiting. And he couldn't even see why.'

'But you could?'

'It was *obvious*. If he'd left Bill where he found him, there'd have been no problem. Bill would've kept painting and Alex could've kept buying. But he wanted to hype it into something more, build Bill up as a cultural superstar. Profile articles, chat shows, the bloody works. That's the trouble with Alex. He's got such a little mind.'

'Did Bill have a problem with drugs?' Enough to jerk her gaze back.

'He had a problem—with booze. He didn't do drugs. I'd have known if he did.'

I believed her; she'd have no trouble recognising the signs. 'You don't think he died from an overdose, then?'

'Well—I couldn't say it's impossible. I hadn't seen him for nearly a month—he was down in Adelaide with Alex. I didn't even know he was back.'

'Did Alex come back with him?'

'Yes. I saw him last night.' A sneer on the *him*. 'He came around to tell me about Bill.'

There were several things I wanted to ask at this point, but I settled for, 'Did he say anything about drugs?'

'No. He just said they didn't know yet what he died from.' Her eyes narrowed, gave the impression of looking me up and down without actually doing so. 'If you ask me, I think he knew more than he was saying. But then, it's hard to tell. Alex is so close to cracking *right* down the middle that you can't make sense of half of what he says.'

My eyebrows went up, and she smiled. 'You think I'm a dreadful bitch saying things like that about someone I work with. Well I don't work with him any more, the partnership is over, so I can say what I like. Alex has been neck-deep in shit for a long time. He owes more people more money than even he probably realises. And if the wrong people came to hear certain things—' So comfortable was she in her own drama that the pause for effect was automatic, '—I could just about feel sorry for him.'

Difficult to make out what she was hinting at here. She might even have been implying that Bill had found out something he wasn't supposed to, yet somehow I didn't think so. 'You mean he's on the verge of bankruptcy,' I said.

'Worse than that, but yes, basically. He was counting on Bill to haul his nuts out of the fire, and Bill kept making noises about going home. Back to the Territory.' She paused again, leaning forward slightly as she waited for my next question.

'Did they argue about it?' I asked, and she was nodding before the sentence was half finished.

'Hammer and tongs. Every week or so Alex would give Bill one of his pep talks about commitments and seeing things through, and Bill would say yes, fine. Then he'd get pissed and announce that he was going home, and ask Alex for the money to get there. It used to go on and on. Once he just took off, and Alex was in a panic for a week looking for him. Eventually he turned up—he'd been staying with some old derelict in Redfern. My God, didn't the shit hit the fan that time . . . '

I pretended to listen while she went into detail, wondering if it mattered how far her view of things could be relied on. It was clear to me that her main objective was to create a bad impression of Alex—which was why she'd agreed to talk to me in the first place—and at the moment everything else was secondary in her mind. I decided then that there were only two more things I wanted to ask her.

'This might sound odd,' I said, 'but did Bill like to . . . dress well? Expensively, I mean.'

She looked at me blankly for a second. 'Oh Christ no. Jeans, T-shirt and thongs wherever he went. He made a point of it, said he wasn't a bloody peacock and no-one was going to dress him like one. The only decent clothes he had were ones I'd picked out for him, and he never wore them. Of course Alex had to agree with him—said it'd go against his image.' She glanced at her narrow-banded watch. 'Is there anything else? Because I—'

'Just one more thing.' I didn't really know why this was important. 'Did you ever see him wearing a silver tie-pin shaped like a rose?'

For the first time, an unplanned expression crossed her face. 'I never saw him wearing it. But he did have one. I gave it to him—for his birthday, this year.' Her mouth compressed, and her head jerked ever so slightly. 'How did you know about that?'

'His uncle told me it was found with him.'

Five minutes later I was thanking her as I backed out the door. I'd found out all I felt she could tell me.

There it was on page five of the evening paper: Tragic Painter's Death. The body of a man discovered yesterday morning on the Opera House steps has been identified as William Burragai, an Aboriginal artist from the Northern Territory . . . I scanned the next few paragraphs, which told me nothing I didn't know already, and came to a halt at the last line. Believed to have died of a massive heart attack.

For the rest of the night I mooched around the house, pausing at intervals and thinking: heart attack? Well, maybe. It can happen to anyone; people are having them younger and younger; also, it's a handy euphemism for a metabolism pushed to the point of non-function by chemical intake. But Amanda Thomas had been quite certain that Bill Burragai didn't do drugs, and alcohol won't usually kill you that quickly.

I didn't know much about Alex Bradford, the second name Uncle Mooroo had given me, but I suspected that getting to see him was going to be more difficult. I'd been lucky to strike Amanda at the right moment; Bradford had no reason I could see for wishing to discuss his dead source of income with a total stranger. I rang his office anyway, and was told by an irritable answering-machine voice to leave a message. I did this, without much hope.

TV was more than usually depressing that night. News, current affairs and a brace of American sitcoms, followed by the latest in glossy mini-series about people with lots of money killing each other, committing suicide and having crises. I stared at the screen, a triumph of technology reduced to a commonplace aggravation. A jet lumbered unseen over my patch of the city, and I wondered how it was that we got bored with miracles so very quickly.

The phone rang at about nine-thirty. Less than a minute later, I boggled at the receiver before slowly replacing it. Alex Bradford had just asked me to have lunch with him the following day.

The restaurant was full of unobtrusive waiters, potted palms and tinkly piano music. Sir's table had been reserved; Mr Bradford had been delayed, but should be arriving in a few minutes. Would sir care to see the wine list?

I declined and sat back to wait, wondering what it was about restaurants that vaguely offended me. Something to do with the elaborate ritual surrounding the simple act of paying large amounts of money for small amounts of food and alcohol. I wondered if I was imagining the sideways glances of two women at a nearby table, the lowered voices: see, I told you *some* of them have got jobs . . .

I'm not usually prone to that kind of paranoia—if paranoia it is—and I knew it had a lot to do with the image of Bill Burragai that I couldn't get out of my mind. How had he felt in places like this, with his jeans and T-shirt and thongs, his skin, his hair and his features? For some reason I found myself thinking of Bennelong, taken across the ocean in the great winged ship to meet the King . . . paraded in front of the bloated and jaded upper class like a new species of monkey. I heard again Amanda Thomas' voice. Brilliant. So vivid. Fresh, exciting, different. A new diversion in a world grown bored with miracles.

'Leonard Billingsley? Alex Bradford. Sorry I'm late, bloody telephones.'

He was almost the exact opposite of what I expected. Short, a little beefy, yet his face was somehow bloodless under what I was irrationally sure was a hair transplant. I stood up, let him shake my hand. 'Have you ordered?'

'No—I haven't been here long.'

'Fine, fine. Terrible about Bill. Were you close?'

I'd explained to him on the phone that I was inquiring on behalf of an uncle, and hadn't known Bill personally. 'No,' I said, and left it at that, because he was already speaking again.

'Terrible thing. He had a brilliant future ahead of him—but then, you never know, do you? Just like that.' The waiter reappeared with menus, and after he'd gone, Bradford repeated, 'Just like that,' and I remembered what Amanda Thomas had said about him being close to crack-up point. Hard to tell behind his tinted lenses, but I noticed that his eyes didn't match his voice. I wondered again why he'd been so willing to meet me; I wondered, too, how well I'd get away with saying as little as possible and letting him do the talking.

Then, 'I believe you spoke to Amanda Thomas yesterday,' he said.

'That's right, I did,' I replied, hiding my surprise. A muscle twitched in his smooth-shaven cheek.

'Yes, well. She may have given you a false impression. She's very good at doing that.' He gave a grimace that passed for a smile, and I knew what I was meant to think: women! bloody troublemakers, the lot.

I nodded as if in agreement, still asking myself how he knew I'd seen her, and then it hit me. She would have rung to tell him that someone was curious—suspicious?—about Bill, to make him stew that bit more. I didn't know exactly what his position was, but at the very least I was damn sure he wouldn't want to be the subject of bad

141

feeling and rumours in the Aboriginal community. And so he'd decided to speak to me himself, find out what she'd said, and leave his own impression. There was, I reasoned, no harm in playing this for what it was worth.

'She told me you and Bill were on bad terms.'

'That doesn't surprise me.' He swilled his wine around in his glass, looked at it critically. 'The fact is, Bill and I had our differences of opinion, and Amanda liked to use them, d'you follow? Divide and rule. She'll have told you we no longer work together.'

'She mentioned it.'

'Well, basically that's the reason. She saw a chance to make a fat profit from Bill's talent and she wanted me out of the picture. So she worked on him.'

'Right,' I said, and paused as the waiter sidled back. 'She told me he wanted to go back to the Territory,' I added, when our orders had been taken.

'*She* wanted him to go back. Or maybe she just wanted a bone of contention, I don't know. She kept filling his head with it. But it just wasn't possible. He'd gone beyond that, and I told him so. He'd begun to grow, develop—there was no going back and he knew it. You should've *seen* where he was living—a bloody shantytown, that's what it was. Nice enough place for a holiday with a four-wheel drive, but my God, he was an *artist*. He no more could've gone back than a butterfly can go back to being a caterpillar. You can't deny talent. You've got to make the most of what you've got in this world, and he'd taken the first steps.'

I said something in agreement, and soon our crepes arrived. They looked pretty, with their unidentified but colourful smattering of salad and twist of orange, and smelt of nothing. The taste was similar. 'She said he had a drinking problem,' I added after a moment. Bradford swallowed a mouthful too quickly and gestured with his knife.

'That's what made it so easy for her to get to him. She'd fire him up when he was on the booze. She had—other ways—of getting him to listen, too.' A glance to see if I'd taken his meaning. 'I think he felt something for her, you know. Until he realised that Amanda uses what she has to get what she wants, and what she wanted was him dancing to her tune.'

I thought of the silver rose which Bill had never worn, but which was the last thing his eyes had seen. And the undertone in Bradford's voice, which was unmistakable: jealousy, stark and simple. 'You had some overseas exhibitions planned?' I said, making it a question.

'London and New York. Can't go ahead now, of course.'

'Amanda said he'd stopped painting.'

'Just a lapse. A dry period. Naturally, she made more of it.'

'She said it put you on the verge of bankruptcy,' I commented.

His fingers spasmed briefly on his fork. 'Yes, she would have said that. Things were at a low point, there were temporary problems. Actually, he died owing me quite a lot of money.' Not that it matters in the least, said his sorrowing look—but don't hope to squeeze anything out of the estate, cousin.

For the rest of the meal I listened to him talk. About the necessity of vitality in the art world, the mechanics of making talent work for you, the importance of its development. Then, over coffee, I asked him the one remaining question I wanted him to answer.

'Did you know Bill had a weak heart?'

Bradford looked up from his dissolving saccharine as if the question surprised him. 'No, I had no idea. Never showed a sign of it. Of course, his drinking . . . I tried to get him to stop, you know. I knew he could if he wanted to, that was the thing. He didn't need it. He wasn't what you'd call an alcoholic. He just couldn't *see*—'

He stopped in mid-sentence and stared at me, as if suddenly recalling who he was talking to. In that second I saw the rage, the resentment. Here he was, left in the lurch. After all he'd done, all the sweat and labour; he, Alex Bradford, had offered Bill bloody Nobody riches and international fame, and all the ungrateful bastard could do was crawl into a bottle and die.

'No,' I said quietly, 'I don't suppose he could.' Then I stood up, unable to stomach the thought of breathing the same air as Alex Bradford any longer. Ignoring his startled questions, I walked out of the restaurant and took a relatively fresh breath of Pitt Street. I kept walking, wondering how long it would take me to reach Redfern, and if the rest of my thinking would be done by then.

'So now you tell me,' said Uncle Mooroo. 'Why did he die?'

I thought about it, as it had come together in my mind. Because he wanted to. Because the magic had been taken from his heart and turned into cash. Because he woke up one morning and found himself to be a piece in the squalid game of other people's lives. Because there was no home to go to any more. Because he had been taken from the solid red earth and pitched headlong into a glittering world full of exciting promise; but the glitter crumbled at a touch, the excitement was as shabby and fleeting as teenage masturbation. And the promise was as hollow as it had always been.

None of it new. Not the first or the last. We who grow up in this world, never knowing any other, take it for granted that it is a more or less satisfactory place to be, and so for most of us it is.

'He died because his heart stopped,' I said. 'His heart stopped because he wanted it to. He wanted it to because he knew too much.' And he dressed himself to show what he knew, and how much it meant. An expensive, superbly crafted body bag.

Uncle Mooroo nodded slowly. Then he reached into his pocket and drew out a crumpled envelope.

'He sent me this,' he said. 'I got it the morning you found him.'

Inside was a single piece of paper. Across the middle, in large, clear letters, was written: 'In memory of Bennelong, first victim'.

I looked at Uncle Mooroo, saw the terrible, ageless sadness in his eyes. But no tears; tears are for sorrows that can be expressed.

Daybreak's first glimmer found me on the steps of the Opera House; found me, regarded me not too unkindly, and passed on, dragging a dazzling sunburst in its wake.

Robert Wallace is the pseudonym for Robin
Wallace-Crabbe—artist, bantam hen breeder,
and writer.

He is the author of many works including
*Australia Australia, Feral Palit, Payday, To
Catch a Forger, Flood Rain.*

He currently lives near Braidwood, New South
Wales.

Robert Wallace
BEE STING

The windows gave onto playing fields beyond which the waters of Western Port were flat, and a surprisingly brilliant blue. A fishing boat was heading towards French Island, possibly to try its luck beside the tidal rip outside Cowes. The Reverend James Matheson breathed in the all-pervading smell of boy, gazed out the window, watched a car ride the anti-speed humps.

An early bird. Like Matron who was returning from her walk.

It was visitors' day when guilty parents pretend to have devoted the intervening time to thought of nothing other than their scions' ultimate good.

There was another boat too, possibly put out by the launch moored behind French Island. The boys spotted the launch first—it was unusual to anchor so far from the shore—a flashy craft, more suited to the big game fishing grounds up north. Now this small boat, aluminium from the way the sun glinted off it, powered by an outboard running on idle, was heading towards the school's beach with one person at the tiller and the bow absurdly high.

Too awful, thought the Reverend James Matheson. Partly about the aluminium boat—that it had not been crafted of wood, steamed planks held by copper nails—mostly about everything else. For his life had become one of regret and worse, more so with each passing day. And of pain. He shook his head in wonder at the pain because there at the centre of his vision was the headmaster's daughter.

Matheson had been going through a turbulent patch, theologically, pondering that old chestnut, the actuality of this God of his. And the more Matheson considered the subject the less visible the old man with the beard became and the more nature itself turned into the deity.

Mostly, the Western Port Grammar Chaplain—who, regarding it as 'helping out', also taught some English—believed he caught a glimpse of God's physical reality when peering into the tinted centre of flowers, particularly red ones, past the stigma and down the stamens to that scented depth.

Within the chapel dedicated to the founding headmaster, a red brick Gothic monstrosity with stained glass honouring the dead of two wars, God was no airy fairy idea, hell no, he was that judgmental patriarch who, nevertheless, is with you in the valley of the shadow of death.

'Oestrogen.'

'Sir?' Donald Martin was standing at the next window along, gazing upon the sunlit scene with as close as possible to the same intensity as Matheson. But stealing a glance sideways from time to time, because it was unsettling for a boy of fourteen to observe a hero falling to pieces, particularly since, at such a young age, it was hard to tell if what you saw was real or just another of your own fantasies.

'Oestrogen, Donald.'

'Yes, sir.'

'You've been taught about oestrogen, I expect?'

'Not precisely, sir.'

'Then why sound as though you know?'

Half a dozen paces separated the pair of them. Most of the other boys in Collinson House were out there in their groups of two and three, scrubbed, hands in pockets, waiting for relatives. The car which had been coming up the drive, a top-of-the-range Mercedes, gold, was resting now, and its owner's Gucci loafers crunched on the raked gravel as he pretended joviality, punching his son rather hard on the upper arm. Making a man of him. That was Williams, an old boy, thick as a post, rich as Croesus—in timber, bricks and mortar, hardware stores. Very aware of himself, and of the world as audience.

The headmaster's daughter, come down from the city two weeks ago, driving her own recently acquired old model VW 1600, and apparently a fugitive from the workplace, or from love, or from her own silly mind, was standing there for no reason, one had to suppose, other than to be seen by the mothers and fathers as they arrived. Well, the fathers would most certainly notice her.

Because of the oestrogen.

Donald hadn't responded to the Chaplain's rebuke. He had gone into himself, which was the boy's way. Intense. But he remained on guard at his window, sticking like glue to Matheson, as he had done all year.

'Oestrogen, Donald, is a hormone . . . any the wiser?'

''Fraid not, sir.'

The headmaster's daughter was all breasts and bottom; like some fruit come ripe too quickly, it was hard to pick up the notion of bone from the girl. She was small, her legs quite slim, a great mop of curly black hair added to the effect, as did the big eyes, the full lips, those round pink cheeks. She was juicy indeed. And, Matheson hoped, it must have been the additional hormonal stimulus of the pill which caused her to bloom so fully, so quickly. At a time when anorexia was in vogue, those of the boys' sisters who were prevailed upon to make the journey down from Melbourne to Western Port tended to be as skinny as waifs begging on Calcutta street corners.

Matheson feared girls, although he had long been something of a girl watcher, justifying this unecclesiastical hobby by theorising that girls were the flowers of his own species, created in tempting form to attract the bee with the sting in its tail, so pollination might take place.

'Even at fourteen, Donald, you must have become aware of the difference between girls and boys.'

Donald stiffened; he didn't enjoy talking about sex, particularly not with adults—already the headmaster had given the class a pretty thorough if belated introduction, complete with slides showing the working parts of a flower, and of your standard male and female mammal. The words, 'the erect penis' coming, as they did, with difficulty, provided the headmaster with the satisfying distraction of asking Williams and Sgro, who had collapsed giggling, to wait outside his office. Saying, he'd show them if there was a funny side to sex.

And now here was Donald's hero, the school Chaplain, introducing the subject. Would the Reverend Matheson find it funny?

'Don't want to talk about it, aye?'

'It's not that so much, sir.'

'Take Bridget down there for instance, not so many years ago she was a bean pole, not unlike yourself, Donald. Look at her now . . . breasts.' But then the man began to cough, as though something had stuck in his throat. Next he was doubling over and going red in the face till finally he had to stagger along the corridor to where there was a wooden bench right at the far end. He slumped there, head in hands.

'Should I fetch Matron, sir?'

'Nothing to bother about, I'll be all right . . . ' Gulping air, lifting his face so he was gazing at a ceiling marked where grubby tennis balls had bounced against it.

Finally, apparently recovered, 'Well, Donald, where were we? That's right, hormones—these chemicals inside us, acting, emphasising in the case of oestrogen, the female side of things.'

More coughing. 'Just a touch of spring fever I shouldn't be surprised.' Matheson vanished through the nearest of two doors leading into his quarters—one for the bedroom the other the study, rooms interconnected by an internal door. For most boys a summons to see the Chaplain was as bad as a sex lecture from the headmaster because he'd sit you down in there and ask about spiritual things, and you wouldn't have a clue what he was talking about. He'd try and discuss morality, for instance, or why one ought to tell the truth.

As if God cared about telling the truth!

There were photographs of Matheson in cricket gear, his claim to fame. And a funny painting which made the boys wonder.

Donald, while gazing down upon the headmaster's daughter, was also noting the aluminium boat, now beached and being pulled up the sand by a man. Too far away for details, particularly with a sea haze veiling the bay's long sweep, still water lapping the tidemark, those dunes held in place by a sparse growth of succulents and tussocks. He narrowed his eyes in concentration, focusing on the swell of the girl's breasts, trying to associate them with adventure.

No luck.

His scrutiny remained objective, scientific, despite the fact that after lights-out the dormitory was alive with fantasies about this girl.

The headmaster's daughter, Bridget, not only did she have very large breasts but she tended towards tight black slacks pulled up between her buttocks; there was no denying her femaleness.

Donald didn't like the look of her, all that soft flesh. Yet her being out there when the parents were due interested him, just as he was fascinated once he realised that the girl was gazing about anxiously, as though she too might be expecting a visitor. Yet it wasn't so simple. Couldn't be. Bridget was waiting, sure, but at the same time she was pretending her presence on the gravel beneath Collinson House's windows was entirely accidental, as if she were pretty bored, actually, and at a loose end.

Not a particularly good piece of acting.

'What would you say she's doing out there at this hour, Donald?'

'Sir?' The boy surprised by the Chaplain.

'It doesn't strike you as strange?'

The visitors were gone, and boys confined to their dormitories rather earlier than usual—because of the circumstances.

The desk in his study was wide, ink-stained and undistinguished, except in as much as it was old. Matheson sat there, considering. His chair creaked when he tilted it back. He was staring at a framed reproduction of Cranach's 'Cupid Complaining to Venus' in which the goddess, resplendent in necklace and hat, holds fast to the branch of an apple tree while Cupid raids a hive. Cupid the honey stealer.

Matheson had purchased the print around the time he first entertained doubts about God.

Now it had taken on the importance of an icon.

Bridget had travelled by ambulance, dead.

The headmaster, as much concerned with the school's reputation as upset by the passing of his daughter, was engaged in a PR exercise with the police, and with reporters.

Yet, despite foreign presences, never in Matheson's memory had the school seemed so quiet. And never had he, within his own being, been so pulled and pushed about.

In the Cranach, Cupid is weeping because, as it states in a Latin quatrain painted over the blue sky in the top right-hand corner: 'As the child, Cupid, plunders honey from the hive, the bee fastens on his finger with a sting; and so in like manner the brief and fleeting pleasure which we seek injures us with sad pain.'

Matheson thought: only too true.

Unmarried, he had deluded himself into believing the trick to be a vigorous life, an occupied mind. Not that he was a High Churchman dreaming of a celibate priesthood along Roman Catholic lines. But now, oh dear, he had felt the sting, tasted the honey, its sticky sweetness within corrupting his soul.

Further proof of God and nature being one.

No doubt he would be expected to conduct a memorial service.

As a distraction Matheson turned up Donald Martin's latest excursion into fiction—a fresh piece appeared every other day! Strange boy. Fourteen years old and he'd written: 'A body lay on the steps. One hand resting just above the level of the water and a narrow watchband was visible below the cuff of a light-coloured coat. Dark hair curled damply to the nape of the neck. The legs were a little appart; the new sole of a woven brown leather shoe faced upwards . . .'

On automatic, and using a red pen, Matheson crossed out the 'ing' of 'resting' and wrote 'ed' above it in his scrunched-up hand. He wrote 'sleeve' after 'light-coloured coat' and deleted a 'p' from 'appart'.

She had been discovered by Mr Williams of the gold Mercedes who claimed to have entered the chapel in response to the headmaster's suggestion on some earlier occasion that, 'being in the trade', he might have something useful to offer in the way of advice regarding rising damp along the southern wall. That would have been half an hour, maybe more, after Matheson abandoned bowling at the nets to those of the children fortunate enough not to be visited by parents. As was usual during net practice, Donald Martin hung about, taking his glasses off, wiping them on his shirt tail, putting them back on: an old man in his habits and bearing, not the sporting type at all.

If he was short on knowledge in the sphere of biological science, Donald Martin made up for it with his writing. He kept a detailed diary. It was this great work—there was a fresh volume produced each term—which gave the boy a certain standing in their closed community. The exercise book in which he was currently working was usually clutched in his hand as he shambled about the place, held in awe by the rest of the students ever since, the previous year, Charles Sgro had snatched the current volume and run off laughing, taunting. But when, having collected a crowd, Sgro opened the book—there was the record of their lives, of each day's weather, of the petty dramas, but written in Mandarin! The language of Donald's mother, a Chinese from Sarawak, married to Stephen Martin, an Australian working with a Malaysian oil exploration company. At least Mandarin was what Donald claimed the language to be.

When, eventually, at the insistence of the police inspector, Matheson entered the chapel with the late sun boring in through the uninspired Rose window—Western Port Grammar's answer to Chartres—he had been dressed in his cricket whites, a university blazer on top. As requested he checked the items on the altar, its cover of embroidered lace cloth, candles, silverplate crucifix. Even counted the stacks of hymn books just inside the main door. Then checked the other doors, making quite a show of attempting to remember which should have been locked, which open—how long after morning service had he left the building? All this under the scrutiny of Inspector Keogh, a Papist from the way he was regarding this red brick heathen temple. And an expression on his face while talking to the Reverend James Matheson which did more than imply that in the eyes of the law, being Anglican gave you no status at all. Matheson supplied the names of boys with whom he'd practised cricket, then, thank God he remembered to mention the aluminium boat coming across the bay, motor on idle.

'Would it have been low tide or high tide?'

'Low tide, sir.' How had Donald Martin managed to get past the constable on the door, for heaven's sake?

Keogh: 'What've we got here?'

'His parents live overseas, Inspector.'

'Teacher's pet.'

'I wouldn't say that.'

'A bit of a swot?'

Donald: 'It came across about the same time Mr Williams arrived.'

'Mr Williams . . . that name again?' Keogh had one ear gone out of shape as though he'd boxed. But he wasn't a large man, his suit hung loose about a wiry frame. His face was hepatitis yellow-grey. His belt not threaded, the top of his trousers was puckered from being drawn in by it.

It was the Bursar, Paterson, bustling in some minutes before, who verified about Mr Williams and the damp wall.

Asked to reconstruct his day Matheson was astonished to discover he couldn't actually recall a great deal of what he'd done. Other than conduct the morning service. And then he'd been standing up there at the windows, alone except for Donald Martin. Oh yes, that coughing fit as well. No need to mention about the coughing fit. And Donald didn't say anything about it either. Inscrutable. Of course there'd been the spell of Matheson's bowling at the nets—he hadn't forgotten polishing the ball's leather casing on his inside leg, working on that in-swinger the students found so hard to handle.

'Did you look into this matter of the boat?' he asked Inspector Keogh.

'Tide's come up, no trace. Just have to take your word for it . . . yours and the slope kid's.'

Donald Martin flinched.

Keogh: 'Anyway, with the wind come up the way it has, we've got waves to contend with now.'

Matheson: ' "Take my word!" What exactly are you trying to say?'

'I'm telling you the tide's come up.'

'Check with the blasted launch then, that's where the boat came from.'

'Would if I could, but I've already been into that. Thorough . . . In-the-know Keogh's what they call me. Famous throughout the land for attention to detail. The fact is, Reverend—is that what you call yourself when working for this kind of an outfit?—the fact is, various of the boys have mentioned this launch lying there for a few days. Only when I pushed them on the angle of an approach from the sea you understand . . . but right now there isn't a launch on Western Port like the one you're all talking about. Not even over at Cowes. Fishing craft, sure, and a million yachts. But no up-market launch.'

Which Matheson thought a pity. The launch and its tender had represented possibility.

Inside the chapel while Keogh kept on at him and Donald stood a little to the side as was his habit, observing—had there been the hint of cordite on the air? Or was that something suggested by honour rolls, by the stained glass with their message of Empire and the fallen? Matheson found it hard to say. Because how could he think at all with the outline of where Bridget's body must have lain demanding everybody's attention.

Keogh had explained how one bullet, a .22 with a hollow point, had gone in through her left breast. That one the neatest, as Keogh had put it, enjoying detail, because it had left a surprisingly small hole and not much blood had leaked. So little in fact that Keogh concluded the victim was killed instantly by the head shot—going on to speculate how the chest wound must have been for the form of it. The head shot was not immediately evident, it seems, since the barrel had been held behind Bridget's ear and her long hair covered the powder burns as well as soaking up quite a lot of blood. The words 'head shot', echoing, bounced about the transept. Matheson collapsed on a pew, coughing again.

It would be a couple of days at least before the police could be specific as to the murder weapon though Keogh couldn't help thinking, or so he said, that it must have been a pistol, 'target model most likely, on account of you wouldn't be able to hold a rifle up to nobody's ear like that, and her not respond? It'll be to do with sex, this one, mark my words. Girl like that—breeding age—ripe for it. Lust's to blame for all sorts of . . . there's jealousy to start with, then the rest. No, sex . . . has to be.' For some reason Keogh had chosen to stare straight at poor Donald Martin while pronouncing on the motive for the crime.

And those eyes behind the thick lenses, they hardly blinked. Donald's mind having switched to recording mode.

Now returned to his study, the Reverend James Matheson, gazing at Cranach's cupid with the stung finger, was wondering if in truth Bridget might not have been a sacrifice to the Lord, to the grey bearded old man with stern and unforgiving eye, who seemed more real than, and to have nothing at all to do with, Christian love. And then, mind wandering, he wondered at the diminutive size of the breasts of this Venus in the reproduction, compared with those of the headmaster's late daughter.

Hormones. Matheson wondered if the headmaster had ever noticed the myriad forms in which his daughter's sexual maturation had evidenced itself. And next thing, quite suddenly, he was casting his mind back to the gold Mercedes negotiating the speed humps along the drive. Mr Williams at the wheel. And the way Williams had alighted from the car. How he'd postured, like a cockerel—one might have been excused for anticipating spurs.

Bridget there already, standing out the front of the row of pseudo Tudor red brick buildings that were the three houses, Collinson in the middle—commemorating General Collinson who'd led a charge somewhere in Africa. Bridget watching the animal antics of rich Mr Williams. Her body unconsciously responding to pushy Mr Williams. Bridget's eyes meeting those of Mr Williams. Not a word spoken between them.

'Lord, that I might, just once, know the mind of another.' Matheson shook his head, as though to free himself from this ridiculously personal interpretation of an individual's relationship with the Almighty.

Had that really been it . . . ? The pair of them, the headmaster's daughter and dreadful Mr Williams—oh so vulgar Mr Williams—performing something akin to a love dance?

Mr Williams arriving early. Mr Williams so recently and spectacularly divorced.

There was a knock at the study door.

It was Matron. She enjoyed an evening chat, particularly after some disruption to school routine. She enjoyed a sherry as well.

Matheson approached the sideboard—his own, a family heirloom—to pour the woman a drink from a cut crystal decanter. Matron wore her hair, black turning grey, cut short and parted like a man's. She was tall, extremely thin, wore no make-up. Once the boys were in bed she liked to smoke. In fact, in an environment where she was just about the only adult who did smoke, people tended to sense about her the smell of the weed, it clung to the fibres of her cardigan, to her flannel trousers as well. She had a cough to go with the habit; hear it in the evenings after lights out and you knew Matron was lighting up.

'A turn-up for the books.'

'For the papers.'

'The papers too, yes, Chaplain . . . ' Accepting the proffered glass, taking more than a sip. 'Ah yes, lovely. Headmaster won't like the papers.'

'He'll have to lump it then, won't he? Strange, when you come to think of it, Bridget ending up the way she has.'

'Dead?'

'Actually I didn't mean that . . . may I offer you another?' Why did they go through this farce of formality, why didn't he simply place an occasional table beside her chair, leave the decanter on it—a drinking straw too? 'And an ashtray?'

'So kind.' She grinned at him, the smile of someone who'd had to carve life out of the unyielding stone of Melbourne society where women should be small, blonde, and say 'yuk' to anything irregular. 'So, Chaplain, what then did you mean?'

'I suppose, watching her grow up, such a pretty girl, bright as well . . . of course the headmaster's residence.'

'Why not say it? It's not the blasted residence, is it? It's the man. I mean, a girl, alone with that man and a school full of boys!'

'Hardly ever, Matron, she was away at school herself most of the time.'

'Interstate, so holidays didn't coincide, that sort of thing. Stuck in this dump . . . a week here, a week there, the boys ogling her, their dirty thoughts almost tangible. And she, nothing to do but play tennis up against a wall.' Matron's eyes were, as always, fixed on a spot just wide of his left shoulder.

'Curious thing is I was having . . . myself . . . well I wouldn't exactly call them "dirty", but thoughts only this morning. She'd developed into such a . . . how should I say . . . such a feminine creature.'

'Knockers.'

'I beg your pardon?'

'You are I expect referring to the size of her breasts.'

'Well, well, well, Matron, you are a forthright woman.'

'In my line of business what else would you expect?'

Matheson, to his surprise, had gulped his own drink.

'God only knows,' Matron went on to say, 'what the boys will make of a murder. And, it couldn't be a worse time, with this recession, children not taking up the places parents reserved for them at birth, others being withdrawn. Bursar tells me of fees in arrears. And then this, anybody looking for the chance to back out will take it. Let's face it, Chaplain, the old school ain't what it used to be. Not that it was ever much, mind, but it has gone down hill . . . less money because we're not attracting the right economic class of student, apart, of course, from Williams. Declasse Grammar . . . the name . . . that's what we'll be known as. Headmaster with his head in the air, the glorious past. Rubbish the glorious past . . . how about the ignominious future? And what a development site! The only freehold this size left with a bay frontage.'

By the time she poured a fifth sherry and was asking for the umpteenth time if he minded terribly if she smoked—what could he say?—Matron had lost her monopoly on the Chaplain's concentration and he found himself counting the apples on the tree branch Venus was grasping in the reproduction. Was she raising that arm for the sole purpose of displaying a shaved armpit, or was there something more to this crude compositional device?

Twenty-four apples.

Suddenly he was struck by the way in which the abundant fruit thematically repeated the demure and understated orbs which were the breasts of the goddess.

Now he was conscious of a certain stiffness in his shoulder; had he been bowling faster than usual?

He said, 'I heard Paterson, the Bursar,' —clarification because there were also Patersons, twins, in Form Two—'talking about land, its value . . . and some parents apparently, those with debentures or whatever it is, are in favour of moving the school.' For something to say.

Matron was splashing sherry while attempting to aim the three-quarters empty decanter at the glass.

She wet her cigarette.

'Damnation,' wiping fingers on her cardigan then licking them clean. A great deal of cat in the woman.

Matheson was considering the signature on the Cranach: a writhing winged snake with a crown on its head, a ring in its mouth—this painted on a stone which itself seemed like a dead echo of the fruit and the woman's breasts.

It really was a most extraordinary picture.

'Tell me, James . . . ' Matron slurring her words ever so slightly. Matron calling him 'James' for the very first time. Matron looking him straight in the eye. 'She'd arranged to meet Mr Williams, hadn't she? Or he'd arranged to meet her, rather—the little slut. In the chapel. In your chapel! They must have been getting on together up in the city, don't you think so? Nymphomaniac and the older man. But you'd thought . . . since you'd slept with her too. Did you have to feel so bad for succumbing? So absolutely rotten? An eternity of hell and damnation in exchange for becoming just another knot in her hair? Oh yes indeed, you poor boy, don't think I can't understand how it is. And then I happened to see you—sheer chance—in your cricket whites, sneaking in through the side door of the chapel. Who would blame a woman of my years, with not enough to interest her, for asking the question: Why?

'But I'd never have suspected such an outcome.'

Matron, drunk, was an unattractive sight. She'd stayed considerably longer than usual. Donald Martin watched through the glass panels in the dormitory door as she shambled off to her quarters. The rest of the boys were asleep yet the room was far from quiet; there was a surprising variety of noises issuing from noses and mouths. And one of the boys, the second youngest, Piggy McDowell, was whimpering like a puppy in a pet shop.

Donald continued his vigil at the door. It was a warm night but he had his dressing gown on nevertheless, because it was a dark garment, slippers too. He could see right up to Matheson's doors: the one into the bedroom through which he had actually slipped an hour earlier, surprised at his own audacity; and the other giving directly onto the study.

He had not expected it to take so long for Matheson to emerge.

But when he did there was a curious quality to the man's being, the way he held himself, like someone psychologically prepared for the scaffold. Yet a furtiveness as well. Donald expected he knew what this nocturnal journey would be about, because he'd discovered the gun in the Chaplain's bedroom during an unhurried search carried out after slipping the bolts on both doors, and with an open window giving onto the fire escape. There was no way a boy could get caught with an exit like that.

This secretive young fellow who believed life's purpose to be the writing of a journal in Chinese characters now watched the Chaplain head for the end of the corridor while outside moving lights indicated where police were searching the beach.

The glass of the building's tall windows was rattling in the sea wind.

Donald slipped back in through the bedroom door. The gun was gone. And then he slipped out the window and descended the fire escape. He crossed the rear courtyard and came along the side of Collinson House, the south side where hydrangeas grew, their flowers pale balls against the black wall, both blooms and boy in the shadow of a waning quarter moon.

For cover the Reverend James Matheson was sticking to the long hedge of cyprus defining the shape of the Chapel end of the football ground. And then he came to the groundsman's house and the long, green painted shed where mowers, rollers and line markers were kept. These provided him with more cover and the opportunity to gain the unmade road leading to the boathouse and ramp.

Donald watched as this man he'd idolised sprinted across the open space. Then he followed, trying to close the gap but still intent on keeping a safe distance as the trail led into the thickness of tea-tree scrub, then up the leeward side of the dunes. Donald puffing now, not being a healthy boy, wheezing. Matheson's long strides making easy work of the soft sand.

And then Matheson was standing there, staring out to sea, and the police were between him and its loud and broken surface, and Donald was peering at this silhouette that had one of its hands moving backwards and forwards in the air, mechanically, as if it were holding something it didn't wish to be holding.

The hand, it was grasping a gun! It was thrusting the thing towards the Chaplain's head as though against the force of a magnetic field.

'Oh no . . . sir! I thought you were going to throw it away!' Donald running forward. 'Not this, not this . . . please!' Donald wanting to arrest time. Donald shouting. Donald weeping, falling, getting to his feet again. But his voice unheard with the wind blowing in off the sea and the water roaring.

Then Donald was grabbed from behind, held by the arms. A hand clamped across Donald's mouth.

A face against his own face, a voice, surely the voice of Inspector Keogh! And it was saying: 'Leave the poor bastard be now, boy, to his agony . . . because however you look at things it's too late anyways.'

Then Keogh talking to himself rather than to the boy: 'It's the innocents, see, they don't understand . . . not even the potential for evil within themselves. Instead they get lost in the detail.'

Marele Day grew up in Sydney and graduated
from Sydney University with BA Honours.
She has travelled extensively and lived in
Italy, France and Ireland. Her first novel,
Shirley's Song, is a comedy set in Ireland. She
then began writing thrillers. *The Life and
Crimes of Harry Lavender*, featuring Australia's
first female private eye, Claudia Valentine,
was published in 1988, and was followed in
1990 by *The Case of the Chinese Boxes*, in
which Claudia features again.

Marele Day

UNPLEASANTNESS AT THE BIG BOYS CLUB

Corpse at Opera House
A body lay on the steps. One hand rested just above the level of the water and a narrow watchband was visible below the cuff of a light-coloured coat. Dark hair curled damply to the nape of the neck. The legs were a little apart; the new sole of a woven brown leather shoe faced upwards. No marks could be seen on the head or hands, but beside the face lay two items, a train ticket from Adelaide and a small silver rose. A dawn walker had called the police from The Rocks station: they arrived as the mist was lifting from the Opera House.

'Eddy, Eddy,' called Mrs Levack as she breezed into the flat, 'it's in!'
Mrs Levack plonked the paper on Mr Levack's stomach which overhung his trousers by a good few centimetres. He looked a bit untidy but he was at home and a man's home is his castle. When he went out to bowls, all spruced up in his whites, he made a different picture altogether.

It hadn't taken Mrs Levack's beady eyes long to find the item they were looking for. She had excellent eyes for a woman her age and was very proud of them. 'It's all the bleeding exercise they get,' Eddy would say. 'Peering here, peering there, minding everyone's business but your own, spying on the neighbours.' 'Well, it helped solve a murder case once, didn't it?' snorted Mrs Levack. 'Yes, Mavis,' Eddy said tiredly. Everyone at the bowling club, everyone in the street, in fact everyone in the whole of Bondi knew how Mavis Levack had helped solve the murder of the boy who died in the flats opposite.

Eddy read the item intently, reread it then looked up over his glasses. He'd held off getting the glasses for a long time what with Mavis going on about how good her eyes were, but finally he had to admit defeat. However, other opportunities for small victories presented themselves and Eddy wasn't slow in taking advantage of them.

'Doesn't say anything here about the famous sleuth Mavis Levack,' he said triumphantly.

'No,' she frowned, 'I'll have to ring the papers about it. They've called me "dawn walker" and they didn't even use capitals.'

'Probably that New Age journalism,' remarked Eddy.

Mrs Levack pursed her lips. 'Heaven knows what they teach them at school nowadays. They wouldn't know punctuation if it reared up and kicked them in the face.' Mrs Levack sailed into the kitchen and put a couple of eggs on to boil.

'Mavis,' called Eddy, 'they just say "a body". How's a bloke supposed to know whether it's a man or a woman if they use that non-sexual language?'

Mrs Levack came back into the loungeroom carrying a spoon. 'Well it wasn't all that easy to tell. It was wearing women's clothes, I mean no self-respecting man would wear woven shoes, but it had a boy's haircut and the face was a bit grubby. You know what, Eddy,' she whispered confidentially, 'I think it was one of those travesties.'

'Those what?'

'Travesties. You know,' her voice got even lower, 'men who dress up in women's clothing.'

'Transvestites,' he corrected her. 'And why are you whispering? There's nothing wrong with men dressing up in women's clothes,' said Eddy, 'we used to do it all the time in the army. Just a bit of good healthy fun.'

Mrs Levack had a rather peculiar look on her face. Mr Levack thought it best to get back to the matter in hand. 'Funny they don't mention a handbag. You'd think a transvestite would carry a handbag, wouldn't you?'

'Handbag?' Mrs Levack sounded startled. 'Perhaps a mugger took it. I'll just go and check the eggs, dear.' Something was up. Mavis very rarely called her husband dear.

She thought he'd never leave. He always went to the library of a Wednesday morning but this morning he'd wanted a kipper with his egg. She didn't mind the extra cooking but today Mrs Levack had other fish to fry. And they weren't red herrings.

As soon as he'd gone she left the washing up, got out the vacuum cleaner and pushed it against the door so that Eddy wouldn't take her by surprise when he came back.

She closed the venetian blinds in the bedroom then fished the handbag out from under the bed. Eddy would probably take a dim view of her removing evidence from the scene of a crime but as she discovered the body she thought it was only fair that she should have a head start in solving the mystery.

She'd had a peep in the handbag on the bus on the way home from the Opera House but when she saw the gun she snapped it shut and remained po-faced all the way back to Bondi, the handbag sitting on her lap like a time bomb. Worst of all she'd had to wait till Eddy was out of the house before she could examine it properly. The suspense was killing her.

Gloves. It was best to wear gloves while examining evidence. She went through the drawers but there was not a glove in sight. Nothing.

Think, Mavis, think.

She sat on the bed absentmindedly stroking the back of her hand. Hands were another thing she prided herself on. Sorbolene every day and never allow harsh detergents near them. Detergents. Mavis, you silly old duffer, of course you've got gloves.

They were still a bit damp despite the fact that she'd rolled them in a teatowel to get them dry. Well, washing up gloves were better than nothing and she didn't have all day.

Despite the cumbersome gloves she managed to snap open the handbag. She'd have to be careful taking the gun out in case it was loaded but at least wearing the gloves she wouldn't electrocute herself.

It was a gun like the ones in the Dick Tracey comics, it didn't look real at all. Still, Mrs Levack wasn't going to take any chances. She didn't know how to tell whether it was loaded or not so very gingerly she put it under the pillow. It was safer that way and if it went off accidentally the sound would be muffled.

Next thing she pulled out of the handbag was a compact. Mrs Levack always used loose powder and a puff. The girl in DJ's at Bondi Junction had told her that loose powder was more suitable for a more mature skin. She hadn't always cared about her appearance but things had changed now that she'd taken up part-time employment. She got a decent perm and Shirlene gave her a facial once a month. Freda at the club said next thing she'd be taking up aerobics. Working at the flagship of Australian culture meant you had an image to keep up, said Mrs Levack. 'Struth,' said Freda, 'you're only doing the cleaning, not conducting the Sydney Symphony Orchestra.' It didn't matter, said Mrs Levack, it was important for a woman to have a career. Heavens above, you can only play bowls so many days a week.

There was lots of other make-up in the bag but none of it looked like evidence so Mrs Levack just left it.

Next item of significance was an address book, always a mine of information in the television shows. It was difficult looking through it with the rubber gloves on but Mrs Levack managed by blowing on the pages to separate them. One of the pages came loose. That meant only one thing—the opposite leaf had been torn out. That missing page was probably an important clue. It was a disgrace the way people tore pages out of books, no respect for private property.

Mrs Levack stopped. She realised she'd been shaking her head and talking out aloud. She felt silly. She hoped she wasn't getting that disease, what was it called? She couldn't for the life of her think of the name of it.

Mrs Levack rummaged on through unimportant items. At the bottom of the bag she hit pay-dirt—first, a scrap of paper with a phone number on it; then, nestled in the folds of the lining, one of those paper umbrellas used to decorate drinks.

After a great deal of wrestling with the rubber gloves she managed to get it open. On the black umbrella were musclemen in various body building poses. As she turned it round to examine it she noticed that the men moved. Ingenious, remarked Mrs Levack, hopefully to herself. The last detail she noticed about the umbrella was the chain around the edge.

But the links of the chain weren't links, they were numbers. Mrs Levack had a hunch. She picked up the scrap of paper and compared the numbers on it with the numbers on the umbrella. They matched perfectly.

She went to the phone and dialled. Brr, brr. Brr brr. She looked at the mahogany clock on the sideboard. Quarter to eleven. Then she remembered. Alzheimer's. That was the name of the disease. Brr, brr. The phone rang on and on then it stopped. She waited for someone on the other end to answer but all she heard was an irritating noise.

Then she heard an even more irritating noise—the sound of the door hitting the vacuum cleaner. Eddy! She dropped the phone and raced back to the bedroom. 'Flamin' hell!' she heard. 'What's the woman trying to do, cripple me?'

She just had time to whisk the contents back into the bag and fling everything under the bed before she heard him coming. 'What's the vacuum . . . ' He stopped short. Mavis was sitting on the bed with her hand to her chest and she was panting. He rushed over to her. 'Gawd Mavis, are you all right? Will I call Dr Mackintosh? Why are you wearing your rubber gloves? Have you gone funny? Mavis?'

All that running around, even in your own home, it wasn't easy being a private investigator, 'I just . . . I had a bit of a turn,' she said between breaths (the gloves, Mavis, the gloves, you'd better explain about the gloves otherwise there'll be even more questions) ' . . . while I was doing the washing up . . . '

'No wonder you had a bit of a turn, woman. The washing up, the vacuuming, you can't do everything at once. Lie down for a while, come on.' Eddy went to fluff up the pillows. Mrs Levack looked horrified. The gun! She'd forgotten about the gun. Which pillow was it under? She had to put Eddy off. 'Oh for heaven's sake, stop fussing!'

But Eddy was not going to be put off so easily. 'Mavis, do as I tell you, lie down.' She knew when his voice got this determined tone there was no point in arguing. Meekly she lay down and even more meekly did she put her head on the pillow. Mrs Levack lay perfectly still, afraid any movement might trigger off the gun.

'Better?'

'Yes thank you, Eddy,' she replied, hardly moving her lips.

'I might as well have a lie-down too,' said Eddy getting onto the bed.

What had got into the man? In all their married life he'd never had a lie-down in the morning. Mrs Levack's breathing had returned to normal now but it was Eddy who sounded like he was panting.

Mrs Levack continued looking at the ceiling, wondering which one of them had the gun under their head.

'You all right?' said Eddy, after a while.

'Yes thank you.'

The next thing, she felt Eddy's hand stroking her arm. What was the man up to?

He cleared his throat and put his arm round her shoulder. He hadn't done that since the day the dog died. 'Ah, I thought we might . . . you know . . . have a bit of how's your father.'

They hadn't had a bit of how's your father since before the dog had died. She'd always been rather partial to it and she didn't want to pass up the opportunity, heaven knows with Eddy it didn't arise all that often, but there was still the problem of the gun. All that heaving and hoing, what if the blessed gun went off and shot one of them? No, she couldn't take the risk.

'But Eddy, what about AIDS?'

'AIDS!' Eddy spluttered, 'AIDS? Where would we get AIDS from? Unless of course you . . . '

'Of course not, Eddy,' said Mrs Levack hastily. She thought it wiser not to mention the bowls Christmas party.

'Anyway, you needn't worry, you've got your rubber gloves on.'

He snuggled up closer to her and Mrs Levack started feeling frisky. His voice got softer now, almost like a pigeon cooing. 'I got a bit worried about you there for a minute, Mavis. I don't know what came over me, I thought what if she goes . . . '

'Oh Eddy.' Mrs Levack felt as fluffy as a schoolgirl.

'Mavis?' Mavis could feel something pressing against her. It wasn't soft like Eddy's stomach though it was in the same general vicinity.

'Yes, Eddy?' she said eagerly.

'Will you take your teeth out?'

'Oh Eddy.'

She hardly gave the gun a second thought. At least if she was going down she was going down in a blaze of glory.

Mrs Levack could hear Eddy snoring. At least neither of them had died in their sleep. It was a strange thought to wake up to, then she remembered why. She sat bolt upright, getting her head off the pillow as quickly as possible. She turned around and very, very carefully lifted her pillow. There it was. She reached under the bed for the handbag and as she opened it to put the gun back, she noticed again the scrap of paper with the phone number on it. She took that out. It was 5 o'clock. She put her teeth back in, went to the phone, and dialled.

It answered almost immediately. 'Big Boys.'

Now what? What would Angela Lansbury do? Keep them talking, see what you can find out. 'Hello, can I speak to . . . the boss?' Mrs Levack could hear disco music. It sounded very loud. 'Frankie won't be in till nine, can I fix you up, sweetie?' Mrs Levack pursed her lips. He didn't even know her and he was calling her sweetie. 'Well, perhaps you can . . . lover,' she hesitated. She found it somewhat distasteful to be calling this person she didn't even know 'lover' but in this business you have to be ready for anything. She thought of the paper umbrella. 'I've got some catering items to deliver, and I've misplaced the order form, can you tell me your address there?'

He gave her the address. Oxford Street, Darlinghurst. She also asked him the hours of opening. 'Till the last one passes out,' is what he said. From his conversation and the noise in the background Mrs Levack was getting quite a good idea of what sort of club Big Boys was. She was not completely unexposed to the kind of goings-on nowadays, she passed through Oxford Street on her way to work and she saw the photos in the newspaper of that Mardi Gras parade they have. Men in brassieres that were coiled like bedsprings. Some of them in tights with their bottoms showing. Chains and funny little leather suspender belts. Special dresses with slits in unusual places. Well at least they knew how to sew, you never saw things like that for sale in the shops.

The next morning Mrs Levack left for work earlier than usual. At Oxford Street she got off the bus and went to the address. It was a set of stairs between a clothes shop and a takeaway food place. There was a man lying on the bottom step in a big overcoat with a trail of some sort of liquid coming from underneath him. Two young people came down the stairs. They both had very short, very white hair. One of them was zippering up her black leather jacket but Mrs Levack had time to see rather large bosoms. She couldn't believe her eyes, beneath the jacket the person was completely naked! The two of them walked down the street, got on a big motorbike and roared away. Mrs Levack shook her head. The passenger wasn't wearing a helmet even though the wearing of helmets was compulsory.

'Excuse me,' she said, stepping over the gentleman in the doorway. She went up the stairs and knocked on the door but no-one came. She gave the door a little push and it opened.

The smell! It was like walking into a giant ashtray. When Mrs Levack's excellent eyes got used to the dark she could make out two figures embracing. Good heavens it was going on everywhere. She wondered if she'd made this comment out aloud because they put their tongues back in their own mouths and looked in her direction.

'Sorry, darling, members only.'

'Large members only,' sniggered the other one.

Mrs Levack sniffed, she had no idea what they were talking about. 'Is the boss in? I'm the cleaner,' she said.

The one wearing the most clothes spoke. 'The boss isn't in and *I'm* the cleaner, darling, what do you think this is?' he said brandishing the nozzle of a vacuum cleaner.

The sniggering one started prancing around. 'I'm a bit of fluff,' he giggled, 'we all know what vacuum cleaners do to fluff, don't we?' He seemed to think it was hilarious. Drugs, thought Mrs Levack. She was sure Angela Lansbury didn't have to put up with this sort of carry on.

'Is this the . . . the,' she said to remember other clubs on the way here, 'Tool Box?'

'Big Boys.'

Now it was Mrs Levack's turn to giggle. 'What a silly old duffer I am, I've come to the wrong place.' As she turned to leave she saw a large figure looming in the shadows near the far wall. She continued on her way. When she got to the door she turned back. The figure had disappeared. 'Sorry to have bothered you,' she said cheerily, 'bye-bye.'

Standing at the bus stop she felt very satisfied with herself. She'd cased the joint. Now that she had an idea of the layout she would come back. Tonight. Maybe the boss would be there tonight. Maybe the boss was there all along. Maybe the boss was that large ominous figure lurking in the shadows. There was something familiar about his shape. Orson Welles? Or was it that other chap, what was his name, Brandon something? Or was it something Brandon?

The bus pulled up at the stop. Mrs Levack showed her pensioner's pass and sat down at a window seat. It was shaping up to be a bright sunny day in Sydney. But Mrs Levack wasn't thinking about the weather, she was deep in thought.

She was at the steps of the Opera House before it came to her. Of course, Marlon Brando, how could she forget. Must be the Alzheimer's. Oh dear, she hoped she was going to last the distance. How was she going to organise Eddy if she had the Alzheimer's? Mrs Levack hurried along to work; her little detour had made her seven minutes late.

Along with the shopping that morning after work she purchased a few extra items. She worked at the sewing machine while Eddy watched the midday movie. At five past two he called out: 'Perry Mason's started.'

'In a minute,' Mrs Levack called back, guiding the black fabric through the machine.

'Mavis? What are you up to?' yelled Eddy during the first ad break, 'You've missed the murder.'

'In a minute,' Mrs Levack called back.

Perry Mason was just about over by the time Mrs Levack finished on the machine but it was worth missing it just this one time. She had a nice little black outfit now. One that you wouldn't see in a shop. It looked quite nice on, except that it showed the cellulite.

'Just going round to Freda's, dear,' she said. There was that 'dear' again.

'Why've you got your overcoat on? It's not that cold out.'

'At our age it's as well to take precautions, isn't it dear? Don't wait up.' As she bent down to give him a peck on the cheek she felt something slide loose.

'Hang on,' said Eddy imperiously from his lounge chair, 'what's that?'

'What's what?' asked Mavis. She had that same look on her face she had when she called royal flush and only had a pair.

'Under your coat.'

'What coat?' She could feel the butter in her mouth melting rapidly.

'I've had enough mucking about, Mavis, undo your coat.'

Mavis knew that Eddy had had enough mucking about. She also knew what had caused the trouble. Reluctantly she undid her coat and exposed the source of the trouble.

'The dog chain! What the bloody hell are you doing wearing the dog chain round your neck, and you haven't finished getting dressed! What's come over you woman, are you losing your marbles?'

She'd have to reveal all, he had her backed into a corner. Well count your blessings, Mavis Levack, she said to herself. At least if you're backed into a corner he can't see the bottom cut out of the fishnet tights.

She thought about Miss Marple and Angela Lansbury. It was all very well for them to carry on sleuthing, she sighed, they didn't have husbands who wanted to know the whys and wherefores of everything. They could walk out of the house dressed however they liked whenever they liked.

She told Eddy everything, about the handbag, the club and the mysterious figure that looked like Marlon Brando. Probably Orson Welles, commented Eddy when she got to that part, more shadowy, mysterious.

'So I have to go and see what happens at the club,' she concluded. 'It's the only lead I've got. Someone might recognise the handbag and tell me something.

Eddy of course was all for handing the matter over to the police but Mrs Levack thought she had gone too far to backtrack now. They'd ask all sorts of difficult questions such as why did she take the handbag in the first place. Besides, the police were always a bit dumb and everyone, even Perry Mason, did things behind the police's back.

She almost had him convinced. Full of bravado she walked towards the door. 'I'm off then, bye-bye,' she said brightly.

'Oh no you don't,' bellowed Mr Levack. 'No wife of mine is going to a club like that by herself.'

'How many wives do you have, Eddy?' retorted Mrs Levack.

'Enough of your cheek, Mavis, you're not going to that club by yourself and that's that!' Mrs Levack glared at her husband. 'I'm going with you,' he announced grandly.

This was a twist to the plot. 'But Eddy . . . '

'No buts about it, I'm going with you.'

'But you haven't got the appropriate clothes,' she said, dismayed.

'Don't you worry about that, Mavis Levack, don't you worry about that.'

He heaved himself out of the chair and went into the bedroom. Mrs Levack saw him pull down his old army duffle bag from on top of the wardrobe, then he pushed the door to. She'd always wondered what he kept in that bag, not that it was any of her business. She had tried to look in it once but the knots were too tight. And she'd almost fallen off the chair, bringing the duffle bag down with her.

'Mavis,' Eddy had opened the door a fraction and was poking something out, 'is this your hairspray?'

What do you think it is, a Molotov cocktail? 'Yes, dear,' she said. What was he going to do with it? He had hardly any hair to spray.

Ten minutes later Mrs Levack knew exactly what he had done with it. He'd hairsprayed a wig! A wig that made him look like Lana Turner—well actually he was a long way from looking like Lana Turner but that was the first thing Mrs Levack thought of. As for the rest of him, there were more feathers than you could poke a stick at. He looked like a chook that had been in a fight except that chooks didn't usually wear silver lamé skirts with the zipper undone to accommodate their fat bellies.

The person at the door reminded them that this was a gay bar but Mr and Mrs Levack had no trouble getting in. Mrs Levack twirled the little black Big Boys umbrella, said she was Frankie's mother and she'd been here thousands of times. 'And your girlfriend?' inquired the doorperson, looking at Eddy. 'She's my husband,' replied Mrs Levack.

Once inside it was a different kettle of fish. You couldn't see that much, not only because it was dark but also because there was this flashing light that made the whole thing look like the television when it goes on the blink. But in the glimpses that you caught it was very risqué indeed. Mr and Mrs Levack didn't look a bit out of place except that they were about 50 years older than everybody else.

Eddy went to get drinks. There was nowhere to sit down, the bar stools were occupied and there weren't any tables and chairs like at the bowling club. Mrs Levack hoped her feet weren't going to start playing up. She wished she'd brought the Homypeds but that would have meant a plastic bag as well as the handbag. She was hoping someone might recognise the handbag and she didn't want anything detracting from it. Also, she'd rather taken a liking to it. Such a big roomy bag, even with the gun in it.

Eddy came back with a Campari and soda in one hand, and a can of Fosters in the other. 'Gawd, the price of drinks nowadays, how can they afford to get drunk?'

'They're on drugs,' said Mrs Levack in a matter-of-fact voice. 'Where's the Reschs?'

'Sorry Mavis, bloke didn't even know what I was talkin' about when I asked for Reschs. You don't mind the Fosters, do you?'

'That'll be fine,' she said, 'take the top off for me will you, Eddy?'

Eddy obliged. They stood around sipping their drinks and trying to tap their feet to the house music. 'Well,' said Eddy after a while, 'what do we do now?'

Mrs Levack wasn't sure what they should do now. She was hoping someone might say something to her and she was looking for Orson Welles. She felt sure he had something to do with all this, he just looked the type. 'Suppose we should mingle. I'll go and make myself more visible and you . . . ' She looked him up and down, 'you shouldn't have too much trouble.'

Mrs Levack moved about in the crowd. Mostly young men with moustaches like New Zealand cricketers, some young women and some in between. Occasionally she spotted an older chap. If anyone looked at her, and lots of them did, she smiled back. 'Enjoying yourself, Gran?' said a man with a moustache. 'After some rough trade?' said another. 'Love the outfit, do you think your mother would make me one, too?'

Mrs Levack said yes to everything, even though she suspected they were talking in code. Occasionally she caught a glimpse of Eddy through the crowd. He was at the bar talking to a grey-haired gentleman wearing a polo neck skivvy. The grey-haired gentleman was wearing lots of rings and was smoking through a cigarette holder. Despite the wig, feathers and lamé skirt Eddy was leaning on the bar in a very masculine stance. They were talking as if they were old mates.

No-one seemed to be commenting on her handbag so she started to make her way back towards Eddy. It looked like the gentleman was pointing out something to Eddy. Just before Mrs Levack got to the bar the gentleman headed off in the direction he'd been pointing. Mrs Levack watched him disappear through a door in the back wall. You couldn't tell it was a door at all, it looked the same as the wall. In her mind's eye Mrs Levack marked the spot with an X.

'Mavis, there you are,' he said sipping his second Campari. This one had the Big Boys umbrella on it. The gentleman must have bought it for him, thought Mrs Levack, Eddy wouldn't be drinking with such gay abandon if he was paying for it himself. 'You'll never guess what, I'm standing here minding me own business when who taps me on the shoulder but Bobby Watergate.'

'Very interesting, Eddy.' She had no idea who Bobby Watergate was but guessed it must have been the grey-haired gentleman.

'We was in the Army together, he was one of the boys. You wouldn't of remembered him but you would remember Frank Carmody. Remember Frank?'

Mrs Levack had never met Frank Carmody but she'd heard all about him. In the early days it had been Frank this and Frank that. Bit of a lad Frank was if she could believe all Eddy's stories. Getting up to all sorts of shenanigans.

'And guess what, Mavis?' said Eddy slapping his thigh through the lamé skirt, 'Frankie runs this place!'

Mrs Levack hadn't seen her husband so excited since the wet T-shirt competition at the Bondi Diggers. Frankie. Well that set the jelly, didn't it?

Then Mrs Levack noticed that Eddy was twirling something between his fingers. It was a silver rose.

To say that Mrs Levack had a flashback would be putting too fine a point on it. It was hardly a flash. It was more of a grope through a long dark tunnel. To another silver rose.

The one lying beside the corpse at the Opera House.

'What's that, dear?' she said with no hint of emotion in her voice. 'What's what?'

'What you've got in your hand.'

'Oh that. Bobby give it to me. It's like membership of a club. The Rosebud Club. If you're a member, you get to take part in club activities, you know, like at bowls.'

'Let's have a look at it, shall we?' It didn't sound like Mavis' voice at all, it sounded like a doctor.

'You wouldn't like it Mavis, just us boys hanging around chewing the fat.'

'I don't suppose I would like it but that's hardly the point. I have a mystery to solve. I'm dressed like most of the boys here so I could slip in unnoticed.'

'But Mavis,' protested Eddy, 'it's exclusive, most of the blokes here don't even know about it.' Mavis had her lips pursed and Eddy knew what that meant. Wild horses wouldn't budge her. 'Look, tell you what, I go in there first, have a word to Frankie and get them to let you in.'

Mrs Levack thought about it for a minute. 'All right.' Mr Levack looked relieved. He started to walk away. Mrs Levack felt strong and confident, the sort of feeling that comes from having a gun in your handbag. 'Not so fast, Eddy. I'm coming with you.'

It seemed to Mrs Levack that she had spent hours outside that door in the wall. She'd heard Eddy say 'Rosebud', saw the door open a fraction then watched him disappear.

She squinted at her watch in the dull light. Only ten minutes had passed but it seemed long enough for Eddy to chat to the boys and get her an introduction.

She tapped on the door the way Eddy had. After another eternity it opened a fraction. 'Rosebud,' she said but the door didn't open any further. In fact it started to close. Mrs Levack rammed the handbag in the door so it couldn't close completely.

'I am Eddy Levack's wife and if you don't let me in I am going to start screaming.' Mrs Levack pushed her way into the inner sanctum.

Despite her excellent eyesight she couldn't believe what she saw.

Eddy was hanging from a noose. Standing underneath him was a man. She couldn't see his face because a hangman's hood was covering it, but she recognised that shape. It was Orson Welles. He had a whip in his hand. He was torturing Eddy!

Without giving it a second thought Mrs Levack whipped the gun out of the handbag and aimed it at her husband's tormentor. Eddy started making gurgling noises and waving his hands. 'Hang on, Eddy, I'm coming!'

'Drop it, c'mon drop it,' she said to the man with the whip.

'Look,' he said, 'you've made a mistake . . . '

'No,' said Mrs Levack, '*you've* made a mistake. First that one at the Opera House and now my husband, you won't get away with it you know.'

'Look, it's not what you think.' He made a step towards her. Mrs Levack closed her eyes and squeezed the trigger.

In that instant she found out that the gun was loaded. So did Frank Carmody.

When Mrs Levack opened her eyes she saw his body lying on the floor. When she looked up she saw Eddy grunting and gesticulating wildly. He wanted to say something and he wanted to say it badly.

She dragged a chair around, took off the shoes that were by now killing her and climbed up on it. A knife, thought Mrs Levack frantically, I haven't got anything to cut the rope with. 'I'm sorry, Eddy, I've got to find a knife. Will you be all right for a minute?' She climbed down off the chair again. Eddy was grunting and pointing at the chair. 'Yes, Eddy, the chair, what about it?' He was very red in the face now, he kept pointing at the chair then at himself. Finally Mrs Levack got the message. 'Of course, Eddy, what a silly duffer I am, the chair, of course.'

She slid the chair under his feet so he could stand on it. He loosened the noose and stood on the chair catching his breath before untying the knot, the same kind of knot as on the duffle bag.

He stepped down off the chair and examined the body. 'You've flaming killed him,' he roared, 'you flaming killed him.'

'But . . . I saved your life, Eddy,' she said in a bewildered voice, 'he was torturing you.'

'It was just a bit of fun, like we used to get up to in the old days. I told you you wouldn't like it, Mavis, but you had to come and stick your nose in it, didn't you? Can't a man have a bit of fun with some old mates without his wife interfering?'

Mrs Levack looked around the room. The walls were painted black and there were all sorts of strange contraptions, she couldn't really see the fun side of it at all. Plus now she had another dead body on her hands. 'I'm sorry, Eddy, I was only trying to help, really I was . . .' She started to cry.

'There there,' Mr Levack put a comforting arm around his wife, 'don't upset yourself. You can't make an omelette without breaking eggs,' he said philosophically.

'What a strange thing to say, Eddy, you always like your eggs boiled.'

Eddy brought her in a cup of tea and the newspaper. He was good like that, not that she got sick much but if ever she did Eddy would always be there with the cups of tea. He'd wanted to call Doctor Mackintosh but Mrs Levack thought it wasn't really necessary.

'Couple of items in the paper that might interest you, dear,' he said emphasising the 'dear'.

One item stated that police had charged an Adelaide man with the murder of his wife whose body had been found on the steps of the Opera House.

Mr Robert Watergate, the dead woman's uncle, informed police the dead woman had left her husband and come to Sydney looking for work.

In another unrelated incident Frank Carmody, proprietor of the Big Boys club had been shot dead. The murder weapon had not been found and police were asking anyone with any information to come forward.

'This should be an easy one for you to solve, Miss Marple, you already know who did it. Shall I call the police for you?'

Mrs Levack picked at her blue crocheted bed jacket and slunk down further under the blankets. 'Please, Eddy, I'm not in the mood for jokes, I'm feeling a bit off colour.'

Martin Long studied music but went on to make a living in journalism—as music and film critic, feature writer and leader writer, and later as a university information officer. At the same time he dabbled in musicology and published work on English lute music. On retirement from full-time employment he discovered that what he liked doing best was writing fiction. The outcome has been a set of novels featuring a mild-mannered detective, Wellington Cotter, who disentangles good from evil in late nineteenth-century Sydney.

Martin Long
THE TARPEIAN WAY

Her lover was waiting in the stage door foyer as she came running down the Green Room stairs, in peril on her high heels.

They kissed briefly under the benign regard of the attendants.

'Taxi's on the way,' he said, taking the coat she carried.

But when the glass doors closed behind them she cried, 'My God! It's *freezing*.' (Her party dress of ruffled silk taffeta covered her from cleavage to mid thigh.) He helped her huddle into the coat.

There was no-one to be seen in the concourse, the vast wide tunnel that lies under the imposing front steps of the Opera House. The concert hall, the opera theatre and the playhouses had in turn disgorged their audiences. Few would want to linger on a night as cold as this.

Once out of sight of the stage door they kissed again, this time in earnest. They held the embrace until car headlights shone at the far end of the concourse. He gently disengaged himself.

'Stupid party,' she said as the taxi drew up. 'I'll only make an appearance, but I do have to go. I still wish you'd come, my darling.'

'Not invited.'

'Doesn't matter.'

'Nobody knows me over here. I can't stand that sort of party—where I know no-one and everyone else knows one another. Even more so when they're all half drunk before you get there. I'll walk to the bus. It's only a step.'

When the taxi drew out he chose to follow after it into the open air rather than traverse the gloomy length of the concourse. He walked briskly, hunched against the cold, with his hands thrust into the pockets of his duffle-coat. The sound of his footsteps on the pavement made an imperfect echo: not an echo but an accompaniment. Then there was a man's voice close behind him.

'She's still a beautiful woman, isn't she?'

He stopped and turned, astonished. The other man, tall, gaunt and dishevelled, seemed to have sprung out of the asphalt. He, too, had his hands buried in the pockets of an overcoat.

'You mean Clara Markham?' the man in the duffle-coat said. 'Of course. But why "still"? She's young.'

'She'll be thirty-three on October the twenty-seventh next,' the other answered without hesitation.

The man in the duffle-coat shrugged and walked on. The man in the overcoat caught up and kept pace beside him. 'And she has more than beauty,' he said. 'Genuine talent. She had enviable reviews.'

'I know.'

'And her performance grows in stature and confidence every night.'

'You've been there every night?'

'Except Saturday. That was sold out.'

'Good Lord!' The first man, amused, stopped and cast a glance over the other's threadbare coat.

'She seems to have lived down the scandal.'

'Scandal? Oh, that. It was ten years ago.'

'Nine years, seven months and twenty-three days—from the crucial event.'

'It's all in the past.'

'All in the past. Water under the bridge, you were going to say perhaps. But the past isn't like that. It doesn't flow away and disappear. The past invades the present and endangers the future. But you are right, the scandal did her no harm professionally. At first it was mere curiosity, voyeurism. They would say "Isn't that the girl who . . . ?" But you see she did have talent. And beauty. She conquered in her own right, and now she can swim in a bigger pond, play Hedda Gabler at the Sydney Opera House and enrapture the critics. But she had to change her name. She was Clare, not Clara, and Markham is neither her maiden nor her married name. A fabrication.'

'A stage name. A common enough thing. You make it sound like some sort of alias.'

'Still, the real purpose was concealment . . . Your name is Gordon Ross, isn't it?'

'How did you know?'

'I take an interest in everything that concerns the woman who calls herself Clara Markham.'

They had crossed the forecourt and were within yards of the blackened cliff-face that divides the shining Opera House from the green Botanic Gardens, like a boundary between two centuries. Ross considered ways of ridding himself of his adhesive companion. He consulted his watch, looked in the direction of the bus stands and said 'goodbye' in a decisive manner.

'It would do you no harm to stay and listen for a while,' the stranger said quietly. 'I can tell you things about Clare and Paul Steward that you don't know. Things that nobody knows.'

Ross had turned away, but now he hesitated. At the time of that episode he had been far away from Adelaide and all he knew of it was hearsay. By unspoken agreement neither he nor Clara ever mentioned it. Yet at the back of his mind there lurked always a furtive curiosity.

'You knew Steward?'

'Intimately. Both before and after the event.'

'Who *are* you?'

'Call me Ishmael.'

Ross laughed, but the stranger's set expression did not change. Ross observed him with more attention. The seedy appearance of the man was at odds with his stilted loquacity. He seemed to be between forty and fifty, but not well preserved—he might be younger than he looked. He had deep-set eyes, an aquiline nose, a thin mouth locked between deep creases. His features had a rigidity about them, like those of a man in constant pain. His unkempt hair, worn rather long, hung loosely from a balding crown.

The stranger's eyes were turned to the wall of rock and the steps leading to the top.

'I wonder what fancy prompted the forefathers of this city to name that path along the edge of the cliff the Tarpeian Way,' he said. He seemed suddenly to have forgotten his obsession with Clara Markham. 'Do you know the legend of Tarpeia?'

'No.'

'She opened the citadel of Rome to the Sabines for the promise of gold, but the Sabines killed her. Treachery is despised even by those who benefit from it. The Tarpeian Rock was the place where the Romans executed criminals.'

'Very interesting, I'm sure. You were about to say something else.'

181

'Betrayal takes many different forms—falsity, faithlessness. It occurs not only among nations but among men and women. Yet traitors sometimes prosper . . . yes, I have something else to say. Come with me.' He went towards the steps. Ross was left with the choice of walking away or following. Despite himself, he followed.

'I come here in the daytime,' the stranger said as they walked up the worn and weathered steps. 'You get an unusual view of the Opera House. And I watch the people that come and go from it. You know, Gordon . . . may I call you Gordon?'

'You can call me Julius Caesar for all I care.'

'He was betrayed, too . . . you know, everything might have been so different for Clare if she had gone to gaol.'

'You said you were going to tell me things that nobody knew. Anyone could tell you that there wasn't a chance in the world of Clare being convicted of anything serious, in view of the medical evidence. The man had beaten her black and blue. There were bruises and abrasions around her neck. He had tried to strangle her.'

'Tried to strangle her.' He had that trick of plucking words from the other's mouth, then weighing and measuring them. 'Have you ever thought about that? Steward was a strong man, as tall as you; his wife is no Amazon, as you know. What could have stopped him if he had really wanted to throttle her to death?'

'You know quite well, she fired a shot from a revolver, just to scare him.'

The stranger swung about and thrust both hands, thumbs and fingers outstretched, towards Ross's throat. Ross instinctively clutched at the other's wrists.

'That's what you do when someone tries to strangle you,' the stranger said. 'You don't reach for your gun, even if you happen to be carrying one, and Clare certainly wasn't carrying one. In fact she was half undressed. You haven't thought about this much at all, have you? Even the police had the wit to ask questions about that.' He returned his hands to his overcoat pockets.

'Clare told them that she broke away from her husband's grip and ran to another part of the room, where there happened to be a loaded revolver,' he went on. 'She seized it and fired a shot at random, "just to scare him"—as you said. But unluckily the bullet struck the wall, was deflected, and entered Paul Steward's skull through the right temple. It followed that it was just bad luck that she shot and wounded Steward. That chip on the wall, together with the bruises on her neck, saved Clare. The case never went to trial: the magistrate ruled that no jury would convict. She came out of it a heroine to some, and as for Steward, he was a monster.'

'What did Steward have to say for himself during all this time? Nothing. Steward lay in a hospital bed with a bullet lodged in the frontal lobes of his brain and his mind a complete blank about the whole thing. The irony of it was that he would have been well qualified to describe what had happened to him. Steward was a physiological scientist, held in high regard. It was for him, not Clare, that the brilliant career had been predicted. He could have told you that the frontal lobes of the brain can be damaged or destroyed without causing death or even loss of mental faculties. The bullet and the bone fragments were too close to vital tissue—the optic nerve in particular—to be removed, so they left them there rather than risk blindness or death. After that there was nothing left for Steward, brain-damaged and rejected of men. His life would always be in peril, but if he lived for a year and a day—which he did—Clare was safe. After that she couldn't be charged with manslaughter, even if anyone had had a mind to do so.

'Steward came out of hospital with his physical faculties intact, though he suffered from blackouts and what are politely called "personality disturbances". Most of the time, though, he could tell a hawk from a handsaw. The only person who had any sympathy for him was his brother. Owen Steward was an unusual man, a "loner" as they say, unmarried, something of a recluse. He had a farm on Kangaroo Island, and he took Paul there and cared for him.'

'If you're trying to work up *my* sympathy for that brute you'll have a hard job,' Ross said.

'Of course. And yet there was so much more to it than anyone knew—apart, of course, from Clare herself. More than Paul Steward himself knew, until his memory came back. It did come back, a fragment at a time. It began when he returned to the flat. Clare had gone, taking everything that was hers—except for the gifts that Paul Steward had given her. Silver jewellery, mainly. She likes to wear silver, to offset her dark beauty, as you no doubt know. Pieces of silver. It puzzled Steward, this rejection. Then, standing there with those pieces of silver in his hand, he remembered the letter.'

He gripped the tall upright bars of the iron boundary fence and stood gazing down into the empty forecourt.

'He remembered standing in that same place with the letter in his hand, reading it in disbelief. He had come upon Clare earlier as she was writing it. She finished it quickly, sealed it and stuffed it into a handbag without a stamp or address—a curious, furtive thing to do, he thought. When she went to change her clothes he found the letter and opened it. It was a love letter. She had secretly betrayed him with that man Clissold. That was terrible enough, but what stunned him quite as much was the evidence of hatred—hatred towards him, her husband, conveyed in the letter. She often wished he were dead, the letter said. Steward was out of his mind; he rushed in and confronted her then and there, while she was still half undressed. It was the sight of her in that half-naked state that drove him to greater frenzy—the thought that she had been defiling her body with that man and at the same time pretending affection to him, Steward. She was unrepentant, defiant. She stood and poured out venom: accusations and lies. It was unbearable to him. He had to stop that awful flow of words. That was why he put his hands on her, just to stop the words.

'Then the frenzy left him and he felt suddenly ashamed of his loss of self control. He had let the letter drop. Now he picked it up and began to read it again, unable to believe the things it said and implied. The letter, of course, was never seen again. What a difference it might have made—the clear evidence of her adultery, of wishing him dead. It would have planted the seeds of doubt. Once planted, doubt will grow and grow unless there is hard evidence to refute it.'

'It wouldn't have made any difference with me. Look, you talk like somebody out of the Ark—all this stuff about adultery and betrayal. Betrayal is the wrong word. People make mistakes, they change, split up, form new relationships . . .'

'Relationships. What a cold and comfortless word! I suppose you're the sort of person who'd say that she had "boyfriends". They weren't boys and they weren't friends. They were grown men and they were paramours. People have invented words to match their own false standards. Clare made solemn vows before God when she married Steward; it was a church wedding. She concealed her liaison with Clissold. I call that betrayal, and I call it betrayal when someone allows another's reputation to be destroyed by default.'

'That's not the way I see it. And you've left a few things. Clare had bruises on her other than the ones on her neck. Neighbours heard her screaming. Steward was a violent and brutal man.'

'He was a *passionate* man, a man easily hurt. A blow can be equivalent to a cry of pain.'

'Bullshit. Look, I don't have to listen to this. You can go and spout your poisonous meanderings to someone else.'

He turned and strode toward the steps, but the other man still kept pace beside him.

'You speak about Steward in the past tense,' Ross said, curious about one point. 'Is he dead?'

'Long ago.'

'Can't say I'm sorry.'

'Pray that no-one says that about you after you are dead.'

'I don't make a habit of half-killing defenceless women.'

'Defenceless. There's also the matter of the revolver. The revolver belonged to Steward. There was no argument about that: it was registered in his name. What sort of man, people said, keeps a loaded revolver in a secure block of flats in a peaceful city? Another black mark against Steward. But you see it wasn't true.'

'What do you mean, it wasn't true?'

They were back at the foot of the cliff. 'I'll tell you,' the stranger said. But instead he began to cross the road in the direction of Man-o'-War Steps. Ross wanted to turn on his heel and go, but again that lurking half-guilty curiosity compelled him to follow.

'It wasn't true that Steward kept a loaded revolver in the flat. In fact he had never even bought that gun: it had been his father's. He put it unloaded in the back of a drawer and forgot all about it. Yet somehow it came to be loaded and ready to hand when Clare wanted it. If the court had known that, those seeds of doubt would really have germinated. Had she staged the whole thing with that end in mind?'

'That's ridiculous. She wasn't a prisoner. If she wanted to be rid of Steward she had only to walk out. Or *was* she a prisoner? You can imagine that man threatening to kill her if she left him.'

'Yes, an interesting question. Only she could answer it. Are you going to ask her?'

Ross answered quickly, 'No.' The other man turned his head and regarded him without speaking. Ross felt a surge of anger, clenched his fists but kept them in his pockets.

'She would have had good reason to stay with Steward,' the stranger said. 'The man Clissold was married; Clare was a nobody then; she'd never played a speaking role on a professional stage. Steward provided a home and money to spend. Let us suppose you are right: the incident was not engineered deliberately. In that case she fired the shot in blind rage, not in self defence. Just how did the gun come to be in her hand? Have you thought much about that? Be patient while I describe the scene. The bedroom turned a corner, so to speak. Imagine a rectangle with a smaller rectangle cut out of it for a bathroom—*en suite*. The re-entrant part of the room formed an alcove lined on two sides with wardrobes. That was where Clare retreated. The wardrobes would have been open—Clare was getting dressed. Where was the revolver? In Steward's clothes, she said. But that wasn't so. It must therefore have been among her clothes.

'Steward never saw the gun in her hand. He was standing side-on to her, in the main part of the room. He had picked up the fallen pages of the letter and had begun to read it again. That was the last thing he remembered, until he found himself standing in the same place with the silver ornaments in his hands, months later, and his memory began to come back. She fired while he wasn't looking. So who was the defenceless one? Did the bullet go wide in the first place because she meant it to or because she wasn't a good shot? I imagine it was the first time she had ever fired a revolver. The bullet grazed the wall at the entrance to the alcove; it wasn't all that much off target, if Steward really was the target. The picture grows more confused, doesn't it?'

Ross had to make an effort to keep his voice steady. 'This is only what Steward said. You seem to believe everything he told you.'

'I know these things to be true.'

Ross made a scoffing sound. The stranger continued unperturbed.

'After it was all over Clare obtained what the civil law calls a divorce from Steward, though Steward never consented. He never renounced those vows. Clissold, too, gained a divorce. They married, but Clissold was betrayed by her in his turn.'

By now they had moved onto the old stone mole that encloses Governor Lachlan Macquarie's little boat harbour—Port Lachlan as they called it in the 1820s.

After a pause the stranger said, 'Somebody should have warned you that Clare is a sorceress. Those who have made love with her are never released from the spell. Clissold went to pieces. He is dead.'

'*Dead*? We—Miss Markham's lawyers have been trying to find him.'

'Clissold was no longer part of the world that keeps lists and notes addresses. His body will never be found, but he is dead.'

A sudden coldness that was not of the weather descended on Ross. He summoned his nerves and muscles into alertness.

'You're Owen Steward, aren't you?' he said. 'The brother.'

'Oh no. I'm Paul Steward. I thought you would have realised that before now. You're not what I would call a quick-thinking man.'

'But you said Paul Steward was dead.'

'He suffered a sort of death when Clare betrayed him. It was Owen who died—was killed. A tractor overturned on him. The money from the sale of the farm barely covered debts, and Paul Steward became once more a wanderer on the face of the earth.'

'You're insane. What was the point of all this?'

'You don't know?'

The man's hands were around his throat, and this time it was no pretence. Ross tugged with his hands at the man's wrists, flailed with his feet and knees, but his assailant had the lunatic strength of utter single-mindedness and was heedless of pain.

He felt consciousness draining away. If he was to survive he had only seconds in which to retaliate. His sole superiority lay in his greater weight. He hurled his body forward, trying at the same time to entangle the man's feet with his own. They were on a narrow unfenced causeway, with the black waters of Farm Cove lapping on either side. Ross did not want to continue the struggle under water, but neither, he guessed, would Steward. Stewart evidently sensed the danger of losing his footing and turned away from the edge, twisting until his back was towards the farther end of the breakwater. But he was stumbling, and Ross used his little remaining strength to push his advantage. He could see what Steward could not: the gap where a flight of steps led down to the water, and just beyond it a tall stanchion, the only modern structure on the breakwater.

Steward's feet avoided the steps but his head came up against the metal post with a jar. It did not seem a heavy blow; nevertheless the grip around Ross's windpipe suddenly relaxed. Ross shook himself free and sank down on hands and knees. At the same time a thin high cry came from the other man's throat. Ross looked up to see him standing with his hands raised in front of sightless eyes. Steward took a few stumbling footsteps, crumpled, and pitched head foremost down into the well of the steps.

After nine years, seven months and twenty-three days, Clare's bullet had done its work at last.

Garry Disher grew up in rural South Australia. He has travelled widely and now lives in Melbourne, where he is a full-time writer. His books include novels, short story collections, the *Personal Best* anthologies, books for children and writers' handbooks (including the Allen & Unwin title, *Writing Professionally*). His short stories have won awards and have been published overseas and widely in Australia. His crime fiction includes a story in the first *Crimes for a Summer Christmas* anthology and the novels *Kickback* and *Paydirt* (Allen & Unwin).

Garry Disher

THRESHOLD

'It's not that we're smart, Sunshine, the bad guys are dumb. Detective work, investigative procedures, it's all garbage. The reality is wrong addresses, phone numbers with the digits transposed, drinking shit-house tea in ugly sitting rooms so you don't offend potential witnesses—who invent things anyway, tell you what they think you want to hear.'

'Yes, sir,' I said.

'Yes sir. No sir. Turn right at the next set of lights.'

'Yes, sir.'

It was seven o'clock in the morning and we had a double homicide in Hawthorn. It was my first homicide on Vestey's crew. Everything I'd been told about him was true. I sat tense and buttoned-up and didn't trust myself to speak.

'No, boyo,' he said, 'most cases are broken in the first twenty-four hours. More often than not your crim is caught in the act, or his wife dobs him in, or he forgets to clean the blood off his shoes, or he gives himself up. Feeling lucky?'

'Don't know, sir.'

'Don't know, sir,' Vestey muttered, and he settled into the icy solitude that unnerved me more than anything else about him. He was burdened with perpetual anger and a hard searching mind, and for a week now I'd been feeling the force of it.

'Next left,' he said, closing the Melways, 'then two streets down.'

'Sir.'

He was respected at 412 St Kilda Road but not liked at all. He was too secretive and private for that, and too straight, somehow. He viewed everything and everyone with frank disbelief. He loathed judges, magistrates, lawyers, criminals and time-serving cops. The very day I joined his team he'd been on the front page, pictured in front of the latest gun-amnesty haul, throwing a challenge at the world.

'Rigby Street,' he said.

It was one of those broad leafy streets where the houses start at half a million dollars. Vestey didn't have to tell me the number. An ambulance, divisional vans, and a huddle of neighbours were blocking the street a hundred metres down. I parked the Commodore and we got out.

Vestey seemed to know all about it. He led me along the side of the house to a vast garden at the rear. 'Numero uno,' he said.

The first body was lying half a metre inside the back door. The head rested on the outstretched left arm; a narrow watchband was visible below the cuff of a light-coloured coat. The right arm hugged the stomach. Dark hair curled to the nape of the neck. The legs were bent a little at the hips and knees, the toe of one woven brown leather shoe appearing to chase the heel of the other.

In other words a configuration of sleep—except no-one would choose to sleep on a cold porch floor, the hand clasping the stomach had done a poor job of holding the blood in, and there was a small entry wound in the temple. A case of wrong time, wrong place, I thought, taking note of two items lying near the body: a small shoulder bag with an Ansett tag on it and a tiny rose cast in silver. The spiky metal had torn through classy black wrapping paper, probably when the woman fell.

Vestey made no move to go in so I stood there with him, looking at the body. After a while he grinned at me. On that face it was a brief, bleak spasm. 'Okay, Sunshine, first impressions.'

'Sir.'

I knelt next to the body. The entry wound displayed the classic stippling effect, pinpoint haemorrhaging caused when unburnt powder and tiny metal shavings are driven into the flesh. 'Shot at point-blank range, sir.'

'An effect of which,' Vestey said, 'is sound suppression. Let's see who she is.'

He crouched next to me, wrapped a handkerchief around his hand and removed a wallet from the woman's coat pocket. It was crammed with cards. 'Nina Galt, of this address.' He looked at me. 'Ansett ID. Check the case.'

I did what Vestey had done, wrapped my hand in a handkerchief, but he curled his lip as if I was overdoing it. I found a uniform in the suitcase. 'Some kind of flight attendant,' I said.

Vestey returned the wallet to the coat pocket. 'Not that it matters, poor bloody bitch.' Then I saw him reach out, clasp the dead woman's slender hand above the watchstrap as if to comfort her, and rotate her wrist. The watchface was cracked, the hands stuck at 7:03. 'Time of death. Just like in the movies, eh, Sunshine?' He stood, brushed at his knees. 'She's been here twelve hours, long enough for *rigor* to come and go. Okay, give it your best shot.'

'Sir.' I pointed at the suitcase near the base of the steps. 'She arrives home from the airport yesterday evening, opens the back door, goes in, and he's waiting for her. Pops her one in the stomach, she falls, he pops her again in the head.'

'Don't give me *pops*, mister. Why the back door?'

He was right. People generally let themselves in by the front door. I looked away, hunting for an explanation. A light had been left on above the back door. There was a small bluestone building in the garden behind us. One of the uniform boys was standing watch over it. A hundred years ago it had been a stable but now there were curtains in the windows, creepers on the walls and brass fittings on a Brunswick Green door. 'Maybe she rents the stable. She's friends with the owner and was calling in to say hello.'

Vestey likes to drape his long frame in dark, expensive double-breasted suits. He brushed at invisible lint. He was elegant and dangerous-looking, as if he'd just stepped out of a cognac ad. 'The rose, Sunshine. The sexy black paper. Rushing in to say hello before she even unpacks her bags. That tell you anything?'

He didn't wait for an answer but stepped past the body and disappeared inside the house. I turned around in time to catch the uniformed constable disguising a grin. I ignored him and examined the garden, a sizeable area of fruit trees, wattles, wrought-iron chairs and a lawn that needed cutting. Instead of a fence there was a bluestone wall on three sides. A block of flats showed above the wall at the back. Apparently a woman who lived there had noticed the suitcase late yesterday, noticed it was still there this morning, and made a 'you'll-think-I'm-being-silly-but' call to D24.

Vestey was back in the doorway. 'Communing, Sonny Jim? Think the answer's floating in the ether? Come and apply some lateral thinking in here.'

'Yes, sir.'

I followed the vigorous, thrusting shape into the kitchen. Now there were five of us there, counting a nervous DC from the local CIB, Sally waiting with her fingerprint kit, Mack snapping pictures.

Six, counting the second victim.

She was dressed for a Sunday afternoon in Lygon Street, designer tracksuit and Reeboks. She'd fallen onto her side in a foetal position. Masking tape bound her wrists and ankles and two strips of it had been pasted over her mouth. Her eyes were wide and alarmed, as if she'd seen what was coming. There were no marks on the body. There was no blood.

Without looking at anyone Vestey said, 'The coroner? Crime-scene unit?'

I happened to be looking at Sally when he said it. She was watching him covertly. I'd seen women do that, grow distracted and covetous around him, even if they wouldn't admit it. 'On their way, sir,' she said.

'Fine. So instead of contaminating the crime scene why don't you all bugger off outside until they arrive?'

He didn't mean me. The others began to troop out, trying to look bored. 'Mack,' Vestey said, 'there's a crowd gathering in the street. I want you to take a few candids. Maybe our boy's hanging around, catching the action.'

'Sir,' Mack said, going out.

Vestey turned to me. 'Feel along the hairline.'

'Sir?'

'On the job training, Sunshine. Don't worry, you won't disturb anything.'

I knelt on the slate floor, steadying myself for a moment by holding the dead woman's shoulder, then edged my fingertips from her temple to the back of her head—almost as if I were working shampoo into a lather. The hair was fine and clean; I could hear the soft scrape of my fingers at the roots.

I found it where the skull meets the spine—a small patch of sticky dampness. I jerked my hand away, stood up and stared at my fingers.

Vestey may have thawed a few degrees, for he called me by my name. 'Well, Mr Niall?'

'He made her kneel on the floor, sir, then shot her in the back of the head.'

I stared at my fingers as I said it.

'Wipe them, for Christ's sake. What else can you tell me?'

I took out my handkerchief and rubbed hard at the blood. I had it on the tip of each finger. 'It's a pro hit, sir.'

'I know it's a pro hit. I expect our esteemed Commissioner could tell me it's a pro hit. I want to know what sort of forensic joy we can expect out of this, if you catch my drift.'

I felt my face grow hot—it was the lingering sensation of the sticky blood and Vestey bearing down on me regardless. I thought of other head shots I'd seen, the classic splash pattern of bone fragments and brain tissue. 'As with the first body,' I said, 'there's no exit wound, meaning a small-calibre weapon, probably a .22. If he used hollow-points—'

'All we'll get are fragments, meaning we can't match them to any gun, meaning the brain will be porridge. Well done.'

I peered around at the slate floor. 'Maybe he left a shell casing behind.'

Vestey looked at me pityingly. 'Explain the tape.'

'To stop her from struggling?'

Vestey's handsome lean head swung down close to my face. His white shirt looked very white inside his dark suit coat. He smelt faintly of soap. He smelt clinically clean, like a surgeon, only no surgeon was ever this sharp and glittering. 'So why didn't he tie the Galt woman?'

'He wasn't expecting her, sir.'

Vestey nudged the taped ankles with his black shoe tip. 'Meaning this one's the intended victim, yes, yes, but *think*: why the tape, why the kneeling down, *why the formality?*'

I snapped the word, I couldn't help it: 'Execution.'

Vestey relaxed. He almost smiled. 'Give the lad a great big hand.' He looked bitterly at the dead woman. 'Execution. Know the rationale behind execution, Sonny Jim? You're a varsity boy, you've got letters after your name, enlighten me.'

'Punishment.' I was still bristling.

'Punishment. To teach a lesson. To restore honour. This isn't just a shooting, it has a signature on it, it's symbolically meaningful. It says this is what happens if you transgress the unwritten law.'

I thought I understood him. He hated criminal posturing. He hated the banality of the code behind this execution. I nodded. 'I see.'

'You still here, sport? We've got a dead dyke with connections—how else do you explain the execution—the little friend who walked in when she shouldn't have, and you're standing there with your mouth open?'

He said all this for the entertainment of the pathologist, who had just come into the room. Professor Quennell glanced at me sympathetically, nodded at Vestey, and opened his black bag. We watched him draw on latex gloves, hook a stethoscope to his ears and crouch next to the body.

'She's dead, Prof.'

Quennell ignored Vestey. He listened for a heartbeat then switched on a micro-cassette recorder and started talking: 'Preliminary indications. The deceased is a white female, aged approximately thirty years, bearing no visible wounds, but—' he bent over and sniffed at the woman's head, '—the hair reveals traces of cordite, and—' he touched the back of her head without hesitation, '—there is a possible entry wound concealed under the hair at the base of the skull . . . '

To look useful I got out my notebook and drew separate floor plans of the kitchen and the adjoining porch, showing each body in relation to furniture, doors and walls, and marking distances and angles. Then I looked around the kitchen. It was a copper, pine and skylight kind of place, with a vast refrigerator and farmhouse style stove. Potted ferns leaked over the edges of the pine benches.

At one end of a shelf of tattered cookbooks above the refrigerator was a shallow cane basket heaped with bills, receipts, postcards and letters. I lifted it down and began to sift through it using the tip of my pen, pausing at a postcard of a Gold Coast beach. It was a long-distance shot, the sand crowded with sunbathers. The word ME had been scrawled breezily in red ink in the top right corner above a red arrow angling into the anonymous mass of sunbathers. I flipped the card over. It was postmarked a week earlier and said simply, 'See you Monday.' Yesterday, I thought. It was signed 'Nina'. The rest of the message lay in the big red kiss and the tiny heart that dotted the *i* in 'Nina'.

I put the basket back on the shelf. I didn't want to hear the homophobia in Vestey's voice again, the note of ugly hate, so I didn't mention the postcard. 'Got a name, sir,' I said. 'Rosemary Joyce.'

'The silver rose,' Vestey said. 'The name Joyce do anything for you, Sunshine?'

'No, sir.'

'Let's just say it's known to the police. How does 7.03 pm yesterday grab you?'

Vestey was addressing the pathologist, who'd just withdrawn a thermometer from the dead woman's armpit. Quennell noted the temperature and went on recording, ignoring Vestey. 'Two factors affect this reading: the body is lying on a cold surface, slate, and the back door has apparently been open for several hours.' He bared the woman's waist where it met the slate. 'Skin coloration in the region of the trunk indicates that gravitational sinking is well advanced.'

'And we're not,' Vestey said. 'Come on, Mr Niall, we're twelve hours behind.'

By now the rest of Vestey's crew had arrived. While they searched outside, I took the sitting room and study, Vestey the bedrooms. I was glad of the solitude; I needed to shake off Vestey's voice. It had been living in my head all week, didactic, withering, full of hard judgements.

I glanced around the quiet, curtained rooms. I formed an impression of good taste and the money to support it. The floorboards gleamed, the rugs were muted and thick, a smell of polish clung to the simple, expensive chairs and cabinets. The ceilings were high and the entire wall space of the sitting room had been given over to turn of the century oils and watercolours. In the study I found filing cabinets, bookshelves and a massive desk topped with scuffed, ink-stained leather. A computer crouched cold and mute on a portable stand. Neither room had been disturbed. They might have witnessed nothing more violent than a sneeze.

That's when I found the money. As I remember it, I noticed a gap at the top of the desk drawer and eased it further open with my pen. The money was fanned out over the surface of a writing pad as if it had been tossed in there carelessly. I looked, touched, gathered it up, I don't know why. A hundred and fifty dollars in twenties and fifties. Not enough to wonder at.

'No-one to see, Mr Niall. No-one to know.'

Vestey's voice was low and goading but somehow a chill came off it. I didn't move. He approached me silently, smiling a little. He stopped. We looked at the money. 'Neither of us earns much. The job is thankless. Come on, sport, what do you say?'

He reached out and took a fifty-dollar note. He folded it, never taking his eyes off my face, and slipped it into my top pocket. 'We could do ourselves a favour,' he said.

I tried to read him. Almost the first thing he'd ever said to me was, 'Give them the eye, Sunshine. Define them. Nail them.' He was doing it now. But it was more than that, somehow. He was making me his, I could feel it. A kind of aversion gripped me. 'Nup.' I took the note from my pocket, handed it to him and backed away. 'Nup.'

He half smiled. I watched him straighten the note, snap it with both hands, drop it in the drawer. 'Incident passed,' he said.

He continued my instruction back at 412 St Kilda Road.

'Always start with the victim, Mr Niall. Family. Known associates. Find me someone with motive, means and opportunity, the classic triumvirate. Don't look startled, Sunshine, I can read. Take motive.' He touched his forefinger. 'Revenge? Money? Sex? One of those. Means: the gun. If you can't find me a gun, find me someone with that signature, pow, in the back of the head. Opportunity. Find me someone who wasn't definitely somewhere else at the time.'

I began to drift. Vestey looked like a magazine cover, but he worked in a clutter of open drawers, overblown files and bent paper clips. His pinboard was famous. He never cleared it. Memos, cards and newspaper clippings were tacked on top of one another like dusty scales, all of it stirring like a forest whenever you walked past it.

'You with me so far?'

I straightened in my chair.

'Welcome back. Check parking infringement notices, cab companies, stolen car reports, the airlines. Talk to the neighbours. Take Mack with you to the funeral, get some snaps of the grieving mourners. Above all, concentrate on the Joyce woman. This smacks of a hired gun brought in to settle a grievance. I want to see every bit of information the moment it comes in. When you turn up someone who can help us with our enquiries, we pounce immediately, no farting around. We need evidence, Sunshine, physical evidence tying culprit to victim, culprit to scene. Motive, means and opportunity amount to fuck-all if you haven't got evidence.'

The voice wound through and around me. When the briefing was over I went upstairs, opened files on the victims, hassled the lab people, ground a phone into my ear, all the other things that Vestey had taught me to do. Every thirty minutes he asked me for an update. 'We're losing time, Mr Niall. Evidence. Find me evidence.' I felt that I was existing on a knife edge, that I'd miss something vital and let the culprit slip away.

Sally's report came in first: no fingerprints that shouldn't have been there. Later ballistics called to confirm Vestey's suspicions: no bullets, only unidentifiable fragments. The pathologist grumbled that he wasn't ready to file a report yet, but he was prepared to say that both women died at the same time and he had no reason to doubt the 7:03 time on Nina Galt's watch.

There was nothing in Nina Galt's background to excite attention. She'd been renting the converted stable for six months. Her job entailed regular lay-overs in various Ansett destinations, sometimes for days at a time. The last one had been Brisbane, hence the postcard.

So I concentrated on the Joyce woman, as Vestey advised, and by mid afternoon had come up with an inheritance and an estranged husband. The inheritance was Joyce Constructions, a shadowy outfit named in two royal commissions. The husband was a nasty piece of work called Liam Quinn, who'd worked his way up from union muscle to son-in-law. I pulled Quinn's file and found convictions for demanding money with menaces, assault and resisting arrest. His photograph showed vacant eyes in a good-looking face. Rose had been twenty when she married him. Eight years later, when her father died, she'd dropped Quinn's name, settled an allowance on him, and told him to get out. He lived in Fitzroy now. I rang the Fitzroy CIB, who told me that Quinn moved in a world defined by the TAB, corner pubs and his mother's house in Richmond. He often got drunkenly sentimental about his marriage, and he gambled, got into fights and was a general nuisance.

'I like it,' Vestey said. 'Let's go and shake his tree.'

Ten minutes later found me accelerating past a dozy tram in Brunswick Street.

'Steady on, Sunshine, set an example to the citizens. You were saying about Hobart?'

There was an unusual degree of tension in Vestey. It made me nervous, made me think I'd overlooked something. 'Quinn spent the weekend at the casino,' I said. 'On Sunday evening they barred him from the gaming rooms for being drunk and abusive. I asked them to check his phone account—he called Rose Joyce three times that night.'

Vestey was still tense, as if I should have told him all this before. 'Airlines?'

'Listed on Ansett's 4.50 to Melbourne on the day of the murder.

From memory the flight takes just over an hour, giving him plenty of time to pick up a gun and be in Hawthorn by 7.03.'

'His first big case, and the lad's on a roll,' Vestey said, settling back in his seat. He didn't speak again but sat concentrated and still. I had no idea what he was thinking or what he expected. His rank meant that he didn't have to do this sort of hackwork, but he was a coal-face cop, not a pen-pusher, and I also guessed that he didn't want me to stuff things up.

I slowed a block short of Quinn's but Vestey told me to keep going. 'Right outside the front door, Sunshine, large as life.' He'd become hard and sharp again. 'It brings on the attitude. Have I explained the attitude? Defiance, the sulks, resentment, sometimes all three at once. You'll see what I mean. You take the front. Give me a minute, then knock. If he comes out shooting, you know what to do.'

Quinn's house was the kind of two-storey glass and cement-brick structure that gets called a townhouse in the brochures. I contemplated the tasteless front door while Vestey went around to the back of the house. I pushed the buzzer, waited, pushed it again. I pounded on the door with my fist.

I was stepping back to look up at the upstairs windows when I heard the first shot. It was the second shot that got me running.

I rounded the corner and paused, upholstering the .38 I'd signed out before we left St Kilda Road. It was all sundeck and glass at the back of the house. The sliding glass door was open and I had a clear view across the kitchen to the bottom step of a staircase showing through an archway at the other end. Vestey stood a short distance from the archway. He was half crouched with his back to me, tensely regarding a body sprawled at the base of the stairs. As I watched, he straightened, stepped past the body and darted a quick look up the stairs. Apparently satisfied, he began to climb them, his gun extended.

It hadn't occurred to me that Quinn might have friends there. I went in fast and low, through the archway, and into each of the ground floor rooms. Nothing.

I returned to the body. I could see that it was Quinn. He wore underpants and needed a shave. I stood back, trying to work it out. There was a gouge in the wallpaper near my head. Vestey's first shot had missed. I wondered how he was going to justify this. I wondered what he'd want me to tell the board of inquiry. I could hear his voice winding through me.

That's when I spotted the gun. Quinn had dropped it in a patch of dustballs and shadows at the base of the stairs. It was a little Colt, a .22 revolver, the kind of gun you'd use if you wanted a quiet, clean killing.

'As I told you,' Vestey said, coming down the stairs. 'The bad guys are dumb.'

In the days that followed, Vestey rode high at 412, despite his aloofness. Even I earned a couple of friendly winks in the corridors.

But I was worried sick. There was an outcry in the civil liberties camp, Quinn's mother and brothers cried 'set-up', and internal affairs kept going over my statement with me. There were TV cameras, abusive phone calls, my name in the paper for days at a time.

I needn't have worried, though. Vestey had commendations a mile long, the gun was real and loaded with hollow-points, and Liam Quinn was the prime suspect in a double murder inquiry. We came out of it with a pat on the back.

Typically, Vestey had no thanks for anyone. 'Police culture, my son. Take a group of unimaginative, undereducated men, give them a job that sets them apart from society, make them feel overworked and undervalued, and you can rely on them to stonewall and close ranks when the outside world gets too nosy.'

I couldn't work him out. I knew all about feeling different, undervalued, I felt it every time I walked down the street. I liked the idea of a police culture, even if bad cops did get protected sometimes. I concluded that Vestey had a kind of puritan's distaste for excess, deviance, manipulation and dishonesty of any kind. He must have been offended every minute of every day. It made me wonder if he had a threshold.

Life went on. We still had to prepare for the coronial inquiry. 'I don't want any "death at the hands of a person or persons unknown" about this one, Sunshine,' Vestey told me. 'This isn't going to be another unsolved mystery for a self-ordering society, a juicy story for the daily rags. We can lay this one on Quinn. I want a solid, clear-cut submission, no fuck-ups.'

'Yes, sir.'

So I went back over the material step by step, extracting the relevant evidence from the mass of detail, constructing a character and motive profile of Liam Quinn, building a logical case. It was meticulous, satisfying, calming work. I double-checked everything: the physical evidence; Quinn's movements; his state of mind in the period prior to the murders.

I came unstuck with the airline. It was the fiftieth call of the day and I wasn't in the mood for mistakes. 'How could it touch down at 6.55 if it left at 4.50 and it's only a one-hour flight? Check again.'

'I have checked, sir,' the Ansett clerk said. 'It's all to do with putting the clocks forward. Tasmania was two weeks behind the eastern states in putting their clocks forward. They're synchronised now, though.'

I went cold. 'He has to collect his luggage, get home, get a gun, get to her place. No way could he have shot her.'

'Sir?'

'Never mind.'

I hung up.

For some reason then I thought of the mother. After the shooting of her son, Bridie Quinn went on every current affairs programme. Everyone at 412 mocked her, and Vestey had things to say about Irish clannishness, said because I was Irish I'd know what happens to the truth when mother love is involved, yet I'd been impressed by the woman. It wasn't only her singular and unapologetic grief, it was her absolute conviction that her son was innocent. 'Liam Michael,' she said, 'would do a lot of things but he wouldn't do this.'

The thing is, it took me a while to think clearly. My first instinct was for self preservation. I didn't know how I was going to explain my carelessness to Vestey. I could hear his voice peeling layers off me until I was worse than nothing in his eyes, a slapdash cop who couldn't get his facts straight. It didn't make it any better when I thought more about it and realised an innocent man had been shot. The hassle was Vestey's but I was implicated in it.

That brought me by degrees to thinking about Liam Quinn, his mother and her grief and vehemence, the way she spoke about him in the present tense: 'My boy doesn't use guns. He might punch someone, but he doesn't use guns. He's been set up.'

It's not that difficult for a policeman to come by an unlicensed gun. Vestey could've been holding on to it for years. But I needed evidence and I found it in the proof-sheets at the *Herald-Sun*'s photo library. The front page photograph was no help—Vestey is obscuring the table on which the amnesty guns are displayed—but the photographer had shot two rolls of film that day. Several of the photographs clearly show four .22 pistols among the handguns. The guns were melted down several days ago, Vestey's orders, but I've checked the paperwork. It lists three .22 handguns destroyed, not four.

For a while I thought Vestey may have intended to replace the gun after he'd used it. He knew it would be destroyed and there was no ballistics evidence to link it to the murders. He may have hoped the murders would remain unsolved—explained as someone settling an old grievance against the Joyce family, perhaps—but when he saw that my inquiries were leading me to Quinn, he took the opportunity to retrieve the gun and plant it by Quinn's body.

But Vestey's not the sort to improvise like that. I remember the way he guided me through the investigation, pointing me where he wanted me to go. I think he had Quinn marked for the murders all along. He simply waited until all the factors were right. The one thing he hadn't anticipated was Quinn's trip to Hobart. I remember Vestey's anxiety about it, and the flight times, and the way he relaxed when the timing seemed to fit.

I don't mind admitting that I feel spooked now. It's like I'm being watched, like footsteps are behind me only there's no-one there. I don't know whom to approach with all this. I don't know who'll listen.

And until a moment ago I couldn't even tie Vestey to the women. I couldn't see why he wanted Rose Joyce dead unless she was very bent and he'd turned vigilante, and that didn't seem likely.

Not Rose Joyce.

That's how he wanted us to read it.

Nina Galt.

The evidence has been here all the time—a dusty postcard, curling at the edges, all but obscured under the yellowing clippings and notices on Vestey's pinboard. Anyone would have forgotten they had it there. I wouldn't have looked twice at it myself if I hadn't noticed a red ME scrawled in the sky above the harbour, a red arrow isolating a tiny figure on the Opera House steps. She'd sent him the card two years ago. It doesn't take two years to fall out of love with one person and in love with another. It doesn't take two years to learn how to hate, either. Vestey has a lifetime of hate behind him.

Janette Turner Hospital was born in Melbourne in 1942. Her family moved to Brisbane when she was seven. She now divides her year between Australia, Canada and Boston. She is Adjunct Professor of English at La Trobe University and also at the University of Ottawa. She is frequently writer-in-residence at MIT Boston. She has won a number of international awards for her novels and short stories; her most recent publication in Australia is *Isobars*, a collection of stories.

Janette Turner Hospital
A Corpse At The Opera House

A body lay on the steps.

From the distance, Dennis assumed that something had fallen into the water—a hat perhaps, or a scarf—and someone was reaching for it, ankles hooked around iron railing and concrete socket. Otherwise, unaccountably, the figure was engaged in a slow head-first slide into the harbour. Dennis kept walking, though walking into the wind was difficult, and though, curiously, the body on the steps never seemed to get any closer. Of course that was nonsense; or else it was a spatial illusion cast by the deserted stretches of concrete and water and by the grey dawn light. Then suddenly he was close enough to see one shoulder jutting upwards like a stuck kite, its arm awkward. The other arm, the right arm, hung forward and down across the steps, reaching, its hand trailing in water.

Instantly Dennis knew whose arm it was.

Even before he saw the small silver rose lying on the step beside the head, he knew. He felt stunned and dizzy and ill, and yet he felt simultaneously that he had come upon some dreaded inevitability. *So this is it, then*, he thought, and nausea lapped at his edges and moved the body slightly and slapped against the concrete abutment.

It seemed to him now that he had known from the second he glimpsed the body in the distance, and its staying in the distance had been an avoidance trick of his mind. It seemed to him that he must have known before he set out on his walk. Yes. He thought he must have. And yet he stood there transfixed, ill, the Opera House behind him, the first ferry of the day sluicing its way out to Manly. He watched the ferry wake catch the forearm and the pale fingers and lift them, play with them, bounce them, toss them up and down twice, lay them to rest again across the bottom step. The hand had a life of its own.

Dennis couldn't move. It was only the fifth time he had seen her. *The bastard!* he thought. *He's done it. He's actually done it.*

Then it occurred to him with sudden dread: *They'll think I did it.*

He turned to run but the wind was against him, the ferry wakes were against him, the tide was against him, there was something viscous and weighty in the air, there was something wrong with his muscles, there was something malfunctioning, some fuse had blown in his nervous system, he couldn't move, he couldn't breathe, he woke with a cry and clutched at his thudding heart.

Oh God, he thought. Oh God, thank God, a dream.

Just the same. Something *was* going to happen, he knew it.

But who could one tell?

And what would one say?

Excuse me, officer, I have this intense premonition, this certainty . . . No.

Officer, I can hear a murder approaching on burning cat feet, but I'm not quite sure who the killer is. Or who the victim will be.

The dream was only his fifth sighting of her, though he had begun to notice her name all over the place. *Lilian's,* he saw on a bar tucked in between two office buildings in Regent Street. *Lilian's Lingerie,* he saw in a shop window, and he stopped to stare in at silk underthings and drifts of intimate lace. *Vote Lilian* he read on a poster over a bin of student newspapers at the university. He turned back, startled, to pick up a copy, but it was a different Lilian. The student elections had nothing to do with her. With his Lilian. With Henry's Lilian.

The first time he had seen her—or rather, the first time he had been *conscious* of seeing her—had been in the hallway outside his office at the university. He collided with her. She was just coming out of Henry's door, as a matter of fact, and instantly, because of a certain aura of agitation and distress that she gave off, Dennis sensed that the merry-go-round was going round on the old go-around, *hey ho,* that green and lush and endless-as-ever grew the rushes-O, but why did the sweet green girls never learn-O, what kept them stepping to the same old Misery Rag?

Why, he wondered, didn't they drop out of the dance?

'You dropped something,' Dennis said.

'Pardon?' The young woman turned back. Her cheeks were flushed. She stared blankly at Dennis, and he handed her, without looking at it, the letter that had slipped from one of the folders in her arms.

'Oh,' she said, blinking. 'Oh my God. Thank you.' She focused on him then, making a clear effort to concentrate, and said with a rush of words and more gratitude than the slight occasion seemed to warrant: 'Thank you very much. It's very kind of you. Oh God, of all the things to drop. How can I thank you?'

How does Henry do it? Dennis wondered, mesmerised. Where does he find them? Does he have some private referral service that scans the incoming student population for the most delicately formed translucent faces? What do they see in him? What *do* they see in him? Dennis had a fleeting image of himself as the kind of man (a Henry kind of man) who could answer a green girl's rhetorical question lightly and urbanely. How about letting me buy you a drink? he might say with a quirky smile and a Henry-like lift of one eyebrow.

'Well,' she said. 'Well, I don't know, I'm in a bit of a state at the moment, I'm afraid. Look, I'm really terrifically grateful for your . . . but I don't think I'd be . . . I don't think I'm much of a . . . I'd be lousy company, to tell you the truth.'

Good God. He'd *said* it. With totally uncharacteristic and involuntary recklessness, he'd *said* it.

'But, ah . . . if I could postpone . . . ?' she wondered. There was a flighty nervous edge to her voice.

He focused on the little silver pendant—a stemmed rose—that hung between her breasts.

'Till next week then,' he said lightly, astonishing himself. He could feel his heart jumping around like a chook in a sack. 'Same time, same place, the chips will be called in. How's that?'

She laughed, then bit her lip, then covered her face with one hand. 'Same place, no. Believe me, no.' She leaned her back against the wall and closed her eyes. 'I don't believe this,' she said. 'I don't believe it. Talk about suckers.' (Him? Herself?) She shook her head, giving up. 'Uh . . . look . . . ' She remembered she owed him something, she was under some sort of obligation. 'Um, I work part-time as a waitress at the Opera House. If you want to . . . The main restaurant. There's a lounge bar at one side. If you want to drop in?'

He could tell she hardly knew what she was saying, that she didn't know how she'd got herself into this, stuck with him.

'Listen,' he said, mortified. 'For heaven's sake, I was joking. I don't want to have a drink with you.'

'Oh,' she said in a small voice.

'What I mean is, you don't owe me a thing.' She pressed her lips together and he thought she might be going to cry, oh no that was silly, students these days were about as likely to cry as to wear bone corsets, but nevertheless he felt an urge—almost, but not quite, as great as his ineptness—to offer her a kleenex, a shoulder, to touch her cheek. He rushed into words. 'Of course, I'd be *delighted* to have a drink with you, delighted, I just don't want you to think, you know . . . ' And he floundered on, *ridiculous, not obligated, think nothing of it*, rhubarb, rhubarb.

'No, really, I'm very grateful,' she said. 'You don't know how rare decency is these days, you don't know how . . . Next Wednesday, okay? Ask for Lilian.'

'Ah Lilian.' Henry said, opening the door, startling them. 'Still here?'

'No,' she said coolly. She turned and walked down the hallway, head high.

'Great presence, eh?' Henry grinned. 'Silly girl. Dennis, me lad, you ready for squash?'

Dennis raised his gym bag.

'Good, good,' Henry said. 'Just got to lace my Adidas on. Come in.'

Dennis watched Henry sprinkle deodorant powder into his court shoes, then pull the criss-crossed laces loose all the way down. He stuffed his feet into the shoes and tightened the laces, hole by hole, intently. 'Lilian in one of your classes too?' he asked.

'No,' Dennis said.

'But you know her?'

'Yes,' Dennis said, for reasons unknown and unpremeditated.

'Troublemaker. Have to keep a wary eye.' Henry finished lacing his shoes and stood up and bounced lightly on the balls of his feet. 'Very bright but nervy, the worst combination.' He pulled his squash racquet from a cupboard, swept it across air, and smacked it against his left palm. 'Of course, in the short run, there are few things as irresistible as a neurotic woman, don't you agree?' He swept the racquet back through air, and forward again, to a feather landing on his fingertips. 'That hum like a high tension wire, that febrile possessiveness, *mmmm*'—he trampolined the grid of strings appreciatively off his crotch—'nothing like it. Trouble is, they never know when enough's enough.'

Dennis said nothing.

'I swear, they get more demanding every year.' Henry bounced the racquet lightly off Dennis's stomach. 'You be careful now, Dennis me lad, or she'll eat you for breakfast.'

At the door to the gym, he said, 'They expect too much. They expect way too bloody much.'

Sharon, Henry's wife, called the very next day. 'Hi,' she said huskily.

'Hi,' Dennis said.

'Haven't seen you for *ages*. Miss me?'

Dennis said nothing.

'Poor Dennis,' she said. 'Poor darling. How *are* you?'

'I'm fine. And you?'

'Oh well, can't complain. Henry's first is being difficult again, so what's new? Otherwise, I'm terrific.'

'Good. That's good.'

'The girls are starting soccer,' she said brightly. 'Henry insists. Little liberated women, he says. He wants them to be all-rounders like him.'

'Hmm,' Dennis said. 'That's great.'

'And Louise was over last night with that new boyfriend, I suppose she told you? My gosh, I haven't seen you since the dinner for her twenty-first, lemme see, six weeks ago?'

'Four.'

'What? It can't be, oh God you're right, I can't believe it, it seems *ages*, I don't know where the time goes.' And Sharon chatted on brightly of this and that while Dennis, waiting for her to get to the main and sorrowing point, asked himself why he fell so constantly and so passively into this role. Habit mainly, he supposed. Familiar structure after chaos, the comfortable old niches, all that. And the fact that he was so good at it, an expert, a veteran sorrower.

'Dennis?'

'Yes, that's great,' he said. 'Wonderful.'

'You weren't listening.'

'Sorry. Mind wandered for a minute maybe.'

'Um, Dennis?' She dropped her voice into the come-hither registers. 'Hmm?'

'Can we have lunch?'

'Something wrong?'

'Well . . . ' She sighed. 'At squash last night. Did Henry, you know
. . . Did you notice anything?'

'How d'you mean?'

'Well, was he . . . *different*? Preoccupied or anything?'

'Nothing out of the ordinary,' Dennis said.

'I think he's having an affair.'

'I wouldn't worry about it, Sharon,' Dennis said.

'You don't think so?'

'I'm sure so.'

'I think you're wrong,' Sharon said. 'I don't know if I can cope
anymore, Dennis. I think this is serious, there've been little signs for
months. Last week I warned him that if anything was going on again,
I'd reached my limit. I'd leave and take the kids and kick up a fuss
that'd make the History Department scandal look like a church
service. *Then* what would happen to his chance of being dean?'

'Well,' Dennis said drily. 'He got the message. You can take it from
me, it's over.'

She bridled. 'You mean you *knew*? You mean people *know*?'

'No, no, I don't mean that. I mean it's an instinct I have, I've
known him so long—'

'Oh yes,' she said bitterly. 'We know where your instincts got *you*.
Fat lot of help your instincts—'

'Believe me, Sharon. In this instance, you've got nothing to worry
about.'

'You *did* know. I hate you,' she said. She slammed the receiver
down, but the phone rang again before he reached his kitchen door.

'You knew,' Sharon accused bitterly. 'And you didn't tell me. I
can't *believe* you, Dennis, I can't believe you, I really and truly can't
believe you. You take my breath away. I can promise you, I won't
take things lying down the way you did.'

'No,' he said mildly. 'I can't imagine you taking things lying down.'

'People *know*, don't they? I'm the joke of the Economics Department, I'm pitied by the whole Economics Department, right?'

'I wouldn't say that. No. Not at all.'

'A womaniser, a pants man, is that what they say? All those
undergraduate girls pitying me, all those bitchy career women snick-
ering behind my back, all those rotten little protégées and graduate
students tut-tutting, "His wife's such a *touchy* woman . . . " Oh, I
know the kind of thing they'll be saying, I'll give them *touchy*, right
up their tight little—'

'Sharon, for heaven's sake, you're getting all worked up over—'

'Believe me, Dennis, if you had any idea of half the things I heard about *you* after we split, you'd never—'

'No doubt,' he said drily.

'People *talk*, Dennis.'

'They do, yes.'

'They talk about me, don't they?'

'I never pay attention to talk.'

'But they *know*, don't they?'

Dennis was silent.

'I'll kill him,' she said, and slammed down the phone. It rang again in exactly ten seconds. 'Who is she?' Sharon asked.

'I'm afraid I can't help you there,' Dennis said.

'I'll kill him. I swear I'll kill him.'

Dennis said mildly, 'Do you want to have lunch first? Or after?'

'Who is she?'

'Sharon, anything I think I know is mere instinct, I don't have two facts to rub—'

'Okay,' she said. 'Lunch tomorrow. You can tell me everything you think you know then. I'll pick you up.'

'I brought the photographs of Louise's party,' Dennis said. 'Just got them back. Haven't looked at them yet myself.'

Sharon brushed them aside. Her eyes were puffy. 'I was lying awake last night,' she said, 'waiting for Henry to come in, and I thought, well this is it, I've got my comeuppance, they'll all be gloating behind their hands and they're right. I had it coming. I made the wrong choice ten years ago, I should've stayed married to Dennis. Then I started to laugh. I was crying, and I actually started to laugh, because I thought, I *have* stayed married to Dennis, Dennis and I have always been faithful to each other, isn't that crazy?' She ran her finger across the back of his hand. 'Dear Dennis,' she said.

He took her hand in his and brought it up to his lips. Yes, it was nice to be needed, to have this ongoing role.

'I'm a shit, Dennis,' she said. 'And so's Henry. I don't know how you can stand us.'

'Oh I don't know,' he said. 'We're all a pretty sorry lot, when you get down to it. And you've got the little girls to worry about.'

'Do you really think it's nothing again?' she asked plaintively.

'I do.' Dennis moved his wineglass in slow soothing ellipses on the tablecloth, rolling the stem up and down the soft inner skin of Sharon's forearm.

'What time did you leave the gym?'

'Oh, around ten, I think,' Dennis said.

'But he didn't get in till two in the morning, he said he was marking papers.'

Dennis's wineglass paused. 'We do have to get our mark sheets in this week,' he said.

'I found a letter.'

'Students get crushes,' Dennis shrugged. 'Professors get letters . . . '

'No, I mean a letter *he* wrote.' Sharon's fingers played jerkily with her serviette. 'It said . . . it said . . . ' *Dear lavish, corrosive, coruscating, and lustrous L.* How could she repeat such words? How could she forgive such silly, such alliterative passion? 'That's why I think you're wrong, because he's never, not before this . . . '

'Obviously he didn't send it,' Dennis pointed out.

'It was a rough draft,' she said. 'It had lines crossed out. It's so reckless, isn't it, to put something in writing?' Her voice trembled a little. 'He's never done that before.'

He wanted it found, Dennis thought. There was nothing reckless about Henry, nothing. Never. He wanted the letter found.

Mmmm, that febrile possessiveness . . .

'So I told him,' Sharon said. 'I'd give him twenty-four hours to end it. If I found he had any contact whatsoever after that, I'd go to the vice-chancellor.'

'Well, he's done it,' Dennis said. 'Cast her into outer darkness, and all that.'

'Who was she?'

'That's not how I know,' Dennis said quickly. 'There was, uh, a phone call, just before we left for squash.' He was not used to lying, not good at it, but the habit of not causing pain ran deeper, and he knew that the meticulously detailed lie was the most convincing. 'Henry kept rolling his eyes at me while this other person talked.' He mimicked this, and Sharon's face lifted, softened, at the vision of some brazen little trollop of a student mocked. 'I could tell it was a woman's voice, a girl's voice, and he listened for a minute and said goodbye and hung up, and then he said to me: *Silly girl. They expect too much.*' This was not a lie, Dennis thought, not really; it was more what you might call a transposed truth. 'So you see. A little flash in the pan, over and done with.'

'Oh Dennis. You're sure?'

'Positive.'

'Do you know who she was?'

'Who they are is irrelevant, Sharon. They never mean anything.'
It's you, he might have reminded her, for whom Henry waded through
the wreckage of two marriages, several kids' lives.

'Dear Dennis,' she said. 'What would I do without you?' She sighed
and reached for the packet of photographs beside her plate and began
shuffling through the prints. 'Oh Louise did look lovely in that blue
dress,' she said. 'She looks so happy. We must have done something
right, mustn't we?' She passed the photographs on to Dennis one by
one. 'Oh, don't the little ones look cute? This is a nice one of you
and Henry.' She passed it on. 'My two favourite men,' she smiled. 'It
says something, don't you think? about the two of us, about you and
me, that we . . . I mean, when you consider the way Henry and his
first, after all these years . . . ' She shook her head. 'Like circling
tigers still, the pair of them. Do you know, I sometimes think she
will murder him. *He* certainly thinks so. He thinks she'd *like* to,
anyway.' She leaned across and kissed Dennis lightly on the cheek.
'I do love you, Dennis. You're so *civilised.* And I do know you're right.
I do know they mean nothing, his flings.'

In the photograph which she handed him they were all sitting at
a table in the Opera House restaurant, the lights of the bridge visible
through the glass windows behind them. His daughter—his and
Sharon's daughter—was cutting through the silver 21 on the cake
and looked very happy, her new boyfriend at her side. The glowing
faces of the little girls—Sharon's and Dennis's little girls—bobbed
above the silverware like pale moons. Henry's daughters from his first
marriage were mercifully absent.

'They still hate me,' Sharon said. 'They side with their mother.
Sometimes I think Dennis'll murder *her.*'

'That's ridiculous, Sharon.'

'He'd like to, anyway. So would I, half the time. Oh, look at this
one,' she said fondly. 'I have to admit, he does look the perfect image
of the family man. He's *beaming.*'

Dennis reached for beaming Henry, smiled at the picture, choked
on a mouthful of wine, coughed, knocked his glass and the photograph
off the table.

'Dennis, for heaven's sake, what . . . ?'

I took this photograph, he thought, dazed.

Under cover of the linen tablecloth folds, he stared again at beaming Henry. Facing the camera, facing Dennis-the-photographer, Henry and Sharon leaned toward each other, their heads touching in a joyfully intimate moment. Henry beamed. Behind him, a waitress was balancing a tray over her left shoulder and reaching in to pick up his glass. It was, of course, an optical illusion, but it almost seemed as though the waitress was murmuring in Henry's ear, curving over him, sliding her right arm along his coat sleeve the way a silk skirt might slither against a thigh—except that it didn't count. As a waitress, the girl was invisible.

Dennis stared at the delicate cheekbones, the downward curve of the lashes, the masses of loose auburn curls that fell over the waitress's shoulders.

He could not believe he had taken the photograph. That he had seen her and not *seen* her. That he had looked right at her and not been conscious of her.

I met her before I met her, he thought dazed. The first time I saw her was the second time. Extraordinary.

'Can I have that one?' Sharon asked.

Dennis felt strangely euphoric. It was so bizarre. It had to be a sign of some kind, it had to mean something. He thought that this was patently ridiculous, but he believed it just the same.

'Wake up, Australia,' Sharon teased. She leaned over and snapped her fingers.

But did it mean that Lilian took on value for him because Henry had a claim on her? If she'd been coming out of anyone else's door, would he have found her so mesmerising? Would he have noticed her? Was it perhaps the *collision* that did the trick, some chemistry of body contact? For that matter, how was it that he hadn't been aware of her before, at the weekly colloquia with the graduate students? Was it true, as Sharon said, as Henry said, that he went around blind? That he lived with his head in the ground?

'*Dennis!*'

'What?' He blinked. 'Sorry, what did you—?'

Sharon laughed. 'I said, can I have that one? The one with just me and Henry in it, playing lovebirds.'

Dennis tucked it into his pocket. 'I'll have a copy made for you,' he promised.

'I like this one too,' she said, handing him another of Henry, alone this time, staring at something across the room. 'He's miles away,' she said fondly. She looked vaguely past Dennis who looked at the photograph. 'But Dennis, why did he stay out till two last night?'

Yes, why? he wondered.

'*Dennis!*'

'Oh I don't know, Sharon. Marking papers, I expect, just as he said.'

'You've *ripped* it.'

'What?' He looked at the photograph and was startled to see that he had torn it in two, right across Henry's face.

'You forgot,' Dennis said. His tone acknowledged the inevitability of this, the naturalness of it, the idiocy of his coming.

'No, I didn't,' Lilian protested, blushing. 'Look, I have to . . . I'll be back in a jiff.' She moved off with a tray full of Bloody Marys, their celery sticks branching from frosted glass like small trees. 'Okay, I forgot it was *today*,' she admitted sheepishly, several orders and trayloads later, 'but I didn't forget you were going to drop in for a drink. I didn't forget *you*. I didn't forget you picked up the registration card.'

'Registration card?'

'In the envelope, remember? Look, I have to—Trish, she's the next shift, phoned to say she'd be an hour late and could I cover. I should be free in another fifteen minutes though, if you can wait.'

He waited comfortably enough, sipping a scotch, watching her, until she joined him. Then he was tongue-tied.

'So,' she said awkwardly.

'So,' he said. His eyes rested on the silver rose pendant.

'From my parents. My twenty-first,' she said, playing with it self-consciously, sliding the charm back and forth along its chain with a thin zipper sound. She began tearing a coaster into a spiral rind of padded paper, watching her handiwork intently. 'It didn't do any good anyway,' she said, 'snitching the registration card. Well, not snitching. It *was* my card.' Her hands paused in their production of paper snake, and her right hand went to her throat, and the silver rose buzzed angrily on its track. 'It was *my* bloody card after all. I suppose you're going?'

He frowned. 'Going where?'

'Adelaide.'

'Adelaide? Oh, the conference. Yes. I'm giving a paper.'

'I was going to give one too,' she said. She was tearing the coaster again. 'The germ of my PhD thesis. At least, I hope it turns out to be the germ. I'm still at the poking around stage.'

'You changed your mind?'

'It got changed for me.' The spiral snake of paper bucked and tore itself off, the pendant rose zigzagged with its silvery ratchet sound, zigzag, zigzag, she picked up the remains of the paper coaster, she began tearing again very vehemently. 'We're such idiots, we're such incredible idiots. It's not as though we don't hear rumours. We just never believe it's going to happen to us.'

'Who's "us"?'

'Women.'

'Ah,' Dennis said. 'Is Henry your supervisor?'

'Was.' She kept tearing, but the paper rind grew wider and thicker. 'It makes me so furious, playing fast and loose with my program, with my career, just because . . . Oh, what am I doing, talking to you? Bad taste, poor choice, conflict of interest, the works. You're probably personal friends, for God's sake.'

'No,' Dennis said forcefully, and then, embarrassed, amended: 'Well, you know. In a sense, I suppose. Over the years, it's inevitable.'

She shrugged and raised her glass. 'Oh well. Learning the hard way, and all that.' She drank a rather reckless amount in one long glug. 'My own stupid fault, no doubt.' But a flash of anger crossed her face. 'It's cancelling my paper that really takes my breath away, cancelling my *registration* even. I can't, I just can't . . . I would never have believed he'd do that. I still can't believe it.' She shook her head. 'I was so stunned when he said it wasn't good enough to present. I mean, he'd seen the early drafts, he'd raved about them, it just didn't make sense. And so I asked him what he thought I needed to do, and he said withdraw from the conference. I was so . . . I couldn't . . . Her hands moved about, searching for words, and gave up. 'I could see the registration envelopes, his and mine, on his desk. He was handling everything, you see, we were going to . . . '

She was replaying something, seeing someone turn his back, walk to the window. *Taking advantage of our . . . inappropriate . . .* His back to her. *Insufficient academic calibre . . . Time to call a halt.* She felt the dizziness again. Was she brilliant (last week's assessment) or no good at all? She saw the registration envelopes on the desk, she saw his back over by the window. She picked up her envelope and walked out.

'He was handling, you said . . . ?' Dennis prompted.

'And then of all the things to drop! Anyway, it didn't do me any good. I got a letter from the steering committee regretting I'd cancelled. Some post-doc from Perth's taking my place, a woman, *surprise surprise*, someone he's been doing research with.' She drained her glass. 'You think you know someone intimately,' she said, still dazed, 'and you find out you don't know them at all. Not at all. You don't even recognise them.'

'Yes, that happens,' Dennis said.

'I try to stay angry,' she said. 'It hurts less.'

A thought suddenly articulated itself in Dennis's mind: *It depends on just how angry you are, and on how dangerous it might be to find out.*

The thought frightened him.

'Or slightly drunk,' she said. 'That definitely helps.'

He said, 'I'm afraid Henry is not a very, is not always . . . entirely honourable.'

She laughed. 'You can say that again. I can't say I wasn't warned, I can't say I hadn't heard the rumours.'

'But he can't cancel your paper without your consent. You can contact the steering committee.'

'Hah. I can just imagine where that will get me.'

'It will get you back on your panel in Adelaide,' Dennis said.

'But it's too late. They've got someone else.'

'It's still worth a try. And if you're not reinstated, you must lodge a formal complaint with the department.'

She looked at him disbelievingly. 'You've got to be kidding.'

'Definitely not,' Dennis said. 'That's unethical behaviour, and there are guidelines.'

She found his naïveté both exasperating and endearing. 'You're nice,' she said gently, the way one might speak to a child, or as though the banal word *nice* designated something exotic and rare and dangerously innocent. 'But you haven't had much experience at being a woman in an Australian university.'

Dennis bridled. 'I do have experience with ethical codes. I do have exper—'

'A complaint would really finish me off,' she said. 'Spurned woman, hysterical student, the lot. I wouldn't have a leg to stand on.' She signalled Trish for more drinks, and gulped her second scotch greedily. 'The good old Sidney-Sparks-Orr-and-Susan-Kemp syndrome, remember? You may—though you probably won't—get him, but only by leaping into the bottomless pit yourself. I want my union card first, thank you. Don't you know that just last year, thirty-some bloody years later, Susan Kemp was denied re-entry at the University of Tasmania? And that was for a brilliant student, remember? No, thanks. I want my PhD before I make waves.'

The silver rose zithered crazily on its switchback track. 'We did have an affair, you see, me and Henry, and that means I have no rights at all.' She bit her lip. 'Oh it all started out very innocuously, course discussions, thesis discussions, the intellectual excitement, the debates . . . well, the mind's the sexiest organ, right? I never thought about where it was heading, it was like, oh I don't know, being caught in a rip-tide. I was on a sort of cerebral high, and he suggested I go to that conference at Armidale last term and *kaboom*, what can I say?' She knocked on her forehead, then opened her hand to show: nothing in there. 'And then he began phoning and writing these extravagant letters, it was a kind of frenzy.' She shivered. 'On both sides,' she said, shivering again. She drank some more. 'Well,'—she licked her index finger and made a mark on the air—'chalk up a lesson on the hard fact of power. I'll tell you one thing, though. I'm going to go to Adelaide anyway. Pay my own way, go as an observer. He just bloody well does *not* have the right to sabotage my intellectual life as well.'

As well, Dennis thought. Nevertheless, he felt full of optimism. Adelaide, he thought. That little restaurant right on the bank of the Torrens.

'Anyway. Enough of this morbid stuff.' She brushed it aside with the back of one hand. 'I'm still mentally inside the paper I'm no longer giving. What do *you* think is the dominant factor for Oz in Pacific trade? The fallout from supply-side economics, or Keating's—'

'Neither,' he said. 'It's the fact of Japan.'

'No,' she said. 'I disagree. It's not the *fact* of Japan. It's the *perception* of the fact of Japan. That's what my paper—'

'Nonsense,' Dennis said warmly. 'Take the car market here and in the States. Protectionism or no protectionism, co-production or no co-production, the simple truth is—'

'Oh shit,' she said. 'Heres comes Henry and his post-doc from Perth again. You know he did that last week, the jerk? The very same night, the two of them sat here drinking for hours. Trish was on too, thank God, so she served them. I wouldn't give him the satisfaction of a single glance at his table. Let's get out of here, quick.'

Crossing the room, she took Dennis's arm suddenly, warmly, and leaned in to murmur something in his ear.

Henry raised a surprised eyebrow. 'Dennis. Lilian,' he said, disconcerted.

'Henry.' Dennis nodded, and swept Lilian out through the door to the windy plaza.

She held his arm until they had moved beyond the reach of the windows, then dropped it. 'Sorry,' she said. 'I shouldn't have done that. A cheap theatrical trick.'

'That's all right,' Dennis said. He thought he could acquire quite a taste for cheap theatrical tricks.

She said restlessly: 'You interested in prowling along the covered walk for a bit?'

'Very.' They walked in a companionable way, chatting, arguing. Ferries passed and a night breeze scuffled off the water. She told a joke, he laughed. He thought that certain things were ordained in astonishing ways. If the first time you saw someone was actually the second time, it meant something. Especially if you had recorded that first time in all innocence and then found yourself carrying it about in your wallet. He saw the boardwalk curving seductively ahead across the three weeks to Adelaide and beyond, its niches bright with little way stations where candles flickered on tables-for-two and flagons of wine.

'We're so perverse, aren't we?' Lilian sighed. 'Human beings.'

'Oh, I don't know. Curious, certainly. Endlessly surprising.'

'That's for sure.' She laughed. 'That's for sure.'

She was silent for a long absorbed time. Dennis thought the bridge, the docks, the ferries, the moon on the water, had never looked so stunningly beautiful. 'Penny for them,' he said at last.

'Oh, perversity still. I was wondering how to account for . . . I mean, when you know someone is a complete jerk, when you know he has no integrity at all, how is it *possible* that you can still miss him?'

'Ah,' Dennis said, and all the candles in all the way stations went out at once. 'So if he changed his mind . . . ?'

'Oh no, I'd rather die. I just mean . . . the emotions are such shambling retarded beasts, aren't they?' She sighed. 'I mean, there's Henry Before, and Henry After, and they're two different people. I can't fit them together. I can't figure out where they join. I suppose I wish I'd wake up and find that Henry After was just a bad dream.'

217

'Yes,' Dennis said. 'I know that feeling.'

'But it won't happen,' she shrugged. 'So there it is.'

Dennis saw the candles relighting themselves one by one, he saw the intimate tables and the flagons of wine. He reached inside his coat pocket and touched the photograph. He smiled and took Lilian's arm.

At their weekly squash games, Dennis played for relaxation and pleasure. Henry played to win, and always did.

There was no such concept as the casual game with Henry. He played hard every time. The week following the encounter at the Opera House (there had been no comment made on either side all week), he played with particular ferocity.

Something curious had happened to Dennis. Instead of answering with his usual competent yet ultimately pliable game, he contested every point in a way that caught Henry off guard.

Henry was shocked. He vibrated. He twanged. He increased the swift and deadly accuracy of his game.

Dennis fought back, stroke by stroke. It was as though a new man had entered the peaceable envelope of his skin.

'Holy shit!' murmured a startled Chemistry lecturer, pausing in the gallery. 'What's got into those two?'

'Coronary occlusion about to occur,' someone offered. 'What odds am I given?'

Beyond the wet sweat of pain around his heart, in his muscles, in his head, Dennis sensed that he played to keep a long row of candles lit.

Henry won, but only just. He left abruptly, without saying a word. Dennis, his chest thumping and burning, leaned against the wall of the court until the red aura in his eyes went away. He breathed slowly and deeply. I won, he thought incongruously. He hummed Mozart as he showered. He hadn't seen Lilian since the walk around Circular Quay, but whatever was going to happen next would happen, he felt tranquil about it. He hadn't even asked for her address or phone number. But then he could always find her at the Opera House. And she knew where his office was. He walked through the city, seeing her name all over the place.

Sharon called the next day. 'Dennis,' she said huskily. 'You sly dog.'

'Hello, Sharon,' he said.

'You didn't tell me there was a woman on the scene, you secretive man. How can you be so rude to *me*? I'm hurt, Dennis.'

'I'd hardly call this a matter for a press release, Sharon.'

'Aha,' she said. 'But there *is* a woman in your life.'

'I hardly know how to answer you.'

'Well,' she said, 'that's not what I hear from Henry. It's all over the department, he says. He couldn't stop talking about it. In *public* together, he says. With a *student*. I'm surprised at you, Dennis, you know that's frowned on. Who is she?'

Dennis said nothing.

'The way Henry went on,' Sharon said, 'you'd almost think he was jealous. I get the impression she's gorgeous.'

'I find her attractive,' Dennis said drily. 'Naturally.'

'What a surprise you are, Dennis, you old roué. What's her name?'

'I thought Henry told all.'

'He doesn't know her name, he just recognised her as one of your students. Oh come on, Dennis, don't be mean, you can tell *me*. What is it?'

'It's Lilian,' he said, unable to resist the taste of her on his tongue.

'Lilian,' Sharon said. 'Lilian. Well, well,' *Dear lavish, corrosive, coruscating, and lustrous L . . .* 'What a sweet old-fashioned name.'

Dennis was amused. He knew that tone. Jealousy would not be the right word for it, however. A jarred sense of entitlement, perhaps; the instinctive raising of territorial hackles.

'Yes,' he said. 'It *is* a lovely name.' He thought suddenly that he would get her phone number from the departmental secretary and call her. 'Goodbye, Sharon,' he said.

At Lilian's number, later in the day, there was one of those damned answering machines. He didn't want to make a fool of himself, so hung up. He looked into the little cubby-holes where the graduate students had office space, but there was no sign of her. He wandered across to the courtyard cafeteria where they ate, and sat sipping abominable coffee and reading the *Sydney Morning Herald* for over an hour. No sign.

Back in the department, he passed Henry in the hallway. Henry seemed full of suppressed excitement. 'You've got Sharon all in a tizzy, Dennis,' he said jovially. 'I do believe she's jealous. She's got a bit of a possessive streak, our little Sharon, as well we know, eh mate? She likes to keep us all on a pretty short leash.' He laughed and went into his office.

A passing secretary rolled her eyes. 'He's acting really strange lately,' she said. 'I mean, we're talking *weird*.'

There was, Dennis noticed now, a sudden cold front, a fog of anxiety in the air. He tried to mark papers but couldn't concentrate. He taught a class, disastrously. He phoned Lilian's number again, got the answering machine, hung up. He phoned again and left a faltering message. He tripped over his words. He sounded like a stammering schoolboy. He went back to reading but couldn't sit still. There was nothing for it but to go for an early evening drink at the Opera House.

He felt nervous. Suppose he'd miscalculated? Suppose he'd completely misread the signs? Suppose he was going to make an idiot of himself?

Suppose he was going to feel pain?

He'd got out of the habit of feeling pain. He'd learned the knack of switching the pain track off.

Afterwards he realised they might have seen him coming, his body angled against the stiff wind that came off the water. He, of course, was blinded by the late afternoon sun off all the glass, the great white sails bouncing sunset at him. He was inside for several minutes, blinking, waiting for his eyes to adjust, before he saw them sitting together, Henry and Lilian, leaning across the small table, intense.

Probably they hadn't seen him. Probably they weren't aware of anything at all beyond themselves.

He did not feel or think anything except a colour. He felt a great pulsing, throbbing, beating *red*, thump thump thump, that filled his eyes and ran along his skin like fire. He lurched toward the door inside it, inside the colour, which moved with him like the rusty clouds that scud around Saturn. He tripped over someone's foot and murmured an apology and a voice hissed urgently: 'Dennis, we have to talk, we have to *do* something.' He tried to focus on the blurred red shape, a woman, someone faintly familiar, hunched into a table-for-one behind thick potted plants. He lurched on outside, into the wind, and the red after-image on his retina defined itself: *Sharon*. He had a fleeting moment of fascination at the idea of Sharon experiencing pain; real ungovernable pain.

Fortunately, he himself felt none.

Thank God for that, he told himself in the red fog of the covered walkway. Thank God, I don't feel any anger or any pain.

The walkway, unlit by a single candle, stretched endlessly on.

In the morning, very early, he walked through the gardens and past the white-sailed mausoleum, that desolate shrine to his silly hopes. He walked like a man possessed, although luckily he felt nothing more than mild embarrassment for his own stupidity. He walked along the harbour edge, along the steps, past Circular Quay, through the empty streets of The Rocks. Her name kept leaping out at him. *Lilian's. Lilian's Lingerie. Chez Lilian.* He had no idea how many bars and brasseries were on her side.

He walked and walked. He must have walked the entire day, or if not, whatever he had done with the day was a blank, because here he was letting himself into his office late at night. The building was quiet as a tomb, the blackness behind his door was palpable. He switched on his light and there was, *aghhh . . . !*

His cry was involuntary. There was something . . . there was this great untidy bulk on top of his . . . There was a body.

It lay across his desk leaking blood on the ungraded papers. Oh God, he thought. Oh God, they'll think I did it. They'll produce witnesses from the squash court, *palpable hostility* . . . He could see the bald spot where Henry always spray-lacquered the hair carefully across, he could see the blood he had often half-wanted to see, colonising his desk blotter with bright red asterisks, slowly spreading, filament by filament, hair-thin spike by spike. He couldn't move, he was going to vomit. *Sharon*, he realised. He would never have thought, he would never have actually believed. Oh Sharon, what inspired, what diabolically brilliant dual revenge! Because Dennis would be found guilty, he had no illusions about that. In fact, in fact, perhaps he *was* guilty. Why couldn't he remember what he had done all day, what did that mean?

But maybe it was Lilian?—because how could she have done that? How could she have gone running back? How could she have seen Henry again? How *could* she? There was Lilian Before and Lilian After, he couldn't join the two in his mind, he couldn't think what he would say to the police, he couldn't hear, but yes he could, he *could* hear the sirens already, he could feel himself lurching, falling, his hand groping to switch the bloody alarm clock off—

Oh God, thank God, a dream.

I'll die of an overdose of my own adrenalin, he thought, trembling. But something *was* going to happen, he knew it, and the alarm clock went on and on and on.

Because it wasn't the alarm clock, he at last, in agitated and befuddled state, sensed. It was the bloody phone that he was groping for in the early morning light.

'Dennis? I hope I'm not calling too early. I got your message on my answering machine.'

Lilian. Was he still asleep, still dreaming, or awake? He pinched himself. He saw the coloured pattern in his carpet, he saw his socks on the floor. Okay, awake. And Lilian on the other end of the line. But he didn't know whether he loved her or wished he had never bumped into her or hated her. He didn't know whether he should hang up with silent dignity, or yell *You fickle bitch*, or blurt . . . well, extravagant and passionate things.

'Dennis?'

'Yes. I'm here.'

'Dennis, it's Lilian. I'm . . . I'm frightened, Dennis. Can I talk to you?'

He said cautiously, neutrally: 'What's wrong?'

'Well, last night, while I was working, Henry came in. He was very strange, very intense, he was like an explosion waiting to go off.' She was talking very fast, in a high breathy way, as though she might not be allowed to finish in time. 'He said I had to sit down and talk to him *immediately*. I said I couldn't, I was working. And he said if I didn't I'd be sorry. He said it so . . . so *intensely*, I felt scared.'

'Yes?' Dennis said. He was blinking. He could just make out little flickerings of hope lighting up like candles along a shore.

'Well, at first he was . . . um, well, passionate. He said he was . . . well, he said lots of crazy things, he said he was going out of his mind but his wife was threatening chaos and he'd had to think and weigh costs and there were the children to consider and he . . . Well, he was more or less raving. Then he wanted me to come up to his beach cottage at Patonga for a week. He said he'd told his wife he was going there alone, to work on his Adelaide paper. He said that would give us time.'

Dennis waited, feeling nothing.

'I'm afraid I half wanted to,' she said nervously. 'Part of me did. But it was so scary, the way he was talking. I mean, he wanted us to leave *immediately*. Just like that. And so, he was so . . . and of course

I'm highly allergic to being hurt again, being made a fool of. Anyway, I managed to sound calm, at least I think so, a bit of a miracle, and I said no, it was out of the question.'

'Then it was like . . . it was Dr Jekyll and Mr Hyde, I was stunned. He said he'd heard I was going to Adelaide anyway. He said if I went, he could promise me I was finished. He said . . . what he said was: *If you go, that's it, your life's over.* I was stunned. I suppose he meant my academic life, well I *know* he meant that, but I . . . it was his *eyes.* Dennis, I was so scared, I stayed at Trish's last night.'

Dennis felt incongruously, deliriously happy. 'Lilian,' he said. He felt immensely strong, very wise, invulnerable, omnipotent, protective. 'Why don't you come over here? I'll make coffee, we can talk. You can stay here if you want. There's nothing he can do to you, you've got witnesses. I'll look after you, I'll take care of things.'

'Thanks, Dennis,' she said. 'I knew if I . . . I just had to talk to *someone,* and you were so . . . But the thing is . . . look, please don't think I'm rude, but I don't want to see anyone, I don't want to have anything to do with the university or anyone in it for a few weeks, it's all so ugly, I don't even know if I *ever* want . . . Right now, I feel I'd rather drive a truck for the rest of my life than have anything to do with academics.'

'Yes,' Dennis said, 'that's understandable. But you can't judge the whole—'

'The only thing I *am* going to do is go to Adelaide, because I refuse to give him the satisfaction, I refuse to meekly fold up my tent and crawl away. But till then, I just want to disappear. I've got a friend with a flat in Collaroy and she's away for a few weeks so I can have the place to myself. I'll just hole up there till a day or so before Adelaide.'

He said urgently: 'Can't I see you before you go? I could come over.'

'I'm going straight back to Trish's,' she said. 'I just came to get my stuff and my messages. I don't want to stay around here because he's got a key, you see. From . . . from happier times.'

'Yes, I see.' He felt a swooping rush of anger to know that Henry was familiar with intimate space that he, Dennis, had never penetrated. That Henry had stepped inside the delicate shell of her life, a bull in a china shop. 'But couldn't I see you at Trish's place? Or meet you somewhere for—?'

'Dennis, please don't think I'm rude, I just . . . I really don't want to see anyone.'

'Yes, I . . . so what will you do?'

'I'll stay with Trish tonight, and I'll take the ferry and the bus up to Collaroy first thing tomorrow. But I'll see you in Adelaide, okay?'

'Okay,' he said reluctantly. 'Take care of yourself, Lilian. If you want to call at any time—'

'Thanks, Dennis,' she said. 'You're such a *good* person, such a *gentle* . . . You're a gentleman, a true *gentleman.*'

But he thought, ungently and deviously: she will take the ferry to Manly, then the bus from the Manly Corso.

He thought that he would go to Circular Quay very early in the morning and wait at the ferry dock till she appeared; perhaps he would ride to Manly with her, if that didn't upset her; but at least he would see her, speak to her.

He took out the photograph and looked at it: Henry and Sharon, with Lilian behind and between, and Dennis, the unseen photographer, seeing all. Or *not* seeing all, in fact. Not then. Not seeing anything. How odd it was that he had only seen her four times, and that the first time didn't count because he hadn't known he was looking at her. In another sense, of course, the first time counted for everything.

It was still not quite light, he had nearly an hour before the earliest ferry would leave, he just wanted to walk, he liked this dawn solitude, he needed it. It was while he was still under the covered walkway, the Opera House sails flashing sunrise, that he saw the two figures, male and female, on the great concrete plaza. They stood very near the steps to the water.

He didn't want to proceed. He also wanted to run, to reach her in time, to stop whatever was about to happen from happening. But now the morning fog off the water intervened and he couldn't see them. He walked faster. There was no-one in sight. Perhaps in his febrile state, he had imagined them?

Then he saw the body on the steps and he knew. He couldn't bear it, he felt ill with dread. The bastard, he thought. He's done it, the animal's done it. He walked and walked but the body never got any closer and then it was in front of him, its broken arm awkwardly angled, the silver rose on its snapped chain, the ticket to Adelaide, grief singing its high shrill deafening note in his head, sirening on and on and on in his police-car bed and his hand slamming the bloody alarm clock again.

Oh God, he thought, these dreams will be the death of me. I can't take them anymore. I'll wake straight into a heart attack.

He was shaking and drenched with sweat. It's because I know something is going to happen, he thought. My unconscious *knows*. A murder is on its way, I'd stake my life on it, it can't be stopped, it's way over the speed limit, its brakes are shot, but what can I do?

He stumbled about his apartment, putting the coffee on. The dream was the fifth time he had seen her. But I *will* see her this morning, he reminded himself. There will be a real fifth time, at the ferry dock.

And there was. He did see her.

He waited near the ticket booth for the Manly ferry, half hidden behind a newsagent's stall, until he saw them crossing the Quay, Lilian and a woman friend, the other one who worked in the Opera House lounge, the one she called Trish. A cab, he thought. They must have come in a cab. He waited until she bought her ticket, and then Trish gave her a hug and said: 'You stay right here with plenty of people around until they start boarding, okay? And give me a call every night.'

'Okay,' Lilian said. 'Thanks, Trish.'

'I'd better run,' Trish said.

And after that, he walked up to her quietly. 'Lilian,' he said.

She started violently. 'Oh Dennis! Oh God, don't *do* that.'

'I'm sorry,' he said. 'I just had to see you. I just had to make sure you were all right.'

She smiled weakly. 'That's kind of you. It's just that . . . ' She zipped the little silver rose back and forth on its chain with nervous fingers. 'I know you meant well, Dennis, but I wish you hadn't come. I feel as though, somehow, I can't even be sure if black is black or white is white. I don't feel certain the Manly ferry will go to Manly, can you understand what I mean? When you can be so wrong about someone, you don't trust yourself to be right about *anyone*, about *anything*, you know? I don't mean to be rude, I can't help it. I just don't want to see anyone for a while, I want to be alone.'

'Yes,' he said. 'I understand. I'm sorry I . . . Will you . . . ? D'you think you could phone me sometimes, from Collaroy?'

'I don't know,' she said. 'Maybe. I can't promise.'

'I'll go then,' he said. But he stood awkwardly in front of her, unwilling to leave, and she did not move away. 'I feel as though—'

he began. But no, he must not say he felt as though he could not live without her, that would frighten her. That would be the worst possible thing to say. He said quite formally, almost primly: 'I will worry about you, Lilian.'

'Thanks, Dennis.' she said. 'I *will* see you in Adelaide, that's a promise.'

But that is so far away, he thought. Ten days, that is endless.

Every day he pictured her, solitary and absorbed, walking the beach at Collaroy. He would stop at Circular Quay, morning and evening, and look out across the harbour toward North Head, beyond North Head, transmitting beams of safety and comfort. Every evening, he would stop by the Opera House. If Trish was on shift, he'd stay for a drink.

'Honestly, Dennis,' Trish would say, amused. 'You've got it really bad, mate.'

'Is she all right?'

'She's fine.'

And he checked the days off with mounting pleasure. He was pleased that he didn't have to deal with Henry. Henry was lying low, working at home most likely. He's either afraid or ashamed to face me, Dennis thought, and the idea pleased him. It occurred to him that he held the trump card for wreaking havoc upon Henry's career. Not that he would play it; at least, not unless Lilian's safety (academic or otherwise) required it. But Henry must be feeling apprehensive, wondering how much Dennis knew. Henry must perceive the deanship and other such future baubles to be hanging by a thread. Henry must be feeling very very jumpy, especially with Sharon tugging on his leash and breathing fire.

These thoughts did not displease Dennis.

Five days before Adelaide, his telephone rang.

'Dennis?'

It was a woman's voice, but not, alas, Lilian's. It was not a voice he recognised. 'Speaking,' he said.

'Yes,' the woman said, 'but the question is, what are *they* doing? Do you know where Lilian is, you stupid blind man?'

'Sharon?' he said startled. 'You sound very strange. I didn't recognise you.'

'Really?' she said. 'Really? Now isn't that interesting?' She sounded drunk, or drugged, her speech slurred. 'But then you wouldn't recognise your arse from a hole in the ground, would you, Dennis? And when it comes to recognising what *Henry's* up to, you score a big fat nothing every time, don't you, my dumb little darling?'

Dennis felt a chill of anxiety. 'What is Henry up to?' he asked.

'The question is what are *they* up to, don't you think? Don't you know where your lavish lustrous Lilian is?'

'Yes,' he said. 'As a matter of fact, I do.'

'You think you do,' Sharon shouted. 'But I'll tell you where she is, my dumb little darling, and I'll tell you what she's doing. Henry's fucking her blind in Patonga, that's what. Henry's been gone five days, up at our beach cottage, his and mine, our happy little honeymoon haven. He had to work on his Adelaide paper, he said. He needed to be alone, he said, now isn't that sweet? And then I find from the department secretary that Ms CoruscatingLavishSluttyLilian is also mysteriously missing for five days, isn't that charming? and I put two and two together, Q.E.D.'

'You're wrong, Sharon,' Dennis said.

'When I put two and two together, Dennis darling, they make four. When you put two and two together, you make a king-size fool of yourself. You've done it before, remember?'

'I know where Lilian is,' he said (though he felt much less sure about it now). He strove to sound confident, the possessor of intimate knowledge. 'She'll be back home a day or so before the Adelaide conference starts. Then she's going to Adelaide with me.'

'Henry promised she would never get to Adelaide,' Sharon said. 'He promised on oath, the lying sod. And then he buggers off to Patonga with her. What are you going to do about this, Dennis?' she screamed. 'What are you going to *do*, you blind spineless idiotic helpless—'

Her voice was getting shriller, shriller, higher, and Dennis hung up, frightened for her. And frightened for Lilian. Frightened for himself.

He phoned the Opera House lounge immediately, and asked to speak to Trish. She wouldn't be in again till Monday, they said. Monday! He couldn't bear it. Could they give out Trish's home phone number? No, they couldn't. He was tempted to do something rash, like drive up to Patonga. Or to Collaroy, where he could wait on the beach till she appeared; or failed to appear.

But of course she would be there. Trish had expressed alarm for her safety at the ferry. Lilian had waited alone. Lilian wanted to be alone.

But why, to examine the matter more closely, did she insist so strongly on being alone? Why had she been so eager for Dennis to leave? Why had she been so very shocked when he appeared?

Was it all an elaborate subterfuge? Was she duping even Trish and himself? Was it all a clever device to take off with Henry? He thought back to the way they had leaned toward each other at the Opera House, she and Henry. It had certainly not seemed to him then an issue of confrontation and threat. Nor to Sharon. Would he never add up two and two and get the right answer? He could feel the red colour swallowing him up and he did not dare to feel anything at all.

By day, he walked and walked, and by night he dreamed terrible dreams. He took to phoning Lilian's number just to hear her voice on the answering machine. Then he would hang up.

He endured, somehow, until Monday, and then he went to find Trish. She has called in sick, they said. She was taking a few days off. No, they couldn't give out the home phone number or the address of an employee.

But this is a good sign, he told himself. It suggests she has joined Lilian in Collaroy. It's altogether too much of a coincidence that she is actually sick right now. It *must* have to do with Lilian. And Trish would hardly be joining them at Patonga. No. Lilian is in Collaroy, and Trish is with her, and that is good news.

Unless it meant that Lilian had felt threatened, felt stalked.

Where *was* Henry? In Patonga or Collaroy? Had he been at Circular Quay that morning, the morning when Lilian got the Manly ferry, had he been watching, following?

Dennis asked the department secretary how he could contact Henry. Rather pressing, he said. To do with the Adelaide conference.

'No problem,' she said. 'I'll be speaking to him by phone today. I can give him your message.'

'Ah,' Dennis said. 'I believe I really need to speak to him myself. If you could just give me his number.'

'Well, he doesn't have one at Patonga. He checks in from a pay phone every couple of days. I could ask him to call you.'

'Look, on second thoughts,' Dennis said hastily, 'I have the address. I'll send a letter.'

'I'll tell him to expect one,' she said.

'Oh no, really,' Dennis said. 'Please don't. I mean, don't bother.

It'll make the matter seem more important than it is, and when he's working on a paper, you know . . . I don't want to distract him.'

'Okay,' she said. 'Oh, by the way, I gave Henry's wife that address you needed, the graduate student's, you know, the one who's transferring to you from Henry. She said Henry told her to get it from his files for you.'

'Yes, I see,' Dennis said. 'Thank you.'

He went into his office and phoned Sharon. 'You are really going off the deep end, Sharon,' he told her. 'Snooping for Lilian's address.'

'What if I did?' she said defiantly. 'At least *my* survival instincts aren't on the blink. I wanted to find out for myself if Ms Lavish Slut was away, and I went to her place, and sure enough: nobody there. And then, Dennis, brace yourself, I drove up to Patonga. I thought I'd stage a little surprise, and what do you know? Nobody there either. No sign that anyone had stayed there at all. Put that in your bloody pipe, Dennis, and see if you can learn to add up.'

On the second day before he was due to leave for Adelaide, Dennis woke from a horrifying dream with the certainty that something worse than any nightmare was about to happen, was happening, had happened. He could not, in actual fact, *remember* the dream, but its aura overwhelmed him. The air in his bedroom was thick with dread.

She returns to her apartment today, he thought.

He phoned and left a message on her answering machine. *Welcome home, Lilian. It's Dennis. Please call and reassure me that you're all right.* If she'd been somewhere with Henry, if he was revealing his vulnerability, if he was making a complete fool of himself, so be it.

He made a fervent little Faustian pact with the Powers That Be: as long as she is all right, I won't even object if she and Henry go off together. I pledge allegiance to the incomprehensible and unsuitable unions that people set up for themselves, I defer to their right to be lunatics, I promise I will feel nothing whatsoever. No anger, no pain, nothing.

Mercifully, he had no classes to teach on this day of reckoning, and he could not bear the thought of running into Henry, who would surely be back, so he would avoid the department. In any case, he could not bear to leave his house in case Lilian called. He tried to read, he paced his rooms, he tried to read.

He called the department. 'Is Henry in?' he asked.

'Yes, he is,' the secretary said. 'Shall I put you through?'

'No, no,' Dennis said. 'Just checking whether we, ah, we've got an appointment. I'll be seeing him later, just making sure . . . Thanks.'

He phoned Lilian's place and got the answering machine. He hung up.

He tried to read. He paced. He left his apartment and walked toward Circular Quay. He walked by the Opera House and looked into the lounge, but there was no sign of Trish. He asked. She called, they said. She'll be in again tomorrow.

They're all back, he thought.

He called the departmental secretary again and explained—absent-minded professor that he was—that he had lost the address of his new graduate student . . . Yes, that one, Yes, thank you.

He went to her apartment and rang the bell. He waited. He rang again. He thumped on the door. He lifted up the brass letter slot and peered into an empty hallway and called: 'Lilian, it's me, Dennis. I just want to know if you're all right.'

There was no answer, no sound, no sign.

It was nearly five o'clock now and Dennis thought it reasonably safe to assume that Henry would no longer be at his office, so he walked to the department where the secretaries were just locking up.

'Oh, listen,' he said, 'there's a book I lent Henry that I need for Adelaide. Well, I need it *tonight* actually, and I completely forgot . . . I wonder if you could just let me in his office for a jiff . . . '

'Sure,' the secretary said. 'He left pretty early, actually. His wife came by to pick him up, as a matter of fact, and he'd already gone. She was pretty pissed off, I thought.' She unlocked Henry's door for him. 'I'm off,' she said, 'so make sure you lock it behind you, okay?'

'Okay.'

He was in the lion's den and he was not sure exactly why. Oh, certainly, he had a mad urge to comb through correspondence, to open drawers, to riffle files, to look for clues, but he was too fastidious, the lifelong habits of scrupulous honour were too hard to break. I will open no drawers, he told himself, arguing with a still small voice. I will only look at what is on top of his desk, that's fair. That's public anyway. Even the cleaning staff could read that.

He picked up books and loose papers: flyers, bills, memos, student essays. He read the notes scribbled on the newly uncovered desk blotter, moving aside—in order to note a phone number—a silver chain that trailed from under one leather corner flap, because the phone number rang a bell, no, not the phone number, something—

Oh God, he thought. He pulled the delicate chain from its hiding place until the silver rose appeared. He stared at it. He was in a state of suspended animation. She was wearing it, he thought, when we stood talking at the Manly ferry dock. He felt nothing.

So that's that then, he said to himself.

They *were* together. She did go running back to him. Human beings, as she had remarked, were perverse, and that was that.

He left the chain and the silver rose in full view on the blotting pad and pulled the door shut behind him till he heard the lock click.

He went home and rummaged in his bathroom cabinet until he found the little bottle of motion sickness pills. There were five left. They would have to serve as sleeping pills, to get him through the night. After that, he would be all right. He swallowed them all, then took the bottle of whisky from the dresser.

After all, he told the amber liquid, I made a pact, and fair's fair. I haven't done so badly after all. Lilian will be looked after, she is safe, her academic career will have a pugnacious sponsor, and Sharon's got her comeuppance, which I must admit does not break my heart.

He descended into a sleep well below the level of dreams and there he stayed until the sirens, no, the alarm, no, the telephone . . . on and on.

'Yes,' he mumbled clumsily. His lips felt as though they had leg-irons on.

'Dennis? Dennis, this is Trish, remember me?'

'Trish,' he said through orthopaedic teeth. 'Lovely to shee you again.'

'Dennis, oh God, I don't know who to call, something terrible has happened, oh God . . . '

There is a particular timbre to panic that cuts through fog.

'What?' he said, more sharply now, sober, fearful. 'What is it?'

'It's Lilian. Oh Jesus Jesus Jesus . . . See, we came back from Collaroy yesterday morning and she was going to stay at my place for the night. She just went over to get her mail and messages, see, oh about two in the afternoon, I think, and she was going to come right back. But see, I went to work, I didn't know, and when I got off and got home, I got off at midnight right? and when I got home she wasn't there. So I phoned her apartment and got the bloody machine, so then I went over and oh God . . . ' She began to sob.

'What?' he yelled. 'What? *What?* Tell me.'

'She's dead,' Trish said. 'She's *dead.*'

'What?'

'I think hit with something heavy, there's this iron door-stopper, there's this great lump on her head and blood and her hair's all—Oh Jesus, Dennis, what will I do? I just freaked out and left her there. I locked up and came home and I just sat here shivering, I don't know how long I've been back.'

'What time is it?' Dennis asked.

'I don't know. Must be nearly three by now, I think.'

Dennis squinted at the digital clock on the kitchen wall. Five, he saw. 5 am.

Trish said, 'What if he comes after me, that maniac? She *said* she thought she saw him in Collaroy. I'm terrified, Dennis. What'll I do?'

'Call the police,' he said. 'You have to call the police.'

'I can't,' she said. 'I can't handle it. I came straight off an eight-hour shift, I'm exhausted, and then I find a dead body, I can't handle this, I'll be hysterical. I'm not going to open my door in the dark, not to the police, not to anyone. I'm not going to call them till it's light, but I had to tell *someone*. Can you call them, Dennis? Please?'

'All right,' he said. Then he said: 'Trish, that will seem very very odd. I mean, I'm not a witness, but I'm involved in all sorts of problematic ways. I just wonder what implications . . . No, *you* must call.' He wanted to say: And don't mention me, don't mention this phone call. But who knew what ramifications might come from that? Who knew what constructions might be placed on such a request? Or on delay? 'I wish you'd call them now, Trish.'

'I can't,' she said. 'I can't. Not till it's light.'

He sat in the dark and thought.

He thought: there will be neighbours who saw me banging on her door. They will think I did it. Then he thought: the chain and the silver rose on Henry's desk, *proof*! And he thought: they will have my fingerprints on them. And he thought: the secretary will tell them I asked for the key; they will say I planted the silver rose.

And he thought: *Lilian*, and something like a tidal wave threatened to smash him and sweep him to a place from which he would never return and he could not, he must not let himself, he must resist, *resist*, he had to feel nothing, he had to walk.

He left his apartment and walked through the still dark and deserted city. He walked and walked. He paid no attention to where he was walking, but as the sun rose he found himself at Circular Quay, he found himself following the covered walkway, he heard the white sails lifting themselves in a haunting unbearable dirge, a Bach chorale, *Lilian, Lilian, Lilian,* they wept in glorious song. He walked along the steps by the water, he thought of margins, of the borderline between harbour and embankment, of Lilian Before and Lilian After, of that thin chain which linked premonition and event, of the fine line between breath and death. He did not even notice the other walker until they almost collided.

Two haggard and sleepless and half-blind men faced each other.

'Dennis,' Henry said, tried to say, 'something terrible—' but a red fog obscured him and forked lightning entered Dennis who sang *Lilian* on a high piercing note of pain and grief, his body roared *Lilian,* his muscles screamed her, he struck out for her, he played stroke by stroke, he gave no quarter, he fought for Sharon too, *take that, take that,* he took no respite until his weary breath buckled up and left him gasping, heaving, leaning on the iron railing at the top of the steps.

A body lay on the steps.

It appeared to be reaching for something, or else it was engaged in a slow head-first slide into the water. One arm was angled awkwardly, broken. There was a great lump on the head where it had apparently crashed against the metal rail, and blood was welling from one ear like red oil.

Oh God, Dennis said in quiet horror.

He prayed for the alarm clock to ring. He groped for it and felt only the iron rail.

This was not a dream.

He felt stunned and dizzy and ill, and he knew that he had come upon the dreaded inevitability. *So this is it, then,* he said aloud, and nausea lapped at his edges and moved the body slightly and slapped against the concrete abutment.

I must telephone the police, he thought dully, and he turned and walked home. There were cars about now, and pedestrians, early commuters. Probably someone would find the body and call the police before he did, and sure enough, when he opened his door, the phone was ringing.

'Dennis?' Sharon said. 'Oh Dennis, I'm so frightened. I did something terrible yesterday, I didn't mean to do it, it was a kind of . . . I just, I just, I'm not even sure what happened, I just meant to confront her, that's all, I just meant to frighten her, I just wanted to have it out, I just wanted to be waiting for her, see, I found her key in an envelope in Henry's desk and I just wanted to but it was when she denied, when she *lied*, I just, I just, and I put it back again afterwards, the key I mean, in his desk, and I went home and I don't know what I was thinking . . . I don't know what I *could* have been thinking, but I think I thought they'll never know, they'll think Henry . . . Oh Dennis, I'm so frightened, I just don't know . . . Dennis, what will I do?'

'Sharon,' He put a shaking hand to his face. A terrible gust of laughter, maniac laughter, came swooping down at him like a tornado, then twisted away without contact. 'These things happen, Sharon,' he said gently. 'We'll just have to . . . we'll just have to . . . ' He could see candles, hundreds of candles, a funeral procession. 'Sharon,' he said faintly. 'I'm sorry, Sharon, I can't talk to you right now. I'm in pain.'

He hung up, and slid to the floor, and put his head in his hands, and sobbed.

Allen & Unwin Original Fiction

THE CRIMES FOR A SUMMER CHRISTMAS ANTHOLOGIES

A *Corpse at the Opera House* is the third book in this best-selling series of Australian crime fiction edited by Stephen Knight.

Look out for the fourth book next summer, *Murder at Home*—another spell-binding collection from Australian writers.

CRIMES FOR A SUMMER CHRISTMAS
Edited by Stephen Knight

'*Crimes for a Summer Christmas* is a rattling good selection of short detective fiction from some of the best Australian writers.' *Sun Herald*

'Australia is certainly undergoing a crime-writing renaissance at present and this collection superbly illustrates the diversity of crime fiction being produced . . . a remarkably consistent collection that proves that the Australian crime story is alive, well and still has many places to develop and explore—in its own very human way.' Stuart Coupe, *Sydney Morning Herald*

Crimes for a Summer Christmas is an immensely entertaining collection of new, previously unpublished Australian crime stories from top crime writers as well as top 'literary' writers new to modern crime. The sixteen contributors are Jennifer Rowe, Peter Corris, Mudrooroo Narogin, Marion Halligan, Elizabeth Jolley, Ian Moffitt, Marele Day, Martin Long, Archie Weller, Renate Yates, Michael Wilding, Nigel Krauth, Kate Stephens, Garry Disher, Robert Hood and John Sligo.

This exceptional collection of short stories has been orchestrated and introduced by Stephen Knight, Professor of English at the University of Melbourne, and long-time crime writing advocate.

QUAKE   SHIVER   CHUCKLE   ADMIRE   ENJOY

MORE CRIMES FOR A SUMMER CHRISTMAS
Edited by Stephen Knight

'A book full of delights, of highly original stories with many a twist in the tail, and it suggests that Australia has something quite distinctive to offer in crime fiction—not only the landscape but a strong dose of wry humour, inventive language and a refreshing absence of moralising.' Judith White, *Sun Herald*

More Crimes for a Summer Christmas builds on the success of its predecessor, with another collection of brand new stories by Australian writers of crime, mystery and psychic violence as well as more 'literary' writers eager to plunge into the seamy world of mystery and crime.

Like the best-selling first volume, leaders in crime writing such as Peter Corris, Jennifer Rowe, Claire McNab and Marele Day are joined by the most exciting new names in this genre including Susan Geason, Garry Disher, Steve Wright and Kerry Greenwood, who all have different forms of mystery to communicate.

Marion Halligan, Richard Hall, Robert Hood, Martin Long, Mudrooroo Nyoongah, Kel Richards, Kate Stephens and Janette Turner Hospital all extend the boundaries of the thriller in this collection.

Stephen Knight is recognised as Australia's leading crime-writing authority whose commentaries on the thriller are quoted and printed around the world.

FAT FUNNY STYLISH FRIGHTENING ENJOY